Cat in an Indigo Mood

Cat in an Indigo Mood

CAROLE NELSON DOUGLAS

BEELER LARGE PRINT
Hampton Falls, New Hampshire, 2003

Library of Congress Cataloging-in-Publication Data

Douglas, Carole, Nelson.
   Cat in a Indigo Mood / Carole Nelson Douglas.
      p.   cm.
   ISBN 1-57490-473-6 (alk. paper)
   1. Midnight Louie (Fictitious character)—Fiction. 2. Barr,
Temple (Fictitious character)—Fiction. 3. Public relations
consultants—Fiction. 4. Las Vegas (Nev.)—Fiction. 5. Women
detectives—Fiction. 6. Women cat owners—Fiction. 7. Cats—
Fiction. 8. Large type books. I. Title.

PS3554.O8237C277 2003
813'.54—dc21   2003001925

Published in Large Print by arrangement with
Tom Doherty Associates, Inc.

BEELER LARGE PRINT
is published by
Thomas T. Beeler, *Publisher*
Post Office Box 659
Hampton Falls, New Hampshire 03844

Typeset in 16 point Times New Roman type.
Sewn and bound on acid-free paper by
Sheridan Books in Chelsea, Michigan

For the real and original Midnight Louie,
nine lives were not enough.

MIDNIGHT LOUIE'S DREAM

THE BEST THING ABOUT DREAMING IS THAT YOU DO NOT know you are doing it until you wake up screaming.

I do not exactly wake up screaming, but all four of my limbs are thrashing to beat the band . . . actually to beat the band of baddies I am fleeing down the endless alleys of dreamland. I can still feel the breath of the hounds from hell that are on my tail.

I lie there on the bed, whiskers still twitching, while I wait for reality to reassemble around me. I wait for the oblong of security light cast through the French door to look less like the shadow of a sneak thief. For the inky blot on the bedroom throw rug to look more like a pair of toppled high heels and less like a chain saw momentarily set down by a serial killer.

Okay, so it was a pretty bad dream.

The pads of my feet are damp with distress. I rub the sleep from my eyes, but still I see alien shapes in the familiar bedroom landscape.

Maybe a familiar shape would reassure my dream-drugged mind, but Miss Temple Barr is in absentia again. What is the use of having a roommate who is off mating in someone else's room?

But I am being selfish. I have left my Miss Temple home alone many a time while I pursued a merry night out on the town, and when the town one lives in is Las Vegas, there are plenty of exciting nights out to be had.

So now that the tables are turned, I have no business complaining.

1

Like the lady poet said a long, long time ago, a dream is a dream is a dream.

Unless it is a nightmare.

The images return in the slow-motion crawl of dawning recall.

I am back in the eternal alleyway, alone, on the lam.

Those mean streets are lit by aged light bulbs that buzz and crackle, threatening to go nova like a dying star, then darken for good.

The wet streets are patent leather slick and reflect whole constellations of light.

Nine relentless Havana Browns are on my tail, leaping from rooftop to rooftop, fanning out on the liquid asphalt streets. Lean athletic dudes in licorice-brown catsuits. Ninjas with nine lives.

Is the number nine recurring in my dream like an unlucky card?

I hear dice—or teeth—rattling down the cul-de-sacs I race past.

Throw them bones . . . or, better yet, get my own bones moving faster—

Then I see it. A light in the window.

I leap for one or the other—the light or the window or both—before I spot the figure also in the window: a masked lady in lavender-brown, dilly dilly.

She extends eight blood-ruby red claws, all wearing shiny fresh Curare Coral nail enamel.

I leap short at the last minute, and fall . . . into a nettle-patch of flailing Havana Browns, shivs drawn.

Then I wake up, my legs still pumping.

By the pricking of my lamentably non-opposable thumbs, something wicked this way comes.

E-MAIL MAN

LIKE STARS, CYBERSPACE ONLY REALLY CAME OUT AT night.

That's what Max Kinsella thought anyway. Nine to five were not its prime-time working hours. It jived, and jammed, spammed, and buzzed like a beehive only after dark. The Internet was a hobbyist's highway, a global beltline jerry-built for enthusiasts and crooks and cranks.

The Net was better than magic, it was technology in irresponsible hands. Amateur Night at the Alhambra Cyber Cafe and Techno-Theater. Babel and the Byzantine Empire online. A Carnivale of commerce. It was all quite quirky, maddening, enchanting. Sometimes it was even dangerous.

Max stared at the large calligraphy letters wriggling like Technicolor worms on screen.

"To tell is to tempt Illusion. The Master Magician dissolves all doubts," Temple read from the screen aloud over his shoulder.

Another thing about the World Wide Web, Max thought. When it pulled you into its online orbit, you lost touch with where you were. Which in his case was up at two in the morning, hypnotized by a seventeen-inch monitor.

"Couldn't sleep?" Temple sounded endearingly sleepy herself, but even that wasn't enough to counter the siren lure of cyberspace. Especially when it had turned mysteriously personal.

So he didn't immediately answer her, merely spun around to boot up the second computer. She'd want to know what was going on anyway. He never forgot that

3

she used to be a television news reporter, and that's an investigative job.

"When did you get that?" she wondered, yawning at the twenty-inch screen on his 400-megahertz model.

"Last week, when that other one started burping messages like that at me."

Temple leaned near the static seventeen-inch screen, the luminous image of wildly colored letters painting her red hair with blue-green punk-rocker streaks.

"Stained-glass threats," she said. Diagnosed. She was awake enough now to sound clinical.

"I think so too."

"Think what?"

"That it's tacky to send poison-pen messages in calligraphic script via computer. Talk about mixed media."

"Sounds like the parchment stuff Gandolph was getting in the mail before he died. Or was killed. Whichever it was."

Max nodded.

"But is this cybergram meant for Gandolph, or for you now?"

"I started using Gandolph's computer with his name and password, so it could be either."

Temple pulled a stool to the abandoned computer station.

" 'The vagrant brother will be outcast into the Final Illusion.' Same old pseudo-antique gobbledegook. You think we should take these folks seriously?"

"I take anybody who enjoys long-distance harassment seriously. That's where serial killers come from."

"And major national governments," Temple added with the solemn twinkle of a satirist born.

"Exactly."

4

Max was not twinkling back. He suddenly needed a change of mood—and topic. Poor Temple. And she'd once thought that consorting with an itinerant magician who worked nights was chaos enough. That was before she knew about his actual vocation.

Max checked his watch. "One of our favorite old movies is on. Why don't we explode some popcorn and forget about computers and cryptic messages for a while?"

"You mean there's a television set in this joint?"

"Is there a television set?" He knew that his tone of voice promised something truly wondrous in the way of TV sets; magicians were inclined to exaggerate and worry about living up to it afterward. "Let me show you to my parlor."

Fifteen minutes later they were ensconced on a massive tufted leather chair big enough for two across the room from a sixty-inch rear-projection TV, an equally oversize aluminum bowl of popcorn warming their laps. Douglas Fairbanks Jr. appeared to be literally jumping into those laps as the opening action scenes of *The Fighting O'Flynn* unreeled.

"This butter spray is great," Temple said, between the mouth-cramming that popcorn-eating demanded, "but this room is hardly a parlor."

"Den," Max amended amiably.

"Den is right. This chair is big enough for Papa Bear. I guess Baby Bear would get the footstool."

"No, *we* get the footstool." Max wiggled his stocking toes on the upholstered matching ottoman. "Baby Bear can camp outside."

Temple, now fully awake, snuggled beside him. For a while there was only the music-scored choreographed action of the movie's inspired swordplay and derring-do and the contented crunch of popcorn.

"It feels like we're back in Minneapolis again," Temple finally said, a bit astounded.

"You liked that, didn't you?"

"Yeah. I mean, the only exotic thing I knew about you then was your working hours. And everybody in the theater works nights."

Max rested his chin atop her head; that was the only time Temple ever felt that her hair was perfect the way it was, red and curly, just like little Shirley. Why couldn't she be a sleek, sultry, *serious* redhead, like Gillian Anderson on *The X-Files?* Of course, G. A. had bad legs, which was why she always wore pants and long coats, while Temple had what her gym teacher had called "dancer's legs." If only they had been about six inches longer . . . Women were reared to never be satisfied with themselves; it was an occupational hazard.

"Remember how we met?" Max's voice was rumbling above her head like a benign volcano.

"How can I forget? One of my stupidest moves ever. Passing like ships in the night in that hall at the theater, and then running aground."

"We both got whiplash turning to look back. What did you crash into? I collided with a potted ficus tree."

"How can you forget my limbo with the drinking fountain? That really hurt, almost more than the embarrassment."

"You still had a bruise the first time we made love."

"Guess it happened fast, huh?"

"Instantly, for me. I'd never been hit like that."

"Oh, come on. What about the Rose of Tralee in Ireland? She sure hasn't forgotten you."

"That's the problem. Now that you know about that,

6

maybe you can understand why I've risked so much, including you, to keep our relationship going."

"How can a cute meeting in a Minneapolis theater compare with a foreign land, the Troubles, your first love?"

"My first loss," he corrected. "It can't. That's what makes what we have so special. With Sean killed, I discovered I'd lost my innocence in so many more ways than one. I felt Sean's death was God's punishment for sleeping with Kathleen."

"You've never said anything before about God in all this."

"I've tried to forget that stuff, because it's too grim to live with. That was what was so wonderful about meeting you. Something about you . . . I was back in high school again and had a chance to do it right. You are my first real love, Temple. You gave me my innocence back."

She didn't know what to say, which was just as well because she couldn't have spoken over the sudden thickening in her throat anyway. And she suddenly saw that he was right, now that she knew the whole story of his past. They had been giddy and so instantly and unreservedly in love, it had been like the first time. It was the first time, only this time for real. The crazy rented rooms near the theater in Minneapolis . . . finding a place as delightfully skewed here in Las Vegas as the Circle Ritz, a fifties-vintage round apartment building that seemed constructed like a stage set of Honeymoon Hotel just for them. They had even invested in the place together, dammit, like lovers with delusions of becoming a lawfully united couple someday soon.

Only someday soon came when Max had vanished without a word, leaving Temple single-handedly holding the mortgage payments and holding off inquisitive Lieutenant Molina, who was all suspicion and questions when it came to Max. Of course the dead body Max had left behind in the ceiling of the Goliath Hotel when he vanished on the last night of his magician's gig there hadn't helped Temple resist Molina's implications that Max was up to his magic wand in something deadly, maybe even murder . . . by him, or worse—his own attempted murder.

But their romantic past had remained a warm, fuzzy domestic dream no amount of current trauma could dislodge. That was what Temple had been fighting for, without knowing it, all the months that Max was so mysteriously gone, while Lieutenant Molina kept demanding explanations for Max's absence, and then for Temple's unswerving loyalty—dumb, feminine loyalty, to Molina.

But there was nothing reasonable about either reality, except how they had felt, from the first moment.

"Are you smiling, or crying?" he asked.

"Watch the movie," she ordered gruffly, through both teeth and tears. "It's one of our favorites."

It was, of course, and therefore thrilling and funny and very, very romantic. And the Fighting O'Flynn was Irish, but he fell in love with the English girl. The Irish girl was just comic relief.

Comic relief. Didn't Temple wish she could believe that was all the mysterious new woman in town, Kitty the Cutter, was . . . and ever had been?

MAIL MAN

MATT DEVINE STOOD IN HIS LIVING ROOM AT THREE-twenty A.M., fresh home from work, a record two pieces of mail in his hands. Two pieces of personal mail in his lobby box at once. Imagine that.

One was a letter from his mother in Chicago.

The other was a suspiciously small padded mailer from a radio station in Las Vegas. WCOO-AM.

He never went to bed right after getting home from his eight-hour shift at the hotline. Listening to other people's woes and then piloting them through crises ranging from overdosing on Oreo cookies to cocaine was a sedentary job, but it gave the nervous system a real workout.

So Matt left the two provocative pieces of mail on his red sofa seat and went into the triangular-shaped kitchen to microwave hot water for herbal tea.

Amazing how many appliances one person living alone could accumulate as "necessities." As a parish priest, he had only been vaguely aware of what equipped the kitchen or furnished the rectory parlor. Much of it had been donated, thanks to the Catholic parish tradition of raising money for serious needs at church, rectory, and school. So Matt had always taken the presence of stoves, lamps, and microwave ovens for granted, as if they were wild flowers that sprang up in season when needed or wanted.

Now that he had left the dematerialized world of a religious vocation, every way he turned was a speed ramp driving him onto the consumer highway. He was a perfect novice consumer, conspicuous or not. Almost

9

everything that secular people took for granted, from clothing to gadgets, was new—and probably lacking—to him.

Matt took the steaming mug of Red Zinger (Celestial Seasonings; had the brand name attracted his spiritual side?) to his Goodwill sofa (Vladimir Kagan original from the fifties, according to Temple the secondhand shopper) and set it on the melamine cube table (low-cost high-style Kmart, *not* courtesy of Martha Stewart, whose hopelessly homebody taste seemed to be redesigning America back into post-war frou-frou these days).

He opened the package first, expecting a promotional audiotape. Radio stations were also trying to convince everybody they were essential, but he didn't have a radio, only a small color TV on a wire-metal stand that looked like it belonged in an old folks home.

The tape label read AMBROSIA.

That's when it crossed his mind that the tape might be something sleazy. This was Las Vegas, after all, where sex-for-sale offered as many innovations and incarnations as theme hotels.

A letter folded in thirds shook out of the empty package.

It was addressed to him, which made Matt frown, as if he had discovered a dirty wad of gum on the sole of his shoe. Almost no one knew his address, and he was happy with that situation. He was probably the only man in America who got no junk mail, none specifically addressed to him, that is. There was always the "Occupant" stuff that would dog an apartment address through all its generations of tenants.

"Dear Mr. Devine," it began.

He read on, his wariness changing to wonder.

Finally he just sat there, balancing the unusable tape in one hand and the letter on the palm of the other. The tape weighed heavier.

He set them aside and used the table knife he had brought from the kitchen to open his mother's letter. (Did he *need* a real letter opener? Should he buy one? Where? Pier One? A stationery store in the mall? Or save money and stick with the table knife? Decisions, decisions.)

She usually hand-wrote her letters on blue-lined notebook paper, tear-off sheets she folded into inexpensive business envelopes.

But this envelope was square and pale blue. The smaller sheets inside had a faint image of a butterfly in the upper left-hand corner.

He raised his eyebrows. Looked like Mom would know where to get a fashionable letter opener these days, now that her niece Krys had drawn her into the shopping mall distractions.

He was glad to see his mother expressing some personality; she had spent so many years repressing it. But as he read, he found himself biting his lip.

She had been thinking—always a dangerous pastime, he thought wryly. He read one paragraph over, then over again.

I was thinking about what you said when you came for Christmas, about your real father. You said that he might not have died in Vietnam like his family's lawyers told me when they gave me that settlement. I was thinking that since you were so successful in finding your stepfather, maybe you could look into finding out about your real father. I've written down all I know, all I can remember.

11

Maybe you will see some clues in that. I realize that you're not here in Chicago to do anything, but maybe you could suggest some ways to start looking.

No. The last time he had gone looking for a man who had gone missing, a man who did not want to be found, the man had died. Been murdered. Horribly.

Now his mother was asking him to hunt down a dead man, so how much worse could it be? A lot, if the man were still alive. A lot more than either of them could handle.

Meanwhile . . . he set aside his mother's letter and picked up the audiotape again.

He supposed he could listen to it. What harm would that do? No doubt *that* little question often led teenagers to their first heavy-metal rock album. But first he'd have to find someone with a tape player.

Someone? Only one person he knew was nearby and handy and definitely armed with a sound system. His accelerating pulse made it impossible to tell if this was merely a good idea, or a dangerous one.

First thing in the morning. He would have a reason—an excuse?—to see Temple.

WAIL WOMAN

THE PARKING LOT FELT LIKE A GIANT BLACK SQUARE on an inactive chessboard: empty, yet possessed of an odd aura of expectancy.

Carmen Molina advanced into it like a bold pawn making the first move: big steps, strides even, her velvet work clothes hanging slack in the Blue Dahlia's tiny dressing room while she left in her jeans and tennies, key ring jingling on her finger.

Still, she moved to the echoes of Gershwin and Porter, big songs that drew power from intimate, tautly controlled renderings: "Someone to Watch over Me" . . . "The Man I Love" . . . "Body and Soul" . . . "Night and Day" . . . "Smoke Gets in Your Eyes," and her current favorite, "Begin the Beguine."

The trio had run through the whole repertoire that evening, for an audience that had hunkered down and listened like well-paid extras in a big-band movie. No drunks, no druggies, just good little groupies. The Blue Dahlia's clientele liked the setup, anyway; liked not knowing if the singer might show tonight, or if they were going to get instruments unaccompanied by voice. The performance schedule had to bow to her job responsibilities, but it also gave her a certain vintage persona: mystery chanteuse from some unfilmed sequel to *Casablanca,* where the saxophone, the girl singer's voice, and the room were always smoky.

Carmen chuckled, hearing an echo from the hard asphalt. If the audience knew about her daytime gig as homicide lieutenant C. R. Molina, she'd lose all her mystique. She wondered sometimes which was the role, and which the reality: blues singer Carmen or detective C. R.

Her well-aged Toyota sat alone near the lot's border, a familiar silhouette usually hemmed in by other vehicles when she left at midnight in her civvies, like Cinderella seeking and finding her homely pumpkin long after the ball was over and Prince Charming had been eluded.

But it was after three now. She and the band had celebrated a stellar night by noodling around with new wrinkles to the repertoire and a truly knock-'em-dead version of "Begin the Beguine."

Like a thirties cartoon character, she could hardly keep a rhythmic bounce out of her steps. *I got rhythm. Who could ask for anything more? Night and day. Smoke gets in your eyes.* Great songs.

She veered toward the driver's side, then her steps skipped a syncopated beat.

Someone had strewn a broken trash bag right beside her car. A leaky trash bag. The distant streetlight ran its rays over a slick rivulet of liquid.

Yuck.

She'd have to haul it away; it was too close to the car door for her to get in without stepping on it . . .

And then she got closer.

Her hand was digging in the shoulder bag at her side. She wasn't sure whether it hunted a firearm or a cell phone or both. Both were there, but a glance around the parking lot had her pulling out the cell phone first.

Might be watching, but discreet enough to keep distant.

She stayed put for a few seconds after making the call. A homicide cop didn't often discover her very own dead body. But a cop's gotta do what a cop's gotta do.

From the torque of the torso, the victim had fallen—or been dumped—here while the music was being made inside.

She went close enough to check the body for heat and heartbeat. Neither, of course.

She glanced at the driver's door of her car.

It wasn't often that a homicide cop's vehicle was part of the crime scene, either.

She read the lethal graffiti, two words spray-painted on the sun-faded paint: *she left.*

14

Maybe "she," whoever she had been, had. But Carmen Molina couldn't leave.

"Long night," Detective Morris Alch said about four A.M.

Molina nodded.

"You eat here with anyone?"

"No."

"Kind of late to still be at a restaurant."

"It's part jazz club, and the group was jamming. I was the last to leave. From the customer lot, at least."

"The pits about your car."

"Yeah. I'll get it back soon enough, after it's been through the 'body shop' at the morgue."

He laughed at her pun. Horror and humor were the Abbott and Costello of police work.

Molina glanced at Alch's partner, Merry Su.

That was it; the whole name.

The woman was almost shorter than her name: ninety pounds of ace girl detective; a China doll so adorably diminutive it was a shame not to keep her on a shelf.

But Su was resilient, and the firmly middle-aged Alch made a pragmatic partner more inclined to playing father-figure than Romeo or Lancelot. They were turning into the department's most effective team. Molina counted herself lucky they had been "up" for assignment when she had called the murder in.

They were also the pair she could most trust with her silly little secret: The homicide lieutenant was a crooner on the side. But no need to confess prematurely. The boys in the band knew better than to mention her intermittent role as torch singer unless they had to. They could all tell the truth and not quite tell it, just like an L.A. lawyer.

15

Unless things got ugly.

She glanced down where the dead woman had lain, body twisted as if she'd been turning over in her sleep and had been flash-frozen.

Strangled and stabbed. Classic signs of a perpetrator known to the victim.

"She left."

Classic motive for domestic violence.

But why *here?* Why *now?* And why beside *my* car?

Nothing classic about those facts of the case but the question marks.

MOOD INDIGO

WHEN SHE LEFT MAX'S HOUSE IN THE UPPER-MIDDLE-class gated community, Temple found herself driving away from the city and its heavy morning traffic.

She quite literally didn't know where to go, but once she turned onto the highway to Lake Mead, her choices narrowed one by one until she found herself by her namesake landing, Temple Bar.

Three O'clock Louie's restaurant wasn't open until lunchtime; tourists scarfed up the cheap and plentiful breakfasts along the Strip before heading to the hinterlands for day tours and lunch.

Lake Mead wasn't a walker-friendly body of water, like the hundreds of tree-rimmed lakes in her native Minnesota that attracted joggers, bicyclists, and dog-walkers in droves.

No, this was a large, fiercely blue expanse of water forced by the great wall of Hoover Dam to flood an even fiercer expanse of red desert rockland.

The effect was alien, like red Mars sporting a

16

landlocked sea. People didn't stroll along the shoreline in this demanding sun-baked environment naked of shade. They arrived on wheels and swiftly embarked on boats or Jet Skis.

Temple sat in the idling Storm, parked as close to the shore as she could get. Hers was the only vehicle out here, although within hours tour buses and campers and minivans would hunch wheel-well to hubcap, glittering in the sun.

Now it was quiet and cool.

She turned off the motor and sat in the silence.

She had just left Max, but she was thinking of Matt.

Her hands rested on the steering wheel, as if she still wanted to go somewhere, but she wasn't sure where.

Her left hand was bare of Max's ring. He had dismissed the opal's unlucky reputation when he gave it to her in New York City less than a month before.

Now it was gone. Stolen by a stage magician who had also disappeared. Déjà vu all over again, as language-mangler Yogi Berra or Hollywood mogul Sam Goldwyn ("an oral contract isn't worth the paper it's written on") had said, but maybe somebody else had. No one had a lock on anything anymore, including ignorance.

Shangri-La the lady magician had left town, maybe even the planet. With her went the ring.

Temple glanced at the tote bag in the seat next to her. It occurred to her that she always carried such a big bag ("such a big bag for such a little lady," bluff strange men had been known to remark) not just because she could pack a lot of her working life into it, but because it made an ersatz companion for a single woman. Always a comforting bulk in the otherwise empty front passenger seat.

It did pack all her essentials: her day planner,

17

sunglass case, bulging wallet, notebook and pen case, a cosmetic bag for sunscreen and makeup touch-ups, and a pair of tennis shoes now that she had played Nancy Drew often enough to think that she might have to make tracks fast—and now that her trademark high heels were becoming a luxury her lifestyle could no longer afford. Geez, to hear Max talk about how much danger she might face from the mysterious Kitty O'Connor, love of-his-schoolboy-life turned psycho, Temple might have to start wearing combat boots.

"Never!" she told the lake, gripping the steering wheel as if it threatened to wrench out of her grasp.

Her fists unclenched and fell to her lap.

There was something else nowadays in the clutter of her tote bag: the box holding the delicate crushed-opal cat necklace Matt Devine had given her.

She carried it around under the delusion that she really ought to give it back to him and would someday.

She continued to carry it around because she knew she never would, and everyone should have some talisman of paths not taken, some visible reminder of temptation and guilt. God! She was starting to think like a Catholic!

Max must have been reared Catholic, but he never mentioned the church. The Church, it was, in Ireland. Temple suspected that he blamed it for complicity in the Troubles that had made his life a shambles and a secret. He had put his religion behind him like his family, both too dangerous to confront.

So where was her sense of guilt coming from? From Matt? Was guilt contagious, like a flu bug? Could you get it from proximity, French kisses, osmosis, daydreams?

Temple thrust her lacquered nails into the wilderness

beyond the tote bag's always-open and inviting maw.

She found the small square cardboard jewelry box and hauled it out into the light of day: cotton batting on which coiled a thin gold chain with a central cat-shape etched in a mosaic of black opals that shot red and green sparks onto the car seat.

First, she had felt guilty because Matt bought her a Christmas present when she hadn't bought him one. A second later she had felt guilty because she had spent her Christmas far away, growing closer to Max again, so close that she had accepted a ring from him as well as a resumed intimacy. And right after that, she had felt guilty because she had avoided telling Matt that their stuttering relationship had run out of gas just when he was finally getting his foot on the accelerator.

And, finally, like all women in whom it was ingrained from puberty onward, she was guilty because the gift had "cost too much," although social custom still decreed that man gave and woman accepted, from candy and flowers to engagement and wedding rings.

She touched the winking figure of the black cat, almost hologram-elusive in its crushed opal outline.

It had cost too much, and money, for once, had nothing to do with it.

She closed the necklace in her palm, and closed her eyes.

He hadn't asked about it, would never mention it again.

Just as she would never wear it again.

Just as they would never mention the . . . incident it had played a part in.

Which never would have happened if she had told Matt the minute she got back from New York that she and Max were a couple again, had coupled again. If she

19

hadn't been trying to spare everyone's feelings, which was a very female and, she gathered, a very Catholic thing to do. No wonder the nuns at Our Lady of Guadalupe had been so *nice!* They were doubly cursed. Maybe niceness was as dangerously infectious as guilt.

Temple felt tears welling behind her eyes, yet her sorrow had a warm nostalgic core, like the necklace warming in the close custody of her fist.

So. It never should have happened, that close encounter with Matt after his stepfather's ridiculous funeral. Except that it had; he had reached for her in ways that he had maybe never imagined, and she might have but never had dreamed could be so . . . inexplicable.

Okay. Analyze it, she told herself. What had happened? Simple biology. A man, a woman. Kisses and clothing shifting all over the place, intimacy, excitement . . . but nothing any teenager hadn't tried before senior prom. Nothing like serious sexuality. Still, given Matt's repressive background, "nothing" meant a lot.

The Virtue Policewoman in her had raised a stern hand to stop the crime of the heart in progress, but the Social Worker advised against rejecting Matt's much-too-long delayed foray into foreplay. And poor, startled, slumbering Sleeping Beauty had been way too stunned and breathless and touched and turned on to do anything sensible but enjoy the big moment.

That was the problem; Matt might still be a babe in Toyland when it came to sex, but Temple was not. She knew solid from shabby. She knew all relationships have ups and downs, and hots and tepids. She knew Lady Godiva from Reese's Pieces.

Nobody had ever made love to her like that before,

and nobody ever would. Because that moment had begun Matt's new vocation, sexual human being. And that convert's intensity, that pent-up celibate energy, the dimly sensed spiritual drive behind the sensuality, that unholy lack of inhibition smoldering beneath the surface, well, Mae West was wrong. Goodness had everything to do with it.

"Goodness," she said aloud.

Her musings had created a receptive state that felt emotionally bottomless, but sexually shallow. Simple sexual fantasy was too empty a response to such a mystery. There could only be one revelatory, transforming moment like that per customer. A moment worth remembering, if she could manage to forget it for a few decades first, and get on with the rest of her life.

Something bounded atop her car hood.

Temple jerked to full alertness, feeling caught in the act of something illegal.

A black cat nosed the windshield. Big black cat.

"Louie?"

Another guilt pang. Once you take that puppy out for a walk it doesn't let you stop. She'd hadn't thought much about Midnight Louie lately.

Temple stirred herself out of her reverie and looked around. No more cars in sight, no activity. Just the cat.

She unlocked her door and got out.

The morning felt cooler than the car had under the glaring glass dome of early sunlight.

The cat walked to the fender to sniff the hand she extended.

She still clutched the necklace. Uncramping fingers revealed her palm, hot and moist. The cat figure's sharp edges had scribed red indentations across her heart and head and life lines.

21

A black cat's paw patted at the dangling chain.

Temple's other hand stroked the smooth sun-warmed head.

"You *are* Louie." She nodded at the restaurant name, Three O'clock Louie's. Spuds Lonnigan's cat. A group of old prospectors known as the Glory Hole Gang in their wild west-of-Vegas youth now ran the restaurant. "I better get home to *my* cat Louie and see what he's up to."

Three O'clock twitched his grizzled muzzle and turned so that her stroke followed his spine to the base of his tail and up to the very tip.

It must be nice to be a cat in the sun, Temple thought, with nothing to do and no place to go and no memories worth immortalizing and not a smidgeon of guilt for the roads (both taken and not taken) in your whole supple body.

WILD WOMAN

IT REALLY BEGAN WITH A DAME.

But then, it always does.

I had decided I needed good raw meat, so I was back at my old stand, the stand of canna lilies behind the carp pond at the Crystal Phoenix Hotel and Casino, that is.

I was not setting up shop again, honest. I was just resting and thinking about a midafternoon snack.

I am well aware that my purported daughter, Midnight Louise, is the house dick, can a little doll be a house dick, around here nowadays.

So there I am, lounging among the lilies trying to catch a few Zs when the leaves of the lily-next-door part, trembling.

She is trembling too, all the way to the tips of her full-length fur coat.

That coat is as white as a magician's rabbit and her face is also a pastel tribute to the Easter season: pale pink nose, blush-pink inner ears, sky-blue eye, sun-yellow eye.

Yup. The lady is either wearing one color-changing contact lens, or Mother Nature gave her two-tone vision.

I am not sure which exquisite orb to look into, but she does not notice my schizophrenic attempts to focus.

"Are you Mr. Midnight?" she asks in a soft, quavering voice.

"On formal occasions, yes."

"I suppose this is a formal occasion," she decides,

23

mincing past the carp pond without a glance at the afternoon's seafood selection.

I realize that her pure-white coat, while not as fluffy as a Persian's, declares her a purebred. I have seen a lot of good-looking dames in my time, but this little doll has made a career of it. She is a lean, fine-coated lady and from the look of her, she is in big trouble.

"Have a seat," I say, brushing off a flagstone with my second most useful appendage.

She settles uneasily on the indicated spot, swishing her luxurious train nervously. Her long nails work in and out, lightly scratching the stone.

"And what can I do for you, Miss—?"

"Furbelow."

I had noticed.

"That a last name or a first?"

"My, ah, friends call me Fanny."

"I bet they do. What is the nature of your problem?"

"A gentleman friend is missing."

I fix my gaze on her. "You are sure this is not an intentional absence?"

"Wilfrid would never leave without saying goodbye." She stretches a long silken rear gam and with her tongue straightens the seam where you can see pink peeking through.

Wilfrid. What a wimpy name! "I can believe that. What is your . . . uh, occupation, may I ask?"

"I was a showgirl, but I am retired from the ring, and now serve as a lady's companion."

I nod. This dame has pedigree written all over her, but she seems to get around a bit too much for one of the pampered darlings of the blue-ribbon set.

"That is how I got here," she adds accommodatingly. "A former ringmate begged her mistress to take me along for a beauty pageant they are holding in the hotel today. I had heard there was a house detective here."

"Indeed there is, and he is at your service." I feel no qualms at usurping Midnight Louise's role, since she usurped mine. Even in the feline world it is usurp or be ursurped.

"Did Wilfrid have any visible means of employment?" I ask.

She nods, the spidery edges of her coiffure brushing a canna lily leaf.

"He worked as a domestic. Our pets were neighbors. He was not . . . purebred, but he was a real gentleman, and I can assure you that the only reason he is missing is that something has happened to him. I am so worried!" she adds in a breathy rush, her composure shaken for the first time.

Lucky Wilfrid the Wimp. "When did Slick Willie go missing?"

"Two nights ago. The next morning, when I repaired to my facing window to greet him, I saw the blinds were still drawn shut. I am afraid that his pet is missing also, but that is merely a symptom of the real problem. As soon as Wilfrid was let out each morning, he came to call on me. We were going steady, you might say."

"So his . . . employer is absent as well?"

"There is no sign of life at his residence. None."

"Have you considered the usual vacation? Human beings . . . er, pets, are often not considerate enough to advise others of these alterations in habit."

Her head shook on its long elegant neck. "Wilfrid is usually accommodated at the medical compound when his pet is running off by herself."

While I am contemplating this missing purrson report, I notice an agitation among the nearby lily leaves. I have a pretty good idea what it is, and rise to meet the enemy.

"Ah, Miss Louise. I am interviewing a client in the inner office. Perhaps you would be so good as to fetch some refreshment for Miss Furbelow."

Midnight Louise reacts in a predictable manner: She lofts her back like the St. Louis arch, and hisses like an irate Cardinals fan.

"I know you were not expecting company, Miss Louise, but I am sure that Miss Furbelow will appreciate whatever you can rustle up." I turn to my client. "My girl Friday. She is new at the job."

Miss Midnight Louise's private response to me is unprintable, but her golden eyes narrow as she takes in Miss Fanny Furbelow and I can see that she is curious. She may be a knot off the old snarl, after all. I grin and watch her slink off in no good grace, but without boiling over like a pot of unwatched water.

"Your office has a lovely view," Miss Fanny comments morosely.

I cast my eyes on the fancy fish cavorting in the pond. "Is Wilfrid much of a sportsman?"

"No." She sighs. "He is content with the domestic life. But he is no pushover, Mr. Midnight." Her odd-colored eyes narrow. "Nor am I. I must find out what has happened to him."

"And so you shall, if I have anything to say about it. Ah, would you care for a cup of broth? Shrimp today, I think."

Miss Midnight Louise is back and grudgingly nosing the rice bowl filled with Chef Song's daily offering toward my guest.

"Oh! I have not been able to eat a bite since Wilfrid disappeared. But perhaps a little chicken noodle soup . . ."

Miss Furbelow laps delicately while Midnight Louise squints fiercely at me over her head. "It is won ton," she mouths. "What a bubblehead."

"Miss Furbelow is distressed," I tell Louise, leading her a safe distance away.

"I suppose you believe everything that bleached blond has told you."

"Her coloring is perfectly natural."

"Yeah, sure!" Louise jeers. "If you call people selling your parents into enforced breeding 'natural.' Okay. I bet you believe everything that albino babe has told you."

"It seems pretty cut and dried. Her boyfriend is missing and his house is deserted. Certainly the case is worthy of investigation; he may have been left behind in an empty house. He may be starving to death even as we speak."

"You hope! I have seen you eyeing Miss Furbelow's furbelows. And why are you so anxious to take anybody's 'case'? I thought you were retired."

"Nonsense. I was simply assisting Miss Temple Barr with *her* cases."

"Which are mostly under the covers now, I understand," Miss Midnight Louise notes with a leer.

For one whose romantic life has been surgically truncated she certainly feels empowered to comment on the habits of those not so restricted. I tell her so.

"You are just burned up," she sniffs, "because your precious roommate is rooming with a dude of her own species instead of you."

"How do you know this?"

"You are out of touch, *Père* Louis. I am the one with my nose and ears to the ground nowadays. Which is why you will need me if you intend to actually

27

investigate this missing purrson report."

"I see no need to involve you—"

"Do not worry. I will not interfere with your so-called romantic life. Though I doubt this dollie is about to take up with an out-of-practice gumshoe when the love of her life is missing. *If* you believe her story, that is."

Our discussion is interrupted by a plaintive "Mister Midnight?" from my distraught client.

I return to her side. "It is nothing, dear lady. Just a consultation with my gal Friday about office protocol," I whisper in her ear. "Clerical workers take so much direction these days."

"I know," she says mournfully. "It is so hard to get good help."

"I will need your address."

"Nothing more?" Her limpid blue . . . gold . . . eyes . . . eye gaze into mine.

"Ah, a retainer fee will not be necessary. You are obviously good for it." I decide to stop while I am ahead, and while Midnight Louise is still out of hearing range. "Now, there is nothing to worry about. Midnight Louie is on the case."

A soft rake along my spine spurs me to add, "And Miss Louise will assist. Do not expect to hear from . . . er, us, for a day or two while we investigate."

"But Wilfrid—"

"He will be fine. I suspect his irresponsible employer has taken an unscheduled trip and neglected to inform her neighbors of the event. People can be so thoughtless. No doubt she never thought of you keeping vigil in your window."

"That is what I do now. I am a window widow."

"Tut-tut. No tears." I escort her out with an

avuncular lick on the ear.

"Tears!" Louise is waiting by the canna lilies when I return. "More like eye-stain! Those white hussies are prone to running mascara."

"It is possible there is something in it."

"It is always possible that there is villainy afoot," she concedes, "but you are too quick to believe every sob-sister with a sad story."

"Someone has to."

RADIO MAGIC

MATT MANAGED TO WAIT UNTIL ALMOST NOON TO call Temple the next day.

"And aren't you up bright and early for a night owl!" She greeted him cheerfully enough, but sounded a bit groggier than an early-bird robin should at high noon.

"I wanted to catch you before you went out, in case you have something scheduled this afternoon?" His explanation had turned into a question.

His careful reluctance to assume nothing about her schedule, to pre-deny all interest in its specifics, warred with an overriding compulsion to know what she was doing, with whom, every moment. Matt wasn't used to being bounced between the wildly conflicting extremes of rationality and romance. He realized that he'd best serve himself by appearing calmly normal when he was the opposite. Did everyone go through this charade?

"I'm not going out for a while," Temple said. "What's up?"

"Um, I've got this . . . letter from my mother that's rather interesting. About my real father. And I could use your tape machine. I've got a tape I should hear."

"Oooh, news from the Chicago past? Come on down!"

Matt's relief exited on a sigh as he hung up. He'd been right to use the mystery of his parenthood as the primary lure. Temple couldn't resist speculating any more than she could resist dispensing advice. He certainly knew her, if he didn't quite recognize himself these days.

He picked up the tape and the letters from the table,

30

keys to contact with Temple. He'd known her for almost a year now, and he'd known for most of that year that he found her attractive. He hadn't known that he was in love with her until just after New Year's, only days after she'd resumed her interrupted relationship with Max Kinsella, "the mystifying Max." The magician's stage name was a remnant of the past now, but it lingered like a haunting refrain, which was probably a line he had heard in one of Carmen Molina's vintage torch songs.

At least Kinsella hadn't moved back into Temple's place at the Circle Ritz; there would be no way for Matt to slake his thirst for Temple's company if he had.

He hurried downstairs to her floor; no telling how much time they had. In the short hallway outside her door, he paused. He put his palm on the coffered mahogany, sensed her presence inside like an actor preparing for his first entrance onstage.

Then he knocked.

The door opened almost instantly, and yes, Temple looked the same: loose red curls too adult for Shirley Temple, a petite cyclone of energy and warmth with very honest eyes at the center of that engaging storm.

She was in her usual rush to do three things at once: finish getting ready to go out, deal with him, and feed the newly arrived Midnight Louie his umpteenth snack of the day.

"Here." She handed him a tin of smoked oysters. "Spoon this over Louie's Free-To-Be-Feline. There's coffee in the carafe. I'll sit down with my mug and check out your letter, if that's okay."

"Sure," Matt found himself lying.

He'd hoped for a quiet tête-à-tête, not being drafted into dishing a noxious dollop of seafood over the cat's dry health-food pellets.

Louie, a massive black cat hunched over the shallow glass bowl, eyed Matt soulfully.

"Short shrift. I agree with you, my lad. And a little bribe on top doesn't do much to make up for it."

"Wow!" Temple, reading, was commenting from the living room.

Matt poured himself a mug of black coffee and followed his letters in there.

"Your mother has undergone a huge change of attitude. Now she *wants* you to look into your real father's background?"

"And now *I* don't want to do it." Matt sat on the side chair at right angles to Temple.

Temple was always to be found either in full career gear or out of it. Now her bare feet were tucked under her. She wore a loose aqua knit top over close-fitting tights or leggings or something. Her red hair was comfortably tousled and she looked about fifteen years old.

She hardly seemed like a woman he couldn't get out of his mind, night and day. Day and night.

Then she glanced up at him, and the clarity, perception, and humor in her Civil War eyes— Confederate gray sometimes, and sometimes Union blue—nailed him to his chair.

"First *she* didn't and *you* did; now she *does* and you *don't*. I told you; life is all timing. Or the lack of it."

She could have been describing their own ill-timed relationship, except with them it was first she *did* and he *didn't* and now *he* would and *she* couldn't.

If none of it made much sense, he was beginning to discover that this was more often the case than not in the real world.

"And this letter from the radio station," she went on.

" 'Ambrosia.' Get real!"

"I thought I should at least listen to the tape, which is why I need your machine, and someone to run it. It sounds like a maybe-job offer."

"Radio counseling. Not too different from hotline work. But . . . radio's an entertainment medium." Temple shrugged, then jumped up. "Come on in the other room. The receiver's in there."

He knew it was in there, and he knew that a couple of weeks ago she would have called the other room the "bedroom."

He'd had visiting privileges there before, in the most casual way, once when they were going out together. Now it was taboo territory.

"It might take a while," he began to caution her.

"Hey, this is portable. We'll move it out."

"You can put a tape in this?"

"Sure. Tape. CD. You can even sing karaoke on it."

"No kidding?"

"Yup. Has a feature that strips the voice out but leaves the instruments. You sing solo."

"I just want to hear what WCOO is all about. Maybe this is just some advertising scam. Offering everybody their fifteen minutes of fame on the air."

"I don't know." Temple returned, carrying the squat black machine. "The letter said someone recommended you."

"And they had to get my address somewhere."

"Probably from your boss at ConTact. Maybe that's the recommender."

"But why not mention it to me?"

Temple plopped the receiver on the living room floor near an outlet and plugged it in.

"Sorry this is makeshift. You put the tape in here, and

33

there's your volume control. That's it."

Matt stared at the crowded faceplate of buttons and labels. "Looks like the control com of the Starship *Enterprise* to me."

"You'll get used to it. Gotta go get ready for a buzz by the Crystal Phoenix. I've been neglecting my duties as freelance Public Relations Whiz Kid, and the theme-park makeover at my biggest client's hotel-casino."

"How's that going?"

"Great, I hear! But I'm a cynical ex-news reporter. I don't believe in anything I don't see for myself."

"Speaking of not believing in things you don't see for yourself, what's, uh, the friendly neighborhood magician Max doing these days?"

Matt could have kicked himself for the ensuing silence. He had time to deliver about four swift ones before Temple answered.

"Uh . . . the usual Mystifying Max stuff. Being mysterious."

"I was just wondering. If he was going to vanish again."

"Not this time. I think he's back in Las Vegas for good."

Or ill, Matt mentally inserted into another long pause before Temple spoke again.

"I've really got to get ready. You don't mind if I leave you alone?"

She realized it was a loaded question the moment it left her lips. So she stood there, quizzical smile fading. She had already left him pretty conclusively alone by resuming her relationship with Max Kinsella, errant magician.

Matt moved to reclaim his mug of coffee. "Go ahead. Do you what have to. I'll be all right."

Talk about banal double meanings.

She gave him a last, wrenchingly uncertain smile and returned to the bedroom.

"Just hit 'Play,' " she advised, closing the door.

Matt sat before the stereo on the polished parquet, a faint lemon scent tweaking his nostrils, feeling vaguely like a worshiper in a media-age church. Louie came over to investigate the intruder on the floor: the machine, not him.

He punched "Play" and kept his fingers on the volume button, in case it was too loud.

A woman's voice floated into the room, mellow, the tones as pear-shaped as a Rubens nude. Ambrosia welcoming her petitioners to the seven-to-midnight shift at WCOO—"We Care Only about Others Radio."

Matt braced himself for smut, at worst, or schmaltz, at second worst.

Oddly enough, Ambrosia avoided both traps. People called in, shared their troubles or joys at her mellow urging. A lost love. An anniversary. A sick baby in the hospital. Then Ambrosia picked some soft-rock anthem or bathetic ballad perfectly attuned to the moment: Kenny Rogers's crooning about a time you weren't there for a thirty-something wedding anniversary. "You Light up My Life" for an absent girlfriend. "Feelings" for a lost love.

Despite her inciting radio handle, Ambrosia was romantic rather than raunchy, and managed to sound sincerely sympathetic.

After a few minutes, Matt turned down the volume. He could hear the muffled shut drawer, the muted hiss of running water: Temple going through whatever motions needed in her own little world, which was as removed from his now as the orbit of another planet.

Yet the mundane sounds of her passing through time and motion so near and yet so far, made him edgy. His skin felt so supersensitive that his clothes irritated it as he stirred.

He realized he was staring at the closed door like a mute animal, gazing until it opened for him. Ambrosia's professionally hypnotic voice was no competition for Temple's slightest unseen gesture.

Nuts! The entire phenomenon was nuts.

Matt glanced at Midnight Louie, who was watching him with the same concentrated stare that he himself had given the bedroom door. The cat's pupils had dilated to fill half his irises.

"I guess you go through something like this regularly, despite your unelective surgery last fall, huh, fellah?"

Louie lifted a paw and patted his knee. Honest to God, like he understood.

Silent masculine commiseration, Matt could choose to think. But that idea was as ridiculous as the obsessive longing that gripped him now.

Maybe an operation could fix him too.

DEAD DAHLIA

MOLINA FACED AN OFFICE FULL OF LOOSE ENDS: CRIME scene photos; detectives' reports; Alch and Su sitting across from her, asking as many questions as they answered.

She studied the overview photo now front and center again. A woman's body, twisting in death, her half-visible face frozen in an unvoiced scream. It reminded her of the artist Munch's agonized Expressionistic figure from the painting called "The Scream," the one

36

that novelty manufacturers printed on large blow-up balloons and sold as a symbol of modern angst for entertainment value.

"I could see the ligature mark in the parking lot," she said.

"The . . . implement was gone, but not forgotten," Su noted. One of her mandarin-orange-enameled fingernails expertly flicked a photo from its place in the pile into full view. "Interesting. Some sort of cord, possibly wire with nodules along the length."

"Barbed wire."

Alch nodded. "You could call it that. But not as sharp as the varieties you customarily think of."

"Do you know how many varieties of barbed wire there are?" Su's dry but eager academic voice added. "Hundreds."

"And Nevada uses every one, I bet," Molina predicted.

"Maybe." Su had not yet finished her research.

"Stab wounds?" Molina asked. The medical examiner's report would contain it all, but the clinical detail often obscured the humanity of the death and the motive, the feel of the death scene.

Su leaned forward. Alch never did, but he answered. "Another oddity. Some tiny defense cuts on the hands. Not many. She was choked to semi-consciousness first. A stab in the throat after she was dead."

"Ah." Molina nodded at her detectives. The gratuitous blow, not the killing one, testified the most. Neck-dashers wanted to silence. Maybe they wanted to silence the victim. More often they wanted to silence the internalized voice in their own heads, the one that said they would die unless they killed.

"And did she leave anything?"

Alch shook his head. "We rousted the restaurant staff and the band within thirty hours. None of them admit to recognizing her description, although we don't have a photo a civilian could see past to recognize someone with. They all left from the small employee parking lot on the west side of the building, just as you indicated, Lieutenant."

He gave her a particularly boyish look from under graying eyebrows. "You said you were there alone, and the last customer to leave. You patronize the place often?"

"You're a good detective, Morey. I'm a music buff. That's why I go there. Not everybody shares my enthusiasm."

"The band guys say they stayed late to jam."

"Yeah."

"And did they let you listen in on the session, 'cause you're a regular?"

"Yeah. I'm a regular."

"That's what they said too. They said you left when they knocked off, about three A.M."

She nodded. "It's my only vice, Morey. I've got a great sitter for Mariah, stays all night."

"Solitary vice."

Molina shrugged. "In my position—"

Su was tapping her lethal nails on the glass desktop, impatient to talk about something of substance, like wounds or possible suspects.

Alch got the picture. In her position, Molina couldn't socialize regularly in the cop bars around town, and didn't care to anyway. She didn't dare date inside the department, and her hours and single parenthood kept her off the streets, except on occasion when she went to the Blue Dahlia.

If she had to, Molina would let Alch and Su in on her avocation. But not unless it was absolutely necessary. Carmen worked as a pressure-reliever only because she was a figment of everyone's imagination. The moment she became too real, she would have to die.

And Carmen Molina really didn't want two women to have died in the Blue Dahlia parking lot that Friday night.

"So we've got a mystery woman," Alch summed up, gathering the scattered materials into the manila folder and rapping it sharply on the glass so no untidy ends poked out.

Molina nodded. " 'She left.' A lot of women have, and have ended up dead for it. Just make sure that we don't end up with a mystery killer."

WILD WOMAN, PART II

THE RADIO STATION SAT UNDER A GIANT'S ERECTOR set of metal, an Eiffel Tower of the communications world. The one-story building was oddly insignificant for the spire of electronics it demanded, like the little church in the vale attached to a Gothic flying buttress.

Matt parked the motorcycle as discreetly as he could: A silver streak called a Vampire is hard to hide. He entered a tiny reception area that was equipped with a desk piled with mail and one low sofa for visitors.

"Oh. You must be Ambrosia's three-o'clock." The girl at the reception desk was exactly that—gangly, pierced at earlobe and nostril, wearing a garishly clashing knit vest skimpy enough to show her navel, also pierced.

Matt felt like he was in a massage parlor, although he

had no, um, firsthand experience of such venues.

The girl eyed him approvingly from under eyelashes tipped with cobalt-blue mascara.

"I'll let her know right away." She hit a button on the desk phone while Matt studied the chaos. Music, not totally strident, played over a speaker.

He cleared his throat, even though he didn't have to say anything . . . yet. He'd worried about dressing appropriately for the interview, but saw now that radio was not a visual medium. Khaki shirt and pants might be a bit unimaginative, but they certainly weren't too formal.

He checked his watch. WCOO wasn't far from the ConTact offices, but he did have to leave for errands by four.

"Go right in," the girl announced proudly.

He went through the only door, a bland expanse of wood.

The other side was as jumbled as the lobby: a rat-maze of cubicle walls.

"Hi! You're Matt. I'm Leticia Brown. Come this way and we'll . . . talk radio."

She laughed and led him down the narrow corridor. Matt followed, wishing he had a white rabbit for a guide instead of this amazing being.

She was the most dazzling woman he had ever seen, bar even Kitty O'Connor, the femme fatale of the alley behind ConTact. The memory jangled Matt's nerves like a thrust of broken glass at his veins; a phantom pain that, along with a scar, were eternal reminders of a bizarre assault. But the memory of the woman Temple had christened Kitty the Cutter in a fit of black humor faded before Leticia's majestic presence. The impressions reeled in his mind: caramel-colored (and

40

lots of it visible) skin; perfectly applied and perfectly obvious makeup highlighting dark brown-black eyes that tilted like a cat's under winged brows; burnt-orange highlights in jet-dark hair that were probably tinted, but who cared because the color would have made Titian throw away his brushes in the futility of capturing it. Bold perfect teeth, Witeout bright against that café-au-lait skin. The effect was overwhelming, especially when you factored in that the possessor of all this pulchritude weighed about three hundred pounds.

Matt was used to considering his own good looks a curse; what would it be like to be the perfect woman in everything but the all-important size, he wondered.

What she wore was loose and flowing and didn't do a thing to disguise her bulk. He wasn't sure that she didn't like it that way. Her movements were brisk, adept, and in charge.

She led him into a jewel-box-size office crammed with papers and CDs and tapes, and indicated a frail-looking chair.

"Nice to meet you." A plump amber hand bridged the desktop clutter, a hand beringed and braceleted as if wearing costly welts.

He shook it.

"Whew! Are we talking the wrong media for you!" She sat back to admire him, her chair whining at the weight shift. "I suppose we'll have to do billboards."

"Wait a minute. I don't even know what exactly we're talking about."

"Exactly that. Talk, my man. And music. And emotions. Did you like my tape? I'm Ambrosia."

"*You're* Ambrosia?"

"I'm a producer here too. But Ambrosia is my baby, and Ambrosia is a hit. That's the deal. I thought about

41

adding a real, honest-to-goodness counselor to the mix, and your name came up—"

"How?" Matt figured he better interrupt her or he'd never get a word in edgewise.

"I was interviewing one of the passing-through celebrities. He overheard me and Dwight discussing the idea afterwards, so he recommended you."

"A local celebrity recommended me? Who?"

"Mr. Flamingo, the great Domingo himself. You know, that conceptual art weirdo who got the whole town in a flap over plastic lawn flamingos? I figure that man knows the public pulse."

"That's very nice of Mr., ah, Domingo. But all my counseling work has been private, not public. I don't know about hundreds of people listening in. Look, Miss Brown, I'm even anonymous at the hotline; we use pseudonyms."

"Thousands and thousands listening in," she corrected him, leaning forward until the chair squealed for mercy again. She propped that siren's face on chubby fists. "Oooh, tell me. What's your hotline pseudonym, honey?"

"Ah, Brother John."

"Brother John." She tasted it, rather than pronounced it. "Brother JA-on. After that old school song?" She proceeded to sing, rather well, "Are you sleeping, Brother John?"

"*Frère Jacques,* right?" Her laugh was a tenor saxophone solo. "Far reach, *mon ami.*" Somehow, the voice made the name seem . . . slightly lewd. "All right! This is a music medium as well as a talk medium, after all.

"Brother John," she repeated, wrinkling her nose. And a lovely nose it was too, bare of ring or stud. "I see

42

your point. Maybe that's kind of . . . bland. The Brother John Show. Naw—"

"Hey! Bland Brother John might not be interested in any show."

"Might not be interested in doing a radio counseling show! Led into by a hit like 'Ambrosia in the Evening?' We are talking possible syndication here, and Brother John might not be interested? You *are* an interesting cat. Maybe you're all looks and no brains. But you see what I mean. 'The Brother John Hour,' it sounds like the Crystal Cathedral or something. Religious radio." Her nose wrinkled again.

"What exactly are your counseling qualifications anyway?" she asked as an afterthought.

Matt took a figurative, but deep breath. "I've worked at ConTact hotline for almost a year. Before that, I was a Catholic priest."

"Go on! Get outa here! You? Huh. Makes sense, then. Brother John. We'll give you a try. An audition, okay? Trial run. At least you're used to working nights, right?"

"When would you want this 'show' to run?"

"Ambrosia rules from seven to midnight. I guess we could stand an hour of genuine counseling then."

"The midnight hour—"

"The Midnight Hour! That's it. Baby, you got marketing vibes. Yeah. Okay. Brother John I can stick for now. 'The Midnight Hour *with* Brother John.' Got it. And then we do the billboards. Yeah."

"Uh, about the audition—"

"Oh, yeah. Take an hour or two. Me and Dwight— you'll like him; skinny white dude like you—will play we're typical call-ins; you counsel. That's all. You'll ace it. Got a nice voice. Not too professional, you know? Real sincere. That's the key to my show. And

43

then we do those billboards. Oh, baby . . . I feel like a Hollywood producer. Any questions?"

"A lot. Like—"

"Oh, yeah. Pay. What do shrinks get these days? I haven't seen one since I tried hypnosis for my weight. Say, what? Um, a hundred bucks a night. Naw, two. And we wanta go over the weekend, say five nights a week. Monday and Tuesday are dead anyway. That okay to start?"

Matt tried to do mental math and an examination of conscience at the same time; each canceled the other out. Like Scarlett, he would think about it tomorrow. Rearranging his seven P.M.-to three-A.M. shift at ConTact would be easy compared to adjusting to the idea of counseling as entertainment. Still . . .

"I'll audition, and if you like—"

"What's not to like?"—she glanced down at a notepad on her desk—"Matt? Or should I say, Brother John, you devil, you?"

THE DEAD DON'T TALK

MOLINA SAT AT HER DESK, STARING AT THE CRIME scene photos from the Blue Dahlia. She had seen thousands of these: cut-and-dried, seriously unaesthetic photos that gave the word "graphic" a chilling new definition.

Lieutenant C. R. Molina was used to them. She saw details, clues, a puzzle, a crime scene, a case, a body. She didn't see a person. No one in crime work could see a person in every dead body and survive it. Oh, sure, the victim was a person when Molina interviewed survivors, or mentally pictured arresting the killer.

44

But that person appeared in the other photographs, the ones supplied to newspapers and run in obituary columns. These crime scene memorabilia were evidence: photos of abused and forsaken and unfeeling "remains" hastening toward earthly dissolution. To think of them as anything else was to court insanity.

Carmen though, *Carmen* who sang old standards and watched black-and-white movies and wore silk-velvet dresses that had not required underwear originally, had never discovered a dead body before. A victim, a case, a puzzle? No. Carmen took it personally. Her car, part of the crime site. Her car, defaced. Her place of work and recreation and escape . . . tainted. Touched. Discovered.

Molina should tell Alch and Su about her involvement, of course. But to tell was to kill Carmen. And Carmen was her only escape from the years and desktops of photographed remains.

The knock on her open office door was deferential.

Alch stood looking in, head lowered, expression quizzical. He resembled a graying Hardy boy.

Molina waved him in, toward a chair.

"Must be weird," he commented, eyeing the array of photos. "To find a body."

"I've seen a lot of bodies in a lot of conditions."

"But not unexpected like that. As a witness."

She nodded, volunteering that much. "It was a shock. Don't know why. I've seen a lot more gruesome crime scenes."

"But you were called in there. You knew what to expect."

Molina leaned forward, braced an elbow on her desk, fanned her supporting hand over her mouth. She nodded. "Makes you wonder if I was *expected* to discover the body."

45

Alch relaxed in the chair. "Made me wonder. I didn't know about you." He looked up, carefully. "Just how much of a regular at the Blue Dahlia are you?"

"There are a couple of restaurants I hang at. Mexican place. The B.D. But . . . my patterns aren't predictable. You know the hours."

He nodded. "It's a long shot. Still, if there's something in it—"

"If there is, he waited until I was in the right place to do the job."

Alch shook his head. "Nuts. But they all are. 'She left.' That mean anything to you?"

"Just the obvious. We all know abused women are most vulnerable just after they finally leave their abuser for good. Why do we say 'their abuser?' Isn't he the abuser of us all? Creeps who need to control other people to death, in order to feel alive themselves, are everybody's problem."

"You assume that's the motive here?"

"The message, anyway."

"You really want to go to the autopsy?"

"Yeah. It's been a while."

"Well, I advised the M.E. you'd be coming."

"Oh, good." Molina stood, swept the photos back into their folder. "He'll have the place lined with all the burn victims he can dig up."

"Me," Alch said on the way out, for he disliked autopsies much more than she did, being much more of a romantic, "it's the drowning victims I don't like. Luckily, there aren't a lot of those in Las Vegas."

It had been more than a year since Molina had donned plastic goggles and latex gloves to stand over a stainless-steel autopsy table, trying not to smell the

46

odors that decaying flesh is heir to.

All medical examiners were sadists in one thing: harassing civilians who ventured into their grisly arena. Even a veteran cop like Molina was grist for their private horror show, though they especially relished novices, like reporters or would-be crime writers. In real life, as in the TV show *M*A*S*H,* black humor was the only sane way to deal with constant carnage.

Rusty Bahr was one of those men who had outlived his youthful nickname. His hair had waned to the earline while his yellowing eyebrows had waxed long and bushy enough to imprison a princess.

Privately, Molina called him "Grizzly," which did suit his line of work as well as his burly appearance.

He looked at her now over the trifocal lines in his goggles, a tall empire-builder of a man she could easily imagine taming darkest Africa in the nineteenth century. Medical examiners, like trial lawyers, had a knack for self-dramatization.

"This particular corpse stick in your craw, Lieutenant?"

The food metaphor was part of the morgue comedy revue.

"The body was found in a staged scene."

"Killed there too?"

"That's for forensics to say. But the marking was on a nearby vehicle, not on the body, so far as we know."

"Pretty straightforward body." Bahr glanced at the waxy flesh from which the first mannequin-grip of rigor mortis had long since fallen.

Fresh kills like this were a mockery of the human condition. Naked, immutable; a preview of the fate to which all flesh comes. After visiting the morgue a few times, and the decaying body vault, Molina had decided

47

how her particular world should end, as Robert Frost had asked in his short, macabre poem. Not in icy flesh imbedded in earth, but in fire. In Matt Devine's choice for Clifford Effinger: cremation.

"Her clothes," Molina said.

"Bagged and tagged upstairs. We deal with the story scribed into the derma, Lieutenant, into bone and body tissue."

"The ligature was fatal? The stab in the throat an afterthought?"

"Looks like it."

"Strange pattern."

He nodded, bending nearer the mottled flesh of the woman's throat.

She was not a young woman. Not the glamorous, model-thin young thing so picturesquely slain on camera in a zillion TV shows and films.

The medical examiner would exhume the facts dormant in this body: time of death; actual means; age; weaknesses; trauma.

Molina would put the medical data into a socioeconomic framework. Already she had observations: mid-fifties; middle-class, starting to lose the battle of the bulge but not particularly worried about it. Most telling detail: the base of the third finger on the left hand pinched in, as if it had worn a corset for many years. A wedding ring.

She Left.

Many had tried and failed, but the graffiti artist/killer said that this woman had succeeded, at least for a while.

It was an epitaph for too many women across the country, for too many daily newspaper front-page stories: bodies of women who had left, and too many sisters left behind who had not yet summoned the courage to leave.

The medical examiner picked up an electric implement with a small circular saw at the end. It began whirring like a can opener. The slicing of the cranium to expose the brain was about to begin.

Behind her, Alch cleared his throat.

Curious fact: autopsies usually shook men more than women. She knew Alch would leave very shortly. She would stay, and every moment she stayed the dead woman she had found sprawled by her car would become a dead body, would become a case number, would become more an event she could decipher in the course of many days' work, and less an affront to her very soul.

GRIPEVINE

"THE FIRST TASK OF THE CANNY OPERATIVE IS TO SCOUT the victim's place of habitation."

"You mean where he lived."

"Lives. We do not know that anyone is dead here."

Midnight Louise is too busy checking out the traffic on the Strip to object to my correction.

"That neighborhood is seven miles from here," she says. "Already we are losing money. How much did that dame slap down for a retainer anyway?"

"Er . . . enough for me to know and you to forget about. I handle the money, kit. Got it?"

"I do not 'got it,' that is the whole point. But I am not in this for the money anyway."

"Oh?"

"I thought I would like to see how you operate . . . when you are not dishing out the dopamine to the dames, that is."

"Dopamine? Are you implying that I need the aid of drugs to fascinate the ladies?"

"You are a catnip user."

"That is a legal aid to . . . circulation."

"Yeah, Pops. To your social circulation."

"Do not tell me that you do not take a little nip now and again."

"Not a bit. Not a sip. Not a dip. I believe in holistic medicine."

"Wholistic?"

"I believe in natural highs."

"Such as?"

"The fresh air of springtime."

50

"I see what you mean," I say as an air-conditioning truck goes by.

What it actually is becomes clear in a moment: It is a Dust Devils housecleaning service truck pausing at a red light. The rear door of the van trails a vacuum cleaner cord and thus is handily ajar.

"Come on, kitten! Move your tailpiece! Our limo has arrived."

I charge the idling van, Midnight Louise fierce on my own tail. That babe is so competitive she would imprint on a cruising great white shark . . . just because.

I pry the door open and leap into the cluttered dark, counting on my darling would-be daughter to be close behind.

She is. And talkative.

"How do we know that this dust-buster bus is heading in the direction we want?"

"We do not. But every time it stops for a red light, someone jumps out and checks the intersection." I am silent for about six beats.

"I take it this 'someone' is I?"

"Where did you learn such impeccable grammar? Let us say the 'someone' is the junior member of the firm."

"Let us say this job sucks."

"Perhaps. But somebody has to. Oops. We have stopped. Hop to it."

Thus, via frequent stops and my encyclopedic knowledge of the Las Vegas street map, Midnight Louise and I are conveyed to within a mile of our goal, at which time we forsake the Dust Devils van for a bit of fancy footwork.

"Now I get it," she observes between pants as we mush along to the lively Miss Fanny Furbelow's neighborhood. "The secret to your success is a memorized guide to the streets of Las Vegas."

"There is a lot more I know that is not obvious."

"So I have noticed."

"Now hush! We have arrived. See! The matching windows. And, if I am not mistaken, the lissome widow even now keeps vigil at her lonely station."

" 'Lissome widow.' Dial a twentieth-century dictionary, mein papa. 'Lonely station.' I bet *she* did him in."

"First, we reconnoiter the alleged victim's domicile."

Miss Midnight Louise is already sniffing around the back door of the house next door.

"Someone left. I would say more than two days ago. I detect a clump of . . . hmmm, this is a commercial brand of cat food, Pops. Unfortunately, my palate has been accustomed to Chef Song's ministrations."

"An Asian chef feeds you Italian soup?"

"Not 'minestrone,' Daddio. 'Ministrations.' You know what ministrations are . . . you just pucker up your lips and ministrate."

I am not about to answer that one.

So I dutifully sniff the back stairs.

Say!

A clear "footprint."

"Not just food, my dear. Also a lilt of litter scent. Pretty Paws, if I am not mistaken. The divine Yvette's brand, that allows no piece of litter to cling beyond its time. The missing Mister Wilfrid's employer spares no expense for her domestic help."

"So she is a saint. They are all dead, too, are they not?"

"The fact that the owner is gone does not mean that the lady or even her feline companion are, er, goners in the existential sense."

"Cut the theorizing. Can you crack this door?"

"Why must I do all the difficult jobs? I found us transportation. Perhaps you can get us entry. It would be a good exercise."

"Fine," she says, "but the back door is locked. I shall return."

With that threat, she stalks off around the side of the house, and I settle down for a long winter's nap. No doubt the chit will soon be back, begging me to enlighten her to the fifty nifty feline ways to gain illegal entry.

HEARD IT ON THE GRAPEVINE

MATT STOPPED AT A DISCOUNT ELECTRONICS STORE TO buy a shelf unit stereo.

He had never heard that phrase until he got there, and he wasn't sure what he had bought when he left after arranging for the item's delivery to Electra Lark at the Circle Ritz. Motorcycles weren't useful for bringing home big, heavy sound equipment boxes.

What Matt needed had been a machine to record and play back Ambrosia's show on the radio.

What he *thought* he got was a combination tape player, CD player, juke box, and Atari slot machine, a high-tech melange of buttons and digital light-up visuals with two accompanying speakers that looked and sounded like Darth Vader's helmet-head: black, bristling, and booming.

The setup also came with an instruction book a quarter-inch thick. Matt hoped that was because it was in three languages, none of which he could seem to translate, including English.

Matt suspected that all he had really needed was a cheap boom box, but even the term "boom box" had sounded immature and obnoxious. The earnest yet superior salesman had eagerly pointed out the advantages of the mini-tower system, so Matt had nodded and produced plastic. By the grace of Chase Manhattan Bank and his own ignorance he was another four hundred dollars poorer.

But . . . for poorer, for richer.

The first thing he did when he got back to his apartment was to get out his address directory—a notepad with a pharmacy phone number logo that had been dropped into his grocery store bag—and dial most of the few numbers recorded in it.

First was landlady Electra Lark, to see if she'd mind accepting delivery on the mini tower unit in the next couple days.

"I love getting packages!" she insisted, as if he had offered to do her a favor.

Then he called Chet Humphries, director of the ConTact hotline, to discuss a change in hours to accommodate his audition tomorrow.

"Is this because of that radio station inquiry?" Chet's scholarly voice asked over the phone.

Chet was a retired college psychology professor who found running the hotline fended off the retirement blues.

"Yes. They sound pretty serious at the radio station. Want to use my ConTact 'handle.' I don't know how you feel about my . . . "

"Great idea! We need to reach out, not just 'be there' for those who know where to find us, or have the will to call."

"But . . . the underlying motive is completely commercial."

"People learn a lot about interpersonal dynamics even from those freak-show TV talk shows. Eighty percent of it's mummery, but that twenty percent of classic dysfunctionalism comes through loud and clear."

"Very loud," Matt said dryly. "So it wouldn't bother you if I did this . . . show?"

"Not at all. It is media, my dear boy. Any sophisticated listener knows that's always to be taken with a grain of salt."

"I don't think their target audience is the sophisticated listener. If I do commit to this midnight show, I'd have to work ConTact from—"

"Three to eleven P.M. instead of seven to three A.M.," Chet said promptly. He managed shifts for a variety of full and parttime workers. "You'd have to finish up a full workday with another hour of the talking cure. That okay with you?"

"Yeah, if I can get used to the idea of helping people as entertainment. Doesn't exactly fit my previous calling. But I'm used to working nights now. Kind of like it."

"You're a good counselor; you should do fine with a radio clientele. They need someone with real ethics, like you."

"But am I a good showman? That's part of the job."

"Do your best, youngster; that's all any of us can do."

Having taught for so many years, Chet had an arsenal of fondly avuncular titles suitable for students. Some people would have found the habit condescending, but Matt enjoyed the sense of being back in school again. In a very real sense, he was. Civilian school. Secular school.

He hung up, multiplying figures on a blank page of the notepad. Another essential item of civilian life he didn't have: a pocket calculator. Luckily, he still knew his multiplication tables, and his scratching pencil had come up with a mind-boggling formula: At two hundred dollars an hour, five nights a week, Matt would be making four thousand extra a month!

Hey! He'd have his Christmas present-buying spree paid off in . . . three weeks, not including the belated present of Temple's necklace.

He grimaced as he looked at the figures. She hadn't given it back yet. He hoped she wouldn't, but could understand her reluctance to keep it. She was engaged to another man now; he'd have to get used to the idea.

His gaze lingered on her phone number, one of three on the all-important first sheet of the notepad: his boss, his landlady, his . . . no words could summarize what Temple was to him.

He turned to a fresh page and carefully printed in Leticia Brown's name and phone number. Door number four: the radio station. What would lie behind it? A brave new world? Or a booby prize?

While he was sitting there, being wistful, the phone startled him by ringing.

My, he was getting popular.

"Hello?"

"Frank here. Bucek."

"Oh, Frank. I'd almost forgotten I'd called you."

"I get around, out of the office. Anyway, I was able to look into that party you wanted checked out. I got intrigued when you suggested she might have something to do with that scam to rip off the casino. You know, when I first came to Vegas and ran into you again."

Matt knew. The shock washed over him again: his spiritual director from St. Vincent Seminary, *the* formidable Father Frank Bucek, aka Father Frankenfurter, a civilian himself, with a wife and job in the FBI.

"I probably shouldn't have asked—" Matt began, falling into the guilty mode of a confessee.

"No problem. We're always interested in that kind of terrorist activity, especially after Oklahoma City. But we came up pretty empty on this Kitty O'Connor, at least under that name. Some activity in Ireland years ago. Some hints she showed up in South America. All pretty innocuous. She's not a major player. Sorry."

"*I'm* sorry—sorry I bothered you."

"Don't be. You're in good company."

"Company?"

"Your Lieutenant Molina contacted me for a rundown too."

"She's not *my* lieutenant."

"Your local city cop, then. She's pretty tenacious."

"I thought all law enforcement people were."

"Nope."

"Thanks. I appreciate the information."

"Hey! I'm not done. I also ferreted out a subversive group in your neighborhood."

"IRA?"

"Naw. Ex-pat priests. The Corpus organization for former priests doesn't have a chapter in your area; not too many ex-priests hang out in Las Vegas, but there's an informal group that meets in Henderson. Got a pencil?"

"In my hand."

"Write this down: Nicholas Benedict, 555-9543. Got it?"

"Got it. So. They, like, meet?"

" 'Fraid it's tonight. Just heard there's something going on. Look into it. It can't hurt."

Yes, it can, Matt thought. It can always hurt.

CLOTHES CALL

MOLINA MET ALCH IN THE MORGUE'S SMALLISH lobby, looking sheepish.

"I was checking out the victim's clothing."

"I'll get the report in a couple of days." She turned to leave. The smell of the autopsy room, however well masked, lingered like a hidden corpse.

"I think you should look at them." Alch still sounded apologetic, but that would be for deserting her at the dissection table.

Molina raised her eyebrows.

He shrugged before he spoke again. "Maybe I should say . . . smell them."

"I'm not really in the best condition for smelling the evidence, Morey," Molina told him in the elevator on the way up.

He was standing in the elevator's opposite corner, leaning against the wall, as if getting a load off his feet rather than a reek out of his nostrils was the real reason for the distance.

His mustache twitched. "I know. But this smell you can't miss. Only . . . I can't explain it."

The lab was only a few doors away from the elevator, and a technician, who had put away the brown paper bags while Alch was gone, cheerfully produced them again.

Molina, hands enclosed in latex gloves, unfolded them gingerly. With the damage to the body occurring on the neck and throat, the clothing was likely to bear little damage from the crime.

She was glad that Alch had dragged her up here, after all. There was something odd about the clothes—a dark skirt, a blouse, a matching jacket. Navy blue, except for the blouse, which was a strange, not-silk slippery fabric. Polyester. This lady was definitely not upscale.

"She had no purse. No ID." Molina was repeating what they already knew. "Nothing in that line's turned up?"

Alch shook his head. "We checked the trash containers in a mile radius; got the trash pickup schedule. Nothing."

"Someone didn't want us to find out *who* she was, but he sure didn't mind us finding *her*."

"Do you see what I mean about the smell?"

"Yeah. Oh, yeah." Molina's head reared back as the unfolded skirt gave off an odor as strong as a slap in the face. "God, I hate that stuff."

Alch nodded glumly. "Get it often enough in the squad cars. That's why I was so happy I'd made detective. Never have to smell that strawberry shit again."

"Are you sure it's just strawberry? This is too noxious to be just a little strawberry."

"You got it, Lieutenant. It's super-amplified strawberry, that's what it is. Strawberry to die from. They always use it in those car refresher thingies that hang from the dashboard. It's enough to make a guy puke."

She nodded. "Strong stuff. I always thought it was worse than whatever it was supposed to cover up."

"So why's it so strong on the victim's clothes?"

Molina considered this very good question. "They also use it in gas stations' ladies' rooms."

"No kidding! Honest, I didn't know that."

"What do they use in gas stations' men's rooms, then?"

Alch thought. "Uh, nothing. Lieutenant."

Molina restrained herself from comment. "So she was in a gas station ladies' room recently? Makes no sense, but—"

"Check the gas stations in the neighborhood for strawberry air freshener. And their trash bins too."

"Got it." Molina took a deep breath. "Now let's get out of here."

Back in the lobby, they paused by some mutual unspoken consent.

"Maybe that strawberry stuff," Alch suggested, "would help . . . in there."

"No way. If the orange stuff doesn't do it; nothing will. Besides, that strawberry stuff is worse than death warmed over."

"Maybe," Alch said, but he didn't sound convinced.

Molina got home a little before seven to an empty house.

Mariah was attending an after-school basketball game followed by a pizza-dinner out and would be dropped off by the organizing parent.

Sometimes she envied parents their minivans full of screaming kids and the smell of pizza and spilled soft drinks.

She took a shower, using almond-scented gel and shampoo. Better to smell like poison than putrefaction.

Despite it, an odor of orange blossoms lingered, bringing thoughts not of weddings, but of very ripe and hidden death.

She ran her fingernails into a bar of wet Ivory soap, digging out half-moons of scrapings that reminded her of the skin cells so often left behind under a victim's nails.

The house was old, and the shower was a coffin, dark as the deep maroon ceramic tile that lined it.

Anybody could be in the house, sneaking up on her like in *Psycho,* and she wouldn't know it, see it, hear it.

She pulled the big bath towel down from the dimpled, frosted glass door, and stepped out into the bathroom, which felt cold.

"Boo!" said Mariah from the adjacent bedroom.

"Back already?"

"You been at the morgue, haven't you?"

"What makes you think so?"

"You never shower this early, unless you've been at the morgue."

"You're a good detective," Molina said in a tone not too different from what she'd use with an employee.

The big navy towel swathed her torso to the ankles. She wrapped a hand towel around her wet head.

"You look like a swami," Mariah teased.

"Then I will go into the kitchen and foretell what you will *not* have for dinner, *mem sahib.*"

Navy, Molina thought as she shooed her daughter out the bedroom door and shed the damp towel to don her usual jogging suit.

Dreary color for a dreary set of clothes. Nothing about the victim was suitable for a TV movie-of-the-week. Just some poor woman who had attracted the violent hand of some formerly abused child who had grown up into a controlling, homicidal man.

Still the same old story.

She toweled her chin-length hair dry, rubbed hard, as if to shake off any lingering taint of Grizzly's dead body emporium.

In the other room, the TV blared. The night for *Sabrina, the Teenage Witch* and her annoying black cat.

"Soon enough," Molina breathed to herself, bracing herself for stages yet to come in her growing daughter. "Soon enough. But not yet."

She went out to round up the kittens and find out how Mariah's day had been and who had won the basketball game, which was important, because Our Lady of Guadalupe had all the cutest boys on its team.

Molina frowned. Didn't girls play basketball too these days?

LOUIE'S GRIM DISCOVERY

OF COURSE, I ONLY APPEAR TO BE NAPPING.

That is what I tell Miss Midnight Louise when she returns from her tour of duty around the exterior of Miss Fanny Furbelow's beloved's house.

"There is a hole in the back screen door I could enlarge into an entryway, but the inner door is solid wood and locked," she reports, eyeing me with disfavor. (But when did she eye me with anything else?)

"What about windows?"

"There are a few," she admits. "All closed tighter than a pit bull's jaw."

"And the front door?"

"Also solid wood; also locked." She cocks an eye at the adjacent house. "No wonder the Window Widow is so upset. If the resident human does not return, I do not see any way Wilfrid could get out, were he still inside."

We glance toward the neighbor's house, to see Miss Fanny Furbelow's mouth gape wide in a distress cry we cannot hear through the window glass.

Miss Louise sits down beside me, the tip of her tail thrashing to show that she is peeved with both the situation and my calm in the face of frustration.

I stand, stretch, and scratch my neck just to get a rise out of her ruff.

"We are not here to watch what passes for a workout with you nowadays," she says.

"I will inspect the site. See what I can come up with."

She rolls her eyes most disrespectfully.

I admit to myself that I have no hot ideas for cracking into this joint. It is a small, old house of the modest sort, but they are built far better than the trendy shacks sprouting up like postmodern mushrooms in Henderson down the highway.

However, I would much like to enhance my status in the eyes of Midnight Louise, not to mention in those two-tone models of the lovely White Widow. As soon as I am out of sight of both females, I sit down, and scratch my head this time. Maybe I will startle some brain cells into working overtime.

I decide to work this case and this scene from the human angle, rather than the animal, for once.

If Miss Furbelow is correct, and Wilf the Sylph's "pet" went off without any prior planning, something bad may have happened to her. I decide to examine the doors and windows for signs of attempted human break-in.

Midnight Louise does know her Las Vegas architecture. These classic old ranch houses may be unimaginative in style and construction, but they were built to repel sunlight and heat loss, which means that windows are few and far between and all means of entrance or egress are on the small side.

Air-conditioners are hoisted up on the roof in this state, and do not hunker down on the ground alongside the house to act as convenient stepping stones. Also, the ground here is desert-dry, which means footprints rarely leave much of an impression.

Midnight Louise has left no trace, I notice as I pussyfoot around the place. The stucco exterior needs work and the painted wooden frames of the windows are peeling. The hole in the back screen door was made by a cat stretching up to sharpen his shivs.

I doubt that I will have any more luck than the missing Wilfrid in getting the back door to open, especially now that there is likely no one inside. I sit to consider matters. Although my foremost problem is assisting my client in finding out where her missing swain is, I have another dilemma.

Midnight Louise is already crowing about her superior agility in mounting the prow of Cleopatra's Barge to examine the dead guy affixed thereon not long before. I do not like to strike out twice in the pipsqueak's eyes. It is bad form for the masculine gender to let these new-model femi-felines get too uppity.

So I badly need to crack into this house, if not crack the case right this minute. I admonish my whiskers with a wet mitt, a gesture that often assists my thinking processes. I fear that there is nothing for it: I will have to use subterfuge and human help, rather than my solo skills as a street operative.

This is a bit of a comedown from my usual modus operandi, but I suppose I can share some trade secrets with the kit. She might come in handy as a gofer now and again, and there is nothing like letting a female think that she is going to get to do more than she is for ensuring cooperation.

So I rise and amble around the front corner of the house.

She is waiting for me like a rabid panther, ready to pounce on any little failure on my part.

"Well?" she demands in a soprano shrill.

"Tighter than a tick on an airdale."

"I did not think you would knock a door down all by your lonesome."

I sit to inspect my nails, very casually. "I do not want the scene disturbed, in case there is a big-time crime here."

"With a missing house cat?"

"Stranger things have happened."

"Name one."

I do hate it when my figures of speech are asked to stand up and defend themselves.

I nod at the attractive white silhouette, so to speak, in the opposite window. "I believe it is time to learn more of Miss Furbelow's domestic situation."

"Oh, you would just love to turn this case into Froggy Went a-Courting! Is it not a conflict of interest for an investigator to harbor romantic notions about a female client who asks him to find a missing mate?"

"On the contrary. If you read a bit more classic literature, you would know that it is standard operating procedure."

"Classic literature! You are no doubt discussing the volumes at the Thrill 'n' Quill Bookstore, with all the cool dudes and the hot dames on the covers."

"Exactly. Classic literature. Anyway, if you care to amble after me, you will see how the old hand uses human nature to work for him without pay."

She is so silent after this, that when I arrive beneath Miss Fanny's window I am not even sure that Midnight Louise has followed me.

Miss Fanny wiggles her airy eyebrows at me, but I shake my head to show that I have found no answers across the way. I lean up against the house wall and call for her to come out.

She shakes her head, but I persist. I watch her glance over her shoulder now and again, as if undecided. Finally, she disappears.

"What is the purpose of this pantomime?" Midnight Louise asks sourly. "A road show of *Romeo and Juliet*?"

"Please. I am working."

"Yes, I can tell. No doubt this house would fall over if you were not leaning up against it."

"Can it, sister. I heard something around the front."

"Are you claiming an incestuous relationship with me?"

"I am claiming no relationship. That is a just an expression."

"No doubt from one of those seriously out-of-date books you lounge around on at the Thrill 'n' Quill. You would be more in keeping with the tempo of the times if you called me 'girl,' as in 'you go, girl, go.' "

This is too much. This is the last whisker! I sit right down and curl my upper lip.

"Listen, squirt. I do not lounge on anything but my laurels at the Thrill 'n' Quill. I go there only on business to consult my, er, librarian, Ingram. As for calling you 'girl,' I am given to understand that would be the supreme insult. I do not mind tossing the casual insult, but I do try to avoid the socially irredeemable faux pas. And now you tell me that 'girl' is okay?"

She shrugs, looking very pleased with herself, which is nothing new in her arsenal of expressions.

"Times change, Daddy dudest. 'Girl' is now considered a term of empowerment. I guess you could call it discrimination reversed."

I shake my head, hoping that the rattling I hear is water in my ear rather than my brains hitting a dead end.

"Look. I do not care about terminology. I am more worried about termination at the moment."

Her ears prick. "You are saying you suspect serious

68

foul play in the disappearance of Wilfrid?"

"Now the . . . ahem, girl gets it! And first I have to talk to Miss Fanny again."

Midnight Louise puckers her black-velvet brow and says no more for the moment. I think I have faked the kit out. I was not born yesterday, as she is too fond of reminding me.

I trot to the front door to find a pretty picture installed there: Miss Fanny Furbelow sitting on the stoop with her long white train fluffed around her dainty feet.

"Just shoot me with a Hasselblad," Midnight Louise mutters, but it is under her breath. "What a coquette."

"A lovely girl," I say pointedly, before trotting over and getting down to business. "I assume you are here because I requested your presence."

Miss Fanny nods, looking a bit confused.

"I also assume your . . . pet . . . is at home to let you out."

"She is a retired meter maid and is usually amenable to my requests, since I am fixed and only go next door."

I nod, well pleased. "Good girl," I say. Hey, if an uppity, ultraliberated snip tells me this is okay, I will use it to the max, if not to the manx.

"Now, the next thing we must get your, er, pet to do is to come out after you."

Jeez, I do not like using the term "pet" for humans. Apparently a movement is afoot to grab every denigrating term in the book and flaunt it. I do not need to prove my superiority to humans by calling them "pets." The difference is obvious to any trained observer.

Of course such an observer cannot be human.

Please do not waste time calling me a feline chauvinist. I am impervious to politically correct cant. Or can.

Meanwhile, I have two dames on my hands, both of the "girl" persuasion.

"Oh," says Miss Fanny. "I do not think I can get my pet to do everything I say. She is very independent."

"Nonsense," Miss Midnight Louise spits. "These humans are pushovers if you know how to handle them."

"For once we agree," I say with a small smile. "All right. It is obvious that your 'pet' has one soft spot."

"Where?" Miss Fanny asks with wide-open blue/gold eyes. "I am soft everywhere, of course, but she is soft only in certain places, which I have selected for private pummeling when I am in the mood."

"I am not interested," Miss Louise spits, "in your private dependency relationships."

"You," I say, gazing deeply into Miss Fanny's eye/eyes, "are her soft spot. Therefore, we will put you in danger."

"Daddy dearest! This is the client. We do not risk the client."

"I understand that, gentlest girlie," I grit right back at the little spitfire. "We merely make the gullible pet believe that the soft spot is in danger. Therefore"—I turn to Miss Fanny in a businesslike mode—"you will 'disappear' for the nonce, while Miss Louise and I have hysterics by your window. When your loyal body servant comes to the scene of the disturbance, we will subtly lure her to the neighboring house, encouraging her to think that you are trapped therein. She will obviously leave no modern method of entry untried in her fever to enter the place."

70

"Oh!" Miss Fanny's odd-colored eyes melt into caramel and blueberry syrup as she gazes upon me. "You are so clever. I have only to play hide and seek for a while, then, and leave it to the professionals?" She looks trustingly from Louise to myself.

I pat her gently on the, er, flank. "Exactly. Now, do you have some special hiding place in the vicinity?"

"I do rather enjoy the arbor under the oleander bushes in bloom."

"Excellent. Off with you, and leave the rest to us."

She scampers away, tail high, wide, and handsome.

"You are quite an operator," Midnight Louise admits. Or accuses. Sometimes I cannot quite tell the difference.

"Thank you. Girl."

"I did not say 'operative.' I said operator. There is a difference, but I am sure you are unable to discern it."

"Whatever. Now comes the hard part. We must attract the pet's limited attention span, and lead it where we wish it to go. Are you ready to scream yourself hoarse, if need be?"

"I am ready to walk a tightrope on my hind legs, if need be. I believe you are climbing up the wrong tree, but if you are willing to pussyfoot out on a limb, so am I. I do so like to watch things fall."

I say nothing in response. We return to the widow's walk window, now empty of a piquant little feline face, and proceed to yowl in tandem and hurl ourselves up at the glass.

It takes only ten minutes to draw Miss Fanny's meter maid to the window.

"Goodness," she mouths through the glass. "The neighborhood cats are getting very vulgar."

In another ten minutes she begins to worry about

71

her precious Fanny.

In five more she opens the door, only to find us serenading the dickens out of her postal box.

"Go away, you alley cats!" she cries. "Fanny! Come home."

But Fanny does not come home, having strict instructions not to.

I jump off the stoop, run toward the neighboring house, then stop, fix the meter maid with my best please-I-have-to-park-here eye, and wait.

"Go away, that is right!" she admonishes me. "You do not belong in this neighborhood."

She has got that right.

I race to the next door house and begin gouging track marks in the stucco under the window.

Belatedly, Louise runs over and does likewise.

"Why, you crazy cats. It is as if you are trying to tell me something."

Yes, Timmy's mother. You did this a thousand times on *Lassie* and that was only a dumb dog. Come on, lady; you are old enough to have seen *Lassie* on TV. Just call me Classie, because I am a cat.

"Oh, my," she says. "I hope my little Fanny hasn't got caught under that house."

Her fanny is not little, but I refrain from commenting on that fact. Ever the gentleman. Before you know it, she is knocking on the front door, next door.

"Monica. Monica, are you home?"

Soon the knocking has her knuckles red. I yowl as if facing a firing squad, and, after a withering look, Louise unleashes a howl that could raise the dead.

"Oh, dear. Something must be terribly wrong. They say animals can sense earthquakes."

Her hands wring, then try the front door latch.

Lo and behold, it opens as if a friendly zephyr has blown through.

"Oh, Monica! You left your door open. How careless. My Fanny must have pushed it open, then shut, and became trapped in your house while you were out."

Miss Meter Maid is one of those people who live alone and talk to their cats and themselves. I am grateful for this; it allows me to learn much about the situation.

"You were always too trusting, Monica. Fan-nee! Fan-nee!"

I brush by her, Louise hard behind me.

My nostrils have told me what poor Miss Meter Maid is incapable of discerning. Something has died in this house, and recently. I fear that it is bigger than a mouse.

Miss Midnight Louise brushes past me, eyes narrowed in a very ungirlish way. "Death on the premises. Do not let her see. I will check out the bedrooms."

I resent this supplanting of my natural leadership role, but have no chance to object. Midnight Louise is a shadow disappearing down the hallway.

"Oh. Where is my lovely Fanny? Monica? Say you are here, please. And that my cat is all right."

I spring after my renegade partner. I do not want the crime scene disturbed.

But I need not have worried.

Midnight Louise has stopped dead at the bedroom door, staring at something out of my sight.

"We have to let the human 'discover' this," she mutters, "though it will be too much for her. You were right, Pops. There is one very dead homicide victim in here. I was convinced it was a member of the other species, but no such luck."

I stare past her shoulder into the room. The floor is old-fashioned wood planking, but a rag rug lies rumpled beside the bed.

On it, dead center, and definitely dead to the world, lies a handsome tiger cat.

Louise and I mew piteously, and brace ourselves for human hysteria.

We are not disappointed.

Although she is discreetly hidden outside, in very short order Miss Fanny Furbelow will discover that her widowhood is now a fact, not a fear.

BROTHERS KEEPERS

HENDERSON, NEVADA, WAS ONE OF THE FASTEST-growing communities in the Sunbelt.

Although it seemed only a stone's throw from the Goliath and other behemoth hotels hunkering along the Las Vegas Strip, it felt like another world.

Matt cruised the Vampire along these clean streets bracketed by upscale two-story homes, the next generation of Sunbelt building after decades of single-story ranch houses. Even the widest-open spaces focused on reducing suburban sprawl now. Imposing as these homes were, they sat on stingy lots, almost seeming to rub stucco shoulders with each other.

He didn't have a clue to what these posh-looking places would cost. More than he could imagine, he figured, and they were probably far less fancy than he thought.

The ex-priests were meeting at a major intersection on the fringe of this human ant farm, at a church, of course. Catholic, of course. Maternity of Mary.

Despite reasonably warm weather, no children played on the weedless front lawns, no garage door gaped open to display cars or clutter.

Matt reached the right address: a boxy brick and glass building whose purpose was suggested by a prow of sharply angled glass. A stained-glass cross was inlaid into the sun-repelling bronze film that overlay the window-wall like technological-age gilt.

What struck him most, though, about this new-built church with the unlived-in look was its relative smallness compared to the looming cliffs of stone and brick that still anchored the old Chicago neighborhoods. Even Our Lady of Guadalupe's desert-architecture modesty in the Hispanic neighborhood dwarfed this neat, pristine, and somehow shrunken house of worship.

Matt felt no urge to visit the church proper. It would be open, bright and soaring like the mandatory "great room" in the houses that surrounded it. He preferred a more serious interior, a sense of history, not histrionics.

He was, he realized, probably becoming an old fogey, a hidebound conservative. So he let the Vampire swoop into the parking lot, toward a low wing attached to the church that was far too small to be a rectory or a convent or a school.

At eight o'clock at night only a few cars populated the parking lot. Saturday evening mass attendees were long gone, heading to the parties they expected to keep them up so late that Sunday morning mass would be unthinkable. All that remained on the cooling asphalt were a couple minivans, teal and forest green, an aging Volvo station wagon, a blue Cavalier, a couple of Honda Civics.

Matt eased the Vampire between the two minivans, hoping to shelter it from potential thieves. Henderson's obsessivecompulsive newness didn't rule out old failings like petty crime.

Matt glanced back as he walked away to make sure a street light would discourage lock-pickers. The Vampire's sleek silver hindquarters were just visible, making it look like a thoroughbred parked among plow horses.

Matt had left his helmet hanging from the handlebar, risking theft. If you couldn't trust a Catholic church parking lot, what could you trust? Besides, he didn't want to walk into a meeting of ex-priests looking like an escapee from *The Wild Bunch.*

He walked into a room like a thousand he had walked into before.

Bare vinyl tile floors. Large collapsible tables usable for anything from a conference to a buffet. Metal folding chairs in that peculiar unnameable brown-gray color that were made to numb rears in record time. Serviceable beige blinds were already hanging slightly askew on the big horizontal windows. Decor by Institutions Anonymous.

No wonder it felt like he had crashed an Alcoholics Anonymous meeting. Especially when he spotted the big aluminum coffee urn on a table by the wall, flanked by stacks of Styrofoam cups, plastic stir-sticks and packets of noncalorie sweetener.

The coffee would be oily and black; everything you put in it would have chemical identification chains longer than your own DNA. The fluorescent overhead lights would make everybody resemble most-wanted criminals, and the chance of something significant being said was zero to none.

Even the men in the room fell into weary stereotypes. Were priests so predictable? He hadn't thought so, but he recognized types from seminary, only aged twenty years beyond his peers.

The Really Nice Guy with glasses and acne scars. The Earnest Thinker with shock of graying hair and a mustache. The Brilliant Theologian with bald head and whiskey nose. The Progressive Cleric, he of the graying pony tail and lively expression. And where did Matt fit in? Young Father Who-Would-Have-Thought-It? More than one parishioner brave enough to watch a rerun of *The Thorn Birds* had looked at him with an edgy speculation.

"You must be Matt."

Progressive Cleric came over to shake his hand. Naturally, he clapped Matt's upper arm with the other hand. Progressive Cleric had been a charismatic athletic coach too. Young people had adored him. He was so cool for a priest!

"Welcome," the man went on. "I'm Nick Benedict."

They all gathered around then—Really Nice Guy, whose name was Jerry. Earnest Thinker, aka Paul, squinting through his trifocals, pumping Matt's hand. Brilliant Theologian, saddled with the overtly Catholic name of Damien, abstracted and just cool enough to make the shecn on his bald head look like glare ice from a Chicago winter. The man closest to Matt's age, around forty, was tall, slightly overstuffed and had a mustache. Norbert.

Matt let some coffee drip into a Styrofoam cup while he gathered his wits. Except for Norbert, these guys were all at least twenty years older than Matt was. He didn't belong here. This was a mistake, but he was stuck with it.

Folding chairs shrilled protest as they were dragged into a circle on the empty floor.

"We start with a group therapy go-round," Nick said, grinning. "No props but java and honesty. We're used to it, but it might be off-putting for a newbie."

"I'm not a 'newbie.' I'm . . . an ex-oldie."

"Oho! Matt's seen the therapy square dance." Paul expertly balanced the flimsy coffee container on his knee. "A veteran."

"I hadn't expected to be the youngest," Matt said.

"We hadn't expected it either," Jerry put in gently. Jerry would always be the peacemaker.

"Yeah," Nick said, laughing. "You must have just

been coming in when we were going out. Kinda like me and smoking; I started just when the Surgeon General's report saying we shouldn't smoke came out in the sixties. Are you as contrary a jackass as I am, Matt?"

"Swimming against the tide. The best always do," Damien put in. With authority.

Matt dragged his own tortured chair into the circle, wishing he dared leave.

But it was his turn to talk. "Yeah. There were almost more women in seminary than men when I went in. Just . . . getting the theological education, of course. Not expecting to be priests."

"Women priests!" Brilliant Theologian Damien looked pained. "God help us; that may be all we have left."

"I suppose gays are still one step below women in the church hierarchy," Norbert noted.

Matt knew that many gay men had entered the priesthood after the first wave of priests had left in the sixties, but the unspoken policy had always been "don't ask, don't tell," long before the military thought of it. He supposed one way of coming "out" was leaving the priesthood.

Nick shook his trendy head. "Don't scare Matt. We're really a pushover group. Being an ex-priest makes it hard to look down on anybody for any position—political, personal, or sexual. For a start, why don't you tell us why you left."

"I can't."

They gazed at him, unconvinced and waiting.

"Not without saying why I entered. It's not a concrete process, like going in a door and out a door, is it?"

Paul nodded. "We talk about it in terms of either in or out, but it's never that simple."

79

"It's a revolving door, Matt." Nick grinned. "Not a door that just opens and shuts, but one in eternal motion. Believe it or not, sometimes you can feel more a part of the church after you've left."

"Politics," Damien grumbled.

"Lots of politics," Nick agreed. "Everywhere."

Matt was shocked to find himself in the company of men who enjoyed discussing theories and verities again. Why had they all made the wrong life choice, then, if they were so smart?

"How did you leave?" Norbert asked, nursing his coffee cup.

"The hard way." Matt laughed softly. "I was laicized."

"Good for you!" Nick looked ready to clap his arm again. Luckily, he was three chairs away.

What a relief to talk to people who know what that word means, or even how to spell it. Being laicized was an achievement. Most priests just left, but Matt had gone through the official process of asking to leave, and had been granted permission. The difference was like getting certified as a conscientious objector in the Vietnam War, rather than just fleeing to Canada to escape the draft.

"I don't know how 'good' it was," Matt added. "That was just how it worked out. I came to see that my vocation, sincere enough when I was young, was really an escape from an abusive family situation. I was looking for a heavenly father. I was afraid of being a father. I was hiding in the Lord."

"Isn't that what He's there for?" asked Brilliant Theologian.

Matt felt momentarily trapped into giving the catechism answer, but didn't. "Then why wasn't that

80

enough?" he said instead. "For any of us?"

Silence. He was the raw recruit, freshly AWOL. They were veterans of leaving without leave. Father figures, except none of them appealed to him in that way anymore. Maybe he didn't need the roles of Father, or even Son, in his life anymore, in himself.

"I'm . . . embarrassed," Matt admitted. "I came to the priesthood after everybody else was losing faith. I feel like a throwback. Like a fool."

"There's no fool like a holy fool," Brilliant Theologian joked.

Matt shrugged. "If only I could be that blessedly idiotic."

They sat silent in their circle, on metal chairs, cosseting ersatz coffee cups.

"Maybe I shouldn't have come," Matt said.

"Look," Nick said, "there aren't that many of us in this area. Las Vegas is one of those oasis cities: one bright dot in the middle of nothing. Literally nothing. Norbert drove in from Arizona. Jerry's from Booma, California. I'm from Tonopah and Damien's from way up by Reno. We may seem a rather paltry group, but we're all we have. Everybody's case is individual. Like, you're the only one among us from an abusive family."

"Thanks. And it wasn't that abusive a situation. It was one guy. My stepfather. And he was a piker. I'm talking yelling, a little hitting, nothing demonically sadistic, just—"

"Just enough to make every living thing around him cringe constantly," Damien said, nodding. "I had an uncle like that. It's not good, Matt, even if it doesn't set a record."

Matt nodded. "I've been working on that. That's why I'm here in Nevada, actually. He, my stepfather, just

81

loved Las Vegas. I . . . found him. And that's when I found out that he wasn't the main problem, not really."

"You're not blaming yourself?" Nick's wrinkled brow showed concern made incarnate.

"God, no!" Here, such expletives didn't sound like swearing, just emphasis. "And it wasn't my mother's fault or mine. It was the times, or, rather, the behind-the-times. A man was head of the family, right or wrong. A woman had to have a man in her life, right or wrong. A kid had to feel responsible, rightly or wrongly. I understand that I fled to the vocation. I accept that maybe that's why that option was there, that maybe it was always a temporary sanctuary instead of the lifelong commitment I thought I was capable of making. I thank God for giving me an out when I so desperately needed one, but . . . I grew enough to know that I was hiding, not committing. So I made my case and left, with the blessings of the church. Who could ask for anything more?"

"An ex-priest could," Nick said, laughing again. "Why are you here?"

"My spiritual director from seminary—my ex-priest spiritual director—told me about this group. And, I'm at loose ends now that I've left the priesthood. There's so much I don't know how to do."

"Like?"

"Earn a living. Set up a place to live."

"We all have to adapt to that," Damien said impatiently.

"And, uh, to women."

"Yeah, I bet," Jerry said. "But what's new? I bet they've always flocked all over you."

"Maybe. But that's the very thing I was running from. Women meant marriage and kids, at least those were the

82

only two options a Polish Catholic boy could come up with . . . "

They laughed, with him.

"But I don't see how—" Matt went on.

"How? How's simple."

"I don't see how to do it *right*. How to do what we asked every Catholic teenager in our congregations to do: stay pure, meet a nice girl, marry her, go to bed with her, have children. I mean, how does anyone do it in that order? Nowadays."

The laughter lasted longer this time, but so did the silence afterward.

"Specifics." Damien pulled out a pipe and sucked on it, but never lit it.

A phallic substitute? Matt wondered.

But the observation distracted him from his own situation.

Why should he give specifics? Why should he name names, including those for his conflicting feelings? Why should he expose himself?

"Okay. There's this woman." Another laugh. "She and I were . . . meshing. Not . . . literally," he said into the face of more laughter. Boys will be boys, even ex-priests.

"And then, her . . . old boyfriend comes back into the picture. And . . . she joins him. I don't understand—"

"What's not to understand, Matt? An old boyfriend?"

"An ex-lover. I'm not that naive. She had been living with him when he vanished. I think she expected that they would get married."

"Women always do."

"She's not a rote 'always' kind of woman. She had made a commitment. She meant it."

"And him?"

83

"He looked like a total rat. Walking out on her without a word. Only she never believed he had. She thought something had happened to make him go. And she was right. When he came back, there were extenuating circumstances."

"Then it's a happy ending. Go with it."

"He's not . . . good for her, no matter the sincerity of his intentions."

"And the sincerity of your intentions?"

"I . . . I really care about her. But I was working out this thing with my stepfather and—"

"When did the old boyfriend come back?"

"Around Halloween."

A bark of appreciative laughter from Damien. "Appropriate."

"So . . . why didn't she take up with him right away," Nick wanted to know, "or did she?"

"No. That's what's so maddening. She didn't go running back to him. We were still . . . well, friendly. And then I went home to Chicago for Christmas, and events with my stepfather and my mother came to a head. I was finally working free of the past, ready to, I don't know, to meet her on her own ground. And—"

"And?"

"He showed up in New York. She was visiting her aunt there for Christmas. He threw a ring at her. Not a diamond. He . . . took her to bed."

"The romance was back on."

"And I'm off, sitting here, wondering what happened. It doesn't seem fair. I mean, I was within hours of being ready to consider a serious relationship with her—"

"How wonderful for you," Nick said.

Matt, reliving the trauma of his own story, could still read the sarcasm despite his anguish. And he *was*

84

expressing anguish. The cagey acolyte had become an eager convert, bleeding all over their group therapy circle like a hereditary hemophiliac. And now, seasoned sharks scenting fresh blood, they were turning on him.

"No! Not wonderful. I'll live with it if I have to, but I don't understand."

Laughter.

He was spilling his guts, and they were amused.

The anger came in a tidal wave; luckily, rage tongue-tied him, so the others went on talking, unaware. Or maybe they weren't so unaware.

"You are a classic case, you know that?"

"Classic?"

"Do you have any idea what you put that poor woman through?"

"Put *her* through?"

Sage nods from several of the circled chairs.

"We all do it, Matt," Jerry said. "We get so wrapped up in the angst of leaving our vocation. We weigh each hair, struggle through faith and fury. Examine our consciences until they are shredded wheat. And women, whew, that's a big one."

"Speak for yourself," Norbert said.

"All right. The big one is sex, gender aside. Maybe we've been pure as the driven communion wafer. Maybe we've stumbled and felt like hell. Still, we're not priests anymore. We can do anything we want. Anything we think we can do.

"And we can't do squat," Jerry admitted. "We're conscience-bound. You don't throw off maybe decades of holy celibacy just because you can."

"So we meet a nice woman," Nick said, "and we tell her, eventually, our little problem."

"Which is that *she's* the devil we've been avoiding all

85

these years." Jerry shook his head.

"Speak for yourself." Norbert's chorus made Damien shoot him a poisonous glance.

"Anyway," Nick went on, "we explain so carefully that we have to go through a lot of soul-searching to decide if we can make the transition. Are you getting this, Matt? Are you hearing the underlying message we're still sending?"

"But we can't change overnight," Matt protested. "We took the celibacy seriously, most of us. We have to take the . . . non-celibacy just as seriously."

"What do you believe in?" Damien snapped. "Premarital sex?"

"No! Well, I can see it's not as cut and dried as that—"

"You'll get married first, then, and then you'll find out if you can hack marital relations at all?" Jerry suggested. "Fun for your bride, all right. Might as well play Russian roulette."

"What about children?" Norbert wanted to know. "You said you had a fear of having them. How can you be sexually active and remain in a church that forbids birth control?"

"I don't know . . . things hadn't gotten that far."

"They'd gotten far enough. How far? Anything confessable?"

"No, not really."

"Not even in intention, if not in act?"

"It's . . . hard to say. She's an honorable woman—"

"And you respected her previous relationship, even if it was unsanctioned by marriage?"

"Yes! She loved the man. She expected permanency, or hoped for it, or she wouldn't have consummated the relationship. I know that."

"So . . . you didn't interfere, did you? You let him

walk back in and resume his old role of lover. Let *him* take the risk, not you."

"No! He'd been back for a while and she still hadn't . . . taken up with him again. I thought—"

"You thought you could string her along forever, with no promise of anything concrete until you had worked through your problems."

"Well, yes. But my problems—"

"—were so much more delicate, so much more serious, so much more spiritual, more important than hers."

"I didn't think of it that way."

"You didn't think, Matt. You didn't think of the woman you say you love."

"Would you have married her?" Jerry.

"Of . . . course."

"In the Catholic Church?" Damien.

"Well—"

"Is she Catholic?" Nick.

"No. But . . . a fallen away Unitarian could be anything."

"A mother? Does she want to be one? How many kids?" Jerry.

"I don't know."

"Do you want to be a father?" Norbert.

"I told you that I don't know if I should be," he said between clenched teeth.

"Well, then . . . " Nick.

"Well then, what?"

"What were you really prepared to do with her?" Nick was obviously head teacher around here. Head interrogator. Head devil's advocate. "You don't know. Do you know you could get married in a renegade Catholic ceremony? Birth control would be A-okay. But you wouldn't be really in the church. Or why not try the Unitarians; they are a very accepting sort. They'd overlook your orthodoxy. Or a true Catholic ceremony? You're eligible, you played by all the rules, but could you promise to accept all the children God sent you after what you've said here about your upbringing? Could you live with that? Could she live with your uncertainty on every matter relating to sex and family that there is? You are separated by a chasm from most people, my son, and from most women by the Grand Canyon.

"It's no mystery why the other man reclaimed her. You weren't ready to commit to any woman. And, in her heart of hearts, she knew it. Better to cast her fortune with an invisible man than an uncertain one."

"You think it was that calculated?" Matt said. "I don't. I think the other guy did what he did before: swept her off her feet. He's a pretty charismatic guy, a performer by profession."

"It's him. Or it's her. But it isn't you, is it, Matt? You're just the innocent bystander." Nick again.

Matt had long since set the Styrofoam cup with its silt of black on the bottom on the floor. He understood the dynamics of group therapy; he understood they were giving him a probably needed crash course in tough love. But it hurt, and it wouldn't have unless a good part of it was the truth.

"I've always avoided close relationships with women," he realized. "My mother and I grew distant because we shared a secret we couldn't admit to anyone else, and then we finally couldn't admit it to each other. Girls at school . . . well, I had my vocation to keep me warm—and aloof. I really didn't know how to be a good Catholic and not have children who would then have to

88

endure what was done to me. Kids pick up the patterns they most hate, they most suffer from, because that's what growing up wrong does to you. So . . . the priesthood was the only option. I know that now. So did the diocese that gave me my laicization. It certainly wasn't for my being a priest who couldn't live without women. That was the last thing I wanted to confront."

"With your looks—" Jerry sounded puzzled.

"With my looks, they were always coming around. Still are. Only now I don't see that as quite the threat."

"Now it's a perk?" Norbert asked archly.

Matt laughed. "Not quite that, either. Now it's a recognizable risk."

"And you were ready to take a bigger risk with one particular woman, only you were too late." Jerry sounded sorry for him.

Matt nodded. "That's why I'm here, I think. Realizing that I did something to ruin my own chances. Except, it was *not* doing something. And you say we're all like that? It's not just me."

"No way, brother! We are so arrogant about women," Nick said genially. "We'd have to be to choose to live without them in any significant way, except for of course, our sainted mothers and the Virgin Mary." His arms lifted to indicate the cradling arms of the church around them: Maternity of Mary, after all.

"Think about it from a different perspective, Matt. If it's such a big decision to decide to consort with one, what does that make her?"

"A . . . temptress. A demoness." Matt spoke slowly, thinking not of Temple, but of Kitty O'Connor. Something he was saying gave him a glimmer into the demon that drove her hostility, but he couldn't quite name it. "And the relationship has to be all my way."

89

"If you need to play it by strict Catholic theology." Jerry.

Matt looked up. "How many of you abide by church teachings still?"

They looked at each other.

Damien closed his eyes. "I don't know why I come here. I can answer that question 'yes,' but I can't answer for my brother priests. The priesthood has fallen so far."

The silence was long, like at a family dinner table where there are deep political divisions and everyone finally learns to hold his tongue so that it doesn't slash into someone else.

Finally, Nick spoke. "Even the ex-priesthood, Damien, or especially the ex-priesthood?" He smiled at Matt as if to apologize for the tension in the bare little room. "You see, Matt, except for our father confessor, Damien, who has no trouble with the rules, we'd have to guess that you are the one-most-likely-to. You and Jerry, there, who lucked out by marrying an ex-nun. They could explore all their angst, and the mutual insult never seemed unnatural."

"It is not insulting to demand moral standards in another person!" Damien dug into his suit coat pocket until he pulled out the pacifying pipe again.

"Demand?" Jerry asked.

"If you don't demand, what do you get? A situation ethics cafeteria."

"I don't know why you come," Norbert said suddenly, his genial air of mock dissent turning suddenly serious and weary. "We're here precisely because we discovered that spiritual values are not tidily painted in black and white, or in bad and good, or in male or female, for that matter."

"You should never have been ordained," Damien

said.

"But I was. And who's to say I was not a better priest than any one of you, my sexual orientation notwithstanding?"

"It's not a contest," Nick said, as wearily.

"It is to close-minded people like Damien," Norbert shot back before turning to challenge the older man again. "I don't get why you come to these meetings. To go away and look down upon us stumbling human beings?"

"Am I close-minded, or are you simply trying to justify your own perversity?"

Matt stirred restlessly, wondering if he'd have to act as literal referee. The two men seemed ready to hurl themselves into physical as well as philosophical combat.

"Don't scare our newbie," Nick put in softly. "This group wouldn't be useful if we didn't differ. And why *do* you come, Damien? We're a disgraceful bunch of failed sinners, by your lights."

"And why didn't *you* stay in?" Norbert jabbed. "Or wasn't everything so perfect for you, either?"

Damien clutched the pipe in his hand, his thumb tamping down on the unlit tobacco as if to crush it.

"Let's get a last cup of java," Nick suggested, rising, and then stretching as disingenuously as a kid.

The homely gesture disarmed the rising tensions. Everybody else stood, bent the kinks out of their backs.

Everyone else but Damien and Norbert, who sat still and sullen in their chairs, like kids robbed of a neighborhood brawl.

Matt joined the dispersing majority that was acting so unconcerned about the ugly fissure of antagonism in their midst. He was struck by the thought that each of

91

the two men represented the most liberal and conservative faction, the literal past and possible future, of the church. But which was which? And which man's values could he better coexist with?

Maybe the answer was both, or neither.

Correct moral values. They didn't advertise, did they?

BREAK-IN

A SIMULTANEOUS SCRATCHING AT ONE OF THE FRENCH doors leading to the patio and at the front door opposite found Temple clutching her TV remote control like a weapon. Eight o'clock on a Saturday evening. Who would come calling so stealthily?

She'd just muted the sound during a commercial, or she wouldn't have heard either modest noise. Was this a concerted social call, or what?

While she debated which unknown to confront first, the scratchers, again acting in eerie concert, decided to bypass her entirely.

The locked front door cracked open like a Christmas walnut, while, simultaneously, the patio door split to admit a slim-jim shadow of night.

Home invasion! Temple thought, wondering what Asian gang she had antagonized lately.

But though both her invaders wore ninja-black and moved on soundless feet, neither was remotely Asian, or gang-like, since they came forward alone.

Temple stood, torn between two primal urges: the succulently steaming take-out pizza box advancing from the front door in Max Kinsella's custody . . . or the disturbingly limp object dangling from Midnight Louie's mouth.

Apparently both her beaux had resolved to treat her to a surprise snack.

"Smells terrific," she told Max. "Put in on the kitchen counter. I'll be right there. And Louie—" She turned to the cat. "Put that down right where you stand. It does *not* smell delicious."

"What has that alley cat dragged in now?" Max was coming over, sounding both proprietary and annoyed.

"I'm afraid to look," Temple admitted. "Cats will sometimes bring you their dead prey as a present."

Max shot her a look. "Lucky for you I'm not a cat." He bent to inspect Louie's offering, but the cat minced backward. "Come on, kitty, give up the goods. How'd he get up here anyway?"

"He climbs, somehow, then comes in through the bathroom window, which I leave open a bit. I can't understand why he came by the patio, or how he got that French door open."

"Those doors are jokes," Max said, going down on hands and knees to capture the cat.

"Louie doesn't like to be crowded."

"So I see." By now Louie was backed up against the French door, watching Max crawl toward him.

Temple could have sworn his whiskers raked back at a smug angle.

"That's it," Max cajoled. "Give up the nice bit of . . . yuck."

Temple squinched her eyes shut. "What is it? Animal, right? Dead?"

"Dead, all right. Soggily so." Max rose and approached, his hands cupping the trophy.

"How can you handle it?" she demanded.

"I've handled worse." The dome of his top hand lifted to reveal a limp oleander blossom wilting on his palm.

93

"A dead flower? Why on earth would Louie drag that in? It looks like it's been off the stem for days."

"Then you don't want me to put it in a vase."

"No way." Temple shook her head at the cat, who was fastidiously grooming his face.

"It was a nice gesture," Max said from the kitchen.

"You approve of something Louie's done?" She followed him in, lured by the aroma of Roma tomatoes.

"Absolutely." Max turned from the cupboard, one of her recycled florist's vases in his hands, filled with velvet-petaled pansies.

"I'm not going to ask how you did that."

"Good. The pizza's getting cold."

They occupied themselves pulling out the plates, knives, forks, and paper napkins that hot pizza required, but never managed to transfer the whole mess to the round card-cum-dining-table near the French doors. Instead, they leaned against the counter and gnawed away on the hot slices right out of the box.

"What brings you over here, really?" Temple asked.

Max shrugged between bites.

"Another message from the Synth?"

He shook his head.

"Nothing's happened?"

"Nothing, except it's Saturday night, and I'm glad you're home alone."

"Not exactly alone."

His dark eyebrows lifted as if awaiting a confession.

"The cat."

"Oh, him."

"That's no way to write off a cat. Next time he'll visit you with something ickier in his mouth."

"Oleander is poisonous," Max mused, staring at the neon clock on the kitchen wall.

94

"And he must have had that flower in his mouth for a long time!"

"Don't worry. The leaves are toxic, not the flowers. Wonder where he got it."

"Las Vegas is crawling with oleanders."

"But not in bloom right now."

Temple frowned. "Let me see that flower again."

Max produced it from behind his back.

"It's wet now, from Louie's mouth, but it looks dessicated. He must have picked it up somewhere."

"And mistook it for prey?"

"I'm glad he did. I don't want any door-to-door lizard-delivery service! Speaking of doors, why did you come scratching on mine?"

"Used to be ours."

Max was leaning his elbows on the white countertop, grinning up at her in the impish manner that always caught her off guard.

"Well, technically, it still is."

"So I thought it was time we spent a Saturday night at home, like we used to."

"You mean, just doing nothing?"

He nodded. "Just doing nothing."

"The couch-potato number? TV, pizza, and—?"

He nodded, glancing around. "Place doesn't look any different, except for the feline delivery boy."

"Max. Did you think I'd have . . . company?"

He paused before answering. "I think you have company now."

"Really! Are you jealous? Worried that—"

"Don't put question marks into words, Temple. That just makes them bigger. I wanted to see you, that's all. On home ground." Max straightened and looked beyond her into the living room. "My home ground too."

He was right, Temple knew. He'd been gone so long he had ceased to seem at home in the place they had bought together less than two years earlier.

"And you're not alone anymore." He nodded at the black silhouette still washing its face and watching them from the living room. "My animal instincts were right. I do have to reclaim my territory, after all."

LOSERS WEEPERS

A THIN DRIBBLE OF WHAT LOOKED LIKE TOBACCO JUICE was all the coffee urn was dispensing.

Matt tossed his stained Styrofoam cup and turned as a departing group member paused to say hello and goodbye.

Damien talked earnestly, and tediously, about a list of recommended books. Matt was tired of reading about being all that he could be, whether it was Thomas Merton's *The Seven Story Mountain* or Alex Comfort's *The Joy of Sex*. Or maybe *The Joy of Sex was a Seven Story Mountain*.

"You're out of coffee and they're finally out of steam," Nick noted, coming up after Damien, clutching his pipe, had faded away. Nick zipped shut his windbreaker and pulled on a tweed cap. "Cheer up, Matt. The worst is over. And the first time is always the worst."

"That sounds like . . . sex. I gave them a red-carpet invitation, didn't I? Why is knowing that everybody else has made the same mistakes as you have supposed to make you feel better?"

"Misery loves company."

"Then you're saying that misery is as good as it

gets?"

"No, no. I'm saying that we all have to go through an awkward adolescence when we leave the priesthood, and some of us were much older than you. Call it vocational acne."

"I never had acne," Matt said gloomily.

"Of course not. You never had anything that would have been a detriment to an active teenage social life, except an allergy to the opposite sex. You ever think that life is exceedingly perverse?"

"I never had an allergy to the opposite sex; I wanted to avoid being human in general. Apparently I did a darn good job of it."

Nick shrugged and waited while Matt pulled on his sheepskin jacket and tried to figure out how old the older man was. Iron-gray hair and metal-framed bifocal glasses enhanced a face that must have been all nose and chin before age had softened the features. Matt detected the faint moonscape pitting of acne scars.

It wasn't fair; he himself had a enjoyed a golden adolescence, but he hadn't used it for anything but running away from life. At least the other men here had run *to* something. Hadn't they?

"Cold out." Nick clapped his palms together as they emerged into the dark parking lot.

Matt couldn't help checking for the ghost of Kitty O'Connor. The muscles in his stomach had tensed.

"People don't realize the desert gets cold at night," Matt agreed.

"No, to most people Las Vegas is just one big, hot, bright, noisy oasis. Boy, a deserted parking lot is kind of spooky! Only my car left and that motorcycle. That's not . . . yours?"

Matt, having spent a couple hours splitting the finer

hairs of truth with a hatchet, didn't know how to answer him. "It is mine, and it isn't. My landlady loaned it to me, but it was given to her."

"Been around."

"Used to be His."

" 'His'?" Nick didn't know how to interpret the capital *H* in Matt's tone. In their circle, capital He's and His's meant the Deity. "Ah." Nick suddenly understood. "So you get the motorcycle, on loan, and he gets the girl, for keeps."

The words struck Matt so sharply that Kitty the Cutter might as well have been there. "Thanks, Nick. Nice way to put it."

"Sorry. It's just that I get a much better picture of your rival when I see that machine."

"He's not a rival if he's won. But—"

"What?"

"Maybe it's part of my malady. Despite everything, I have this wild, fervent conviction that if Temple and I are meant to be together, we will be. Call it an act of faith."

"That's just it. Infatuation is the ultimate act of faith. A manic state. Delusional. Frustrated infatuation is a manic-depressive state. One minute you're positive everything will go your way; the next you're pounding your head on the sidewalk, hoping the worms will crawl up and eat you."

"This is normal? This is what men and women are supposed to go through?"

"And boys and girls, which you and I have tried mightily to head off in our priestly pasts."

"Yeah, but . . . I had no idea they felt like this. It's not a sane state. I can't believe all the advice I was handing out to 'master their feelings' and 'do the right thing.' "

98

"You think it was bad advice?"

"No. Just pretty impossible to follow when your heart and mind and body and soul are all acting like they have St. Vitus's dance."

Nick leaned against the cast-iron railing that bracketed two crummy concrete steps down. Matt settled against the opposite barrier, even though it felt like a chilly rack.

"Tell me about this girl," Nick said.

"Temple." Matt suddenly realized that he had so far sheltered her name from the circle inside.

Nick nodded. "Interesting name. Spiritual almost."

"If you told Temple about 'temple of the Holy Ghost' she'd think you were seriously psychic."

"She has a sense of humor."

"How can you tell?"

"You smile when you talk about her."

"That's scary, isn't it? Seeing one person through another? I do feel she's become a part of me, maybe my better part."

Nick nodded again. "An honor."

"Then how can I live without it?"

He sighed. "You'll have to, Matt, if she's recommitted to her previous love. Look. There's isn't a soul, male or female, walking on this planet, who hasn't cared deeply for someone who's been unwilling or unable to reciprocate."

"You?"

Nick nodded seriously. "I may look like an old codger, but there was this brown-haired girl in grade school—"

"Grade school!" Matt scoffed.

"No, Matt, you don't get it. We get these glimpses. Sometimes we see through people like water in a

99

mountain stream: where it's been, where it's going, how much we'd like to flow with it. Moments of such clarity they cut like glass. And nothing happens. We both flow on, whether we're eight years old or forty-eight. Everybody has a path not taken. A person not known."

"Even priests?"

"Even priests. You're unusual in that you stifled your instincts at such an early age because of your abusive background."

"Then you . . . other guys knew what you were giving up."

"Not really. Mind if I smoke?" Nick pulled a pipe from his jacket pocket.

Matt quickly nodded. He needed to hear what Nick said more than he cared about secondhand smoke.

Nick sucked at the pipe as it took slow fire from a long farmer's match, and smiled when it finally offered enough smoke to expel. "I was not Mr. Cool in high school," Nick began.

"Neither was I."

"But you passed. I didn't. I was precast as either a grind or a nerd, or a seminarian. And I was happy with that life, that commitment. Until I left."

"Why did you?"

"I'd . . . had theological difficulties. I couldn't stand the faces I'd counseled to do the impossible. I get the impression celibacy was not a problem for you. Not for me, either. We were reared in an environment that rewarded the considered act. Desire seemed . . . unreliable, quirky, an adolescent imperative. How strong we felt to conquer it."

Matt thought. Yes. He had "overcome" life. His abusive childhood, any instinct to mate. He was a higher being, next to an angel.

"You can look at me, Matt, and not believe it, but I have enjoyed one of the greatest love stories of all time. Midlife, middle-aged, midcareer." Nick smiled.

"I do believe. The world doesn't have to be telegenic. Haven't I always known that, even while people have envied me my . . . charisma?"

"My wife. She's thirty pounds overweight, and thinks she's fifty pounds beyond the pale. She won't believe that I think she makes . . . oh, Raquel Welch look like a cheap substitute. You ever see this great old forties film, *The Enchanted Cottage?* Two terminally plain people connect, and everybody wonders what they see in each other, except when they go into this cottage, we see them as they see each other. And they're Robert Young and Dorothy Maguire. Love is like that. Love puts this aura on the beloved. Maybe it's a halo. Think what a halo means, an otherworldly spiritual charisma. Attraction is religion, Matt. It's not cheap, it's not tawdry. It's *agape.*"

"A fancy Greek word for spiritual love. If we're in the market for fancy Greek words, why not *eros?*"

"It *is* eros. Love is eros. That's what you don't know until you try it."

"Or . . . you don't try it."

"Your acquaintance with the world, the flesh, and the devil getting too close for you?"

Matt looked down at the concrete steps. "When I first began to think about Temple in that way, I rushed to a priest I knew to confess my 'bad thoughts.' It was really meant to validate his priesthood and my fallibility; I'd been in a position to know his weaknesses and the advantage made me ashamed."

"So you found some shame of your own to show him."

101

Matt nodded. "Tenet of the church: Always make others feel good about themselves before yourself."

"So?"

"So . . . I've progressed—regressed?—to a lot more specifically 'bad thoughts' than the vague piddly ones I confessed. And I haven't told a soul, in church or out."

Nick laughed and clapped him on the shoulder. "Out here, we call that a 'rich fantasy life,' and we don't worry about it."

"What about a rich spiritual life? We used to talk about that in seminary. The odd thing is that what I'm experiencing with Temple is clarifying some parts of my religion I used to take for granted."

"Like what?"

"Like in the New Testament, when Christ walks by the Sea of Galilee and gathers his disciples by asking them to drop their nets and come follow him. I always read about this testimony to his charisma, his sacred mission, and thought, yeah, yeah. Now that I've suddenly been plummeted into this dazzle for Temple, I finally believe it. I believe that in an instant a stranger, or even someone you know fairly well, can suddenly draw, pull, attract, hypnotize otherwise rational beings into mindless orbit.

"And all those times in prayer I sought to find God, reach something so immaterial yet all-encompassing, experience divine love, and utter faith . . . Now I find myself possessed of all the irrationality of faith, but not for God—for another human being, for the rightness of my own belief in that other human being. Beyond the desire, which is so mind-blowing, there's this bottomless cup of unconditional love for her, the world, myself. I can't deny the physical imperative, but it isn't just that. It's . . . a mystery."

Nick was silent for a while. "If the physical pull becomes too frustrating, well, even the church recognizes that in some circumstances it's better to . . . there is self-gratification."

"We spent years in seminary learning to resist it. But even the term betrays itself. How I feel, I know I could relieve it but my satisfaction isn't the point. It's finding satisfaction with another, for another, giving satisfaction."

"So after years of saving yourself for God, so to speak, you're saving yourself for a woman who is committed to another man."

"A new secular vocation, huh?"

"You're sure you're not simply afraid of the intimacy and have become infatuated with an impossible situation to avoid facing it?"

"I'm not sure of anything but my love for Temple. Maybe I'm an obsessive personality. Certainly following a vocation in a church that forbids its priests sexuality caters to obsession; hunting down my stepfather was obsessive to a point. Now that I've lost the intensity of that quest, maybe I've just translated the monomania to Temple. It's true that I knew her and we even played at dating and I didn't feel what I'm feeling now. Maybe I imagined that she has any feelings for me at all."

"My poor boy. Your Temple of the Holy Ghost cares for you. She may not be able to love you as you would love her, but at least she is not insensible, insensitive, indifferent. That is a gift. Take it and go elsewhere."

"How?"

Nick inhaled deeply from his pipe of wisdom. "Date other women. How many have you really known? Get some CDs. Leonard Cohen, a poet-turned-songwriter who offers a master class in the bittersweet push-pull of love and desire, of loss and fulfillment. He's Jewish, but his work has an occasional Christian bite. Do you have a VCR? Get *Gigi*, a film musical from the fifties based on a tale by Colette. A girl from the courtesan class, a literal family of mistresses, meets a man of the world. Her love for him makes him innocent again. Wonderful moment. It's a Cinderella story, how a girl reared for sex feels love, and transforms a man reared for sexual distance into someone who can enjoy intimacy. Buy some romance novels, the ones with the covers you wouldn't be ashamed to check out of the library; they make those nowadays and an awful lot of women read them. Find out what women want—or fantasize that they want—when it comes to men, love, and sex. See other women. Live a life. You've a lot of time to make up for. Do it."

"But how do I do it honestly, without sin?"

"What is sin?"

"I know the letter of the law—"

"Put the letter of the law into a sentence you can live by."

"Sinlessness. To love God and not hurt anyone else."

"Including yourself?"

"Including yourself. I suppose."

"Don't suppose. Live! You'll make mistakes. You will 'sin' by some people's lights. But if you love God and yourself and your fellow/sister man/woman, you will not do wrong."

"I see you've mastered the politically correct slash."

"The slash is our salvation. We are not all black or white. We are gray. We are human. We are two genders and one soul. We have choices."

Matt shook his head. Too much. He was to go forth, and multiply his involvement with the mysterious species *woman*. He was to remain true to his school, his

104

vocation, his first love. Maybe he'd got it right at the beginning. A true love: a vocation. A lifestyle: celibacy. A libido: confused. A heart: broken.

Coming here had only compounded his confusion.

And yet, when he thought about it, there was only one bottom line, and always had been since he came to Las Vegas looking to lay his past to rest.

Temple.

COLD CASE

"YOU KNOW THIS GUY, LIEUTENANT?"

Molina was glad Alch was studying the name he had just jotted on his notepad instead of her face.

"Not really," she said evenly. "What's more important is, what do *you* know about him?"

One side of Alch's mustache quirked, a sure sign that he hadn't gotten all the information he had hoped for.

"Rafi Nadir," he said, savoring the unusual name. "Made Sergeant, but he isn't with the LAPD anymore."

"Since when?" Molina kept her voice from sharpening.

"June of last year."

"Retired?"

"He's a little young for that. Forty-one." Alch shook his head.

"Moved," she suggested, rapid-fire.

Alch shook his head again. "Too bad you wanted my inquiry to be 'discreet.' I could have gotten much more if I hadn't been."

"So . . . he's not with the LAPD for a serious reason. Not retired, not moved." She cleared her throat. "Dead?"

105

"Worse than that."

"Worse?"

"Bad case. Civil suit. Lost the suit, lost his job."

"Just last summer?"

Alch nodded.

"Hmm. Any personal data? Wife, kids?"

"Neither. Had a girlfriend a while back, I guess. Nobody much knows where he went, and I get the impression nobody much cares. A rogue cop gives us all a bad rap."

"That's for sure. Your contact's name written down there, Detective?"

"Yeah, sure."

"Give it to me and I'll follow up on a higher level."

"This have something to do with the corpse at the Blue Dahlia?"

She shook her head. That theory would be too farfetched even to mention. "Hardly. A cold case I had in L.A. Wanted to follow up on it, but it looks too cold. Thanks."

She copied a name and number from his notebook and gave him a perfunctory smile to indicate the report was over.

Alch's lips pouted as he slapped his notebook shut.

She'd seen that expression on his face in interviews when a witness's or a suspect's answer hadn't been satisfactory. Good detective, Alch. Too good sometimes.

She smiled at his wrinkled suit-coated back (Las Vegas will do that to wool blends) as he shuffled out of the office. You couldn't trust that shuffle; it looked indifferent, but it meant that he was thinking, hard.

She glanced down at the name and number. This wasn't who she really needed to call, but she couldn't make that unwelcome call from here. A pay phone that

106

was quiet, maybe. Not easy to find. Too bad there was no other way. She knew her next step: She had to call a woman about a man, neither of whom she liked asking for favors, to get the number she needed. Not easy to ask the devil you don't know to find out about the devil you do. She'd just have to make it sound like a demand, rather than a plea.

Something to do with this case? She hoped to God not.

CAT TRACKING

"THIS IS OUTRAGEOUS."

Midnight Louise's tail lashes the walkway until desert dust rises like a genie conjured in a tale of Sinbad the Sailor.

"It is procedure," I explain patiently to the kit.

"She called animal control. She called to have the body removed from the crime scene and disposed of who-knows-how. No autopsy, no investigation. Just swept under the rug, quite literally."

"You know the routine. Our kind are twentieth-century slaves, with no value beside the monetary."

"But this was cold-blooded murder."

"We cannot be murdered, only be 'killed.'"

"Why?"

"I believe the reason came out on one of my early cases with Miss Temple. An elderly lady argued with her parish priest who had said that animals have no souls. I fear that is the common perception."

"I do not care if I have a soul! I care if I am treated rightly, dead or alive."

"I am afraid that souls are prerequisite to being treated rightly, at least in theory, and among humans."

"Huh! If they truly had any souls, they would not allow such perfidy."

"We will do what we can."

"Which is squat."

"Which is a great deal. We know, at least, that Wilfrid was deliberately hit."

"How do we know that?"

"His mistress is missing."

"I do not care about missing humans."

"Ah, my dear Louise. If you are going to care about the missing of our kind, I am afraid that you will have to care about the missing of their kind. Our lives and fates are intertwined, you see."

"Not mine! I belong to nothing human."

"You work at the Crystal Phoenix. You eat the delicacies that Chef Song leaves out for you. You accept the fondness of the management."

"I tolerate. I do not beg. I earn my keep."

"So do we all." I nudge her upright and then into the house again, which Miss Meter Maid has thoughtfully left open for the imminent arrival of animal control, which I happen to know is so overworked it is not likely to show up before morning. "Are we not 'animal control?' And the way I earn my keep, as you put it— though Miss Temple Barr would never be so crass as to call it that—is to assist in matters of a mortal nature. I have much experience in this area, and I predict that we will not find out the why and the who of Wilfrid's attack until we find out the where and the what of his mistress's disappearance."

"And how will 'we' do that?"

I sit down to consider. "There is one sure clue."

"I myself find the weeping widow highly suspect."

I sniff away that notion. "She is just window dressing, pardon the expression. No. I am disturbed by a slight odor I detected on the premises."

"The open can of tuna fish in the refrigerator."

"I was talking about 'slight odor.' Something fruity, but with substantial body."

"You mean the open bottle of wine in the refrigerator."

"I am not talking about an obvious foodstuff at all. I

am afraid we will have to consult an expert in the field."

"An expert on refrigerator odor?"

"Forget the refrigerator! You would think you never ate before, and here you are scarfing up freebies fresh from the cutting edge of Chef Song's cleaver, night and day. No, I am talking about something I once faintly whiffed in Miss Temple's dwelling. But this scent is too subtle for our feline senses. I will have to employ the services of a specialist."

"There is one in Las Vegas?"

"There are several; fortunately, I know the best and the brightest of them all. But first, you are right. We cannot allow animal control to take control of the deceased. We must bury the body."

"What, a sentimental streak?"

"Sentimentality is always best leavened by practicality."

"Huh?"

"If we bury the body, it will not be hauled away and cremated by animal control."

Louise squinches her eyes to old-gold horizontal slits while she pictures the late lamented's corpse. "He was not a small dude. How are you and I going to dig a hole big enough?"

"Once again, the smart operator acts alone only when necessary. Remember, many paws make light work."

"You are going to ask the so-called widow to help? Besides the fact that she is a bit of indoor fluff who has never dug deeper than one inch, and only in Pretty Paws litter where she cannot get anything under her nails but a little dust—no slugs, no worms, no mice skulls. Aside from all that, do you think she will be able to stop sniveling long enough to lend assistance, such as it would be?"

"No, I do not. I was not thinking of Miss Fanny Furbelow. In fact, you and I will have to begin our investigative odyssey by moving the body to a place of concealment in the yard."

"And how will we do that?"

"We must use our brains. We can drag the rag rug, with poor Wilfrid on it, through the door and into the yard. Who will miss one rag rug in this joint?"

Miss Louise examines the rag-rug-cluttered floor, then nods. "This will be hard on the choppers, but I do hate to see one of my kind disposed of by animal control. Okay. Yo-ho heave ho."

To the tune of the Volga Boat Song, we set to our gruesome but noble task.

HOT TAMALE JALAPEÑO DEATHBURGER

MOLINA PICKED UP THE RINGING PHONE, ONE EYE on her watch and one eye on the report in front of her. Split attention span was ever the busy executive's best personal assistant.

"You wanted me?" The male voice was deep, assured, and sardonic.

She didn't have to ask who was calling.

"Not here. You heard of Charley's Burgers?"

"Not in Las Vegas."

"Maybe not in 'your' Las Vegas." She gave him the intersection, wishing she could watch the address's effect on his expression.

Charley hung his sign in a light-industrial area chug-by-shriek next to a railroad track. Not exactly Max Kinsella territory, but then she didn't know the full range of his wanderings. Yet.

"One-thirty," she added.

"You like a late lunch, Lieutenant."

"I like a quiet restaurant."

She smiled as she hung up. She would get there first, and watch him arrive.

But she didn't, damn it.

You had to be earlier than she had thought to beat Max Kinsella at undercover games. So . . . next time she would reset her watch to dawn patrol, if that's what it took. *Next time.* She wasn't sure whether that unconscious assumption worried her, or pleased her.

112

He was leaning, black-clad, arms folded, feet crossed, against a white Firebird convertible, resembling an exclamation point on an empty page. Perhaps a question mark would be more apropos.

Whatever symbolic piece of punctuation she compared him to, it was grievously misplaced in front of Charley's Old-Fashion Burgers. Molina relished the illiterate, hand-lettered sign. She loved the small weathered shack hunkering down all by its lonesome on an off-the-beaten-path road. So did about six thousand other aficionados of the best burgers to be had in Clark County . . . if you didn't mind messy fingers and a skyrocketing cholesterol rate.

Charley's Old-Fashion Burgers was truly a "joint" in the time-honored sense of the word.

And today was a photo-opportunity late-winter afternoon in Las Vegas: pale blue sky and clear desert air, all deliciously perfumed by the greasy, smoky aroma of sizzling ground beef.

Kinsella followed her to the order window. Charley's was mostly a take-out place, especially if the took-to place was an over-the-road truck seat. A tacked-on addition featured a ten-stool lunch bar and a half dozen aluminum and faux-onyx Formica tables and chairs dating from so far back that they'd probably send a vintage-freak like Temple Barr into paroxysms of covetousness. Except that decades of taking cigarette burns and banging around had made the stuff too beaten-up to cherish.

Kind of like an abused spouse.

"Charming." Kinsella kept any discernible tone from his voice.

Even on matters of public taste he had to be a mystery. She enjoyed eying him against the rough background of Charley's Burgers. It was almost as good as a line-up wall with the heights marked in paint-peeling wood slats rather than impersonally neat notches.

With his patent-leather hair sleeked back from his angular face into a discreet ponytail and the black turtleneck sweater, he resembled an escapee from an *Esquire* magazine ad, and somehow looked more Italian than Irish. But maybe it was the sweater that was Italian. It was expensive, that was for sure.

Molina ordered the usual: a jalapeño "deathburger," a side of coleslaw, and black coffee.

Kinsella's eyebrows went up at mention of the "deathburger" and stayed up while he ordered a custom bleu-cheese-mushroom-tomato combo with fries. It figured.

"Too bad Charley doesn't have sun-dried tomatoes," she opined rather snidely.

"I'll live." He looked around the junky neighborhood. Any visible outbuildings made Charley's look new. Cans and bottles gleamed alongside the naked railroad tracks. "What do we do? Sit inside and wait?"

"We eat in the car, we wait in the car."

"Mine or yours?"

She glanced from the sculpted white dazzle of the Firebird to the faded, boxy silhouette of her Toyota wagon.

"Mine. What's the gimmick? You drive a black car by night and a white car by day?"

He shrugged, hands in pockets. The man always seemed posed as artfully as a model, but then a magician's act was all pose, wasn't it?

"Isn't that snow-white charger a bit attention-attracting for a low-profile guy like you?" she pressed.

"You need to take a moment and visualize the Las Vegas Strip in rush hour without a cop's eye, Lieutenant."

She didn't have to do that, she had only to mentally rewind back to her last couple drives on the Strip. White cars bounced back the desert heat, so the rental agencies ran scads of them, and the tourists like to spin around town in a convertible. He was right: in *Viva! Las Vegas,* high-profile *was* low-profile.

She escorted him around to the passenger side of her car.

"Wait a minute," she ordered.

When he turned, she pushed him expertly against the car door, and began patting down his sweater-clad chest.

He submitted, amused. "This is so sudden, Lieutenant."

"Wisecrack all you want, just so long as you're not wired."

"Who'd wire me? This an interdepartmental hassle?"

"No, it's you I don't trust." She detected nothing, and gave the wool a farewell pat. "Nice fabric."

"Cashmere."

"Why am I not surprised? I hope you'll be very happy together."

"Maybe you want to do a weapons search too."

Molina produced her best fake smile. "Sorry, this isn't your lucky day." She lightly slapped his cheek, then opened the door.

She closed it on him, assessing the interchange. The mock-slap had been a bad move; she couldn't afford to be pulled onto the man-woman ground he was always trying to push her onto. She wanted their positions clear: me authority, you citizen under suspicion.

When she got in the driver's side, she saw the manila

folder she had balanced on the dashboard beyond the steering wheel the last thing before getting out.

Kinsella was watching her without expression. "I've been trying to make up my mind whether this is a lunch date or an arrest, but it's neither. It's a meeting with a snitch. Isn't it, Lieutenant?"

"Oh? Been there, done that, by any chance?"

"No way. If that's what you're after." His tone had grown so suddenly curt that he almost sounded British. But, then, he'd lived over there for some time.

"Relax. This won't take long. I want you to investigate something for me."

He actually allowed himself to look stunned. "What the hell—?"

This time *she* shrugged and looked smug. "Nothing big-time. Just a character whose whereabouts I'd like to know." She tossed the dashboard folder into his lap. "One Raf Nadir."

"Ralph Nader? Hasn't he been done to death?"

"Pretty funny. But Ralph's so clean nobody has ever had any fun investigating him. This guy should be at least a little dirty. Raf. It's short for Rafi. And Nadir with an 'ir.' "

Kinsella opened the folder to skim the contents, then looked up. "A *cop*?"

"An ex-cop. And you're not wearing your cat-eyes today."

Beneath a concentration-furrowed brow, Kinsella's blue eyes grew wary. She actually had him off-balance, and drawing attention to his missing green contact lenses only intensified the effect.

"Is it green for nighttime, blue for day?"

He shook his head as if dislodging cobwebs. "Nothing sinister, not even dramatic. I forgot. Copies," he noted of the employment records.

"Keep them confidential anyway. You can understand I shouldn't be doing this."

"What's so important that you're willing to cut procedural corners?"

"It isn't important, but, ah, sensitive. I've got an unidentified dead body and a very slim reason to think this guy might be involved. Then I found out he's not in L.A. any more."

"Lots of people aren't in L.A. anymore. Fire, mudslide, a few too many earthquakes, a fatal tofu avalanche—"

"Anyway, I only want to know where he is, if it's here, or near here."

"I'm not on your staff, Lieutenant. Why pick me?"

"You mean 'pick on' you. Because." She couldn't help making a disavowing face. She hated her logical conclusion as much as he did. "Because this needs to be ultra-discreet. Naturally, I thought of Mr. Invisible."

"Why do you think I'd do it?"

"You've got the time, living without visible means of support."

"All magicians live without visible means of support." His smile reminded her of Lou Diamond Phillips.

Jeez, now he was looking Hispanic. A real chameleon. One handy facility. There was something international about him, probably due to living abroad for so long. Probably due to cultivating a maddening ambiguity.

"I don't want whoever's tracking this guy to smack of officialdom at all. In any way. *Nada.*"

When she said the popular slang expression, the Spanish word for "nothing," it was pronounced

117

emphatically, with the proper accent, the *d* soft as refried beans.

He nodded to acknowledge her serious use of the word.

"*Nada,*" he mimicked, just as impeccably.

Oh, he was whipped cream with hot melted chocolate on top. What an undercover operative he would make. Did make. Would make for her.

"You think this guy is that dangerous?" he asked next.

She waffled in answering that one. To women, maybe. To a man, maybe not.

"I'll tell you what I know, or think. It's not in the record, not directly anyway, although it ultimately got him canned, apparently. He's a sociopath, all right? Ego the size of the Goliath Hotel. He likes to scam his way around everyone, particularly women. Could have charmed the pants off Mother Teresa. He's probably only dangerous when crossed. Getting dumped by the LAPD would make him dangerous. The usual sociopath." She smiled in conclusion. "You know the type."

He smiled back, as pointedly as she had. "To catch a thief . . . "

"Exactly."

"I'm not a rogue cop."

"The cop part is incidental, as well as past history. Otherwise, he's just your ordinary sociopath."

"You make him for the Blue Dahlia killing?"

"I—" Too late, she'd already started answering. "What do you know about that?"

"A too-small, too-vague item in the newspaper, that's all. I read a little. That's why you want me on this. This one came too close to home."

"I want anyone on this who can cut through the red tape and eliminate one far-out suspect, all right? And, yes, I . . . don't like a body in my backyard. Especially one whose killing will go unsolved unless I do something to break through the lack of evidence in this case.

"Look. I'm not asking you to make a citizen's arrest, Kinsella. I just want to know where he is without stirring up any official channels. You seem to have your labyrinthian ways."

"A poetic sensibility is a rare thing in a homicide lieutenant."

"I read a little. So. Will you do it?"

"Why should I?"

"Because I might reciprocate with some information you want."

"Might?"

"Ask me something now."

He didn't have to think about it. "The two men driving the drug truck. What's going to happen to them?"

"The narcs will get them. We don't have enough evidence on the Effinger homicide. One blurred partial print lifted off a bit of duct tape used on the victim's mouth. They'll probably get a longer sentence on the drug charge than they would have on the murder rap," she added bitterly.

He nodded.

"Is your girlfriend recovering from her traumatic experience?"

"Temple's fine. She's tougher than she looks."

"I should know. I was at the emergency room when Devine brought her in after those unfriendlies of yours roughed her up. Even then she wouldn't give me

119

anything on you."

"*Nada,*" he said, smiling reflectively, even tenderly.

It irritated her, and her voice grated when she spoke. "Me, I would have sung like a nightingale in her place, if my live-in had vanished like that without a word. But not her. Not Miss Temple."

"What makes you madder? Her grit, or her loyalty to me?"

"Both, damn it."

"Everybody loves beating me up for what happened to Temple: you and Devine—"

"You didn't see her."

That sobered him. "No. For the best, probably. Then you'd be chasing me for what your real job is, homicide, instead of vagueness unbecoming to a stranger. Why are you so . . . fanatic about that old Goliath killing?"

She found her hands gripping the steering wheel. "It was my last case before I made lieutenant. I don't like open cases."

"It may never be closed, especially now. Tell me something I don't know. You don't know how much I blame myself for what happened to Temple."

"Does it matter if I do?"

He paused. "No. The important thing is that Temple doesn't blame me."

Molina nodded. "It's her life. Now, you gonna do that job?"

"Of course, Lieutenant. I'll get that info so fast it'll make your blue eyes brown. Any honest citizen would."

"Any honest citizen would be no good at it. Food's probably ready. I'll get it."

But he got out of the car and followed her to the window, watching as she paid for the two bags.

"That's my jalapeño deathburger," she said grabbing

one. "I can tell by the round pattern of the grease spots leaking through."

"Smart investigative work." He grabbed the other bag and walked back to her car.

"Look. Lunch is over. You can take the folder and the burger and eat it in your own car.

"Eat this sloppy mess in my car? I don't think so, Lieutenant." He grinned and hopped in her passenger seat.

Damn. She didn't want to chow down this disgustingly delicious mess with Max Kinsella looking like he'd stepped out of an Armani ad, looking on.

On the other hand, how would a man who'd just materialized out of a *Town and Country* magazine eat a Charley's old-fashion burger?

Watching worked both ways, she decided, as she unwrapped the high, wide, and unhealthy jalapeño deathburger. It smelled divine.

JUST THE WAY YOU ARE

"ISN'T THIS PREMATURE?" MATT ASKED, LEADING Leticia Brown—aka Ambrosia—into his apartment. "The audition may have gone okay, but I haven't done a real radio show yet."

"That's the point. We need to launch you."

"I could be the *Titanic.*"

"So modest. Remember, the *Titanic* was top of the line, even if it sunk. You're not gonna sink. They're gonna love you. Too many big egos on radio already."

"But it takes a strong personality to handle all those call-ins, at least judging from the practice run you and Dwight just threw at me. Drunks and compulsive talkers and obscene callers."

"Worst-case scenarios. And you did fine."

Leticia was wearing draped red jersey pants and top, reminiscent of a theater curtain. She stopped dead when she spied the red suede couch curving through his mostly empty living room. They both equally dominated the room, one horizontal, one vertical. Immovable object meets—and coexists with—irresistible force.

"That is a work of art, my man. Where'd you get that?"

"At the Goodwill."

"Looks like a million dollars."

"Considerably cheaper. I warned you; there's not much here."

"What they call 'minimalist' in the art museums. This is a jazzy building, Matt. We should find a lot of great photo backgrounds here. That lobby is spiffy, the kitchen is a hoot, and the pool looks like something from *Sunset Boulevard.* Too bad it's still winter. Billboards are horizontal, you know, and I can picture you floating on that cool, blue water."

"Dead like William Holden? Not very promising for a talk-show host."

"No." She sighed. "But maybe that couch. Subtle vibes of shrinkdom, you know?"

"I still don't see why you need a picture of me for a radio show."

Her bittersweet-chocolate deep brown eyes made his look like weak tea. Now they darkened to jet black. "Huh! You are Ambrosia's Mystery Man, that's why. Got to tease the folks a little. The audience sure doesn't want to see *me* lolling around bigger-than-life."

She turned majestically, taking in the Circle Ritz's odd angles. "*Love* this place. Nothin' square about it, no way. Who's that?"

122

Matt was surprised to see her stop in mid-turn and point to the ajar hall door.

He could see no one lurking through the narrow slit, no Electra, no Temple. Then he saw that Leticia's gaze was focused on the floor.

A single black paw and leg, and a spray of white whiskers like a feline flag of surrender, pushed through.

"Neighbor's cat. Nosy old boy. Midnight Louie."

"Makes himself right to home, doesn't he?" Leticia's chuckle was as deep and rich as devil's-food cake.

Matt, irritated, watched Louie trot across the floor and launch himself at the sofa. Having the black cat around his place was like having Temple eavesdropping on his every move. It brought her front and center in his thoughts, and she was never very far from that position anyway. Besides, he always wondered if Louie was roaming because he'd been displaced at home by a human interloper. Matt didn't like to know the when and where of Temple's resumed relationship with Max Kinsella.

"Don't act so glum, pardner. You see, a cat always knows exactly where he looks best and this one gives that crimson couch a big two paws up."

Leticia stepped back in her black combat boots and framed cat and couch with her outstretched hands.

"That's it: red sofa, black cat, white guy. Only thing missing is me playing the part of the couch."

"You want Louie in the photograph?"

"It's a natural. Look at him. You should look so relaxed. But you will when I get through with you. The other Mr. Midnight there, he's got Silly Putty for bones—Mr. Midnight! Hey. I like that a hell of a lot better than Brother John. We did the right thing."

"What have I got myself into?"

"Show biz." Her laughter filled up the room, warmed its cool, white curves.

"You might have trouble using the cat. He's been filmed for some cat food commercials. Could be a ban on using him in another kind of ad." Even as he laid down the objections, hope spread its wings in his heart. "I'd have to ask the owner about that."

"Ask away. We could even pay the owner. 'sides, one black cat looks pretty much like another. Who's to know? You don't have any spectacular piece of furniture in your bedroom, hmmm?"

"No! That sofa is it. My one . . . statement."

"It is talking loud and clear. Better get going. Nice to meet you, Mr. Midnight."

She bowed formally to the cat, winked at Matt, and flung the door wide before she left.

Matt shut it slowly behind her. The room seemed emptier than it had before. He wondered if previous tenants had held parties here, if voices had lapped against the glassy wall of French doors like waves, rising and falling.

He could almost hear their ghosts.

Matt went to the ess-curved sofa and sat on the outer curve. Louie had curled himself into harmony with the inner curve.

"Kicked out, boy? Or just restless? I guess we have a lot in common these days, which is why you keep showing up here. What am I supposed to do about it? You're the one in a position to undermine the opposition. Maybe you could give him a fatal cat allergy. Cat scratch fever, that's it." Matt patted the velvety head. "Everything would be so much simpler without the real 'Mr. Midnight' back. Is there a focus group for displaced domestic cats? Do you sit in a circle in the dark at night and yowl at the moon? You have to understand; Max Kinsella was in Temple's life long before either of us was."

The cat listened with that noblesse-oblige look the feline kind had mastered for human soliloquies. Grave, but above it all, above the pangs of exclusion and change. Yet he was voting with his feet when he deserted his home turf to consort with relative strangers.

If even a cat may look at a queen, even a cat may not like being trumped by the knave of hearts.

Matt called Temple before leaving for ConTact that evening to report Louie's defection from her apartment.

"That's all right," she said, "if you don't mind. But you're right about Louie's commercial contract. I heard from the cat food PR man today."

"You did? And?"

"Nothing much. They're going to run the commercials of Yvette and Louie that they have in the can and then decide on any new campaign. That could take months, maybe years. But I'll check to see if there's any print media exclusion in Louie's current contract. This radio thing sounds like it's getting serious."

"It got serious when they offered to pay me a thousand dollars a week."

"A thousand a week?" Matt could see her eyebrows drawing together. "Is that enough?"

"A hundred dollars an hour sounds like too much."

"But you've got travel time to and fro, and this is a performance gig. I don't know what's standard pay in radio. On the one hand, I figure they're paid a lot less than we think, as in every entertainment medium, on the other . . . before you sign a contract you should have an

125

agent check into it."

"Photographs, agents; this is getting to be too much hassle. It just balloons. I don't even know what to wear."

"Let me think about it. I used to art-direct photo shoots for actors all the time. In fact, if you don't mind, I could be there for the actual shoot."

"I don't know how Ambrosia . . . Leticia would feel about that."

"WCOO, huh? Seven to midnight. I'll listen in."

"Temple, I don't want you wasting a lot of time on my new job. I know you've got other things to do."

"Yeah, well, that's the great thing about freelance work. It's seasonal, in a way. With the Crystal Phoenix putting me on retainer for this Jersey Joe Jackson action-ride and theme-park expansion, I'm in pretty good shape financially. And so . . . I have a little extra time right now."

She didn't sound happy about it. *So where is Max, then?* he wanted to ask. But he wouldn't.

"I would feel better about this circus if you were along," he admitted. "I feel like an alien abductee in Radioland."

She laughed. "I bet. It's a hectic, crazy business."

When they hung up, Matt felt both pleased and disturbed.

126

A LITTLE WHITE LIE

WHILE I RELAX AT MR. MATT'S DIGS, MY MIND RETURNS to my recent epic effort in stage-managing the scene of the crime, entering instant rerun mode: Although our impromptu burial detail has been exhausting, Midnight Louise and I still have a busy day ahead of us.

We are headed downtown, and the only regular transportation in that direction between here and there is the animal control vehicle, and we do not particularly wish to be on the scene when it arrives to find the advertised body in absentia.

We stake out a likely intersection that offers the cover of some oleander bushes, which are even better for concealment than the potted palm of hotel-lobby legend.

When a white pickup truck idles at a red light, we leap as one into its empty bed.

Well, its almost empty bed. Luckily, the sleeping dog who is lying near the cab has a collar and short chain on to keep it from jumping out of the truck when the vehicle is red-balling it at seventy miles down the freeway. (Dogs are dumb that way.) The chain also keeps it from jumping two hitchhiking cats not three feet away, although the dog, a Doberman-Rottweiler cross that would give pit bulls a bad name, stands up to curse us mightily for several blocks.

"Shaddup!" shouts the driver from the open front seat window.

Midnight Louise and I hunker down so the dog will look like he is kicking up the usual fuss over nothing, and do not so much as fluff our fur over the

127

commotion.

So we provide good cause for this chained-down Rover to broaden his vocabulary for some three miles, before I spot the tarnished lady-with-a-red-lamp of downtown Las Vegas, the fishtailed sweetheart of the Blue Mermaid Motel.

We are fleet shadows over the truck-bed side at the first red light to stop the vehicle in the downtown business area.

I head away from the spectacularly roofed mall over the major hotel and casinos here, toward the older side of town, which is to say seedier, which is to say the more interesting.

Here is where one can find Reprise, an establishment devoted to used records. So I tell Miss Midnight Louise when we arrive before its old-fashioned, narrow glass door with a big wooden frame.

A paper streamer slashing across a display window filled with dusty album covers announces "Vinyl Clearance."

"I thought we needed a nose, not ears," Miss Louise carps.

"You need to keep your mind open and your mouth shut. Let me handle the negotiations."

A brick holds the door slightly ajar. The scratchy tones of some golden oldie album wafts out the crack like the soundtrack of something in which Peter Lorre is murdered, or should be.

Inside, a subtle veil of dust motes drifts in air that is scented with stale cigarette smoke.

A couple customers stand in the aisles, paging through ancient album covers.

I weave my way through the display cabinets toward a doorway to the shop's rear, in which a beaded plastic curtain hangs.

"Quaint," Midnight Louise notes as we slip through the shimmying strands of grass-green, orange, and yellow.

No one seems to be around back here, but I am not worried. I am not looking for the proprietor of this recycled record emporium, one Earl E. Byrd by name.

"There he is!" I announce, as my sharp eyes spot a familiar profile.

Midnight Louise's skeptical look sweeps up and around the room. "You need assistance in the eye department as well as the nose, Daddio."

I shake my head. Kits these days. They think they know it all. "Try under the desk."

Louise lets the airy hairs above her eyes do a doubtful hula. "You mean that dust bunny by the right front leg?"

I walk on over, and bend down to sniff the scrap of white fuzz on its wet black nose. Ick! That is another thing about dogs. Their snouts are always cold and waterlogged. Luckily, Nose E.'s eponymous schnozzola is as petite as the professional sniffer himself.

He yawns, showing rows of teeth the size of nine-day-old kitten claws. "Who's the babe?"

I lean low enough to flip back one of his droopy ears. "That is no babe, that is my, er, temporary assistant. She is very up on politically correct forms of address and such, as well as equipped with itchy trigger fingers."

Nose E. peers at Louise through the fringe of white hairs that has escaped the little red bow on his noggin—a bow that pulls his facial hair into a perky fountain of long topknot. I prefer to think of it as something a Japanese warrior might do to keep his coif battle-ready, but the fact is that Nose E. is Maltese, not

Japanese. Although he descends through the noble wolf-spitz clan which boasts such big-boned members as malamutes and huskies and the Samoyed, oh my, Nose E. is the wart on the end of the family line: about four pounds of silky white hair over three pounds of ridiculously small body.

But while Nose E. is asking about the identity and purpose of Midnight Louise, she is pawing at my back and not keeping her nails in either.

"Sssst! Pops. Gotta talk."

I excuse myself to Nose E. and accompany Louise under a chair for a hasty consultation.

"I hate to tell you this," she begins, "but if that dust bunny is not second-cousin to a long-haired guinea pig, I will eat it. And I could, very easily. That shrimp must weigh less than a squirrel."

"Nose E. is not one to throw his weight around, that is true. But he has the best nose in the business."

"Nose? I have known dust mites with proboscises that were bigger."

"Size is not everything, at least in this case. Nose E. is the primo dope-and-bomb-sniffer in the country. He and Earl E. have attended gigs from movie openings to presidential inaugurations. Nose E. goes undercover as a lap dog, but this lap dog is never napping. He may look cute nestled up to some starlet's implants, but one wrong perk of his paw and the undercover cops are all over anyone carrying illicit drugs or incendiary devices."

"That . . . Mite E. Mouse?"

"When will you learn that appearances can be deceiving? You thought at first that I was a big lazy galoot, and look how wrong that was."

"How wrong *was* that?"

130

"Plenty," I growl. "Now let me deal with Nose E."

So I ankle over to the little half-pint and fill him in on the problem, laying it on heavy about the widow in the window. Dogs are always a sentimental sort.

Soon I have him whimpering into his paws, but I do not want to overdo the shtick, as too much sentimentality will clog up Nose E.'s main asset.

He scoots out from under the desk, shakes himself off, and declares himself ready to follow the scent at the scene of the crime to the ends of the earth.

"An inspiring number of prepositional phrases," Midnight Louise purrs sourly in my ear, "but how far can this cross between a feather duster and an effusion of Fool Whip walk?"

"He is a dog, nonetheless," I growl sotto voce. "Unlike our kind, they like to walk for the sake of it."

"Ready?" Nose E. asks sharply.

"Do you not have to ask permission to leave?" I wonder.

"Naw. Earl E. never expects me to wander any further than the curb-service latrines. Let us go."

With a Lilliputian yap, the Maltese bloodhound is whisking across the floor like an animated toy, stirring up plenty of dust behind him for Louise and me to swallow and spit out. Before we can exit, though, we hear a Brobdingnagian step outside the shop. I take one look at those size-nine loafers coming through the door and yank Nose E. back by his tail. "Cheese it! The cops."

We three dive behind the counter, aware that ours is an undercover mission and cannot be shared with the local law enforcement types, even if it is . . .

"Lieutenant C. R. Molina," I tell Nose E. and Louise in a throaty growl. "Homicide. Bet she is on the same

131

case that we are."

Nose E. peeks around the counter end to eyeball those formidable clodhoppers. He whimpers under his breath and scurries back to our sides. "I am not used to operating at less than human shoulder-height," he confesses. "One misstep and that cop could turn me into a doll-house rug."

"Shsssst," I caution. "I am trying to hear what she is after. You may be the nose, but I am the ears of the operation."

"What does that make me?" Midnight Louise demands in a hoarse mew. "Chopped liver?"

"Loose lips sink ships," I return.

"What do ships have to do with anything?"

"Er, nothing."

Above us, I hear C. R. Molina's voice making inquiries.

First, though, they have to make with the small talk.

"What can I do for you, Carmen?" Earl E. asks.

My eyes widen. Why is he calling her after the name of an opera?

"I am looking for some old music, what else?" she says. There is a smile in her voice I have seldom, if ever, heard.

Huh? Old music. Could that be a criminal type, as in "old Muse Ick?"

"Recorded or sheet music?"

I grow even more more-than-somewhat confused.

"I am really looking for some lyrics. Do not have much. Just something about 'she left.' Ring a bell?"

"There is that seventies hit, 'She's Gone'."

"No. It has to be 'she left.' "

"Where did you hear this fragment?"

Lieutenant C. R. Molina's laugh is uneasy, like all lies.

"Did not hear it. Saw it . . . somewhere."

"Well, heck, Carmen, a lot of those old torch songs are about 'she left' or 'he left' or if you want to update it, 'he, she, or it left.' "

This time her laughter is genuine. "If you think of anything, let me know."

"Must have been mighty haunting lyrics."

"Oh, yeah. Mighty haunting, Earl E. Thanks."

I hear her flat-footed retreat; no snappy little pitter-patter like my gal Temple makes on her high heels. I feel a stab of regret that I am not able to work this case with Miss Temple, as we have so often done in the past. But there are times when a guy has to go it alone, and this is one of them. Well, as good as alone.

I hear Earl E.'s deliberate soft-shoe scrape back to the used instruments area. He is not so young anymore, and moves to a slow, stately time, unless he is jamming on one of the many musical instruments he plays like a hyperactive young maniac.

"The coast is clear," Nose E. announces. He spends too much time lolling on household furniture watching TV.

He scurries for the door and out into the Big World Beyond.

"This guy may know how to use his sniffer," Midnight Louise warns me, "but he has the street smarts of a fireplug. And you know what *they* end up covered with!"

"Do not worry. That is why we are here to protect him."

"If he gets us into major trouble, you will have to protect him from *me.*"

On that note of carefree camaraderie, we three set off on the trail of the lonesome scent.

SHOOT!

"OH, NO," MATT SAID, BACKING AWAY FROM TEMPLE.

"Just the teensiest bit!"

"No."

"It won't hurt. Please!"

He finally stopped, because he was backed up against a kitchen cupboard.

Her fingers were reaching for his face.

"Just a dab here and there, to balance the shadows. Don't think of it as makeup. Think of it as . . . air-brushing."

She dabbed on the concealer and stepped back to admire her work.

"Great!"

"This is ludicrous," Matt grumbled.

"No, it's getting set up for a photograph. Max has done this three dozen times without a whimper."

"Oh, well, if *Max* has done it—" Matt edged away from the cupboard as if expecting another attack.

Temple couldn't help noticing that he was careful to avoid too-close contact with her ever since . . . well, ever since. A good sign, she decided. They were still friends.

She checked her watch. "They're late."

"It doesn't matter. I've got all afternoon. You might not, though."

"No, I don't have a time problem. I just don't want anything to . . . deteriorate."

"You mean me."

"These things are like meringue, infinitely touchy." She glanced at entry area. "That's one reason I've confined Louie to a carrier. Besides the fact that he's

134

been in and out lately like a second-story man, we don't want stray black hairs all over that red sofa, or your new shirt."

She couldn't resist dusting the shirt folds with her other hand, untainted by makeup, in case any Louie hairs had wafted out of the carrier and sped through the air to adhere to the sand-colored silk shirt she had decided would be the best way to go.

"We need to roll these long sleeves up to just below the elbow."

"We?" Matt asked as her actions followed her words. "What if Leticia doesn't like it and the silk's all wrinkled?"

"Then we get out the steamer, fast."

"Steamer?"

"Don't sweat the small stuff. I have one downstairs."

Matt nodded, looking like a dazed five year old in the school play. Which he probably was, at this point.

"Relax. Once they set up the background and we get you settled in it and add Louie at the last minute, the actual photography won't take long."

"How long will the setup take?"

"Oh, an hour or so, if we're lucky."

"An hour?"

"Time will fly. It'll be interesting to watch the photographer set up, all the silver umbrellas and stuff."

"Why do I feel like my apartment is becoming a set for *Singing in the Rain?*"

"Because it is." Temple flashed her breeziest smile as the doorbell rang. "Don't move. You might muss something. I'll be gofer."

She flew to the door and flung it open.

The opening was filled with an icebergian presence: a black woman in white—a large black woman in white

135

with the face of a supermodel.

"Hi, I'm Temple. I was here helping Matt get ready. You must be—"

"Leticia." She pronounced it *Lay-tee-sea-uh*. "This here's Nance, the photo-wizard."

Nance was built like a Big Mac, with a very butch buzz cut of artificially white hair and a rose tattoo on her left bicep, which was also very butch.

Temple wondered how Matt would take this latest wrinkle in his new media career.

Very well, it turned out. Perhaps the dots of concealer had undone him. He watched Nance sling down her aluminum forest of tripods and various bulky black bags that resembled something the mafia would carry violins in, looking like someone who had just as swiftly rejected the courteous notion of offering to help someone else.

"Hey, nice rags," Leticia greeted Matt. She frowned. "I don't like the shoes, though."

He stared down, perplexed that she had so swiftly seen, judged, and rejected something as minor as what was on his feet.

"Well, they're innocuous." Temple too stared at his khaki suede Hush Puppies.

"Innocuous is not what I'm after here."

Temple nodded. "Maybe we need to do something bold. But nothing black."

"Absolutely. Nothing black."

"Barefoot?" they asked each other at the same time.

Two simultaneous nods.

"The barefoot shrink is in," Temple suggested.

"Right on."

"Would you two mind speaking logic?" Matt asked.

"Don't worry about it," Temple waved him off. "Just

136

one of those creative details that have to be invented rather than planned."

Nance said nothing except the occasional grunt as she studied the Kagan sofa like a target.

Matt sat down on one of the kitchen chairs.

"You might not want to do that," Temple advised. "Could wrinkle your pants."

"If this takes as long as you said—"

"You can lean against a wall," she suggested helpfully.

He turned to do so.

"As long as you check to make sure it's not dusty or stained or wet or something."

"Maybe I'll wait in the hall."

"Good idea," Leticia agreed. "That overhead light is really weak. You going to be able to compensate, Nance?"

"Yeah," came the answer.

A woman of few words. Temple and Leticia sized each other up now that they were virtually alone.

"Well, aren't you the cutest thing?" Leticia led first.

"I don't do cute."

"I don't either, but I'd like to not do it at your size rather than at mine."

"But you're gorgeous the way you are."

"Thanks, child, but my calf is a size six. You look like your whole body isn't a size six. You his girlfriend?"

Temple smiled. "Friend."

Leticia smiled back. "You seem to know your wardrobes, girl."

"I thought of white shirt and blue jeans, but with the red sofa that would have been too Fourth of July. So I went for the gold."

137

"Shades of camel. Works inside a red Porsche. Color coordination why you're here?"

"Actually, that's my cat in the carrier."

"No kidding! That is some cat. I liked him the moment I saw him lolling all over that big red sofa. If he could talk, I'd sign him up too. So there's no fuss with using his buns in our photo?"

"No. I just checked a few hours ago. His cat food contract is film-specific."

"You know your legalese too."

Temple smiled, but said nothing.

"You ever work as an agent?"

"No. But I could."

"Hmm."

"Just what have you got in mind for . . . my client?"

"I thought you were friends."

"And so much more."

"This is a test. Ambrosia really pulls the listeners. I get the boys and a bunch of the girls. I thought it was time to give the girlfriends a little something extra. I produce my own show. I call the shots. But I don't have to hog the spotlight. I'm pretty secure. I never mind adding a new wrinkle. Keeps the audience interested. Too bad we're not video-radio, though."

"Yeah, well, Matt's probably more comfortable in an audio medium anyway."

"He's such a sweet, sexy guy, and he doesn't even know it."

"That's why he's such a sweet, sexy guy."

"Just what I need for my Mr. Midnight. Today's woman doesn't want some alleycat dude, where you don't know where that private dick has been. They want a tried-and-true down-home kinda dude they can cocoon with, know what I mean?"

138

"I know what you mean," Temple said.

Apparently their girl-talk was upsetting the natives.

"Ready," Nance spoke up gruffly.

Temple darted into the hall to find Matt, arms folded, holding up the wall. "You can come in now."

"Thanks." He returned to his apartment to find a spawn of electric-cord snakes writhing over the floor amid a forest of aluminum tripods squatting before the sofa, as well as an overhead canopy of open silver umbrellas to right and left.

"A good thing I don't have much furniture in here," he said.

"Just one good piece that counts," Leticia said with a wink, nodding to the big red sofa.

ON THE STREET WHERE YOU LIVE

NO WONDER I LOOK SO MYSTERIOUS WHEN POSING for the camera! I am present in body only, while my mind reviews my recent mastery of crime-scene control.

"Talk about déjà dog all over again," Midnight Louise hisses under her breath.

We have finally hitched and hiked our way back to Wilfrid's house.

This was not easy. We were barraged by Oreo cookie jokes en route. You picture it: a four-pound white dog that looks like whipped cream on legs sandwiched between an escort of two black cats, one twenty pounds of streetwise muscle, the other about eleven pounds of streetwise sass. We are fortunate that someone did not try to corral us into some homeless shelter.

But I have found that maintaining a purposeful pace makes humans think twice about sweeping a dude or dudette off the streets into the arms of officialdom. It is afternoon by the time we again see the windows of Wilfrid's place.

I take charge.

"Louise, you will conduct Nose E. on an olfactory search of the crime scene."

"What will you be doing—your nails?"

"I will be breaking the sad news to the, er, nearest and dearest."

She gives me a dubious look, but does as I have

140

suggested.

Luckily, Nose E. is smaller than one of those Munchkin kittens and can get into tight places much better than the average dog.

My heart is heavy as I turn to approach the Furbelow house. This is the ugly part of my job. Technically, I have been successful in locating the mislaid Wilfrid. Emotionally, better that Miss Fanny Furbelow did not know his fate. So far I have staved off breaking the necessary news. Death by car, by canine, by catfight is one thing. Report that a loved one was deliberately slaughtered by a human is a fate too horrible to long contemplate. These are the creatures that we turned to thousands of years ago in partnership and trust. They outweigh us by ten to twenty times.

It is not as if poor Wilfrid would have testified against anything human. Then again, anything human would not have offed a cat.

She is waiting by the window, a white blot on the glass that reflects clear and endless sky.

As I near I see that her pale lower lashes are damp and spiked like stars.

When she sees me her dainty mitts beat a tattoo on the window, then she vanishes.

I wait by the door, listening to a pitiful wail until it is opened and she bursts onto the steps like a mad thing.

"Oh, Mr. Midnight! Tell me what has happened! I have sensed so many things. My mistress called the animal control people with their horrid truck that goes to even more horrid places and processes. They finally came, but when they went to Wilfrid's house, they did not stay very long—though one would not expect their dreadful business to take very long—and then they came here, and berated my mistress for putting in a false alarm! Is Wilfrid not dead, as I feared? Was he merely in some kind of coma? What is happening, please? Tell me before I go mad."

By now her long nails are raking my topcoat as if I were a mobile scratching post. I step away to save my threads, which she is snagging at an appalling rate. Fine black hairs drift through the afternoon air like soot-worms.

"Dear lady, the situation remains as dire as before. I have merely managed to rescue Wilfrid from an ignoble disposal. I found an oleander bush at the rear that seemed a stately memorial. Is that sufficient? Would you like to visit . . . the site?"

"No! Yes! At least I can visit him."

"Exactly," I say, with several consoling chin rubs. "My associate and I were determined that he should not be subjected to a common grave, or worse, a common incineration."

Mewling with distress, she leans on me as I guide her to the greenery in question. No flowers dot the spiny leaves, but by summer the bright pink blossoms should be swaying in the breeze.

As soon as we are within sight of the landmark, she sprints to its foot, there throwing herself down and writhing in anguish.

"Now, now. You do not want to get sand in your best coat. And beware gnashing your teeth on any fallen oleander leaves; they are poisonous."

Eventually the voice of reason quiets her grief. She sits up, sighs shakily, then begins smoothing her frazzled hair. "He must have been murdered, my poor innocent Wilfrid."

I do not contradict her sad conclusion. Her heavenly blue/gold eyes narrow hellishly.

"I want you to take on another assignment, Mr. Midnight. I want you to find the degenerate animal who did this. The filthy human!"

"Would that he had been filthy, dear lady. He would have left more of a trail. But do not fret. My associates are examining the house even now. I had earlier detected a scent that might lead to Wilfrid's missing mistress. I also noted another scent, far more subtle, so I called in an expert."

"Oh, thank you, Mr. Midnight. I knew the moment I saw you that you were not an ordinary investigator."

"I do have my connections around this town," I say modestly. "No smell will be left unsniffed that bears any resemblance to the trail the killer left within."

"What is this odor?"

Here I wrinkle my brow. "It reminds me of a human food that comes in a small box. I have seen my roommate mix up some when she is feeling particularly punk."

"It is a medicinal preparation?"

"Quite the contrary. She treats it as something that is bad for her, and therefore particularly welcome when she is in a downcast mood."

"I know! My mistress is equally addicted to this substance, and I know it is poison to the canine breed. Chocolate!"

I frown again. I do not mean to repeat an expression, but this is one puzzling scent.

"That is the problem. This scent is not chocolate. It is not of an edible substance, although it reminds me of this boxed stuff my Miss Temple gorges on, on occasion, which is served warm or cold, but I noticed the scent when it was served warm."

"Oh, these humans! With their disgusting, unnatural

habits of heating and icing food. And they think themselves so superior to us for these very eccentricities."

"I know. They are a hard lot to figure. But they are not all bad."

"No. My mistress means well. I try to understand what she wants, but she yammers on so in that unintelligible manner of hers . . . I am sure your mistress does senseless, stupid things as well."

"Sometimes," I admit, but I will go no farther to libel Miss Temple. Sometimes her senseless, stupid human acts have saved my life.

Miss Fanny Furbelow creeps nearer to me. Tears are trembling on her eyelashes and there is a little catch in her voice.

"You have been so good to me, Mr. Midnight. I will never forget your—"

Whatever of mine she will never forget is lost to recorded history. Her baby blue/golds widen to celestial pools as she gazes beyond me. "What is *that?*"

I turn to look. "Merely the best nose man on the West Coast. If anyone can trace the puzzling, human, not-food smell that lingered at the scene of the crime, it is Mr. Nose E. Byrd."

"That is a bird?" Miss Fanny Furbelow's eyelids flutter and she falls against my masculine chest in a dead faint.

Nose E. trots over to inquire in his best baritone bark, "What is wrong with the dame?" His little, round, black, button nose twitches like a psychopath's eyelid. "I am afraid she has been hitting the nip this afternoon."

"Yeah. She has her reasons."

"Do not we all?" Nose E. muses philosophically. "A bad business, this. From what you say, both suspicious scents you report lie close to home. Very close to home. I suggest we investigate Miss Temple Barr first."

"A waste of time," I growl. My Miss Temple is beyond suspicion in my book.

"She is always up to her neck in solving crime," Miss Midnight Louise notes, glancing contemptuously at the prone Fanny Furbelow. She has never thought much of my taste in female companionship. "Perhaps this time she is up to her neck in committing one."

DEAD OF NIGHT

WHEN THE PHONE RANG, MOLINA'S BEDROOM WAS IN that inky state of darkness that owns the hours of three to six A.M. The Twitching Hours was how she thought of it.

She had been tossing and turning since two-something, second-guessing her gutsy decision to let Max Kinsella play bloodhound for her. She risked his learning more about her past than she liked, but she couldn't risk not knowing where Nadir was. Not with "she left" spray-painted on the side of her personal vehicle.

So she let the phone ring twice before lifting the receiver, not to wake up, but to quiet the jitterbug a sudden ring would have on her already antsy system.

"Molina." Spoken like a wee-hours bureaucrat.

"We got another one, Lieutenant."

"That you, Su?"

"Yeah. Alch was against calling you, but I said you'd want to see the crime scene in flagrante delicto."

"Female victim?"

 "Check."

"Strangled?"

"Right."

"Stab wound?"

"Yup."

"Graffiti?"

"No . . . that's why Alch thought it could wait."

Molina sighed.

"It's close, though, Lieutenant. Too close for comfort. That's why Reisdorf and Muñez, who were up for the case, gave us a call."

Molina scrawled the address on the bedside notepad that lit up when you lifted the pen from its support. Notes in the dark were a routine of police work.

"Keep the corpse on site, then?" Su asked.

"Twenty-five minutes," Molina said, already jamming her feet into moccasins.

Her finger was poised to hit the programmed number for Delores as soon as Su hung up.

Ten minutes later she was rushing through the kitchen door into the garage. Delores's husband worked the graveyard shift at a package delivery service, so she stayed up until he went to work. She didn't mind coming over nights to sit the house and Mariah and she *really* didn't mind making the extra money. Her own kids were old enough to be left at home alone.

Knowing what she did about crime in this town, Molina couldn't imagine Mariah ever getting old enough to be left alone at night.

The night air balanced on the cutting edge of forty degrees, chilly but not icy. The crime scene was far from the Blue Dahlia, probably one reason Alch didn't think she should be alerted. He'd worked for her longer, knew her better, but Su was keen and new and had an unconventional instinct for the odd detail.

"She who delegates is lost," Molina told her softly glowing dashboard.

Maybe she hadn't been in a supervisory position long enough to give her investigators their head as much as she should. If those words hadn't been sprayed on her car—*her* car—she'd be home in bed right now, sleeping, and Max Kinsella would have heard nary a word about Raf Nadir.

This scene was the parking lot of a church, one of

147

those cheap cinder-block churches with a chintzy wooden steeple giving the feeble finger to heaven. The name of the church would not reflect a Major Congregation.

Alch was chewing on his mustache, hands digging deep into his trenchcoat pocket, a sure sign of malcontent.

Su paced, her tiny figure jerky and doll-like in the artificial twilight of a single streetlight. Why did petite people have so much energy, like those wired three-pound toy dogs? Maybe they had to make more of themselves to get attention.

Now that the watershed age of forty was loitering with intent to ring her doorbell, Molina was beginning to envy energy.

Asphyxiation was one of murder's more brutal forms, leaving the victim's face twisted with an expression of struggle at the least, or horror at the worst, depending on how much you wanted to read into the still-life that death made of a human body.

This victim looked no younger but more polished than the Strawberry Lady. Grooming details glossed her face and hands. She looked like she belonged in Las Vegas, as the Strawberry Lady had not.

"No writing," Molina threw to the two detectives, to the technicians tagging and bagging evidence, to the distant streetlight. It was not a question, but it wasn't a statement either. It was a hope. Because writing would be a pattern and a pattern had a prayer of being deciphered.

"Nothing in the immediate area."

"There's no surface but the asphalt here, but the church must have a lot of wall. A Dumpster nearby?"

"The uniforms are conducting a search."

"No purse again, no ID?"

"Right." Su stopped pacing to nibble daintily on one of her dragon-lady nails. No matter the length or intensity of the nibbling, Merry Su never shortened a claw. Must have fiberglass in her nail polish.

Molina donned a pair of the latex gloves jammed in the pocket of every jacket for just such sudden occasions. She squatted beside the body, her knees cracking, and drew back the lacquered hair so bleached you couldn't tell whether the hairdresser had been going for blond or white.

"Strangled with something knotted, but the marks are farther apart and softer than the previous victim's."

"As if the weapon had stretched since its last use," Su suggested.

"Or it could be a different ligature," said Alch.

"Different offender," Molina finished his thought. She stood, joints snap-crackle-and-popping. "We need to be sure we're not missing a message, even on the fringes. But at least this one looks like she's been around town for a while. We should have better luck identifying her. These two deaths; they're strangely inappropriate."

"What do you mean?" Su sounded eager to jump on any supposition.

"Well, the woman at the Blue Dahlia hardly seemed the type to go there, especially alone. And this woman hardly seems the type to be visiting some dinky church at the midnight hour."

"At least we should get some labels off these clothes," Su agreed.

That's the indignity of sudden death, Molina thought; in an instant you're judged on your wearing apparel. What would someone think who found her dead in her unimaginative pantsuits, the pockets jammed with latex gloves as if they were condoms for octopuses?

"Over here!"

The uniform's voice wasn't loud, but sharp and urgent.

They swarmed to the edge of the parking lot thirty feet away, where an oleander bush spread its spiky, poisonous leaves and a flashlight pooled like saffron oil on the ground.

Molina saw something sparkling in the dry soil and squatted again without mercy for her knees.

"Jeez." The officer was impressed with his own find, but let Molina's still-gloved hand scoop it up on the barrel of her ballpoint pen. "That thing's worth something."

"Indeed it is." She stared at the circle of gold and diamonds and inlaid opal.

Su was beside her like a Doberman. "Looks too small for that woman's fingers."

Molina nodded. She thought she knew just whose pinky this little piece of plunder would fit. No need to scour the whole kingdom for a candidate; no way, Cinderella.

This ring had someone's name written all over it. Two someones.

"Was it lost here, or left here? And for how long?" Su was like a Pekingese rolling in possibilities.

"Awfully good condition," the uniform noted. "You'd think someone would spot it fairly soon."

"They don't have your keen eyes and methodical ways, Cartright," Molina said, smiling as she glanced away from his ID. "Good hunting."

She let the ring slide into the plastic Baggie Su held out and open for it.

The last time anyone had seen this ring, it had vanished onstage during a magic act downtown. The last person seen wearing this ring had been Temple Barr. The undeniable donor of the ring was Max Kinsella.

She caught the ring in its plastic shroud tight into the palm of her hand, until its sharp contours stamped her flesh like a cold brand.

She would not be the pawn of any man, not again. Her daughter would not be a trading card between the past and the present, not ever.

Enlisting Max Kinsella to track Raf Nadir had been a bold, unpredictable move. Like any move in the game of chess that a life or a career was, it was also dangerous, and somewhat desperate.

Molina didn't like feeling desperate, and especially detested acting on that feeling. But the two men, her two opponents, were also unpredictable, dangerous and desperate, each in his own way.

To catch a thief . . . hire a thief. To destroy an enemy, destroy another enemy. It wasn't nice, but it was . . . efficient.

No matter what Mr. Mystifying Max dug up on Raf Nadir's and her past together—and the risky position that put her in—she now had evidence of something a lot more incriminating from his own present.

To imprison a magician, capture a magic talisman.

She released the ring, eyed its exotic splendor. Thirty pieces of silver must have looked that good to Judas Iscariot once.

RING OF FIRE

"GUESS WHAT?" TEMPLE'S VOICE ASKED OVER THE telephone.

"I couldn't begin to," Matt said.

"I was out on errands and stopped at a couple of resale shops and I found the neatest brown leather bomber jacket, just seamed enough to scream 'Indiana Jones.' I got it because I'm pretty sure it'd fit you."

"Why?"

"Why am I sure it would fit you?"

"No, why would I want such thing?"

"It's a perfect prop for your next promo photo; trust me. You've got to snap up these things when you run across them. Anyway, I have a ton of releases to pound out for the Crystal Phoenix, but when I'm done, I'll run up with it, if that's okay?"

"Sure it's okay."

Matt shook his head as he hung up the receiver. He couldn't decide whether Temple was a frustrated costumer or a consummate PR woman. Either way, he was looking forward to seeing her more than he was any jacket.

An hour later, the doorbell rang.

"That was fast work," Matt said, swinging wide the coffered door.

Except that it was Lieutenant C. R. Molina who stood there bearing arms, instead of Temple bearing apparel suitable for shooting . . . with a camera.

And Molina's arms were concealed, although her actual arms were not.

Matt was sure now that he was Alec in Wonderland.

"Uh . . . what can I do for you?" He wasn't sure whether she was here as an official or as an acquaintance.

"Plenty, I hope. Got a few minutes? You're not due at ConTact for a couple hours."

"Guess you don't need me to answer your questions."

"Sorry." She brushed past him, pausing in the wide archway to the living room as if the Kagan sofa were a stop sign she was obligated to heed. "That is really . . . red."

She moved farther into the room before turning on him. "What's the matter?"

"I never know how to take you. Getting a surprise visit from you is like getting one from the IRS. Is it a friendly, inquiring call, or gangbusters?"

"The IRS never makes friendly, inquiring calls." Molina grinned. "I do. And this is one of them, but I don't think you'll like the implications."

"I never like the implications. It comes of having led a cloistered life for so long."

"Oh, come on! You priests were the worldliest religious order in the church. Can I, ah, actually sit on this?"

"Sure."

Matt watched her, amused. Temple would certainly dismiss the solid-color suit and Molina's blunt Dutch-cut hair, but the effect was rigorously functional, which would serve anyone who didn't want to distract from the essentials of her job.

Molina squirmed a bit before accepting the fact that she was properly supported by the sculptural, armless sofa. Then she reached into her jacket pockets. She reminded him of Captain Kangaroo. He had never seen her carry a purse, a habit that added to her strong air of

153

command of herself, and others.

Nuns who taught school, for instance, had never carried purses either, now that he thought about it. "No frills" was the message: no makeup, no trivialities; no need to produce evidence of my identity unless I feel like it; nothing to weigh me down but authority.

He remembered his grade-school teachers in their full, long, black habits, and the nun who directed the choir who prowled the lines of trilling students, swinging the gigantic, knee-length rosary suspended from her belt-cord. It felt like a lethal weapon, that swinging arm of wooden beads. Sister Mary Lariat, they called her behind her back.

Still, those muffling habits conferred a kind of magical power on their wearers.

In a sense Molina was a magician, bureaucratic-style, though she'd despise comparison to the Mystifying Max: everything came out of the pockets—her police ID, a notepad and pen, maybe even an occasional Kleenex.

Now it was a small, clear-plastic Baggie that emerged, weighed down in one corner by a nugget of metal.

"You recognize this?"

Matt leaned forward on the hard kitchen chair to take it. The room's arched white ceiling provided reflected light. Matt felt something in him lurch: heart or hormones, which he didn't know.

"It looks like—I can't swear to it. I only glimpsed it for a second. Where on earth did you find it?"

She nodded. "Looks like that to me too. Small enough."

"Didn't that Shangri-La woman skip town with her confederates? She's the one who last had it."

"Right." Molina's lips tightened to grimness. "Found it at a murder scene."

"That has nothing to do with Temple."

"Oh, right." She shook her head as if mere babblers should just be ignored. "It was found at what may be the second murder scene in a series. In both cases, neither victim had any personal belongings or jewelry on or near the body."

"Except for this ring."

"Except for that ring."

"That's . . . freaky. That's odd. But what has it to do with Temple? She wasn't the last person in possession of this thing. You saw it taken from her yourself."

"I know who took it from her and I know who gave it to her. What I don't know is much about this missing magician, Shangri-La, and I don't know why this ring would have surfaced—deliberately, I'd say—at this particular murder scene." Molina fidgeted on the sofa seat again, unaware of her discomfort with its severely chic fifties form. "I'm not going to ask *her,* and I'm not going to ask him, at least not until I have more of a notion to what's going on. You know a little about both of them and about everything else involved here. You get to be my guinea pig."

"Lieutenant . . . what do you want? I suppose you *don't* want me to tell poor Temple her ring has been found, and where, but what else?"

"The victims are complete mysteries. Both women, both stripped of personal belongings other than their clothes, which is even odder; each killed miles from the other, one near the presence of this ring. I want to run the facts of the cases by you, see if anything rings any alarm bells. One of them was killed in a church parking lot."

"What does *that* have to do with it? Or me?"

"Don't sound so exasperated. I thought you might have some expertise in that area, that's all."

"Church parking lots? I don't think so." He sighed. "What denomination was it?"

Molina produced a narrow notebook from her other pocket and flipped pages. "More Holy Roller than Holy Roman Catholic Church, admittedly. 'Desert Spring Well of Christ Triumphant.' You frown. Does that mean you know it?"

"It means I've seen churches like it. Tiny, unaffiliated, often either interesting or seriously weird." He stood up.

"I'm not through."

"Neither am I. I want to look it up in the phone book."

He returned from the kitchen with the formidable bulk of the Las Vegas phone book and began riffling the yellow pages even before he sat back down. "Do you know that Las Vegas has more churches per capita than most U.S. cities?"

"Heard that."

"A lot of Baptist congregations, tons of Mormon ones. The usual Catholic, Lutheran, Presbyterian, Methodist, and Episcopal. Then the zillions of Churches of Christ and Churches of God. Inspiring, isn't it? Only one Unitarian Universalist Church, though. I guess we can't blame Temple too much for neglecting to attend."

"I don't care what church Temple Barr would be attending if she were a churchgoer. I should have figured she'd be something wishy-washy like a Unitarian."

"A fallen-away Unitarian," Matt amended, smiling. "Here's the Sacred Well or whatever is, under

'Nondenominational.' I guess! No, I haven't been there."

"I didn't think you had."

"I could have been. I've visited a lot of local churches. Most cities don't have this rich a range."

Molina shook her head. "To each his own hobby."

"What do you want me to do, if not offer expert testimony on churches?"

"I want you to come to headquarters, review the evidence, see if anything seems remotely familiar, or connected."

"To Temple?"

She nodded.

"To Max Kinsella?"

She nodded again.

"I can try, but the odds are—"

"I've been in Vegas a lot longer than you have. I know what the odds are."

He shrugged and handed the ring bag back to her. "Guess Temple won't get that back for a while."

"Maybe never, if these cases aren't closed."

"Really? The police can do that? The ring must be valuable."

"You really so anxious to see it back on her finger again?"

"No. But it hurt her to lose it. You saw that."

"Better you be hurt than she?"

He shrugged again, then changed the subject. "You say the two murders were far apart. Where was the other one?"

"The first one." Molina stood, jamming the Baggie into her bottomless pockets. They never bulged, but they were never empty. If she ever made captain, they should nickname her "Kangaroo."

157

"It happened at the Blue Dahlia," she added on her way to the door. "I found the body. Or, rather, Carmen did. But that's classified information."

She never turned back to look at him, never slowed down. She simply left.

He stood in his open doorway, staring down the empty hallway leading from his apartment, realizing why he had been called in as a semineutral observer. More than *two* people he knew were personally linked to the puzzling murders. Lieutenant C. R. Molina's alter ego Carmen was too.

LITTLE GREEN APPLES

THEY WERE JUST MANILA FOLDERS, BLAND VANILLA-colored posterboard rectangles. He would never even notice them in most offices. But on a homicide lieutenant's desk . . .

Matt found his glance flickering over them even as he absorbed Molina's deliberate, monotone recital of the facts surrounding two brutal murders.

Her manner reminded him of priests who sleep-talked their way through the Anointing of the Sick—a sacrament once more dramatically called Extreme Unction, the last anointing—their droning murmurs downplaying the ritual's mortal nature. Routinely looking death in the face seemed to demand a defensive stoicism.

"There aren't as many serial killers around as the media would have the public think," Molina was saying. "Thanks to all the books and movies, they're the superstars of the crime-entertainment industry: exotic, scary, and masters of bizarre, random murders meant to shock the public. So-called crimes of passion are much bloodier, and more intimate. Only one person, or a cluster of persons, are targeted. Of course we're now in the era of the terrorist-style murder, where anger at the one person targeted overflows to everyone nearby. That's another unsettling pattern."

"But."

"But: These two murders have earmarks of both single killings and serial killings. But: Just as one swallow does not a summer make, neither do two apparently similar killings a serial killer indicate."

"What do you think I can tell you?"

"I have no idea."

"You really want to interrogate Temple, don't you? But you can't, not without revealing the presence of the ring Max gave her."

"Oh, I can do anything. Whether I get results or not is a different matter." Her voice took on the sardonically self-mocking tone it was wont to use lately.

Matt guessed that Temple and her circle of acquaintances had become quite a crown of thorns for Lieutenant C. R. Molina.

"I am loath to think that every murder in Las Vegas has a link to Temple Barr," she went on. "Or to you. Though it's beginning to look like that in this case, too. All I ask is that you review the evidence, see if it rings any chimes of memory. Or suspicion. You've spent enough time around her; you ought to know her methods by now, or lack of them."

Matt nodded and sat forward. He'd rather see the contents of those faceless manila folders than sit here guessing at them.

Molina spread her fingers over the folders, aware of his impatience, yet not inclined to share the evidence.

Her remarkable blue eyes seemed to darken with seriousness.

"Evidence of murder is not pretty; I'm sure you know that. Evidence of violent crime is often shocking to the layperson. Remember, what you're seeing are just remains. You're looking for details, evidence, conclusions visible on the shell of a dead person, not searching for any exit wounds that might indicate the passage of a human soul. All right?"

Matt nodded. Clinical was the only way to go. He could do that. Especially when he thought how ghoulishly jealous Temple would be that Molina had shared her graphic evidence with him and not her.

Molina spun one fat folder around to face him.

He opened it gingerly, recalling the story of Pandora's box. Only these evils were already long since loosed in the world.

"These are taken for evidence," she warned him. "Not for composition, not for aesthetic reasons at all."

The pictures were as raw as advertised.

Closeup after closeup of damaged flesh. Some were at the crime scene. Some post-autopsy. All unsparing.

He shuffled through them, aiming at the kind of detachment Molina's voice had implied. Dead indifference.

"That is the first victim," she said as he studied them.

"Not where the ring was found?"

"No. Though—"

Matt was glad to hear her hesitation. It gave him an excuse to lift his eyes from the photographs. Years of priesthood, intensified by months of the audio interaction of hotline counseling, had honed his ear for what people had been *about* to say as well as for what they actually said.

"Though what?"

"Another funny thing about the two cases. Victim one's third left finger was narrowed at the base and sightly callused."

"As though she'd worn a wedding ring for years."

"Exactly. Yet no ring or jewelry of any kind was found at her death scene. Whereas victim number two—" Molina lifted the Baggie with the ring she had shown him earlier and pushed another manila folder across the glass-covered desktop.

"Whereas victim number two," Matt mimicked, "had a ring, not hers, in the vicinity, and her hands—" He was getting better at shuffling through the photos without being waylaid by shots that made his heart and fingers stop their routine work of beating and riffling.

Matt frowned as he isolated the photos of the second victim's hands. "No ring depressions. Unless the photographs—"

"I looked over the actual body. No ring depressions, although her ears were pierced."

"May I?" He reached for the ring bag.

"I'm trying to trace it," she mentioned as she passed it over.

The ring weighed down one corner of the plastic bag, like an internal anchor. Examining it through plastic was like underwater photography, not quite satisfying. It was a gold band of equal width all around, but the irregular studding of small diamonds, the geometrical slash of inlaid opal, made it more of a fashion statement than either an engagement ring or a future wedding band.

"Count on the Mystifying Max," Molina put in, "to be ambiguous even in the design and purpose of a ring. I wonder if even Temple Barr knows what he meant by that."

"It's sophisticated," he admitted. "Doesn't seem to go with that second dead woman."

"Why do you say that?"

"She looks very Las Vegas; this ring is a work of art."

She nodded. "If you were to remove it from the bag, which I'll thank you not to do, you'd find a designer symbol next to the fourteen-carat gold stamp. Unfortunately, given Kinsella's globe-trotting past, the ring could be from any exotic corner of the world."

Matt nodded, flipping open the first folder, then the second. "This woman was found at the Blue Dahlia; this one at the church parking lot?"

"That's right. The first victim is probably in her early fifties. The second is forty-something. We're not sure because there are tiny scars along her hairline."

"A face lift. Already?"

"You were the one who said she looked like Las Vegas; Las Vegas is full of women who've made a point of making themselves look younger."

"They're so different."

"And one really big difference." Molina pulled a third folder from her desk drawer and tossed it onto the desk, like a winning card in a game of poker.

He opened it, braced for more carnage . . .

. . . and saw a photograph of the side of a car. "She left," read the straggling black spray paint over the driver's side door.

"This looks like—"

"My car," Molina said ruefully. "At least, my car did look that until I had the door repainted after it had been through a forensics examination."

"Body number one was found near your car?"

"Next to it. On the Blue Dahlia lot."

162

"When?"

"You want date or time?"

"Both."

"Tuesday, at about three A.M. I had stayed late to jam with the band."

Matt repeated the differences. "No ring, no makeup. Older."

"Clothes considerably plainer than those on body number two."

"Less well dressed, and found in a club parking lot. Whereas Miss Las Vegas is found in a no-name church parking lot miles away, and only how many days later?"

"Two. Yes, that's awfully soon for a serial killer to strike again."

"Both strangled?"

"We don't know what was used on the first. A knotted scarf—missing, naturally—may have been used on the second victim. It could have been hers. In both cases, whatever strangled the victims was prepared in advance. Knotted at regular intervals."

"Aren't there garrotes that are made like that?"

"There are garrotes made every which way. But the marks on that first victim are puzzling. We've made a list of all sorts of things, and nothing quite fits the size of the knots, or the spacing, which is very close, or the pattern."

Matt stared at the first victim's neck; small, regular bruises circled the skin like a tattooed necklace of beads.

"This reminds me of something."

"A similar death?"

"Nothing grisly like that. Something about the size and spacing of the marks. You tried electrical cord, of course?"

Molina consulted her list. "Number nine: electrical cord; knots too misshapen and too large."

"What about that other kind of cord? Gosh, what was it? Fabric-wrapped. Old-fashioned."

"You're saying she was strangled with vintage cord?"

"I think they still use it on . . . I know! Irons."

"Oh. We hadn't thought of that one, no. I bet it wouldn't knot tightly enough to produce such close-set contusions, though."

"I don't know. I'd have to try it."

"Do you even *have* an iron?"

"Uh, no."

"Then leave the crime reenactment to us, okay?" She leaned down to open the bottom drawer in her desk. "That brings us to the clothes." Two brown paper bags hit the desk like bag lunches for giants, along with latex gloves, his and hers. "See what you make of them."

Matt's gloved hands hovered over the first bag.

"It's okay. Forensics has sucked everything off them they can use."

"It's not that. Clothes are so much more personal than photographs."

"Skip it, then."

"No! Those throat marks are bothering me. It's like I can almost visualize something that would fit them."

"Don't tell me! You're discovering psychic depths you never knew you had."

"No. Not that. It's a memory problem. Maybe something they wore—"

Matt gingerly removed the contents of the first bag. When he was done he had a motley pile: snakeskin-print gray leggings, a purple knit tunic, a yellow jog bra, something lacy and shiny he let remain in a crumpled pile, a hair clip with a purple chiffon bow attached.

"Not exactly church wear," Molina commented.

"These days, who knows? This woman would have worn jewelry."

"And lots of it. You're right. Inexpensive stuff, for the most part. So who would have taken it, and why?"

"And why leave a really fine ring behind in its place?"

"The good ring could have been dropped accidentally. It's clear in both of these cases that the killer or killers went to some lengths to make sure the victims weren't identified, at least not too quickly, if at all."

"So then who they are is a clue to why they were killed."

"Maybe. Only the Strawberry Lady's bag left."

Matt tackled the second paper bag while Molina shoveled clothes back into the first one.

"Why do you call her the Strawberry Lady?" he asked, unsealing the bag. The odor drove his face back a foot. "Never mind. I recognize that stuff."

"So do we all. Rest room, car and inadvertent sinus freshener. And I used to like the scent of strawberries."

"It's really overwhelming coming out of this bag." Matt pulled out more folded clothes: skirt, jacket, blouse, all man-made fabrics like the other woman's. These felt of better quality, though, and the design was more conventional.

Matt pushed the clothes back before he was forced to confront more dead women's underwear.

"I'm no expert on women's clothes. Temple would know about that." He paused in pushing the bag back over to Molina's side of the desk. "Except—"

"Yes?"

"That deodorizer odor. I've smelled it in less

165

concentrated form somewhere else than in a car or a rest room."

"Where?"

"I don't know. But wherever it was, I was there with Temple. I remember afterwards, after getting away from that awful strawberry scent, wherever it was, that her hair smelled of green apple, which was much better."

"Green apple, huh? Did you know that they're using green apple scent as a diet aid? Take a sniff to get over what you crave. That work for you?"

"I don't need to lose weight," Matt said, ignoring her jibe. "And I think you'd better brace yourself. You can't go around Temple on this one. You'll just have to ask for her help."

SINKING FAST ON SUNSET STRIP

THE LAS VEGAS STRIP GLOWED LIKE THE EMERALD City of Oz in the laser-light of the setting sun.

Max had the Firebird's top down, fifty-degree weather or not. He had made the three hundred miles from L.A. in four hours, despite having to drive decorously enough to avoid attracting a highway patrolman.

Getting away from his seclusion in the city, getting on the road and out into the streets of L.A. for some honest-to-goodness, in-person detective work had been like a vacation. The beat blaring off the CD made him want to stop at the Hard Rock Cafe for more racket, for tourist-tacky rock memorabilia and elbow-to-elbow eating, though a giant cheeseburger there probably wouldn't be quite as good as Charley's old-fashion burgers.

He wished Temple could have ridden along, for the drive at least. Of course, she would have wanted to drive the Trans-Am, and then a motorcycle cop would have gotten them for sure.

As he merged with the ever-more-impossible traffic clogging the highway as it morphed into the famed Strip, Max felt the desert wind settle down to a mild breeze like a hunting falcon roosting on a shoulder, hooded and tamed.

Having contacts all over the world had cut the time it had taken to half. In a way it felt unfair, like the easy way out, but he was jubilant with what he had discovered. Not that Molina would be.

Still, it confirmed her edgy suspicions. It validated her turning to him for assistance. It gave him a gilt-edged invitation to ask for favors in return. Many happy returns.

So she should be happy. He certainly was.

For Raf Nadir had proved to be pretty much what Molina had said he was: a high-performing charmer who under the best circumstances would have been an exemplary cop and citizen, but who under pressure would go rogue.

And he had, over something small and stupid, but then guys like that usually did go ballistic over the pettiest problems—the smaller, the more at stake. Five years earlier he had blown his sergeant's rank with a couple of excessive-force suits. Two years ago he had pulled over a Son of Somebody on a DWI.

Max could see the scene now.

The SRK, L.A. model. Spoiled Rich Kid. The car had been a Lamborghini, red, and the kid's high speed was probably internal as well as external, not to mention fueled by a few too many umbrella drinks at too many fern bars.

But a DWI wasn't enough for Officer Nadir. Maybe the kid had been mouthy. Whatever the circumstances, drugs were found in the car.

A lot of L.A. lawyers got together to make a pretty good case that the drugs had been planted.

Maybe they had been, maybe not. The result was the same either way. Nadir was off the force, and what had once been a promising career was now tawdry history.

He moved down with his income. He became a skip tracer, tracking people who were only a little bit more down-and-out than he was. Finally, he skipped town himself. Skipped right from L.A . . . to L.V.

Max smiled as he reined the Trans Am to a stop for an endless red light in bumper-to-bumper traffic.

Molina would like it, and she wouldn't like it. Either way, he was in like Flynn, whether she knew it or not.

It was a good thing that the new car had the instant pickup of three-hundred-twenty-five overmuscled horses. The bullet that grazed the back of his head as he accelerated from the stoplight would have driven through his temple had he been an instant slower off the starting gate.

Naked was the best disguise, Max had always said, and that was true. Unless your cover was blown.

His cover was definitely blown, which is when naked becomes something to die for.

Now was a great time to find out; he was pinned in by tons of throbbing, idling metal vehicles in an open-topped car.

The shot could only have come from two types of

168

weapon: a high-powered rifle fired from one of the massive Strip hotels, or a handgun in a nearby vehicle.

Max tried to maneuver the Trans Am into another lane, but rush-hour traffic was Sardine City. He couldn't put up the top until he hit a red light and could shut off the motor. Meanwhile the back of his scalp stung with the fury of fire ants. A welt of sticky wetness clung to his exploring fingertips like lip gloss.

He checked out the passing hotels, mostly ruling out a sniper. Too far from the street, too likely to be spotted by a gawking tourist. Unless the sniper was dressed to be part of the show.

The people in the cars and trucks around him sensibly had their windows rolled up. Night was coming and it would be cold to those used to a long broiling summer season.

Drive-alongside hits worked best on deserted roads, where the shooter could zoom off at will. Here, everyone was in the same boat, or car, trapped in packs that kept fairly parallel. Unless . . .

Max tried to ignore the short, impatient honks providing an erratic background accompaniment to the traffic jam. He listened for the drone of an engine that marched to a different drummer than stop-and-go traffic.

There! To the right. A hornet's buzz. Only one vehicle was mobile enough to snail-dart through this rush-hour feeding frenzy. A motorcycle.

And not the roar of some souped-up behemoth like the Hesketh Vampire, but the fifty-cc spit-and-choke of a Honda.

The motor's buzz up ahead reassured Max that only one shot was intended—whether as a warning or to be fatal, no one would know but the shooter.

He maneuvered the Trans Am into the right lane. By the time it stopped for the red light 150 feet ahead, at which point he could finally push the button and loft the top into place, the motorcycle sound was a faint whine.

He turned right on Flamingo, peering through the sparser traffic, and thought he saw a black fly-speck shooting into the darkening blue haze of night.

CLOSE SHAVE AND A HAIRCUT

"YOU'RE SURE IT WAS A BULLET AND NOT A RAZOR?"

"Hurled razors. An innovative idea. Let you be the audience stooge in one magic show and you want to innovate the act. Ouch!"

"Alcohol stings." Nurse Temple winced in sympathy. "This could start a new punk hair style: a horizontal part from ear to ear. It's not bleeding much."

"Then I'm incredibly lucky. Scalp wounds are notorious bleeders. The white leather seats on the Trans Am are safe."

"You're incredibly lucky that *your* leather wasn't ruined for good. Where is Moby Dick, anyway?"

"I left it in the Caesars parking lot. It's history."

"You're not going to collect it later?"

Max shook his head, inadvertently scouring his wound on the cotton ball Temple held against it.

"Ouch, again! It's been identified. I'll notify the proper parties, who'll pick it up and drive it out-of-state. They'll leave something else for me."

"Darn! I never got a chance to drive it, either, especially with the top down."

"No more convertibles for me until we can prove my head is no longer a target for somebody."

"Somebody. That's a long list, I bet."

Temple, her ministrations done, tossed the rusty cotton balls in the wastebasket and turned to screw the cap back on the bottle of rubbing alcohol.

Suddenly Nurse Barr of the coolly competent quip under pressure was gone. The cap wouldn't turn on the neck's grooves and the opaque plastic bottle wouldn't fit into the curve of her hand.

It tilted, tipped, slipped. She grabbed for it, but it was Max who caught it.

"What—?" Temple hated being clumsy.

Max set the bottle down and took her hands. It was only in contrast to their steadiness that she realized hers were trembling.

"This is ridiculous!" Temple regarded her shaking hands as if they were alien appendages. "You were the one who was shot at."

"Passenger's nerves," he diagnosed with a smile. "The person who's driving when the car narrowly misses a collision at least can take action, has a sense of control. The hapless passenger just along for the ride feels totally helpless."

"We're not talking a fender-bender here."

"No. We're talking a near-miss with a lethal weapon. I could quote some cliches: a miss is as good as a mile, for one. But I'm not sure that I was meant to be hit; this could have been a warning shot that came a little too close as easily as a murder attempt that missed."

"How can you discuss it so calmly?"

"Your own peril is always easier to take than someone else's, because there you're really helpless. Call it a noble human trait."

"There's nothing noble in a coffin." Temple conceded the fact that her knees were wobbly and leaned against the counter.

The Welles/Randolph/Kinsella house had a truly palatial master bathroom, vast and dark and elegant as an Egyptian tomb.

Tomb. She didn't want to picture herself picking out a casket for Max.

"Hey," he said. "I'm all right, but you're a mess." He pulled her into an embrace that felt good but smelled too strongly of rubbing alcohol to ease her anxiety.

"Maybe if I'd been along, I'd have been better off."

"I told you. I have to do this on my own. It's confidential."

"It's hard to be left out of the loop."

"I really can't tell you the specifics, except that it's not a big deal."

"So what you were doing in L.A. had nothing to do with the shot in L.V.?"

"Probably not."

"At least you're being honest."

"I've always been honest with you, Temple. I've just not always been thoroughly frank."

"Hair-splitter," she accused, then realized the reference was grotesquely apt.

"That's better," he said as she laughed in his arms. "I'd tell you if I could, but this one is really sensitive. I can tell you what I think about the shooter, though."

"Oh, great. I always want to know about shooters."

"The Synth."

"The Synth? That weirdo magician's group? Max, get real. Magicians play with scarves and doves and little white bunny rabbits onstage. They don't shoot people."

"Anybody can shoot people. And don't forget the

172

messages on the computer. They've been coming to this house longer than I've been back. Did you watch those Fox specials about how magic tricks are done?"

"No. Oh, I saw them in the TV listings, but I hate those instant specials: watch animals eat animals; watch people behaving badly; watch accidents happen. Inquiring people want to descend to the lowest common denominator."

"You're an admirable bastion of taste and integrity, Temple, but you are not the average TV-watcher. Droves watched those shows."

"You mean those hokey tell-alls with the masked magician spilling the beans? Please!"

"Those shows resulted in death threats."

"Get real!"

"I can't get any more real than that. Listen." Max lifted her atop the black marble counter top, which iced her backside. But his eyes were so intense she forgot to complain. "Magicians have always patented certain tricks, certain devices that permit those tricks to be performed. They can spend decades perfecting the perfect illusion. When they die, they will them to chosen successors. And they never tell how. If a magician becomes a tattletale, he threatens the brotherhood's very survival. It's serious business. Gandolph's zeal to expose false mediums came close to giving away trade secrets. My resolve to finish Gandolph's work threatens that magical secrecy. Houdini himself felt that push-pull: He hated cheats using our ancient and secret methods of entertaining to bilk trusting souls. But by exposing them he admitted that we all have trade secrets. Our very reason for being diminishes if everyone knows how it's done. They can know it's a trick; they just can't know how we do it."

Temple leaned her forehead on his shoulder. "International terrorism. Magic. You're telling me that one is as much a matter of life and death as the other. That's . . . ludicrous. Even if you had never become involved in antiterrorism, you're telling me that finishing that poor old man's book could be as lethal as turning in an international mass murderer?"

"Everything's dangerous, Temple. It's just a matter of degree. What about what you've been getting involved in lately?"

"All right. I've been an amateur snoop, but before then, everything was so much safer."

Max pulled her away from him so he could look in her eyes.

"Was it? Was it really? I don't think so. It just seemed safer, like all dream worlds. I know. I used to live in one until Sean died."

"When I grew up in the Midwest, worked there, nobody wanted to hurt you, though."

"No? What about your claustrophobia? Kids held you under a box, didn't they? Your older brothers."

"Little kids do things like that."

"Yeah, they do. And so do big kids. You told me about why you left TV news."

"It was that awful suicide-murder scene."

"In the double-wide in Mankato, I know. But did you leave because of that, or because you weren't getting the assignments you thought you'd earned, because of the in-fighting with the other reporters on staff?"

"Well, nobody took me seriously. It's because I wasn't tall enough and thin enough. And blond. Being blond would have helped."

"Really? From what you said, you did a good job. You got some real scoops. Why didn't they get you

174

anywhere?"

"Because I didn't look right. Nobody took me seriously."

"Maybe they took you too seriously."

"What?"

"All the opposition you faced, from the male bosses, the other women reporters. You kept thinking it was something wrong with you. What if it was something *right* with you?"

"Huh?"

"People don't attack you for your weaknesses, Temple. They attack you for your strengths. You went at news stories like you went at those crimes you stumbled across, didn't you? You were relentlessly inquisitive. You had a certain verve, charm, charisma. People saw you cared. They'd talk to you. They didn't need tall, blond, thin. They needed honest, genuine. Your peers blocked your career because they were jealous."

"Of me? Ever since I was in junior high and I realized I wasn't going to grow much higher, that I was going to be the Gidget of the eighties, I just sort of looked at those prom-queen girls and blinked. They were like goddesses to me. So tall and elegant, so sophisticated and smart. They couldn't envy *me;* I envied them."

"Add to their motives your unending innocence. You didn't even appreciate your edge, which double-damned you in their eyes. You've told me about it, when we were in Minneapolis. You've told me about it here, that artist's mistress who commandeered your hat because you had something individual, and she had to be the only individual thing around."

"Okay! So women can be spiteful, sabotaging snobs. I guess it is a danger."

175

"And guys can be violent, sadistic bullies. This is an equal-opportunity syndrome. You're worried and have trouble living with the idea of a few homicidal hitmen who *might* want to shoot me. That's nothing compared to the danger ordinary kids face every day. The peer groups that demand you become a gang-banger or be the victim of them. Look at an abused kid like Matt Devine. It's obvious where his obsession with his stepfather came from. Every day, every hour in your own house, the screaming, the yelling, the quick fist or slap, the beating. Look at thousands of dogs, for God's sake. A dog who starts life as a happy, panting puppy just wanting to be part of the human pack, subservient to a two-legged master, a dog neglected and berated and beaten until, broken, it crawls on its belly to anything human that will recognize it. Danger? It's all around us. You, me, Matt Devine, Midnight Louie. Black cats have been hated and hunted and killed for centuries. And why do they attack us, these bullies? For our strengths, not our weaknesses. For our liveliness and talent and love and potential, which is a slap in the face to so many who have known only deadening days and nights of loss and hatred and failure."

"God, that's a scary assessment of the human race."

"Exactly. And once you see that you'll appreciate the heights the human species can reach. For every two thousand Goths, there's a Gandhi, for every Hitler there's an Einstein."

"For every Big Bad Wolf, there's a Rin Tin Tin?"

"No. But there's probably a Midnight Louie."

"Fun-nee," she said. It came out almost sounding like "Fanny."

176

SHOOTING GALLERY

THE KNOCK ON MOLINA'S OFFICE DOOR MADE HER look up, then check her watch. "Right on time, to the minute."

"I know artists are supposed to be childishly free souls, oblivious to ordinary constraints, but not if you have two kids to support."

Molina nodded to her rather hard and unfriendly chair, and Janice Flanders came to sit there like an obedient schoolgirl. The closed oversize sketchpad lay across her blue-jeaned lap like a tray. Her laid-back Santa Fe style was attractive and reassuring.

"What a relief," Janice said. "I thought the computer simulations had made me obsolete to the police."

"Don't get overexcited. We need a sketch of a corpse."

"Ooh, my favorite."

"And, to sweeten the assignment, also of one very undead guy, only I need him aged about seven years."

"Only seven?" Janice glanced at the black-and-white photo Molina had handed her. "Looks pretty buff here."

"He's forty-one now; encroaching middle age should make a big difference. Most men show it sooner than women. And this man's gone down in the world, from respectable to seedy. Use your imagination."

"Looks like a physical fitness freak. Military, maybe?"

"Police. Not here in Las Vegas. He might have gotten *more* into pumping iron after his big fall. I don't know."

"A computer sim could run through the possibilities much faster, and cheaper, than I could."

"Yeah, but those things always have the personality

of so-called Roswell test dummies. As I said, I want your imaginative touch. You've done so many mall portraits you've developed a sixth sense about facial planes, how they evolve and devolve."

Janice laughed. "Thanks. I think. Oh, and I also owe you thanks for steering that new customer my way."

"New customer?"

"Matt Devine."

"Oh. That's right. You did the Effinger job for him."

"I did, and with good results. He was an interesting subject."

"Effinger."

"Well, yeah, but I meant Matt too."

"He posed for you?"

"Not exactly. I did a quick sketch to warm up. I mean, who could resist those honest brown eyes? He's been a good customer, and I can always use the extra work."

Molina held back the two photographs of the Church Lot Lady she was about to show Janice, not wanting to interrupt this discussion of the living with the bare-faced fact of the dead.

"It sounds like an ongoing relationship," Molina noted.

"Yeah. I was surprised when he came back for another sketch, but, ah, it might be more of an ongoing relationship than you mean."

"Oh, really?" Molina was horrible at female small talk after all her years in law enforcement. Now she wished she had a refresher course under her belt. But she had kept her tone innocent—and yet knowing enough, she hoped—to encourage Janice Flanders's confidences.

"I wondered why he wanted these pseudo-law-enforcement services. He swore he wasn't an ex-cop or a private detective. I couldn't figure it out, haven't yet, really. Except now that I know he's an ex-priest, it makes a little more sense. They're always out there doing good, right?"

"Let us hope so." Molina found her ordinarily nimble mind balking like a gate-shy horse at the mental leap to what Janice was implying.

"Anyway, how could this guy go wrong? I don't know how well you know him—"

Holy cow! Who was trying to pump whom here? Molina smiled disarmingly, or what she thought was disarmingly. She hadn't had much practice in a long while. In fact, disarming smiles were a hazard in her business.

"He's visited in my parish," Molina said casually. "Our Lady of Guadalupe, where my daughter Mariah goes to school."

"That's right! She must be—"

"In sixth grade."

"Time flies. My two are in junior high now; teen-monsters-in-training," she added with enough fondness to undercut the truth of the remark. "You're so wise to keep your Mariah out of the public schools, but then I suppose you know more than I do what's going on there." Janice shuddered for effect. "That's where I put most of my child-support money, private school. So you know Matt socially," she added.

"As much as I know anyone socially. Between this job and keeping up with Mariah—"

"Say no more. The single-mom routine is the pits. I could use a break today. Or tomorrow. I was just wondering, since you're Catholic, if there's anything I should know about Matt, or some place where I could learn what to expect."

"Golly. I'm a lukewarm Catholic myself. All I can say is that you'd expect him to be pretty conservative about adhering to the church tenets."

"Like celibacy?"

Molina nodded.

Janice idly opened her sketchpad and began doodling. She seemed to think better with her fingers moving across paper. She grinned. "Then we have the same problem right now."

"Except for him it's not a problem. *Not* being celibate is a problem."

"By problem you mean 'sin.' "

"In the strict sense, yes."

"Hmm. It's hard to believe a grown man in this day and age—and a good-looking one . . . but, hey, what am I complaining about? A perfectly safe man. Shrink-wrapped, you might say."

"Let's hope not too tightly. So what was his second assignment about?"

Janice rolled her eyes. "One centerfold-gorgeous female."

"Really? Red hair?"

"Black was the color. I hope it's not his true love, but I got the feeling that there was no love lost between them. Are you sure he's not doing investigative work? He sure acts like one of you guys."

"Did he give you a name for the femme fatale?"

"Nope, but I could tell she gave him the willies. He seemed almost superstitious about my capturing her image on paper, like she was an evil spirit or something. Is there such a thing as an opposite-angel?"

"They're generally called demons, or devils, or were in the Middle Ages."

"I was reared by cheerful agnostics. All this religion mythology is pretty alien to me. I find it fascinating," she confided, leaning forward.

Oh, Lord, Molina thought.

Janice ripped the top sheet off her sketchpad with one broad, sweeping gesture and handed it to Molina.

"Warming up again."

Molina blinked at her own image. Unlike her official photos, which made her look like a Russian census-taker, stern and authoritative, Janice had caught her in a listening attitude: relaxed yet wary; analytical, with a hint of humor peeking through. She felt like *Star Trek's* Mr. Spock placed in one of those four-photo quickie booths and forced to assume an uncharacteristically frivolous expression.

"Very nice," she told Janice. "Thank you."

"Oh, it's not the real you." Janice's warm smile made the white-streaked crinkles around her eyes into an asset rather than a signpost of early middle-age. "I'd never get down to that deep a subterranean level in the first try, but it's a start. Now. Are you going to let me see the photos of the corpse you've been guarding, or not?"

BAPTISM OF FIRE

"OOOH, HERE HE IS! MR. MIDNIGHT. READY TO ROLL on your debut show?"

"Roll over and play dead maybe, Leticia."

"Oh, come on, Matt. Don't be shy. You do this every night at ConTact."

Leticia took his arm and steered him toward the control room.

When they reached the door, she had to hang back

181

and give him a playful push inside. And she could push.

"I'll be right here, baby," she promised, following him in. "Mama Ambrosia."

In the background, an ad pitchman pushed a fistful of consonants over the microphone.

"Can we talk?"

"You let me worry about when and what, until you get the hang of it."

He sat in the rolling steno chair and then sat up straighter so his mouth would have a clearer shot at the mike. Leticia perched on the mobile rolling stool she used.

"I can hardly wait to see the contact sheet on those photos of you. Now don't pretend to be so shy. I'm even thinkin' 'bout trying my ugly mug on camera for some promo."

"Your ugly mug? You're . . . unbelievably gorgeous. Why haven't you done photographs before now?"

The question stopped her effusiveness, leaving Matt feeling he'd committed a huge faux pas. Which he hastened to correct, naturally only making it worse. "Is it because you're African-American, but your voice isn't?"

"Now there is where you are wrong. I am not African-American."

"I don't mean to—"

"Of course you don't. But any fool could see I am not African-American. I am black, and white, and Cherokee and French and Spanish and Arabian. Yeah. I can trace all those tiny trickles in my bloodstream. No. I've just always felt that Ambrosia must be universal. But if this billboard gig works for you, and I think it will, then maybe I'll come out myself, hmmm?"

"You ought to," Matt said. "We can't have shy people

182

on an advice show."

"You are so right, honey, now sit back while I do my intro and get ready to rock and roll."

She'd finessed him into the opening moment so he hardly felt it. Then her voice, as magnificently velvety as her black/white/Cherokee/French/Spanish/Arabian skin, segued into a spiel about meeting Mr. Midnight, magic man of milk and honey who would listen to every hurt and offer every help.

Even while Matt cringed at the blatant pitch, he felt the soothing poultice of her perfect voice. If only everyone could medicate with words . . . He had done it before, now he had to do it in front of an invisible audience.

"Mr. Midnight?" came the first voice, quavering and female.

"Yes?" he said self-consciously.

And then it took over, the process. She poured out the thises and thats of her life. Anxieties and hopes. She was a bubbling spring of doubt and indecision. He was the unseen but well-felt rock she effervesced all over.

He used the leading question like a lawyer. He soothed and probed. He discounted her failures and suggested successes. He did all the things he had done at ConTact for months. She chirped her thanks as she said goodbye and he wondered what he had given her besides air time.

Leticia was nodding approval and cueing the tech guy to run a commercial. She turned the sound down to a drone.

"Wow. Okay. Fine. We're cooking. Remember those tryouts. Those naughty callers. They all won't be easy."

"You thought that was easy?"

"You make it look easy; that's the trick. Easy."

183

After the commercial, three more calls came in, all people Dr. Laura would have sniped into sniveling apology for existing. Matt hated that old-time derision. Backing people into a corner and then forcing them to repeat the old self-abusing truisms like the rote little robots they were expected to be. Dr. Laura was popular the way Don Rickles was popular: Everyone liked to see someone else raked over the coals.

Matt didn't believe in dispensing hellfire; there was enough of it here on earth. He wanted to build up rather than tear down. Maybe that didn't sell. Maybe that didn't make for a good show. What was he doing here? He glanced at Leticia, smiling and nodding as if she were listening to jazz only she could hear.

He was all wrong for this. This "gig." My God, how could he back out of it, with all the money they'd spent on photographs and Temple so proud of her art direction and his palms sweating genteelly and his voice going out where everyone could hear and yet he could hardly hear his own thoughts? What good could he do here, except to his bank account, and what was his bottom line but arrogance and greed?

Out of here. He needed out of here.

And then her voice came on the line. The woman-girl who would change everything.

"Mr. Midnight?"

So hokey. So hopeless. How had he been seduced into this travesty?

"I—I don't know where I am," she said.

"You mean in your life?"

"No. I mean . . . right now. I'm in this strange place, and I don't know how I got here. It's like, um, a bedroom, only it's got its own bathroom and we never lived in a house like that, and it's got a radio and a TV

184

in the bedroom and we never had a house like that. I mean, our radio was in the kitchen, only it was broken, and the TV was in the main room, along with the extra beds."

"Why don't you know where you are?"

"Because . . . because I feel so sick!"

"Sick, how?"

"It's cramps, you know. No, you don't know. The worst cramps in the whole wide world." Her breath caught, and then a shriek came over the phone line that seemed to pierce his eardrums.

He stared at Leticia, whose limpid dark eyes rolled with uncertainty.

"And my breathin', it's so rough. Like I had the fever that time, when I was small. I'm not so small now. I don't understand. I'm all swelled out and I feel like I got the runs."

"Listen. Where are you? You got there somehow. You must remember."

"Remember? No. I just remember turnin' on the radio and rockin' to the music. It was the only thing that made the pain seem even-like. I don't understand. I'm sweatin' all over. It must be the fever."

"The room sounds like it's in a . . . motel, is that right?"

"I don't live in no motel. I got a home. Had one. I can go back. If I can just get over feelin' sick like this, I can go back."

"Of course you can."

"I'm so glad you said that. I was listening and I heard you talking and you sounded so calm. I knew you'd say I could go home, just as soon as I get out of this *X-Files* scene."

"*X-Files?* Like the TV show? What makes you think

185

of that?"

"I don't know. Mulder's always waking up somewhere weird and someone weird brought him there and his sister doesn't remember. Do you think I could be Mulder's sister? I don't remember my family much, except for yelling and screaming. I don't want them to yell and scream anymore, maybe that's why I'm doing it now—"

"No, you're talking now. You're talking to me, Mr. Midnight. On the radio. Remember?"

"Oh, yeah. I dialed the number. Even the phone works here. I think a man helped me. A man brought me here. Cigarette-smoking man. I don't think that's good. Cigarette-smoking. It's not good for you."

"But he's gone, the man?"

"Oh, yeah. I'm alone. All alone. Except . . . I think the aliens are with me. That's why it hurts so much, like I'm tearing apart."

Out of the corner of his eye, Matt saw Leticia's hand chop down through the air. Relief surged through him as he realized they were off the air, that a commercial or a song was wafting out to the world, not his voice and hers.

Leticia was hissing directions into her mike, then glaring at him while her luscious fuchsia lips mouthed words he could hardly make out.

Where? they pantomimed. *Find out where!*

Where? He was just beginning to comprehend *what*.

"Breathe deep," he advised the caller, "and if it hurts, short and shallow."

"Oh, it hurts. It hurts!"

During the commercial break her shouts grew into shrieks.

He'd never seen, heard a woman giving birth before.

186

He'd read a bit on natural childbirth. He was aware of activity around him. He was aware of unthought-of activity over the phone line. But he was basically lost in the umbilical cord of communication that connected him and the woman, the girl in the nameless room.

She was panting now, silent.

"How are you?"

"All right."

"Not so much pain?"

"No."

"And what else?"

"I know it's aliens now." Her voice was strangely removed. Remote. Alien.

"How?"

"There's one in the room with me."

He was speechless.

"It's slimy. Aren't aliens supposed to be slimy? And small?"

"No. That doesn't sound like an alien."

"I know it is. It hurt me, like a needle in the navel. I've got to get rid of it! Before it . . . gets me. I've got to, to . . . tell me what to do, Mr. Midnight."

"First, you must remember where you are. Tell me where you are and I can send help."

Leticia was nodding frantically.

Matt glanced at the console through the glass window and saw a Christmas tree of lit red and green lights. They *weren't* off the air! He wanted to shout at Leticia, the sound man, condemn them as ghouls, but it would disturb an already too-disturbed girl.

His hands strangled the mike stand as if it were a mechanical throat.

"I know," she was saying. "I've got to . . . drown it. Kill it. It's an alien. There's slime all over it."

187

"No. That's just an illusion. Remember when Mulder was slimed? You've got to brush it away and then you'll see it's not an alien."

"It's so icky! So stringy. And . . . yes, there's a face in there, but it's unshapen. It's trying to scream. I've got to stop it, because the other aliens will hear and they'll know where I am and they'll come in and slime me and take me away in a ship. I'll be locked up where the bad girls are."

"No, no you won't. Listen, you're on a phone. There's a . . . secret code on a label. Numbers. Read me the numbers."

"Yeah. You're right. Maybe you are right. Do you know what these numbers mean?"

"I do, and if you give me them, I'll get them to Agent Mulder."

"Not Scully. She doesn't believe. She's a doctor. She'd lock me up. With this alien-thing, attached to me like a leech. It's not part of me, it's not!"

"No, but you don't want to . . . destroy the evidence that will help Mulder, do you? The evidence that will help me. I really need those numbers. What's your name?"

"Name? I don't want to say, they might find me."

"What's a name I can call you? Say of a favorite doll, or pet."

"I had a doll. Once. Daisy."

"Daisy. Read me the numbers on the telephone, Daisy, and help will come."

"I've got to kill this alien first. I've thought of how to do it. In the toilet. It's still small, but it's getting bigger every day, every minute. I tried to kill it before, but it didn't work."

"The numbers, Daisy, please, the numbers."

"Oh, all right, Mr. Midnight. I could really use some help. It's, um, 5556389."

"Wonderful! Wonderful, Daisy." Matt glanced at Leticia. Her face was set, but her beringed fingers were circling on each side of her mouth. Matt tried to interpret her sign language. *Talk, keep talking.* Keep her talking?

"Help is coming, Daisy. You don't have to kill the alien. The government wants it for experimentation. You know the government."

"Oh, yeah. And they can have it. Except, it's moving! I'm so afraid. I've got to kill it, or it'll . . . eat me. I'll be right back."

"No, don't leave me! I have to know you're all right."

"But if I don't go and kill it, I won't be all right. Listen, it's screaming now, such an icky-eerie scream, just like in the movies."

Matt heard the faint whine of a siren over the line.

"Hang in there, Daisy. That's the good guys coming. They'll help you."

"Oh, I don't know. I don't know."

He heard a jackhammer pounding. Fists and feet on a door. A sudden cessation of all noise. A girl's shriek. The sound of heavy breathing.

"It's all right." A man's breathless voice hummed over the line. "We've got her. We've got the baby. It's alive."

"Thank God. Be careful with her."

"As careful as she'll let us."

The line went dead.

Matt felt he'd been catapulted out of a plane into a free-fall to earth.

The silence was deafening.

Then music came on. "And I Will Always Love

189

You," the Whitney Houston version of the Dolly Parton chestnut. The Ambrosia touch.

He looked at his watch. Eleven-forty-eight.

Leticia came in from the control room.

"Relax, Brother John. Mr. Midnight is off-duty for the evening."

DANCING IN THE DARK

CARMEN CROSSED THE NEARLY EMPTY PARKING LOT TO her car, the long dry-cleaning bag whispering at her side.

The time was only midnight, but the Blue Dahlia parking lot looked as desolate as it had the last time she had been here. Just a few nights ago.

This time her car was parked under a twin-headed streetlight that resembled the alien ships' creepy periscope heads from *War of the Worlds.* The vehicle's passenger side faced her blankly.

She was almost there when a figure rose from the driver's side, stretching suddenly and endlessly upward like Dracula assuming human form after moonlighting as a bat.

"Don't drop your dry-cleaning while going for the artillery, Lieutenant. It's only me," said Max Kinsella.

"I would never make the mistake of underestimating you. What brings you lurking around?"

"You seem to want your snitches to report in parking lots. This one was handy."

She hesitated before going around to the driver's side. "You could have called."

"I don't let myself be recorded without getting paid for it."

"Don't be so paranoid. You know as well as I do that I don't have anything concrete on you."

"But there's always hope, isn't there?"

She ignored him, shaking the key ring in her right hand until the correct one jingled into the light. The steel door-key glittered blueish. He stepped back as she bent to unlock the car door, and plucked the hanger from her other hand.

She straightened as if he'd jammed a gun in her back, offended.

"Can't let your work clothes sweep the ground," he explained.

She eyed his raised arm and the vintage velvet gown's train shivering in its transparent polyurethane slip an inch off the dark asphalt. "Now I see why Temple Barr puts up with you; you make an excellent coat-tree."

"I have my uses," he admitted.

"Exactly my hope." She unlocked the door, collected the hanger, and swooped the gown inside to hang from the hook behind the driver's seat. Then she shut the door, folded her arms and leaned against it. "So. What have you got?"

"He wasn't hard to track. Downward spirals never are."

"Left a smoking trail, huh?"

Kinsella nodded. The streetlight's indigo shadows made his face into an eerie mask, skeletal and gaunt. She supposed her own features looked like the walking dead in the deep-blue glare. Perhaps co-conspirators required dramatic lighting. But Kinsella looked more worried than he ought to.

His folded arms aped her own protective, slightly hostile posture. "The first six months after his dismissal,

191

he wrote aggrieved letters to the police union, the newspapers, the ACLU, and a variety of fringe rightist rags, which seemed the most inclined to listen to him."

"He honestly felt he had been railroaded?"

"Apparently."

"And you?"

He sighed. "They wanted him out, no doubt about it. He was minor trouble. Abrasive might describe it best."

"Cops need to be tough."

"This one had a chip on his shoulder that he always ached to knock off onto somebody else's shoulder."

"What about his personal life?"

"After his dismissal, he hung out with strippers."

She nodded. "They're pushovers for users. Speaking of which, any sign of drug or alcohol abuse?"

"Drinking. He was too controlled to fool with drugs. With alcohol, he knew what he was putting into himself; with drugs, it's what the cartel lets you have."

"So he was still . . . cautious. Self-protective."

"I didn't find any trace of a wife. He was an angry loner before the incident that got him dismissed. He was an angry haunter of topless bars afterwards, but that doesn't mean anything. Loners always patronize the topless joints; these weren't businessmen's upscale fantasy clubs."

"I'm sure not," she mused.

"Okay. Your turn."

"What do you mean?"

"Your turn to tell me a few things."

"About what?"

"This case."

"*This* case? Why?"

"Because what I found out about Nadir would mean more if I knew what he was suspected of doing." He straightened to scan the deserted parking lot. "Where was your car parked that night?"

"What night?"

"I know you discovered a body here. I know when. I don't know where on the lot."

Her turn to sigh. She unfolded an arm to point to the oleander bushes fringing the lot's far boundary.

"You were parked there?"

"Yes." Her eyes asked a question he could read under the glaring light.

"Your driver's door panel has been repainted. There's overspray on the front wheel well. Obviously, your car was part of the crime scene. What got on it. Blood?"

"Nothing so gory." To that, he said . . . nothing. "Spray paint. Graffiti," she answered the continuing silence.

"The body was—"

"Lying beside the driver's door, maybe two feet away."

"What kind of graffiti?"

"Words. 'She left.' "

He digested the message for a moment, eyes cast down to the asphalt. "Any overspray on the body?"

She squirmed against the car door; easing the pressure. It was a subtle point, well taken. "No."

He nodded. "You think this ex-cop might have done it. Why?"

"You found no trace of a woman in his past?"

"Rumor. People had retired, transferred, quit. They said he used to live with someone years ago. Another cop."

"Pretty vague. You're sure he wasn't gay?"

His eyes narrowed at the humor in her voice. "Sure." Kinsella glanced past her to the car door. "Your

193

estimate was right; he's the kind of egotistical bully who wouldn't take a woman leaving him kindly. What's his connection to this killing?"

"Don't know yet." Molina pushed herself away from the car door, walked into the borderland between streetlight and shadow. "We don't even know the victim's identity. It would help to know if Nadir was in the vicinity."

"Someone is."

"What do you mean?"

"When I was coming back into town from L.A. someone took a shot at me on the Strip."

She couldn't keep her eyes from widening. She thought for a minute, then laughed. "I suppose you had the top down like a tourist."

"Yes, ma'am."

"It could have been anyone."

"Yes, ma'am."

"Your guard was down. Amazing. Apparently, the shooter missed."

"Mostly."

"Anything I should know about?"

He shook his head. "The bullet creased my skull and then got lost in traffic. I think the shooter was on a motorcycle."

"Ooh. Curiouser and curiouser. Could our Mr. Devine be a tad upset at your rocket-like reentry into Miss Temple's life and living quarters?"

"He could be, but he wasn't using the Hesketh Vampire if he was. Besides, he's got his own fish to fry." When she didn't say anything, he cocked his head. "Too busy to read your morning paper?"

"I checked it."

"For the sketch of the other dead woman?"

"Yup."

"Check it again. I'm not the only one who's attracted unwanted attention lately."

"Care to elaborate?"

"Hope." He grinned. " 'She left.' All I have to do is find out who 'she' is."

"All *I* have to do is find out who the dead woman is. You're out of it."

"Shouldn't be too difficult."

"Not with the cadaver dog I've got."

"Why are you smiling like that?"

"Like what?"

"Mona Lisa on Prozac."

"I enjoy irony."

"What a coincidence. So do I."

"Then," she said, spreading her hands like a good hostess inviting a guest to a sumptuous buffet. "Enjoy."

She got in her car, started it, and left him standing alone ("Blue Moon," crooned like a wailing saxophone) in the parking lot, a fading figure in her rearview mirror, diminishing to a dark question mark in the night.

He thought he knew all the answers, but in this case, no one did. Now, where the hell had she put the morning paper?

Newsmaker, Heartbreaker

ONE THING ABOUT LIVING ALONE AGAIN, TEMPLE HAD decided during Max's several-month absence: You always have first crack at your favorite sections of the newspaper.

Maybe because of her three years as a TV news reporter, she always began with the front news section, then moved to the local news, and finally to features. Sports was immediately consigned to a recycle pile where it was handy in case she heard the unmistakable *gack-gack-gack* machine-gun regurgitation sound of Midnight Louie about to deposit a hairball on some particularly cherished piece of paper or furniture.

This was war: Temple would leap up, seize the still-folded sports section and run to the area of the apartment that seemed in imminent danger of dietary bombardment.

Of course Louie would hear her racing to the rescue of the decor, and would begin backing up so she couldn't get the newsprint under his face in time to receive the forthcoming explosion.

If she managed to capture the prize before he could back out of easy grasp under a chair where it was really hard to reach to clean the rug, he would then retreat further to present a secondary spit-up or two in other awkward, hard-to-get-at places.

Too often she arrived only in time to see the impressive projectile arc onto a six-inch span of floor or seat cushion or her latest paperwork.

Sometimes, though, she reached an alpha state in physical and mental terms—she arrived at ground zero before detonation, made her defensive placement and defused the artillery with the face of her least-favorite ball-bouncer who had just been signed up for umpty-zillion dollars right out of high school to win games, do drugs, and abuse women, all in living color through the various newspaper sections that would feature him in the coming years: sports, business, front-page scandal position and, finally, rehabilitated and born-again, the feature page (with family) and sports section (with teammates).

This was one of those occasions when she was up to the upchuck challenge. In the very nick of time, Louie's hairball lay like a black island in an ugly sea of soylent-green (could he have actually eaten some Free-to-Be-Feline?) and strawberry-pink (what was he getting into *now?*).

Sighing, Temple patted the patient for having achieved a successful delivery in an appropriate place, and returned to the living room to read the first section of the paper.

Louie ambled in later to wash his smug face, sitting on the faux goat-hair rug so he could look picturesque while doing it.

He looked up when she hmmmed to herself, but she read on with relative composure.

Not twelve minutes later, she gasped and leaped up.

He looked around, as if presuming that he ought to be assuming his previous position for another ritual retrieval war.

But Temple barely glanced at him as she headed for the kitchen phone. Then she stopped.

"Fingers schmingers! Why not let my legs do the walking?" she asked aloud. "No unauthorized barfing while I'm gone, Louie."

She shook a stem finger at the wide-eyed cat, then headed for the apartment stairwell, the paper's front section firmly in hand.

She wished her emotions were as well under control.

Even as she knocked at Matt's door she realized it was a decadent ten A.M. to her, but more like midnight to a night-worker like him. At least she hadn't rung the doorbell. Maybe she could tiptoe discreetly away . . .

197

But the door opened, and there Matt stood, looking uncharacteristically rumpled, but as wide awake as an over-the-road truck driver on No-Doz.

"You look totaled," she told him bluntly.

"Give me time. I have a feeling I'll look worse."

The phone rang, and he waved her in as he went to answer it.

"No," he was saying, "I'm not interested in a talk show appearance. Yes. No. Yes, I see. No."

Temple marched over and commandeered the phone. She Who Has Beaten Cat to Rug can do anything.

"Hello, this is Mr. Devine's agent speaking. I'm sorry; we're expecting a conference call from DreamWorks any minute. You'll have to clear the line." She hung up.

"Isn't that a bit rude?"

"You bet. It's the only thing these booking agents understand. Don't worry, it only makes them hotter to trot."

"And wasn't DreamWorks, Spielberg et. al., a pretty unbelievably big lie?"

"That's the second-only thing TV talk-show booking agents understand. Pretty unbelievably big lies. And it doesn't discourage them one bit, either. So, strategy-wise, I've just upped your value considerably."

Temple lifted the section of newsprint in her right hand. "This is you, isn't it? They didn't give a name, just used 'Mr. Midnight.' "

Matt sat on the red sofa, looking like a lost sock. "Yes, it's me. Leticia is pleased purple, has been referring phone calls to me for the last hour, and I probably feel about a tenth as bad right now as that poor girl, which is ten times too much for me."

Temple sat down beside him. "How did all this

happen?"

"It's a call-in show. She called. When the situation became clear, I did all I could to keep her from doing something unthinkable. Leticia called 911 then kept our studio phone on the air so the whole world could hear the rescue team break down the motel-room door. Everything. Action radio."

"Hey, you're a hero."

"Then why do I feel like a heel? That girl is seriously disturbed, and now, thanks to *The Midnight Hour,* she's national news."

"Thanks to *The Midnight Hour,* her baby is alive." Temple let herself slump against the stiff sculptural support of the Kagan sofa. "This designer guy must have been a graduate of the Spanish Inquisition. I'm pretty zonked myself. Max leaves town for a couple of days, and when he comes back someone takes a shot at him."

"Where?"

"In the head."

"My God, Temple! I meant where did the shooting take place, but—"

"It's okay. All he lost is about a quarter of his ponytail. You could call it a scalping, but I suppose the official term is that the shot was just a 'crease.' He was driving on the Strip at rush hour."

"Could it have been . . . road rage?"

"Not when you're stopped for a red light."

"Boy, we've both had a night of it."

"Separately, however." She smiled wanly. "It looks like your new show is launched."

"Don't say that! I hate it. Here I sit, realizing that I actually, accidentally might have done some good, and it's going to turn into a side show. I am, to say the least, confused." He glanced at her, and smiled wryly. "But you had figured that out, hadn't you?"

She grinned back. "I mean it, kid; I can run interference for you. You do need representation, and my Aunt Kit knows all sorts of New York types who are up to the job for real. One call, and you've got a friend who knows how to keep the jackals off, or at least how to make them pay for the privilege of sucking the living flesh from your bones."

"Have you grown cynical lately? Oh, by the way, what name did you say your Aunt Kit writes under?"

"Sulah Savage. Why?"

"I . . . just wondered. If I'm going to ask her for an agent reference, it would be polite to know what she does."

"She'd live if you didn't, and polite is not that important in New York."

"I know. I've just got so much to think about all of a sudden."

Temple nodded soberly. "So have I. Did you see the morning paper?"

"No."

"Well"—she opened the section—"here's the story on you . . ."

He nodded impatiently and ignored it.

"And here's the other interesting thing."

"You mean there's something in the news that might take the spotlight off me? Hallelujah."

"Nothing *that* good, but interesting in its own way. Methinks I know this artist's work."

Matt rubbed his eyes and tried to focus on the small sketch near the bottom of the section's back. "Janice Flanders," he agreed.

"I'm just curious, because this story is so vague. I can

see the police are leaking just enough info to get some news coverage in hopes of identifying this poor woman. And why go to a cumbersome, old-fashioned sketch artist? Janice is good; God knows, I know she's good, but this approach makes me suspicious, that's all."

Matt eyed her sideways—even bleary his brown eyes had serious hot-fudge-overdose potential—then spoke abruptly, as if he'd leaped a barrier.

"Your suspicious instincts are impeccable, as usual. There's been a pair of killings. Two unidentified, and deliberately made unidentifiable, women. Molina—"

"I knew I smelled a rat."

"Molina found the first body at the Blue Dahlia."

"In person? No kidding!"

"The woman pictured here is the second victim. The first one is a total conundrum. Molina called me in because . . . oh, who knows why Molina does what she does? But . . . I saw the crime scene photos, the evidence, the poor woman's clothing. And I recognized a smell on the clothes." Matt laced his hands and looked at the parquet floor, which was exactly the same as the forty-year-old parquet floor in Temple's unit. "I had to admit to Molina that I recognized it, and that I thought I had run into it somewhere with . . . you."

"Oh, great. Temple Barr: guide to the smell of a dead woman's clothes."

"Not like that. We were somewhere. Together. I can't pin it down, but I seem to be more sensitive to smells lately. Odd ones, anyway. I suggested to Molina that she have you in to examine the dead woman's clothing."

"Give it the sniff test, huh? That is ridiculous, Matt! What do you mean you associate this dead smell with me?"

"It's not a dead smell. Quite the contrary. It's one of

201

those noxious deodorizing stenches."

"And it made you think of me immediately. Oh, thanks."

"Not of you. Of some place we went."

"Where? New York-New York? Maybe the cigar bar. That had a 'stench.' "

"Temple, I'm not trying to insult you. I was trying to help Molina. I told her if she wanted any more information, she'd have to have you in to ... give an expert opinion."

"Is she going to?"

"I think she'll have to."

"She's going to *have* to rely on my nasal expertise?"

"Possibly."

"Oh, Well. If I can actually identify something—I assume she'll be suitably grateful."

"I doubt it. Molina is never suitably grateful."

"But she does seem to be relying on you."

"Using would be the better choice of words. She has a job to do; she'll rely on whoever she has to."

"I would love to have her *have* to rely on me."

"I thought you might. Here's your opportunity."

"But I wanted it to be for something more ... grandiose than my nose."

"I realize that. I would like something more grandiose than *The Jerry Springer Show* battering down my door."

"I'll call my aunt right away. You need professional help."

"Temple, as it stands now, I *am* professional help. Scary, isn't it?"

"No," Temple said. "Not at all. I'll let you know what Kit recommends. Meanwhile, take notes on all offers, be polite until we can hire a pro to be impolite, and commit yourself to nothing. I hate to tell you this. You need an answering machine."

"Not another 'essential' I can't afford or even operate?"

" 'Fraid so. Time to join the rest of us millennium-yuppie lemmings leaping into automated lifestyles."

He shook his head. "Maybe. I also might have to take some time off from ConTact. I've already got a call in to Chet. My boss."

Temple stood, rubbing her neck, which was stiff, small wonder. "I have a feeling you're going to be your own boss for the meantime."

His eyes summed her up with sudden compassion. "I'm sorry about Max."

"Thank you for meaning that. I'll call Molina when I'm up to it."

"Thanks."

"Mutual favors are what friends are for."

"I'm glad we're friends."

She nodded. "I think we'll both need them. Did you have time to wonder if any of this stuff that's going on all at once is an accident?"

His expression said he hadn't.

Temple came home to find Midnight Louie in the bedroom reclining smack-dab in the middle of her acre of zebra-pattern comforter. If he was counting on natural camouflage, he was out of luck.

She put her hands on her hips.

"Okay. Max leaves town for a couple of days and is welcomed back by a shot in the head. Matt debuts as a radio counselor for one night and prevents an infanticide. So what have *you* been up to lately? Besides Technicolor hairballs."

Louie seemed to award her question serious thought.

He laid back to give some renegade hairs on his right front paw a silent tongue-lashing.

He again offered her the benefit of his wisest, most uncanny look. Then he leaped to the floor, crossed quickly to her row of shuttered closet doors, and pawed open the right one of the middle set.

Temple gazed at her revealed clothes, which were in relatively decent order for once.

Louie stretched up to paw among the dangling skirts and pant legs.

"No claws," she yelled. "That's my personal resale and vintage section; some of that stuff is older than I am and even more fragile."

Temple went over to straighten her abused clothes. She paused, then lowered her face to them and sniffed. A hint of strawberry cologne, perhaps, madame? Yes.

She sat suddenly on the corner of the bed.

Oddly enough, she did feel fragile.

A little fragile, and a whole lot suspicious.

Someone would have to do something about this.

Like Bob Dylan, Matt Devine's fave composer for the wedding-chapel organ, had sung once: Guess it was up to . . . me.

Little me.

UNDERCOVER CAT

IT IS A PAIN IN THE FOOTPADS TO WEND MY WAY back to the deceased's neighborhood, but it cannot be helped.

The "help" needs looking in on.

I find Miss Midnight Louise lounging in the shade by the string of oleanders behind the house, not far from the, uh, place where we deposited the late lamented Wilfrid.

"How is the work detail going, kit?" I ask nonchalantly.

"It stinks," she snarls.

"Yes, well, that is to be expected. Has the widow been coming around?"

"The widow! They were never formally hitched. It was what you could call a common-paw marriage, and Wilfrid's paw was the more common one."

"Shh. Speak not against the dead departed."

Miss Midnight Louise snorts. "What a charade! I must languish here chit-chatting with mourning females while you are out turning the mean streets topsy-turvy with your so-called master plan. I bet you are taking it easy at the Crystal Phoenix while I broil out here with nothing to eat but lizards."

"The weather is not that hot yet."

"Neither is the lunch line."

I shrug. For once Midnight Louise has a just complaint. I imagine the honor guards for the Unknown Soldier sometimes feel so put upon. Despite the importance of their duty, it is mostly symbolic.

"You know that I am counting on you to do the

appropriate thing when the time comes."

"But when will the time come?"

"When I say so. Now, is the . . . project coming along?"

"Somewhat," she grouses. "It is like a watched pot. It takes much supervision and produces scant results. And then I must make *Girl* Talk with Miss Fanny. Who, by the way, has been asking about the details of your colorful career."

"Oh, really?" I do not mean to preen, but my bib needs a washing, so I do it.

"Do not get your chest-hairs in a wad, Daddio Lothario. I have been filling her shell-like little pink ears with examples of your male chauvinist exploits."

"Louise!"

"Do not worry. The little twit actually is impressed by your feeble attempts at self-glorification. Females!"

"I take it that 'females' are a step down from the empowered 'girls?' "

"You will take it whatever way you like, I know that." Midnight Louise sighs and examines her shapely gams, which are stretched in front of her so she resembles that fierce Egyptian figure called a sphinx. "I suppose they also serve who sit and wait, but I am not taking this assignment well. I am used to running my own show."

"But you are! Your presence here is vital, as time will tell."

"I hope so, because if this all comes to naught, I will feel obliged to vent my spleen. You, naturally, will be the most convenient venting post."

She stretches out her pearl-pale nails, unsullied by any colored lacquer. They are as sharp and pointed as the stakes you would nail a vampire with.

I have not seen the insidious Hyacinth of late, she of the curare nail polish, but if claw came to slash, I would not count Miss Midnight Louise out on a one-on-one with anything. Not in the current mood in which I have put her.

If only she saw her honorable role in my master plan clearly.

But she does not.

That is why it is my master plan, and why I am the master.

Before I leave, I throw her one crumb to chew on.

"I may need you to desert your post for a while to aid in another of my master plans."

Her ears perk. "Does it involve danger?"

"Absolutely."

"Then I am your girl."

"Uh, yeah. Maybe."

I Get a Kick from Champagne . . .

"Come into my parlor," the grinning bald man invited, pulling aside a curtain embroidered with the zodiac.

Temple hesitated. "I didn't know professors had parlors."

"Well, only in Las Vegas. Here, the study of magic is both philosophy and practicality. I'm sorry, did my crypt-keeper act scare you?"

"No, Professor Mangel. It's just that I had a close encounter with a magic act recently that was rather unsettling."

"Oh? And call me Jeff, remember?"

"I do remember, which is why I came to you. But I thought you said you only went by 'Jefferson.' "

"I did, but you so charmingly defied me that I liked you immediately. All tyrants cherish cheek, and a professor is a classroom tyrant."

"Lou Grant didn't cherish cheek. He hated it."

"He hated spunk. There's a difference between spunk and cheek."

"What is it?"

"Everything, except the fact that they both end in *k*."

He grinned like a genie glad to be out of a bottle and led her through a maze of mounted posters, display cases, and freestanding magician's cabinets.

"Maybe I should call you Dr. Caligari," she added, shivering at the upright coffinlike structures and remembering that she had once been incarcerated in one.

"Listen. I'll give you some herbal tea and you'll see it all for the flummery it is."

He led her into a small staff kitchen equipped with a microwave, sink, cupboards, and stained mugs. "Is this better for our talk?"

"Oh, yes."

He ran water into two mugs and set the microwave wheezing. "What's unnerved you? That fatal séance at the haunted house didn't do it, but something obviously has now."

Temple sat at the Danish modern table, hefting her trusty tote bag to the teak top. "A friend of mine has been shot at. A magician friend."

"Shot at, where?"

"In Las Vegas. On the Strip at rush hour."

"I meant, anatomically."

"Oh." Temple winced. "The bullet creased the back of his skull. He was stopped at a red light."

"Gracious! Have the police been notified?"

"I don't know. The thing is, he's working on a book. An exposé."

"Exposé of what?"

"Fake psychics who manipulate séances and gullible clients."

"Hmm."

"Why do you say that?"

" 'Hmm' isn't saying much." Mangel smiled, then jumped up when the microwave timer pinged.

Soon steaming mugs of fragrant tea were wafting into their nostrils like Vick's VapoRub into the nasal passages of cold sufferers.

"Peppermint," he said after savoring the first sip. "What is your main concern?"

"I'm wondering if it's true that magicians—and psychics by extension—are so protective of their special effects that they would kill to protect their secrets."

Mangel sipped again from the steaming mug, then puckered his lips thoughtfully. "You know those 'magic acts revealed' specials on TV lately?"

"With the 'masked magician' explaining everything? Kind of hokey. Yeah."

Mangel shook his head, the overhead fluorescent light polishing his bald pate to cue-ball brilliance. "No. Not hokey. Not hocus pocus. Serious. There have been . . . death threats."

"Death threats? So it's well-known."

"The gentleman's agreement that is magic goes back centuries. Each magician honed his special tricks, his equipment. He expected his brother magicians to honor the secrets of his invention. Toward the end of his life, he would pass on his secrets and his equipment to a younger magician. It was a form of Masonry."

"A secret society?"

"Don't whisper, dear girl. We're on the University of Las Vegas campus, drinking tea. But, yes, the loose brotherhood of magicians is a kind of special society. They have their own rules and expectations. They abhor those who violate them."

"And there have been actual death threats over those hokey TV specials?"

"More than threats. There's a price on the head of the masked magician."

"In this day and age?"

He nodded. "Of course, the price is for revealing his actual identity, so he can be subjected to questions and have to answer them. Still, who can say when the self-protective urge becomes the other-destructive urge?"

"If this magician's compact goes back that far, could anyone be honoring it today?"

He nodded. "The art is even more in need of protection now that high-tech media techniques can dissect every millisecond of every move."

"But . . . a magic act. Surely no one takes it that seriously today?"

"The point is that it was taken 'that seriously' yesterday. That's when the unwritten rules were established."

"If they're unwritten, why would they have influence even today?"

"The weight of time. Leave your tea here, and I'll show you something in the exhibit."

Temple reluctantly abandoned her homey, steaming cup of tea. Even though the building on the Las Vegas campus was thoroughly modern, the magic exhibition area had a certain disturbing aura that spoke of secrets long kept and practices that would not bear close examination.

Jeff showed her a book, a huge, thick, ancient-looking book, closed with a metal clasp that resembled an elaborate hinge. Its thick parchment pages revealed ragged gilt edges, faded ink, and odd drawings.

"This is the syllabus, so to speak, of an organization we believe was called the Synth."

"S-S-Synth?" Temple stuttered, for she had come across that word before.

"I know; it sounds like lisping," Jeff admitted with a rueful smile. "But, believe me, it was taken very seriously by generations of magicians."

"Are there magic tricks in here?"

"Hardly. Those were too guarded to be sketched out and written down. No, this book is mumbo-jumbo. It

211

delineates all the secrets and strictures that pertained to being a magician. Blood oaths, ceremonial rituals, lists of professional names—"

"You mean they didn't even go by their right names in there?"

"What magician does?"

"Is there a Shangri-La in the register of magicians?"

"You mean a practicing magician? Contemporary?"

Temple nodded. "She did a disappearing act at the Opium Den downtown."

Mangel's frown emphasized his polished Wizard-of-Oz baldness. "For that," he said, "we need an arcane and infallible method of divination. Follow me."

Temple wondered what weird room they would enter next, but heaved a sigh of relief when she saw it was just an office, equipped with serious stacks of unfiled papers and a computer on and ready.

"This I understand," she said, plopping down in the molded wood visitor's chair, tote bag beside her.

"I'll search some data banks." The computer keys chuckled at the tickling of his blunt-nailed fingertips. Mangel's head thrust toward the screen.

Temple squealed her chair legs around the corner of the desk so she could watch.

The words *Shangri-La* sat center-screen, along with some dates and a place.

"That's the Las Vegas gig," Temple said. "This troupe appear anywhere else recently?"

His fingers made *Shangri-Las* disappear at the click of a few keys. A blinking cursor marked time.

"Nothing in Europe."

More clicks.

"Nothing in Asia."

"Nothing? Not even in Asia? Shangri-La?"

"Well, not under that name. I'm sure that eastern magicians don't go to James Hilton and *Lost Horizon* for their names. Hmm."

"Hmm?"

He peered at the screen. "One reference. In Rio of all places."

"Rio de Janeiro?"

"Brazil." He nodded. "Two years ago."

"Then it's a legitimate act."

"How could a magic act be legitimate? In a sense they are all frauds."

"I mean a known act."

"Even known acts come and go. Look at one of the greatest."

Temple waited expectantly.

"In this very city, not many months ago, the Mystifying Max played his last night at the Goliath and was seen no more."

"Oh."

"You don't seem impressed."

"Was he really one of the greatest? Magician-wise?" Temple hated the use "wise" in this make-fashion manner, but sometimes there was no way around bad syntax.

Mangel nodded. "Original. Always original. No practitioner of what I call the 'elephant effect.' You know, making pachyderms and helicopters and major American landmarks disappear. But an elegant sleight-of-hand and happenstance artist." The professor leaned back in his chair and chuckled without using the computer keys. "No muss, no fuss, that could have been his motto. I find it oddly fitting that he just . . . stopped. No more appearance dates, no retirement announced. It was as if he had never been there. An apt withdrawal for

213

a magician. Either make a production of it, like Houdini lingering on his deathbed for days until dying on Halloween. Or make nothing of it at all."

Temple nodded, sobered. She knew the bleak necessity behind the mysterious career "withdrawal" of the Mystifying Max.

On the computer screen the words *Shangri-La* blinked like a theater marquee. *Her* withdrawal had hardly been the low-profile disappearing act that Max had managed, though Mangel couldn't know about the dead body Max had left in his wake at the Goliath Hotel.

She found her fingers massaging the base of her third finger, left hand. Where was the ring? In Rio? Nothing elegant about out-and-out theft. A wave of rage threatened to clog Temple's throat.

A shill, Max had called Shangri-La and all her works. A cover for a drug-smuggling operation.

But a shill had ripped off, ripped away, the only engagement ring Temple had ever had. Or almost-engagement ring. She thought. Sort of. Max had never exactly made clear what the ring had represented. Another elegant withdrawal?

Temple suddenly realized that the rage she felt wasn't just for herself. The past had ripped away Max's profession. She'd always thought he had been good at it; now the professor's elegy on Max's career added a serious second to Temple's instincts. Max was used to losing, she realized. Relatives, identities, professions. One golden ring would be the least of it.

"What's the matter? Are you being hypnotized by the computer screen?"

Temple blinked. "No, I was just thinking how fascinating it all is. So this Shangri-La could work under

214

many different names?"

"Doing many different acts."

"What about the ... supporting cast? The ninja acrobats—"

"Ninja acrobats? You make me sorry I missed this show."

Temple shrugged. "It was pretty predictable, really, but I'd appreciate your letting me know if she turns up in your database again."

He shut down the computer search, then turned to face her seriously. "You were never fully satisfied, were you?"

"What do you mean?" The question seemed highly personal.

"About Gandolph's—Garry Randolph's—death during the Halloween séance."

"Oh, that. It *was* rather amazing. All those different psychics claiming to have disrupted the séance for their own motives and in their own ways."

"Sort of like gang assault. No one did it, and everyone did it. I did hear Garry was working on his memoirs about his psychic-busting days." Mangel's lively eyebrows did a caterpillar cha-cha. "Maybe somebody else did too."

"You believe it was murder, after all?"

"Let's just say the jury's not in."

"I'll say! Especially since no one was charged."

"I bet you'd get a kick out of looking at my Gandolph collection. Did you ever see him perform?"

"As a magician? No."

"Come on, we'll collect our cooling tea mugs—it was too hot to drink right away, wasn't it? And then I can show you. I have a large ephemera collection."

Temple rose to follow him.

The professor had been right. The tea had cooled nicely. She cosseted the mug, her tote bag straps slung over her shoulder and staying there for once, while they wandered through a gallery of framed performance posters and circus bills and other transitory paper trails of magical careers from the early 1800s until the 1990s.

Huge but light frames swung out from the wall like the leaves of oversize books, offering an album of the art's latter practitioners.

"That's Gandolph?"

"Back in the days when even I had hair."

"He was a distinguished-looking man."

"Magicians need that maître d' sort of dignity. That's why all the tails and white ties."

"And I thought they were there to hide concealed doves."

"The profession was not in high repute in the early days. Gandolph's heyday was the late sixties, before the tie-dyed brigade took over for a while, before psychedelic drugs gave onstage illusion a run for the money. Here he is, performing at the old Dunes."

"Wait! Don't flip that frame!"

"It is a rather good photograph of him."

"Maybe, but . . . who's she?"

"Ah, Gloria. Gloria Fuentes. What they used to call a 'doll.' Look at those long-stemmed legs. They don't make even chorus girls like that anymore, and Gloria was never that. Always a magician's assistant, and Gandolph's main lady until he retired in 'eighty-four."

"Oh my. Do you have a smaller photograph of her I could copy? Any newspaper clippings?"

"I suppose so. Why?"

"I know someone who's been looking for someone just like her."

216

"A theatrical historian?"

Temple mulled it over. "I guess you could say that." When singing at the Blue Dahlia, Molina was theatrical, and you could call a homicide cop a historian of sorts.

Gloria Fuentes was neither of those.

But she was a much younger version of the sketched face of a dead woman in today's newspaper.

"You wanted to see me?" Temple asked demurely over the telephone.

"No," Molina said. "There's something I want *you* to see."

"What a coincidence. I was about to tell you the same thing."

"I suppose you had better come downtown."

"Always such a treat!"

"Your voice sounds a little husky. You don't have a head cold or anything, do you?" Molina sounded solicitous, almost motherly.

"No. It's always husky. And I've been drinking peppermint tea."

"I see." Molina clearly didn't, but wasn't about to admit it.

They made a date for later that afternoon, and Temple hung up. She had called from the lobby of the university building, a sheaf of papers hot off the brand-name copier still warm in her hand.

What Temple herself had to show and tell, she guessed, would be much more interesting than what Molina wanted with her.

IMAGINE SEEING
YOU HERE

TEMPLE SAT ON THE EDGE OF THE INSUFFICIENTLY padded chair, tote bag clutched on her knees.

Lieutenant C. R. Molina was wearing a forest-green suit today that did nothing for her morning-glory-blue eyes. This woman needed a personal wardrobe consultant, but Temple was no masochist. Then again, Molina was career-driven enough to consider personal attractiveness a disadvantage. In public relations, being neat, clean, and articulate always counted for something. Not that Molina wasn't all of the above. It was just that neat, clean, and articulate didn't seem to do a thing for her. In that respect, Molina was rather like a Doublemint Twin on a TV ad: bland beyond belief.

The notion of Molina with a twin sent Temple's mind on a free fall of speculation, so she hardly heard the operative question.

"What *about* my nose?" she asked too late to appear connected.

"Matt Devine speaks highly of it."

"Really?"

"At least he thinks you might be able to identify the source of an odor on a dead woman's clothing."

"Really." Temple's enthusiasm level had plummeted. "I can't say I much care for *eau de morgue*."

"The clothing spent very little time in the medical examiner's area. It's been held in Evidence."

Temple had a deep suspicion that "Evidence" was very near the morgue.

218

Molina produced a brown paper bag very like a large lunch sack—really!—and pushed it across the desk toward Temple.

"Do I get a hint what smell I'm supposed to detect?"

"Mr. Devine said he recalled smelling it when with you."

"Maybe it was at the funeral home for his stepfather's visitation."

"He says not. But he can't remember where. Come on, have a sniff. It can't kill you."

"I suppose you do disgusting stuff like this all the time?"

"Every day," Molina said gravely. "That's right," she encouraged as Temple uncrinkled the bag. "Come on, sniff!"

Temple essayed a delicate inhalation and reared back. "Wow. That bag really intensifies the odor. It's strawberry-scented room freshener. I'd say a pretty pure dosage. Overdosage. Whew!" She began choking on her words.

"We knew that," Molina said wearily. "*Where* you might have smelled it is the question."

"Very bad ladies' rest rooms, like in non-name-brand gas stations."

"Where you smelled it . . . *when* you were with Matt Devine," Molina elaborated. "Or is there something I should know?"

"Funny." Temple clapped a palm to her face and thought. "Hmm. Some car washes have that stuff around. You know, when you're sitting in the miserable little room with sixteen three-year-olds hunting and fishing magazines watching your baby go through the suds cycle on the other side of the window?"

"I don't know. I wash my car myself."

"You do?"

"I have help."

When Temple looked even more speculative, Molina added, "Child labor."

"Oh, right. You have access to that. Louie doesn't wash much but his own body parts."

"I assume we can presume that Matt Devine has never kept you and the hunting magazines company in a car-wash waiting room?"

"No. I haven't washed a car like that in years, actually. But that's where I smelled that pukey ultra-strawberry stuff."

Temple leaned forward to pull out a fold or two of skirt. "Polyester," she diagnosed, making a face. "From about 1978. Polyester was very big back then. Of course! Why didn't you *tell* me it was polyester!"

Temple had to give Molina credit for not answering as if the game of Clue: "Polly Ester in the Laundry Room, smothered with a scented fabric-softener strip."

"May I assume, 'Eureka?'"

"Secondhand store. *Not* upscale. They use it to get rid of that lived-in smell on clothing. It tends to, um, cling."

"And you were in such a place with Mr. Devine?"

"Where do you think he got that racy red couch? You *have* seen it? I thought so."

"I'll do the interrogations. Are you thinking of a particular place?"

Temple nodded grimly. "One place. Occasionally has some neat stuff, but overdoes the ripe strawberries."

"Do you think the management would recognize the outfit?"

Temple pulled out the permanently pleated navy polyester skirt, the floral polyester blouse. She felt sorry for the murder victim already.

"A lot of their business is consignment. They keep meticulous records. They can probably tell you from whose closet this came."

"As well as to whom it sold?"

"Maybe."

Molina nodded, well pleased, if no less sallow-looking. "Can I count on you to take me there?"

"You yourself, Lieutenant?"

"This lead is much too important for mere detectives, don't you think?"

"I don't know, but I can tell you this."

"What?"

Temple fingered the sleazy, used polyester. It *was* wrinkle-free. "This was a modest lady. How did she die?"

"She was strangled and stabbed behind a nightclub."

Temple shook her head, repelled by the brutal facts. "No. Not Miss Strawberry Polyester. Something's wrong."

Molina was silent. When she looked at the brown paper bag near Temple's hands, it was with regret. "That's what I called her, the Strawberry Lady. Maybe you can help put a name on her."

"Maybe. Maybe not. But I can put a name on this one."

Temple reached into her tote bag and pulled out a copy of the newspaper folded to reveal Janice Flanders's sketch, along with a copied fistful of photos from Gloria Fuentes's magician's-assistant days, fishnet hose and all.

Glory days.

Molina looked like she'd seen a ghost, and it wore *eau de morgue.* "You never cease to amaze," she muttered, paging rapidly through the copies. "Where the

221

hell did you find these old photos ?"

"At the university. What do you think of my nose for news now?"

The bolt from the blue of Molina's eyes was sharp, and full of warning.

"Dangerous. I've always thought it was."

"But you'll use it."

"That's my job."

She stood, and the interview was over.

But the case was not. Her desk phone rang before she could tell Temple to skedaddle.

"Molina," she barked at whoever was on the other end.

Whoever it was barked back. Molina sat down again at her desk chair. "When? Well, it's your *job* to be sure! I see. Any theories? Right. Can't wait."

She eyed Temple as she hung up, looking like the wolf that was contemplating tenderloins of Little Red Riding Hood. Hungry.

Molina called someone from her cell phone while they were en route. The same mustached detective Temple had seen on an earlier homicide case—the cover-hunk-model deaths, wasn't it?—drove.

The Crown Vic swung around the corner, tossing Temple and her tote bag halfway across the otherwise empty back seat. She dug the handy metal high heels of her Stuart Weitzman magenta suede pumps into the serviceable carpeting like pitons. She could use some company as buffer.

Molina had not said where they were going, but she maintained custody of the photocopied likenesses of Gloria Fuentes.

"Where are we going?" Temple finally piped up.

"Goldilocks's bizarre bazaar, then Grizzly Bahr's place," Molina growled.

No wonder Temple was confused—she had been casting herself in the wrong fairy tale; no wolf, no Little Red; now she was Goldilocks and had been sleeping in the wrong bed. Oops, fairly Freudian, that notion. But if this mysterious "Grizzly Bahr" was Papa Bear, was Molina Mama Bear? Then who was Baby Bear? Not her!

"Isn't it . . . unusual," Temple tried again, "for you to be out on a case yourself?"

The detective at the wheel slid Molina an expectant glance. He thought so too.

"This isn't a case; it's a circus."

"What was that address?" Molina shot over her shoulder at Temple.

Temple told the driver, feeling that treating a homicide detective as if he were a common cabbie must be against some law. Not that the Crown Victoria didn't have a smooth ride, but the driver didn't reduce speed much to take the corners.

When the car pulled up at the designated address, they all stared at its humble façade. "Many Happy Returns" read a hand-lettered sign above the aging Strip-center's shop doorway. An eclectic collection of household items littered the sidewalk. Temple was sure that there was a statute against exhibiting a used baby carriage next to a rolling bar-cart covered in leopard vinyl.

Apparently Molina and her minion weren't here to enforce paltry city ordinances. They got out and wove indifferently through the slightly abused clutter. Temple followed.

The minute they crossed the threshold, the trail they sought became patently clear. A miasma of strawberry air-freshener hung invisibly over crowded racks holding used clothing hung on wire hangers.

"I remember coming to this place with Matt. We didn't stay long," Temple said. "Sometimes it has something; sometimes not."

She idled over to the display case that also served as pay station. A plus-size elderly woman in polyester-knit pants was arranging new arrivals on the long clothes rack behind her.

A miniature dachshund curled on a pillow atop a stool growled at their approach, and followed up with two sharp yaps of dislike.

"I'll be right with you," the woman caroled over her T-shirt-clad shoulder. When she turned to the foursome, her open features showed immediate perplexity. Finally, her trifocal glasses fixed on Temple.

"I haven't seen you in here for some time."

"No, been too busy to get around to the shops much. This is, ah—"

Temple was mercifully cut off before she could make introductions. "We're the police." Molina waved a clip-on identity badge pulled from her jacket pocket. "We have some questions about clothes we have reason to believe were purchased here."

She lifted the brown paper evidence bag to the glass counter top, obscuring most of the costume jewelry displayed on the top shelf, which Temple had been discreetly checking out.

"Are you the owner?" Molina donned latex gloves and began easing the clothing out of the bag.

"Sure. Bernice Grandy. Been at this location for ages. But what makes you think these clothes came from here?"

An awkward silence. No one wanted to say the joint smelled like fermenting strawberries.

Molina must have found awkward silences useful in her work, because she let this one lengthen into an embarrassment before she broke it. "That's why Miss Barr is with us. I understand that she's something of an expert in the used clothing area."

"Gently worn," Bernice corrected, gently. She struggled into the latex gloves that Molina extended and smiled at Temple. "Now I remember what you got here last! That sixties hot-pants outfit with the cute little marabou jacket."

"Ah, I bought that as a curiosity. Not to wear." Temple eyed her audience, who eyed her back. Nobody believed her. "But you've got a great memory for clothes, Bernice. I thought you might remember these."

Bernice unfolded the items, shaking her head. "Your stuff I remember. It's always different. I never thought I'd unload that size-six sixties outfit, and that was when sizes were smaller than they are today. But this stuff, it's . . . pretty routine. I don't charge much for it and it usually ends up on a discount rack. Hmmm. Size 14."

They waited, while the dachshund sighed and curled into a cozier sleeping position, apparently bored with their business.

"That's interesting."

"What is it?" Temple asked.

"I did get a pile of stuff like this a couple months ago, all in size fourteen. I think somebody died."

"So do we," Molina added.

Bernice didn't quite make the connection that the clothes in question had last covered a corpse.

"Let me get my book," she said, lumbering through

225

the many racks to the back of the store, doffing the latex gloves as she went.

Temple responded to Molina's look. "Bernice assigns a number, price, and description to each outfit so she can reimburse the consignors."

"So there's actually a chance that she might be able to identify where these clothes came from?"

"And where they went, if the buyer paid by credit card or check."

"Didn't look like a credit-card spender to me," the male detective put in.

"If it was cash—" Temple shrugged. "Unless she signed up for Bernice's mailing list, but it'd be hard to tell who was who."

"This the only resale shop that smells like 'Strawberry Fields Forever?' " Molina wanted to know.

"It's the most obvious, for some reason. Resale clothes can smell . . . stale, more so than vintage clothes, because those really haven't been worn in decades. But you should—"

Molina's Medusa look at Temple would have turned fire to ice. "Here she comes. Now we'll find out something."

"—know that," Temple trailed off in a mutter.

At Molina's words, hailing the return of Bernice, the male detective had immediately focused on the arriving hard evidence. Gee, Temple hadn't meant to give away Molina's experience in finding vintage clothes for her Carmen persona.

Bernice hefted the massive ledger to the countertop, pushed her glasses firmly against the bridge of her nose, and began paging through the hand-written entries.

"I'm guessing November."

"We're in a hurry," Molina said.

"Don't get your culottes in a twist; there were at least sixteen items in the consignment I'm thinking of; should be easy—yes, here it is. November twelfth. Hmmph." She stared through the lowest trifocal bar on her lenses at the mounded clothes. "Navy poly suit. Yup."

"You have a record of the buyer?" Molina demanded.

"Might. Now I have to look in the receipts."

Bernice reached under the counter and pulled out a . . . shoe box. "I think this sold before Christmas. Let me see—"

Molina and her minion openly fidgeted, while Temple, unhurried, window-shopped the display case.

Bernice's unlipsticked mouth made a sound between a "tsk" and a smacking kiss. She was nodding as she pulled a small yellow paper from the shoe box. Temple noticed the brand was Red Cross, not exactly her high-flying style.

"Used a check."

"Did you get a name and address?" Molina asked almost breathlessly.

Bernice shook her permed lamb's fleece of white hair. "Nope. It's one of those temporary checks they give you when you open an account."

Temple aborted a smile at Molina's exasperated expression.

"But I got a driver's license number. Will that do?"

Bingo! Cop faces beamed.

"I wonder if I could see that mesh metal belt," Temple told Bernice while the detective was squinting at the yellow receipt, writing down the long string of numbers.

"That'll have to wait until you're on your own time." Molina scotched private enterprise as she stacked the clothes and picked up the brown bag. "Thanks very

227

much for your trouble," she told Bernice.

By then, her minion's notebook held not only what could be the dead woman's license number, but Bernice's name, address, and phone number at work and at home.

All three traipsed outside and stood for a moment in the silent communion of a job well done at last.

"Detective Morris Alch," the man told Temple. "I met you on that cover-boy case."

She almost blushed at having her mind read.

"What a lame operation," Alch said. "Are the used places all this informal?"

"We wouldn't have gotten anything from a regular clothing store," Molina pointed out. "No sales clerk would have ever remembered a particular item." She turned to Temple. "Did that 'sixties hot-pants outfit' reek of strawberry air-freshener too?"

"I didn't know you cared."

"I don't. Answer the question."

"Yeah, but I hung it off the balcony for a couple of days until the smell was almost gone, then I had it dry-cleaned. And I kept it separate from my other clothes for a few weeks until it really aired out."

"The victim didn't bother doing any of that, obviously. I wonder why."

"Maybe she wasn't as sensitive to smells. So. We're done?"

Molina's smile was almost sadistic. "Noooo. We haven't visited Grizzly Bahr yet." She turned to Alch, smile still lethal. "Next stop; you should enjoy this too."

Temple had only visited a medical examiner's facility in Manhattan, but she recognized this one immediately after they had been allowed through a secured door.

Once again her nose for news was causing her trouble. She could smell that faintly sweet, faintly rotten tang in the air, so subtle you thought you were imagining it because you expected it.

Grizzly Bahr lived up to his name: a big, burly man in his sixties with sun-freckled face and hands, and a larger-than-life manner.

"Civilian?" He cast one corrosive glance at Temple from under albino thickets of eyebrow. He might as well have said, "Fresh meat?"

Molina nodded. "Now. What about the second victim's body?"

"That's if you assume these two deaths are connected." Grizzly took relish in pointing that out as he turned to lead them down halls and through doors. Temple tried not to glance into side rooms they passed, but she couldn't help seeing a naked female body on a gurney, a clinician in a laboratory slicing brain material like it was pâté, more technicians taking fingerprints from a headless, legless torso burned beyond recognition.

"You okay?" Detective Alch asked softly, cupping a hand under her elbow.

"Fine. I just seemed to be walking through quicksand for a stretch there."

"Don't look, don't ask," he advised. "And don't breathe through your nose."

Temple nodded. "If I'd known I'd be visiting here I would have brought my Vick's. Maybe I'll just think of strawberries."

"Excellent idea."

By then Dr. Bahr had led his troupe into an examination room.

His white-jacketed bulk, matched by Molina's dark-coated presence, was enough to obscure the figure on the steel table, although Temple glimpsed a vulnerable row of toes.

"Amazing," Molina said. "And you discovered it—?"

"When I brought the body out to confirm the identity against the photocopies you faxed over."

"What do you make of this, Alch?"

The detective reluctantly shouldered his way into the front line.

Temple didn't need to know. She had no curiosity whatsoever, except as to whether she would faint if she had to confront the naked and the dead form of the chorus-girl lithe figure from those old posters of Professor Mangel's.

While she was thinking so hard about how she *might* react if confronted by a dead body, somehow the trio had parted like a human curtain. Temple glimpsed the waxy yellow form of an unclothed mannequin. Across the bare and bony chest were the words, "she left."

No caps, no quotes, no punctuation, Temple noticed, trying desperately not to inventory any other background details.

"How do you explain it showing up now? Tampering?" Molina was asking.

Grizzly Bahr shook his big, shaggy head.

"Not at all. It was always there." Once the silence had held for a suitably dramatic moment, he nodded portentously. "It was written in some kind of disappearing ink. The lights here, or changes in the body's composition, er, decomposition, brought it out in due time."

"Bizarre." Even Molina sounded impressed. "Imagine." She turned to Temple. "A magician's assistant, murdered and marked with invisible ink.

230

Almost as if someone is playing with us. This definitely links the two deaths."

Temple nodded miserably.

"It would seem so," Grizzly Bahr agreed with small satisfaction. "It had better be disappearing ink. I'd hate to think someone was sneaking into my morgue to mess with my bodies. We've got better security than that."

"People actually try to sneak into MEs' facilities?" Temple asked.

"All the time," Bahr boomed genially. "Especially when we have celebrity autopsies."

Temple shook her head. She wouldn't want to try any of these rolling steel beds on for size, even if Papa Bear Bahr presided in person.

CAN'T HELP LOVING THAT MAN

SAFELY RETURNED TO MOLINA'S OFFICE, TEMPLE accepted the offer of a cup of coffee. Actually, she wanted to smell it, rather than drink it.

It was just the two of them, one on one.

"You were helpful at the resale shop. Thank you." Molina actually smiled at her.

"When will you know the identity of the dead woman?"

"Detective Su is running the license now. We'll have a name and address and some vital statistics very soon. Then we have to find out 'who' she was in the larger sense, and what might have made her a victim of homicide."

"Who'd want to kill a poor woman who bought her

clothes at resale shops?"

"The words 'she left' were spray-painted near the body."

Temple nodded. No need to mention that Matt Devine had told her that already. Molina knew.

The lieutenant's fingertips rapped the glass-topped desk. "That's not what concerns me. Oh, it does, but I'd think that you'd find the death of Gloria Fuentes more . . . disturbing."

"That someone would booby-trap the body like that, to reveal the words over a day later? That *is* sick."

"Sick? Or theatrical?"

"Both, I suppose."

"What is our murderer trying to tell us?"

"I don't think 'our' murderer is trying to tell *me* squat. And maybe it's more than one killer."

"The disappearing ink was no afterthought. Who else would have known about the words at the first death scene besides the police?" Molina paused.

Matt would have known, because Molina had told him.

The lieutenant shook her head, heavy blunt-cut hair barely shimmying at the gesture. "I don't get it," she told Temple. "You are either the strongest case of denial I've ever run across, or you know something I don't, and I can't believe that.

"Loyalty is one thing, but you are harder to crack than Susan McDougal. These women were apparently killed because they had the guts to leave someone who was bad for them."

"That's when abusive relationships turn fatal," Temple put in.

"I know that. You know that. I also know that you are not a stupid woman. So why are you sticking with Max

232

Kinsella through thick and thin, and mostly thin? You and I know he's hiding something, that he's up to his phony green eyes in something criminal."

"Things aren't always what they seem."

" 'Things aren't always what they seem.' Things are *never* what they seem. Don't you see that if you continue to protect him, when he gets his comeuppance—and he will—you'll take a fall with him? He's already proven dangerous to know, painfully so." The flat of her hands hit the desktop. "I don't get it. You could have Matt Devine with a snap of your fingers. You know where he's been at least, even if a Catholic religious vocation is foreign to you. He couldn't lie to you to save his soul. So? What's the reason? A bent for self-destruction? Am I missing something here?"

"Yes. I think you are."

"Really?"

Temple expelled a breath of frustration. "Haven't you ever really trusted anyone, no matter what the appearances?"

"Let me think."

"It's not something you have to think about: You know."

"Then, no. Trusting someone was not an option in the place and time I grew up in."

"If you had, you would understand. Since you haven't, you will never understand. And because Max and I had that total trust of each other, it will take a lot to kill it. Someone else's suspicions will never do it. Are you trying to 'turn' me, Lieutenant? Isn't that what you call getting one criminal to betray another? It won't work, because you're not dealing with criminals here."

"You are fast becoming an accessory to whatever

233

Kinsella is up to. You can't deny you're living with him."

"Off and on. When he's in town."

"Oh." Molina grew still. "And has he been in town lately?"

"In and out."

"The times of the murders?"

"I can swear that he was out of town for the second one."

" 'Out of town' where?"

"The . . . West Coast."

Molina nodded, satisfaction glimmering in her brilliant blue eyes. Temple felt a stab of unease.

"You can swear," Molina went on, "that Kinsella was apparently out of town at that time. But you can't prove it. Not unless you were with him wherever on the West Coast he went. For whatever reason. And you weren't, and you don't know why he went there, do you?"

"No."

"What is trust worth when it's a one-way street?"

"More than what it's worth if you've never had it, or given it, at all."

Molina stood, dismissing her, and her position. "You *will* regret this alliance. Someday."

"Not if my eyes were open, Lieutenant, and I promise you, no matter the appearances, they are."

Temple left, feeling as if she'd been spindled, stapled, and mutilated.

Just who was most obsessive about Max Kinsella? Temple thought she had plenty of competition on that score. And that wasn't even counting Kitty the Cutter.

NOT ALONE BY
THE TELEPHONE

MATT FIDGETED BESIDE THE PHONE, STARING AT THE notebook number he'd called a couple times before.

Maybe it was too late to be calling, but he couldn't afford to wait.

He glanced at his watch. Seven-forty. Almost ten P.M. on the East Coast. Definitely too late to call someone he'd never met. But he couldn't wait.

He punched in the numbers and listened to the first three rings, almost hoping no one would answer.

"Hel-lo!" A lively, husky voice. Like Temple's.

"Miss Carlson, this is a friend of Temple's calling. Matt Devine."

"Yes, of course. What can I do for you?"

"Quite a lot, actually. I'm sorry to call so late, but I was tied up and things are reaching a desperate state."

"Gracious. I adore desperate states. Haven't had any myself since I left the theater. Or it left me. Don't worry about the hour. Inquiring minds never retire. Besides, we just get cooking in Manhattan at ten P.M. Now I'm sitting down, with my toes tucked up and warm, and a nice toasty Calvados in my hand. Tell me anything, darling. I can take it."

"Then you should have my new job."

"And what is that?"

"Recently, I've been a late-night radio counselor."

"Not so different from what you were doing before, if I remember rightly, and I've only had one tiny sip of brandy so far, so I remember pretty rightly."

"I'm flattered; you do remember. Anyway, I got this new job and the first night out had a rather sensational call."

"Don't tell me! You're in Las Vegas. Sensational call . . . sensational call. Elvis! Elvis called you and . . . admitted he's an undercover alien for the FBI!"

"I like your scenario better than the real one. No, a very troubled young girl called me. She was giving birth in a motel room and so . . . mind-warped she thought her baby was an alien. She would have drowned it, except that I kept her on the line and got her to read off the motel's phone number. My producer called 911, then kept the line on the air while the firemen broke in and . . . everything."

"The baby was all right?"

"Yes."

"Wow. Sorry to have been flip. It's a family failing."

"I've noticed."

"We Lake Wobegoners aren't allowed to show feelings, so we become quite good at defensive humor. What a dreadful situation. But you proved your credentials your first night out."

"I did more than that, I attracted attention."

"Your producer must be elated."

"She is. Everybody is. Sordid, tragic story; happy ending by Matt Devine. I'm suddenly a celebrity. The talk shows are calling, even Oprah. It's crazy."

"Did you say 'even Oprah?' "

"Yeah—"

"My God, that's *better* than Elvis."

"Publishers—"

"Oh my God, you're even better than a celebrity, you're a *topical* celebrity! There isn't a talk show you can't do. Our unwed parent problem, our mothers-who-

236

kill-babies problem . . . You need a book contract!"

She must have sprung to her feet with excitement; he could hear her come alive over the phone line.

"So Temple tells me. She says I need an agent first."

"You need a good agent; there's a difference."

"Can you—would you . . . help me out?"

"Yup. I'll check with some people I know here. You're lucky you live in Las Vegas; there are some top people there, but you'll want a class act."

"I don't want any kind of act, Miss Carlson. That's the problem."

"Kit. My name is Kit." Her voice and excitement-level had settled down to fairy godmother level. "Not liking the hoopla is not a problem. Liking it too much is. I know where you're coming from, Matt."

"You do?"

"Temple likes you. A lot."

"She . . . I—"

"You could do a lot of good with this opportunity, for yourself and the people who put their faith in you. Think of it that way. But Temple's right. You need help. I'll try to find you some reliable help."

"You make an agent sound like a house-cleaner."

"Not too bad a comparison. The right agent sweeps out all the nasty dirt; keeps things pristine and above-board. Let me call around on it. Give me your phone number and I'll be back in touch."

"Ah . . . wait! I don't have an answering machine. Yet."

"That's so sweet! You *do* need help! You can get the answering machine; I'll get the agent."

"And, before you go. I was wondering . . . if you could recommend some titles."

"Titles?"

237

"Of your books. Temple said you wrote and I . . . wanted to read some of your books."

"A man! A man wants to read one of my books. I am so thrilled. Not that men wouldn't like them, mind you, if they could get past those swooning cover inanities. Dear boy. What to recommend. Don't let the titles throw you either. Let's see. For you . . . *One Faithful Harp.* Or *Black Rue.* I should be backlisted in the superstores, and have nothing new in paper out in the supermarkets at the moment. You do like Irish backgrounds?"

"Uh . . . no."

"Odd. You are Catholic, so to speak. They love the Auld Sod. Well . . . I know! *Iron Maiden.* Spain, the Inquisition, forbidden love. I even have a saintly monk in that one. Fra Anjelico. Like the liqueur. Comes to such a tragic end, as the good so often do. Now: Get an answering machine!"

"I can't tonight."

"Tomorrow, first thing. Promise?"

"I . . . promise."

" 'Bye. Don't worry about a thing. Auntie Kit is on the case."

Matt hung up. Talking to Temple these days made him smile for hours. Talking to her aunt made him want to laugh for at least twenty minutes.

The next call would not be so jocular. This number he knew by heart.

His mother answered on the third ring, sounding breathless.

"I was doing dishes. My hands were wet." She owned no dishwasher.

"What . . . what's the matter?"

"Nothing wrong, Mom. I just wanted to warn you.

I've got a new job here, same work. Counseling. But on the radio. And one of the callers was in severe difficulty and it became kind of a media thing. So I'm calling to warn you, just in case something showed up in a local paper. So you wouldn't be surprised."

"I don't understand."

"I inadvertently helped stop a teenage mother from killing her newborn. It happened over the air. Every talk show in the country wants me to go on it. I don't think I will, but it's like being at the center of a tornado. The radio station people want me to get caught up in the whirlwind; it's good for them."

"What about what's good for her?"

"Exactly. I'm getting professional help. I don't mean . . . counseling. I mean, media control help. But I might do one of the top shows. It's a chance to get my message across."

"And what is that message?"

"That people are human. Sometimes they need help."

"Is that the message, or are *you* the message?"

"I'm trying to keep track of the difference, Mom. And, when this dies down, I've made up my mind."

"About what?"

"That matter of the lawyers and the house needs looking into. Before too much time has passed and nothing can be traced. I'll help you with that, when I can."

"Maybe I'm wrong, Matt. Maybe digging up the past is pointless."

"No. I'm not sorry I found Effinger. I'm a lot better for it."

"Happier?"

He thought of his too-late-recognized infatuation with Temple. "No. But better."

"Maybe I'm fooling myself, Matt. Maybe I want

some Cinderella ending I used to believe in thirty-five years ago."

"Thirty-four. I'm going to only be thirty-four this year."

"That girl on the radio. You kept her from killing her baby?"

"I think so."

"I could never have killed you. I never thought for an instant about an abortion. Never, never! You've got to believe that."

"I do."

"But. I can understand how she might have—I'm glad you stopped her."

"I just wish I could believe that she's glad, too."

"Oh, she is, or she will be."

His last hurdle of the evening was an in-person encounter with Leticia. Ambrosia. Live and in person at WCOO. On site at the radio station.

She apparently had expected a letdown. She met him with a majestic, calm demeanor and a sisterly lecture.

"Now, tonight will be oh-so-natural. No bolt out of the blue. Just a normal Mr. Midnight evening. Relax, bro. Think mellow. Soothe and smooth. Don't think about last night. If any callers refer to it, be vague. Turn the talk back on their problems, no matter how piddling. The motto of this midnight, Mister, is 'Be cool, baby, be cool.'"

On just such stream-of-consciousness calming she eased him into the studio and the forthcoming hour in front of the mike.

Matt's mind couldn't help turning a kaleidoscope of the women he'd talked to during the past few hours around and around in his head: the Three Graces of past, present, and future; his fairy godmothers; his bedeviling

240

genies of the eternal and mysterious feminine.

His friends.

MAGIC IS MURDER

TEMPLE WOKE UP KICKING HERSELF THE NEXT morning, which was better than waking up kicking Midnight Louie. He was lying docilely at her side again, or rather sprawled on *her* side of the bed on his back, curled legs in the air, looking like the ferocious king of the beasts on a tranquilizer dart.

"Well, and what are you dreaming of?" Temple tickled his tummy until he rolled over and regarded her with flattened ears and narrowed green eyes.

"Nothing nice, I guess. Crabby." She glanced at the bedside clock, a loud-red overlarge set of numbers. "Too early to call. Darn, I'll be wondering why I didn't think to ask what I didn't ask about until I can finally call and find out."

Wait until Max stayed over here some night and discovered that she talked to the animals, just like Dr. Doolittle, the fictional character (not Dr. Doolittle, the very nonfictional veterinarian, who tended Louie).

Louie appeared to find the logic of her monologue sadly lacking. He rolled back onto his spine and elevated all extremities again, all except for his tail, which he quirked to the side like a lazy question mark.

"Aren't you the coyest thing?" Temple asked rhetorically. "I should get my camera." She yawned, too sleepy to catch Louie's disarming pose for posterity. All those wonderful Kodak cat moments, lost from here to eternity. *Baaa, baaa, baaa.*

"Those aren't the poor little lambs I had in mind,"

she muttered as the chorus of the Whiffenpoof Song faded from memory.

Temple sat up in bed and braced her aching head on her hands.

She knew what she should be doing: spending every free moment at the Crystal Phoenix as the Jersey Joe Jackson Action Attraction she had envisioned came to pass. A lot of little details were being decided by construction crews, and possibly even Fontana Brothers, which was an even more horrific thought.

But.

So much else was going on.

Matt was on the brink of becoming a media phenomenon.

Lieutenant C. R. Molina was actually, though reluctantly, confiding in Temple the details of a real-live murder investigation.

And Max.

Temple sighed, shutting her eyes and seeing the angry red welt in his scalp.

Max was up to something she didn't totally know about—this time he acknowledged as much—and maybe, just maybe, he was in more danger than he knew or was ready to admit, from the mysterious Synth.

He was a rogue magician now, as well as a rogue counterterrorist. All this new-found rogue-ishness had resulted from his attempt to live a normal life. For her. With her. He was trying to leave two professions that apparently frowned on voluntary withdrawal, and she was the reason for the danger he now faced on both fronts.

So.

She had to fix that, as much as she could.

Her best lead was the Synth, through her connection

to the motley crew of psychics and semi-magicians she had met at the Halloween séance three months ago.

She looked at the clock again. Two numbers had disappeared without her seeing them doing it. Presto change-o. She had a long wait before the hour was decent enough for a business call. Maybe she would enter her thoughts about the murders and the three musketeers—Matt, Max, and Molina—on her computer. Try to get a fix on the big picture.

What could she name the file? Now that Windows95 ruled the cyberspace world, with '98 on its tail, she could give files long, nonsensical, Swiftian names. This one, she decided, would be: M-is-for-murder.wpd. Gee. Sounded like the title of a book. A mystery.

"Yes," Professor Mangel greeted her earnest ten-o'clock-scholar call later that morning. "I hope the material on Gloria Fuentes proved useful."

"All too much so. I'm afraid Miss Fuentes is no more."

"Tragic. But I'll make a note of it for my files. You, ah, wouldn't object if I let the newspapers know her history? Her passing is worth noting."

"I'd check with Lieutenant C. R. Molina before I did that. You'd better tell her you recognized the sketch in the paper. Don't let on that I had anything to do with it."

"Gotcha. The Invisible Woman. You have wonderful magic instincts."

"I do?" Temple felt complimented.

"Definitely."

"That may be, but I also have a rather slo-mo mind at times. I forgot to ask you some crucial information, such as, where I'd find the people from last fall's séance now. I can't even remember all their names."

"You won't have to. Didn't I tell you the reason for the exhibit being rushed to completion? There's a meeting of parapsychological and magical artistes going on right now."

"A meeting?"

"A combination psychic fair and union confab. Anybody who's anybody in magic and illusion is at the Opium Den right now.

"All of them? Like D'Arlene—?"

"D'Arlene Hendrix; Agatha Welk; Oscar Grant, the television psychic phenom show host; Mynah Sigmund and her husband, what's-his-name."

"It's all coming back to me," Temple said in mock-sepulchral tones, "except the husband's name. Oh, well, he wasn't important."

"Poor man. I suppose you're going over there to view the bodies?"

"Probably. I want to find out more about the Synth."

"Anyone who really knows anything won't tell you."

"I know. That's how I'll know who might know something."

"Aren't you clever? If you learn anything interesting, do share with me. I'm just a humble academician; the professionals rarely tell me anything worth knowing. Even the psychics are close-mouthed about their precious practices."

"I'll tell you anything I can."

"And Temple."

"Yes."

"Be careful. Most of those people over there take this stuff very seriously indeed. You might be surprised to find out who is most . . . fierce about it."

"I hope I am, because that's the only way I'll learn anything."

244

BUT NOT FOR ME

"HO-LY SHIT!"

Molina said it once, with feeling.

She followed it with "Excuse me, Detective Su. I didn't mean to soil the air with any expletives. Not because I need to spare your delicate ears, but because I have a preteen daughter at home and I don't want to fall into any bad habits that could be an excuse. You're sure about your facts?"

"Absolutely, Lieutenant. And I agree. Holy shit."

"So. Strawberry Lady, our first victim, was a former nun. A Catholic nun."

Su consulted the narrow notebook that matched Molina's pocket version. "It took some backtracking. They don't exactly advertise the past. But until four years ago Monica Orth was Sister Mary Margaret of the Order of Our Lady of the Cross."

"What was she doing in the Blue Dahlia parking lot?"

"Nothing I can figure out. She worked as a county librarian in Reno the past four years. Moved here just three months ago. Led a notoriously quiet life. Didn't date. Nice middle-aged single lady, seemingly content to stay that way."

"No relationships with men?"

"We've interviewed her neighbors, here at least. She was like a lot of middle-aged women nowadays, whether divorced or never married: content with their jobs and their housecats. Unless she had a racy secret life we haven't dug out, no; no relationships with men, except for the mailman and the carry-out boy at the local Lucky Food Center store."

"Still, it does give 'she left' a different ring, doesn't

it?"

"You thinking some kind of religious fanatic here?"

"Possibly. All intense religions—and Catholicism is an intense religion—produce intense reactions. But what was Monica Orth, Sister Mary Margaret Orth, doing in the Blue Dahlia parking lot at two in the morning?"

"She must have been brought there."

"By her murderer. Who has a thing against women who 'left.' Who left men? Or who left religious vocations? What have we got? The typical man scorned, or the atypical religious fanatic?"

"Too soon to tell, Lieutenant. All I know is that Monica Orth's past fits her present: the pre-owned, plain clothing; the low-profile, solitary life. Apparently her cat died about the same time, only when her neighbor called animal control to report it, the body was missing. Cat body, that is. It's possible the neighbor was hallucinating. She lived alone and kept a cat too."

"Living alone and keeping a cat is not a sign of incompetence. We are not on a witch hunt. This is not the European Middle Ages, Detective. Women are not balmy merely because they are manless."

"No, sir. Ma'am."

"How old are you?"

"Twenty-eight."

"Wait a decade or two before you judge." Molina donned an abstract expression. "Tell me about Gloria Fuentes. Did she live alone and keep a cat?"

"As a matter of fact—"

"No shit?"

"No shinola." Su again flipped a page in her notebook. "She lived alone, but her neighbors at the Shady Palms apartments indicate she had gentleman

246

callers. Her cat was a tortoiseshell called Pyewacket. Weird name! What is a tortoiseshell?"

"It's a color of cat. I don't know exactly what. Brown and something, I'd think. So, is this cat missing?"

"Not at all. A neighbor took it in when it began yowling outside fellow tenants' doors."

"It began yowling three days ago?"

"Exactly."

"When Gloria didn't come home to feed it. So what was Gloria doing outside a church?"

Su shook her glossy black head. "Hard to say. Her neighbors didn't peg her for the religious type. She relished looking like she had been in 'show business' once. Tight pants. High, backless heels. Teased, orange-colored hair. Flashy, but harmless."

"Not to somebody."

"No, ma'am."

"Apparently she also left someone, or something. Take Alch and dig some more around both residences and the job scene. He has a nice instinct for lonely ladies."

"Morey's a sweetheart."

"Yes, he is. You're lucky to have him for a partner."

Merry Su gave her an oblique look through those attractively slanted dark eyes of hers. Razor-slash eyes. Su was wondering if Molina's assessment was personal.

"Youth and experience make a good investigative team," Molina added, thinking: no, not Alch. He's a sweetheart, all right, but not for me. Not yet.

CALL AND RECALL

THE CALLS STARTED JAMMING THE SWITCHBOARD during the last half hour of Ambrosia's seven-to-midnight shift.

Matt watched her fielding phone-ins and programming appropriate songs, every movement efficient, her Buddha-calm voice never indicating for an instant that she was keeping track of six things at once.

Thank heaven he didn't have to select and play the proper background music for every caller with every kind of problem. He didn't know the past thirty or forty years of popular music anyway, although he was catching up fast after a few hours of listening to Ambrosia spin her spells and her platters.

Callers were eased off the air as fluidly as they were drawn into revealing their losses, failures, fears, and hopes. It was first names only and the comforting anonymity of public confession.

When Ambrosia clocked off, she motioned him to take over the hot seat.

"The whole world wants to talk to you, Mr. Midnight. Come on in and assume your headset."

"I'm not sure I want to talk to them."

"Why not?"

"After all the calls I've been fielding all day . . . talk shows and people who want to write true-crime books and so-called Hollywood producers. I don't know how they all got my home phone number."

"People like that want something bad enough, they get it. Are you listed in the phone book?"

"Maybe. By now. Depending on when a new edition

248

came out. I haven't looked. When I moved here last year and got my phone, it never occurred to me that I should get an unpublished number."

"Such problems," she mocked. "The man is popular."

He checked the big schoolhouse-style clock on the wall with its boldly sweeping second hand. He trusted its massive, plain face more than the gilded hands on his wristwatch.

"My friend Temple is helping me get an agent. Then I can get an answering machine and tell everybody to call him, or her."

"An agent."

"You don't think it's a good idea?"

"For you, baby, sure! For us . . . "

"Oh. Well, it's not like I'm expecting a raise or anything, not so soon."

"Oh, but your agent will be." She chuckled. "Let's see what the people want besides you, Mr. Midnight."

Her stately form glided out of the tiny studio like an ocean liner leaving the dock. Matt felt panic clutch his throat. What did they want, all these callers? Not him, really, but something they thought he could give them. He couldn't be getting more alien-baby calls, could he? Surely something like that happened once in a broadcast lifetime? And he was just an amateur at this.

The first voice came bubbling into his ears like effervescent empathy, female and heartfelt. "Is this Mr. Midnight? I want to talk to Mr. Midnight, not some operator. Oh. It's you! That was the most sad and, and most scary thing I've ever heard. Thank you, thank you, for saving that girl."

"It was her baby that was in danger—"

"And if the baby had died, what would have happened to her? What *is* happening to her?"

249

"I tried to get in touch with her today, but she's in the hands of the professionals. Sociologists, doctors, psychologists. They're examining her. You're right; she doesn't have something unthinkable on her conscience. I have to believe she'll be all right."

"Well, you just keep trying to get through to her. The professionals! Where were they when she needed help?"

"They're there, but you have to ask them for that help."

"Well, at least we know where *you* are, Mr. Midnight. Keep up the good work."

The line didn't even go dead. Another voice was harping in his ears.

"Oh, it's a sad story, all right." Male and bitter. " 'Poor girl.' Where's the father, I gotta ask? Did he have any voice in any of this? What about vows? What about promises? And miles to go, and promises to keep? Nobody keeps promises any more. Wedding rings, worthless. Throw them in the sewers, in the bushes. Web rings, that's what people want. Internet. Not interconnection. The world is crazy—"

"The world is crazy, but people are made that way by other people, sometimes. We can't blame the victims . . ."

"Yes, we can! We can when everybody's a 'victim.' Isn't there any responsibility any more? Everybody weaseling out of everything. In the old days, people *paid*. People did what was right, no matter the cost. There were no easy outs."

"You think running to hide in a run-down motel room is an easy out for anyone? Especially an expectant mother?"

"The Virgin Mary was an expectant Mother, and she didn't run to hide."

"She had an angel come to tell her everything was all

250

right. Is that any different from an alien visitation? Which do you believe, that the young, unwed pregnant woman of two thousand years ago saw an angel, or the young, unwed pregnant woman of today saw alien abduction?"

"There's no comparison. Mary was holy; she bore the Son of God."

"And at the time, who saw a Son of God?"

"Joseph. Joseph was faithful. He protected Mary from herself. He saw that she wed herself to Heaven and himself."

Matt was taken aback. Joseph was the forgotten man of Scriptures. God's cuckold, if you wanted to be crass about it, the first celibate, to go by church teaching, an avuncular husband and stepfather to the Lord. A man who made sure Mary remained a Virgin Mother the rest of her days, unto the foot of the Cross.

Then there were the Lutherans, who said Jesus had many brothers and sisters, and that John the Baptist was his cousin . . .

Theology was not what the Midnight Hour was about, Matt knew that much. Nor was finger-pointing, not if he had anything to do about it.

"She was a young girl," he said. "In some societies she would be buried to her waist and stoned to death for the very fact of her pregnancy, never mind who had perpetrated it on her."

"Pregnancy is a holy state; it is never wrong."

"It is initiated by someone who has an obligation to be there," Matt pointed out, "and in so many cases isn't. What about him? What about the father of the child? Where was he?"

"He was everywhere, and nowhere. That doesn't matter. If she had wanted to get rid of that baby before it

251

was born, it would have been her right without getting anybody else's say-so. Maybe it's lucky she called a radio station to get talked out of murder, but hundreds of thousands of babies are murdered every day—"

Gone. Gone with the control booth. Abortion debate was a no-no on WCOO. And Matt was glad of it.

Another voice. Another point of view. "What about birth control? Why aren't our young people educated to avoid that kind of awful trouble before it hits them? Where were her parents? They should have educated her better about the birds and the bees."

Matt felt he had to say the unthinkable. "She had nowhere to turn. Her father was the father of the baby."

A gasp. Radio in the raw. Ignorance unveiled unto the third generation, and who knows how many generations before that.

"You have to understand," Matt told the empty airwaves that were so crowded now with sensation-seeking, sensation-touched souls. "That's why she was in such an incredible state of denial about what was happening to her. It violated everything society says *should* happen. But it does happen."

"Mr. Midnight?" A timorously soft female voice. Matt didn't know whether he was rescued, or about to be subjected to another incredible dilemma.

"Yes?"

"My name is Tammy. I . . . gave up a baby a long time ago. Everybody said it was better for the baby. I was so young, and I hadn't really understood how it all happened. So fast . . . Anyway, I want to say that I can see how she got herself thinking so weird. It's like that. Everybody around you says it's not supposed to be, but it is. You can't stop it, not after a certain point, and that man who said it's so easy to get rid of a baby early, he

252

just hasn't been there. I hope she'll be all right. I hope her baby is all right. I hope my baby is too. Baby. He's grown up by now. He could be one of your callers. He could be the man who has no time for girls who get pregnant, even though some guy had to help."

"It's true, Tammy. Men don't really know. So many of us get into terrible trouble because we just don't really know."

"I'm glad you admit it. When I had my . . . trouble, almost thirty years ago, everybody else was good and right, and I was bad and wrong. They asked who the father was, but they never really cared. Nobody expected anything from him, least of all me. Now . . . I think maybe that was wrong, even unfair to him. We should have asked, maybe. Maybe even have . . . expected."

"He might have been so young he just wanted to escape."

A silence. "Yeah. But we women can't escape. She was right, that girl. We have that other . . . alien in us, and there's no getting away from that, no matter who put it there."

Matt was eyeing Ambrosia and the technician, Mike, through the glass that threw back a faint reflection of himself, his head oddly swelled by the earphones so he looked like robo-shrink.

The calls were so heavy in content and issues. Where was the hopelessly lovelorn girl or guy? The estranged son or daughter? The ordinary day-to-day heartaches you had a prayer of chitchatting about with confidence, and even a certain glib superficiality?

Macbeth had murdered sleep, but Daisy and her sad dilemma had slain the slick sympathy of radio feel-bad/feel-good talk shows.

253

"It's still the same old story." The low, burning voice thrummed into his eardrums. "Men do what they want and the woman gets left with the dregs. Then people want to crucify her when she refuses to meekly accept the burden."

"It's not just a gender issue. Every story is different."

"Every story is the same! You know what I would have done if I'd been driving Miss Daisy? I'd have got me a gun or a knife or a bomb. And I'd have blown some bastard up."

"*Thelma and Louise* was a movie. Blowing people up has never solved the inequities that keep them committing the same wrongs, paying the same price, seeking the same revenge."

"You're wrong. Every act is a revelation. Every nail pierces fresh flesh, no matter the age, no matter the century, or the country, or the person, or the person's gender. It is all retribution."

"You can't believe in a Divine retribution that merciless."

"Who believes in the divine? I can believe in a human worthlessness that worthy of being wiped out."

Matt waited, letting the faint lilt of the syllables sink into his unconsciousness and rise again with a name. Kitty the Cutter was on the air and making points.

"Your viewpoint is interesting, but too dark to cast much light on what most of humanity faces."

Matt the Cutter made the gesture—his own finger slashing across his throat—that signaled Mike the technician to deep-six this caller.

She left without another word, but the scar at his side burned, and he realized that being found by the public meant being exposed to the personal.

A grandmother came on next, mourning the

254

grandchildren torn from her by a bitter divorce, grandchildren alienated by a hostile ex-spouse and a social system that needed to assign rights for everything from birth to visitation to death.

Matt left the studio exhausted, but not too tired to study the dark and light pooling around the Hesketh Vampire before he claimed it for the ride home, to look for a darkness in the shadows that was as bad as anything demented Daisy had seen in her extremity.

MEDIA MAN

TONY FORTUNATO WAS MATT'S IDEA OF A WHITE Russian prince, or a Mafia don in the days when the mob still showed its Old Country origins.

His office was in a smart new three-story building that blazed white and techno-smooth in the Las Vegas sun, a modern mausoleum of enterprise.

From the third-story window, Matt could see the constant construction that was "Las Vegas Today!" bustling below.

"You make a very interesting property."

Somehow when Tony Fortunato—tall, permanently poised on the cusp of sixty, white-haired as a Venetian cardinal—used the word "property," it wasn't as insulting and depersonalizing as Matt would have thought.

Fortunato tapped the tape from Matt's new answering machine on the glossy lacquered surface of his desk. "You've got an incredible number of opportunities here, but I honestly don't know if I can advise you to use them."

Matt breathed a sigh of interior relief. Trust Temple and her aunt. Kit Carlson had come up with an agent not willing to leap at whatever bait was thrown into the primordial media ooze.

"Not even the respected talk shows?"

Fortunato lifted an iron-gray eyebrow. "Even the most respected talk show is media hardball. Every guest is subject to any challenge. What you think, what you are, is on display. Is a target. You say you don't want to exploit this girl Daisy. You also feel a certain obligation

256

to explain her to the larger world."

"I do think that as a society we're too eager to pin the word 'unnatural' on girls—children, really—who've been victimized by our relentlessly sexually exploitive society. What happened on the radio explains so much. What was this abused child who was bearing a child to think, or do? What did we expect of her? More than the parents who failed her, the society that has spent centuries labeling unwed mothers as pariahs?"

"Powerful words and sentiments. Sound bites to go. You'd be a hit on any talk show on this message tape. You might actually get a message of compassion and enlightenment through. But you'd also be a target."

"I? How?"

Fortunato clapped his hands together. "Your background. A former priest. Given the tragic situation of incest and abuse and unwanted birth, how can you, former Father, uphold your Church's teaching against all forms of birth control, even by a woman being raped, by a person with a sexually transmittable fatal disease like AIDS, that a well-made condom could prevent? If that girl had gotten a decent sex education in school, at least she might have told a counselor about what was going on at home. At most she might have protected herself against pregnancy with the pill. Well?"

"Don't you think I've wrestled with these issues, both while in the priesthood and out?"

"Yes, but are you prepared to come down on one side or the other? In public. On the airwaves. You want to defend this poor girl. Admirable! But you will end up having to defend yourself."

"That doesn't seem fair. I'm the messenger, not the message."

"No angels allowed on major network television

shows, Mr. Devine, unless they're fictional. We are all our own gods, as accountable for our feet of clay as for our wings of steel."

"It's all so confusing. I glimpse this golden opportunity to do something meaningful, yet it seems compromised before I even reach toward it."

"Like a certain apple?"

"Then there's the snake of personal gain or aggrandizement slithering through this garden. You must be Catholic, to sling these metaphors around."

"Devout."

"Then . . . you have no personal doubts on these issues."

"Of course I do. But they don't affect my job. I worry about them on my personal time. If you were, say, a pro-choice crusader, I could represent you."

"I . . . can't imagine—"

"Don't imagine, except when you're dealing with your radio flock. Imagination is the road to empathy, and useful in certain callings. In mine, a more pragmatic bent is called for."

"I don't see how you can separate your personal ethics and your professional."

"But these aren't ethics I separate. These are opinions. Philosophies even. Dogma even. But always, in someone else's view, opinion. As long as there is someone else to have an opposite view, I remain human. Which I like very much."

"So do I. If I . . . we, agree to do business together, what happens?"

"First, I investigate your deal with the radio station."

"They . . . gave me a break. Really enhanced my income. I owe them—"

"No. They owe you. They are the employer. You are

258

the employee. They chose well. You benefit."

"I wouldn't want to—"

"Ask what you're worth in the suddenly bear market? No. But I will want to. That's my job. To be your better half. To be your utterly immodest accountant. Don't you deserve to be paid what you're worth?"

"But what I'm 'worth' seems to depend on arbitrary external elements."

"Congratulations. You'll never develop a swelled head with that attitude." Fortunato smiled. "But you will develop a swelled bank account, if I have anything to say about it. Any objections?"

"Well . . . no. I suppose."

"Good man. I get twenty percent."

"Twenty percent!"

"For a man of your modesty, that is a pittance."

"Okay. But only if you give five percent of it to good works. Of your choice."

Fortunato leaned so far back in the tufted leather chair that it threatened to catapult him through the pristine glass down onto the Las Vegas Strip, and laughed. "Done. You may be a tougher egg than you look. All the better."

Surprisingly, Midnight Louie was waiting outside Matt's apartment door, in that age-old position of Adoration of the Doorknob, as if merely staring at it would cause the knob to turn and open the door.

Matt and Louie entered a quiet apartment, but the new answering machine's little red light was blinking furiously on the sofa table. He was tempted to just pop out the tape and forward the day's messages to Tony Fortunato—let someone else, anyone, handle the hail of unwanted calls—but he might have the occasional

259

personal call, so he rewound the tape and sat back on the red sofa to listen to the barrage.

After a long, connoisseur's sniff at Matt's pant leg, Louie leaped up to join him on the sofa.

Five or six names and organizations that meant nothing to him unreeled in a blizzard of fast talk. Then a familiar voice came on: "This is Molina. Give me a call when you can." She recited her office number with almost musical clarity and hung up. Next, the hurried, hard-sell patter of a televangelist's program booker was certain that Matt would be pleased to appear on *The Lord's Corner* to discuss effectively casting out demons long-distance, via voice. They hoped to start an Exorcist's Hotline, inspired by Matt's success with remote exorcism.

"Remote exorcism," Matt muttered as the messages ended on that weird and venal note. "How about remote extraction of gullible people's money?" His watch showed a little after three P.M., so he dialed Molina, curious.

"Good." She interrupted him as he started to identify himself. "What do you know about ex-nuns in the area?"

"Nothing."

"You ever hear any of them being harassed? Or ex-priests?"

"Only by the local constabulary."

"No joking. I haven't got time."

"Are you . . . was one of the murder victims a former nun?"

"Order of Our Lady of the Cross. Familiar to you?"

"No, but a lot of orders work in specific regions of the country. There's an ex-priests' group that meets in Henderson. I could ask there; the members are from all over."

"Don't make it obvious that this is a criminal case."

"Of course not. Which victim was it? The Strawberry Lady?"

"Right. How'd you guess?"

"The secondhand clothes. Most nuns can't bring themselves to shop anywhere else; after a lifetime of habits, when they switched to civvies, they switched to resale store 'uniforms.' Ex-religious have that problem. Can't spend the money on themselves."

"From the looks of your place lately, you seem to be getting over it."

"I've had expert help." He couldn't keep the grin out of his voice.

"Our Lady of the Tireless Consumption," Molina commented, her voice turning briskly back to business. "I'm interested in any cases of stalking ex-religious: nuns, priests, monks, altar boys."

" 'She left.' It would fit. But what about the other woman?"

"Hardly a nun. In fact, diametrically opposed in lifestyle."

"That one still could have left the usual man. Maybe she was being counseled to leave an abusive man by a member of the clergy. Maybe the murders are closely connected."

"Not bad. But Strawberry Lady was working as a librarian. Unless she was guilty of lending self-help books to Church Lot Lady."

"I know controlling personalities facing the loss of their victim can go ballistic, but that does seem pretty far-fetched."

"So do these murders, when you try to link them. If it weren't for the common method of the knotted garrote and the common message, we'd never try to link these cases. Makes me wonder if someone isn't trying to do that for us."

"Common message?"

" 'She left' showed up on the second corpse. In the morgue."

"Make them seem associated, when they're not?"

"Something like that."

"Anyway, I'll ask, discreetly, any nuns and priests I know, if there've been any cases of ex-religious being stalked. I've got some time now. I'm on leave from the hotline."

"Really?" Her intrigued tone lent that small fact a lot of weight. He wondered why. "Let me know if you get anything."

Matt hung up, staring at Midnight Louie, who was staring at him.

Someone stalking former nuns, or priests. He did know someone like that, he realized; had talked to her, in fact, just last night.

LOUIE ON THE SCENT

AS I SUSPECTED!

I knew I had smelled a rat on someone near and dear.

Well, near anyway!

As soon as I can spring myself from Casa Couch I run down the service stairs, bulling my way through two swinging doors by dint of my tremendous physique, and claw frantically at my Miss Temple's door.

The uncharacteristic ruckus brings her at my beck and call.

She gazes down on me with unfeigned wonder.

"Louie! Leave some of the mahogany for the Hondurans . . . what were you doing inside the Circle Ritz. Louie? Lou-ie!"

By then all she sees of me is my tail as I streak for the guest bathroom, bounce off the tiled wall to the top of the toilet tank and leap up in the air four feet onto the tiled ledge of the window that is always left open.

I am down to the balcony and spearing my built-in pitons into the rough-barked palm tree that acts as my emergency exit ladder.

I am moving so fast that I have gained a tad more momentum than I wish and have to hit the hard sandy ground in a roll, curling into a defensive ball and turning head over hocks like a big black coconut.

Or maybe a bowling ball.

Whichever, it is sufficient to knock Miss Midnight Louise off her four prissy pins.

"M. L., you big lug! What are you doing to me besides felinious assault?"

"This is no time for petty recriminations. At least you did what I asked when I called you back to Action Central, and waited here. Now I need you to fetch Nose E., pronto!"

"This is what you had me come all the way from Wilfrid's joint for? Get your own pronto pup! Do you have any idea how long a hike you are talking about? And that is just one way. I have done enough footwork for you to last me several lives."

I run around to block her departing path. "That is just it. We may save several lives if we act quickly. I have discovered the elusive scent from the crime scene."

This stops her cold. "Inside? Where you live?"

I nod.

"Wilfrid's murderer is inside, on your own turf?"

"Not exactly, but his—or her—scent is on one of my compatriots."

"How do you know that one of your compatriots is not the murderer? Just because you know someone does not make her—or him—innocent. In fact, in your case, your knowing someone is a pretty good indication that they are *not* innocent."

"Present company *not* excepted, I suppose?" I shoot back.

Miss Midnight Louise seats herself before she does something she will probably regret, and that I most certainly will. "I will not move one fingernail until you explain yourself. Who is the party who sniffs of murder?"

Two can play at this game. I sit down too. "Mr. Matt Devine."

Can a black cat turn pale? Perhaps not, but Miss Midnight Louise visibly shrinks with shock and dismay. "Mr. Matt Devine? I know him. Indeed, he was the first person to take me in. I cannot believe that he is involved in anything . . . lethal."

"Me neither, but he has been in contact with someone who has been so involved."

"One of your other Circle Ritz acquaintances, then? Such as Miss Temple Barr. Or even that Mystifying Max I hear discussed here and there?"

"It is possible, but unlikely. No. Mr. Matt Devine has been moving in new circles recently. Surely even at the Crystal Phoenix you have heard word of his recent exploits on the airwaves."

"You mean the nocturnal radio show."

"I suppose you cannot force yourself to even pronounce the fact that the show is named after me."

"All right: The Midnight Hour. But I would point out that both the time of night and the hour were in existence long before you were a mote in some tomcat's eye."

"Nevertheless, I deserve credit. No doubt Mr. Matt came up with the sobriquet because of his acquaintance with me."

" 'Sobriquet?' What kind of trashy talk is that, Pops? You have been associating too much of late with that tabloid newspaper trollop Yvette."

"She was unjustly smeared. I will not have a half-pint like you besmirching her betters. Poor Yvette was . . . a victim of assault."

"Hah! So you admit that your gender is a sorry lot."

"I admit that some of my gender are sorry lots, and they should be a lot more sorry than they already are, were I to catch up with them. But that is then and

265

there, and this is here and now. At least we can help nail this predator that preys upon two species."

"Two species?"

"I heard it on the grapevine. Think about it. Wilfrid's, er, 'pet,' was clobbered too. In fact, I suspect that poor Wilfrid tried to defend his mistress and was rewarded with a swift kick into Never-Never land."

I see Miss Midnight Louise shudder for the first time in our acquaintance. "And you think that Mr. Matt Devine has unknowingly come in contact with the fiend?"

"He has been catapulted into a new environment: anonymous callers, midnight confessions, public intimacies."

"These humans are a needy lot. One would think they were homeless." Midnight Louise shudders again.

"So they are, more often than not. But you and I are used to such a condition. We can do what they cannot do."

"How will you translate the importance of scent to a mere human?" she asks, reverting to her usual scornful self.

That is when I know that I have her. "It will be hard, but I can think of no other way. I have to hope that they have the rudimentary intelligence to follow the clues we will lay before them. If we make it simple enough that even a dog could follow it, we can only hope that the humans will tumble to the truth."

"Right." Louise, mind made up, is a fearsome sight. "I will have that dust-bunny of a dog back here in no time flat, Pops. I hope Mr. Matt Devine is the superior human that you think he is."

She turns on a dime and dashes for the nearest main street. It occurs to me for a regressive moment to worry about how the kit will race across town in rush hour and bring back the always-challenging Nose E., but that is her job, not mine.

Mine is figuring out a way to get Them to do what We want Without Knowing that They are Playing right into Our Paws.

That has ever been our classic dilemma, and I will have to await the arrival of Nose E. to address it once again.

FATHERS

"MATT HAS BEEN BUSY SINCE LAST WE MET."

Nick's announcement brought nervous laughter of recognition and unease.

"I don't know how you could do it," Damien said. "Talk to that demented girl, worse than an abortionist, an unnatural mother."

Matt took the words as if aimed at him. "If she was an unnatural mother, she had an unnatural father first," he said quietly.

"How so?"

"I managed to see her. In . . . custody. Her own father was the . . . father. That's why she was in such denial about her pregnancy."

" 'Denial.' The pharisees in the New Testament were in 'denial' about Christ. Is it all right that they turned him over to be crucified, then?"

"They weren't sixteen-year-old girls."

"Well, I think Matt did a heroic bit of situation-saving there," Nick said. "Apparently she called into some entertainment radio program? WCOO? WACO?"

Matt swallowed a smile. He should have realized he'd return as a *cause celebre*. "WCOO. We Care Only about Others."

"Is that the one with that Oprah-type show?"

"Ambrosia. A self-help guru of the airwaves. Actually quite a good amateur psychologist. Anyway, her listeners are devoted to her. And poor Daisy felt encouraged enough to call."

"Must have been . . . hell," Nick said. "Picking up the phone and hearing that awful situation reveal itself.

Makes old-style confessions in dark boxes seem like a picnic. You stopped her from killing that infant."

Matt took a deep breath. "So they tell me."

"How could you be so calm when two lives were hanging by threads over that phone line?" Jerry wanted to know.

"I've had some recent revelations. Really. I ran into a son of an unwed mother from the fifties, saw how bitter he was, how few options he had. My own mother— Let's just say I wonder what the Virgin Mary would have done if she hadn't had an angel to tell her what was what. Maybe she would have thought she'd had an alien visitation too. And she really did."

"Angels as aliens. An interesting conceit," said Nick, with a wry smile. "Makes you wonder if all those deluded alien abductees are simply seeking a touch of grace in this secular world."

"Or if the saints have been deluded," Norbert said.

"What will happen to her?" Damien asked.

"She'll be psychoanalyzed, then possibly charged. The baby's been taken away, for now, at least. I doubt she could get custody without a caretaker family in her life, and her real family are hardly candidates for anything but criminal charges. I'm told there's a high demand for white babies, no matter the background."

"Poor, poor creatures."

"We are, aren't we?"

Nods and silence.

SCOTCH AND SODA

IT WAS ONE OF THOSE THEATRICALLY SELF-INDULGENT places with an obligatory mirror behind the bar, so everybody who bellied up to the faux-leather bumper rail formed an informal police lineup. Most of them belonged in one.

Including himself, according to some.

Max studied his fellow swiggers, an unsavory and ragged chorus line of high and low, narrow and fat, haired and less-so. He fit right in.

Temple would not be enamored of his revised appearance.

Since the Strip bullet had put a crimp in his ponytail anyway, he'd had his hair chopped off to normal street-length, left an inch too long in the back and cut short enough at front and sides to emulate the hedgehog look so popular among media boy-wonders and aging actors with thinning hair alike.

The effect was punk Elvis, but it went with the black velour jogging suit and the heavy gold chain hanging like snarled fourteen-karat spaghetti around his neck. A crude mass of ten-karat gold and diamond chips on one knuckle completed the transformation. He had used enough hair gel to paste down Alfalfa's cowlick. Add to that a heavy dose of the most noxious men's cologne he could find at the drugstore mingling with a lingering whiff of the joint he'd puffed on before entering.

He fit right in.

Secrets was a dump for all seasons. Part strip joint, part pool hall, it served as a crossroads for every loose-ends lowlife in Las Vegas. Nadir had worked as a

270

bouncer here since arriving from Los Angeles four months ago.

Max lit a cigarette, took a puff, had a fourth belt of the cheap watered-down whiskey in its cheaper low-ball glass, then hoisted it to signal a refill.

Behind him, in the mirror, a virtually naked girl tried to leave her DNA on a chrome pole on the bar across the way, which came with hot-and-cold-running strippers. The bartender swiped a damp rag over the water-spotted faux-black marble Formica before reclaiming Max's smudged glass.

"Looks like this place sees a lot of action," Max commented, still looking around.

"Oh, yeah. Why? You looking for anything in particular?"

If the bartender hadn't been in the navy, he ought to have been. The way he braced his thick, hairy arms on his side of the bar implied more tattoos that you could wipe out with a laser beneath his muscle shirt. He reminded Max of a Mexican hairless bulldog, all bulk and undershot jaw, with so much fat piled on his muscle that the hairs were stretched miles apart, especially on his fat head.

"I'm always looking for something," Max said. "I don't particularly need anything."

The bartender waved the empty glass. "Except another shot."

Max nodded, and watched him lumber away.

Not exactly suspicious, but not a good source of information. Max turned to face the room and the carefully spaced tables. The girls who had finished performing on the small stage at one end of the vast, unimaginatively shaped room now undulated among the tables, performing lap dances and more—most of it illegal, even here.

Strip bars reminded him of medieval masters' visions of Hell. Music so loud even your fingernails vibrated, and bad music on top of it, raunchy and tinny at the same time. Predatory people playing out their prescribed roles of users and losers in equal turn. Crinkled bills pushed toward convenient crotches; alcohol and drugs tossed up and down the usual socially acceptable orifices. Victims who masqueraded as vamps; marks who played at appearing to be masters.

A messily drunk stripper wove over to him. Young, with tumbling long curls and a mouth as slack as her eyes. Blown. Pretty in a way that wouldn't last long at a place like this. A lot of strippers were former high-school cheerleaders who had been sexually abused children.

"Hi." She leaned on him as if he were a chrome pole in need of a good polishing. "I can do barstool dances." Her fingers twined around the god-awful neck chain, then pulled tight for balance. He could feel the metal-burn on the back of his neck, and reached out to support her. She took it for acquiescence.

Max guided her bare rear onto the edge of the neighboring barstool.

The guy sitting there turned angrily at the invasion, then looked into Max's eyes. Grumbling, he took his tall beer glass and moved down the bar; far down the bar.

"Jush a drink," the girl was saying. "Jush a drink. I dance for jush another drink."

"What kind of drink?" They had to shout mouth-to-ear to hear.

Her eyes focused for a moment. "Anything. Anything you want. What's you drinkin'?"

He signaled the bartender. Harder to say who of the two of them the barman viewed with deeper contempt.

No moral judgment there, except that of weakness versus strength. Any man who put up with this lush was a fool; any woman too drunk to make the most of the fools around her was a bigger fool.

"Water," Max told the barman when he returned. The bad drinks were obscenely overpriced, but Max added a five and got his plain glass of water.

"I don' remember seein' you here before." She tried to sound coy, but her sloppy pronunciation only made the remark seem phony.

"You haven't." Max diluted her drink with water while she toyed with his clothes, jewelry, hair. She'd stay blown, but maybe she'd be a trace more understandable with an ounce less liquor in her.

"Oh, new. Like I am."

"Is that why you're drunk?"

"I am not!" She tried to pull away in mock indignity, but tripped and wobbled back down on the stool instead. She reached for the glass, chugalugged a quarter ounce of booze and three ounces of city water. She made a face.

"You don't like my looks?"

"Oh, you look jush fine. Everythin' looks just fine." She gazed blankly at the hectic scene. "I'm supposed to bc getting more money."

"Here." He pulled out some tens and jammed them into one hand.

She gazed at the phenomenon as if she didn't know what to do with the bills.

"I think you're out of pockets," he said.

She looked down at her naked body and the teeny-tiny thong bikini bottom. Her hands went to either side of her mouth, a Shirley Temple gesture if there ever was one. "Oh. I'll just have to remember to hold on, I guess." She studied her fist with the wad of bills in it.

Her fist clenched the money, but she didn't even look to check the denominations. She might have lost it all if she had loosened her grip to look. Poor baby.

Max sighed. "So how new are you here?"

"Three months. I think."

His interest quickened. "Does it ever get rough? I used to be a bouncer; maybe I could get a job here."

She frowned. "It always gets rough. Ruff!" She barked at him, giggled. Barked against his lips with her own slack ones. She pulled away, grabbed the glass, swallowed hard. "We don' need a bouncer. We got Raf."

"Pretty good, is he?"

"Pretty bad. He'd like to hit us as much as them." Her baby-doll eyes grew bleaker.

"He doesn't like women?"

She pushed close, pouting, as much for safety as for sex, but the sex was always there, like an obsequious gift. "I don' know. He doesn't like us women. Me. Nobody likes me."

"That's not true. I like you."

"But . . . you're paying to like me." She lapsed into silence, into the deep, dark well of depression beneath the surface oilslick of alcohol.

She was a big girl, maybe five-eight; slim and firm for now, despite everything. But Max couldn't lose the feeling that he was holding a very fragile, undernourished seven year old.

"No, I'm paying to get you out of here."

She reared away, eye-whites showing like a panicked horse's. "I'm not supposed to leave with the clientele." A bit of shocked sobriety leaked through. "I'm not that kind of a girl. We're strippers, not hookers."

"I know. I know the rules."

274

She relaxed against him. Just tell her it was all right, and you could do anything with her, because it had been all wrong for so long.

"But I think," Max said carefully, "that you really need to go home. You do have a crash pad?"

She nodded.

"Why don't you get your things, and I'll drive you there."

She sobered enough to pull back and look him over, some self-defensive reaction kicking in. She frowned again. "I'm not supposed to leave with the customers."

"Leave by the rear. I'll meet you outside."

She clutched the black velour of his jogging jacket in both hands, never losing custody of the bills. "You like me, don't you?"

"I like you."

She pushed herself upright, standing under her own power. Glanced at the watered-down glass on the bar, looked at him, then wobbled away across the floor in her go-go boots.

"That'll be all?" The bartender was standing there, smirking.

"All except the tip." Max tossed a twenty to the water-dewed surface and walked away without a backward look.

Secrets was the usual featureless box on the outside, as if ashamed to have windows to what went on inside.

He found his current car, a vintage Mustang "borrowed" off a fly-by-night used-car lot, and idled it to the building's rear. The chances of the girl managing to hang onto the money, find and change into some street clothes, and remember to leave by the rear door were three to one.

The chances that she would prove a useful source of

information at this point were zero.

But at this point, Max was no longer working. He was . . . being the kind of idiot the bartender took him for.

After twenty minutes, the single door in the building's bunker-like rear cracked open, revealing a razor-slash of light.

Max checked the parking lot: a lot of dead metal with an insufficient number of overhead lights pouring down on it.

He got out of the car, moved toward the building.

The lone woman who came out hesitated like a doe expecting the paralyzing onslaught of headlights any minute.

Max came closer to encourage her.

He wasn't surprised when a powerful forearm clamped around his neck. Sweat and breath mints assaulted his nostrils. The force of the grip bent him backward. His attacker was shorter. So what was new?

Max relaxed into the controlled posture. You could always learn more when you were trapped than when you were on top.

"What the—? I don't have any money . . . "

A deep voice laughed. "I know. *She's* got it all. What an asshole! Now you can just get outa here. Customers don't run off with the hired help, got it?"

A knee in the kidneys made the point.

Max gave with the blow, had expected it. Raf Nadir, he presumed. Better than he had hoped for.

"I was just—"

"You're outa line, bud." Max heard the rage, felt the bullying sadism beneath the bluster. "And you. Girlie. Give me the money. You know the rules. Who are you anyway, asshole?" The punishing grip tightened.

"I'm her brother."

"Oh, yeah. And what's her real name?"

"Shirley," Max said.

"Shir-ley?" Sheer incongruity made the attacker pause.

The girl, whatever her real name, came nearer, hypnotized, helpless. Her fist was still clenched around the bills Max had thrust into it nearly thirty minutes earlier. She slowly, shakily, held it out to the bouncer.

Greed will get 'em every time.

Max spun from Nadir's grip as he reached for the money. He dropped the guy with a double kick to the kneecaps. When Nadir tried to lumber up to an attack, Max returned the courtesy to his kidneys twofold.

Nadir was groaning on the ground, but surprise worked on a seasoned thug like him for only so long.

Max grabbed the girl's outstretched, clenched fist. "Come on!"

"But . . . he'll be mad."

"That's why you don't want to be here."

"But—"

He pulled her toward the Mustang, opened the passenger door, shoved her in. The damn car was too cramped for a man of his height, but he jackknifed himself into the driver's seat, revved the engine, and roared off into the night.

In his rearview mirror, Nadir was starting to get up.

"Where do you live?" he asked her.

"With Ginger and Reno."

"They got a street address?"

She mumbled numbers and a street name, then sat hunched, the money fist clamped to her mouth. "Oh, Jesus. Sweet Jesus. Raf's a bad guy to cross. He's a bad guy even if you don't cross him."

277

Under the strobe-like effect of passing streetlights, she was looking at him, sober enough to be worried.

"We'll talk about that later."

"Later?"

"When you're home."

"Home. The girls are nice."

"But the guys are hell."

"No. Some of them are nice. Really. Just sad little guys. Normal. But then we're supposed to get them to buy drinks and table dances, and they're like lost puppies, they always want to come home with you ... You're not a lost puppy. Why am I letting you come home with me? I'll be in trouble—"

"Anybody going to be there in the next twelve hours?"

"Reno and Ginger have gigs all night. No . . ."

"Good."

"How do you know how to get there?"

"I know Las Vegas."

"I guess you do, if you knocked out Raf like that. He's a tiger. He's been at Secrets since I came. He's scary. Ooooh, I feel sick with all these fast turns."

"Let me know if you're going to puke, and I'll pull over."

"I'm a Harlington High Harlette. We don't puke."

"Glad to hear it. Still, if you feel like saying hello to the pavement, let me know."

She just moaned and wrapped her arms around her narrow midriff. Her street clothes were a pale mint-colored miniskirt and a shrunken T-top. The look should have been alluring, but to Max it was just pathetic. As was her tiny, doll-size purse on a long strap. She was still dressing like Shirley, like a little girl in her Easter best, while the world did its worst with her.

278

The apartment building was three stories, no elevator; the girls' apartment was on the top floor. Junket automobiles littered the parking lot. No curtain hung straight, and a lot of darkened windows didn't have curtains, or even blinds.

The exterior stairs were cluttered with kiddie toys. Shirley lurched up with him, clinging to him, just a sick, scared girl, that's all.

"Got a key?"

Her false nails scrabbled through the baby-doll purse. "I can't find it."

Max took the small box and probed its tight mirror pocket. "One key."

"Oh, how'd you do that?"

"Magic." He opened the apartment door, assaulted by the odor of must and cheap face powder and baby formula.

"Maybe I would visit the bathroom now," she suggested, delicately.

He let her go, watched her stumble over the furniture and clutter to a hallway. Then he checked the window. Miniblinds. Some metal slats askew. He straightened the crooked and closed them tight. The kitchen reeked of open cans not thrown out. He found a bottle of hardened instant coffee crystals in a cupboard and a mug to heat up in the spaghetti-sauce-spattered microwave oven.

She finally came out, clinging to the hall wall, the ridiculous shoulder-hung purse swinging at her hip.

"That doesn't work," she told him as he pulled the coffee mug from the microwave. "Coffee, I mean."

"The effect is psychological."

"It's supposed to make me think I'm sobering up?"

"No, it's supposed to make *me* think I can help you

279

sober up."

She laughed at that, and reached into the tiny purse. "Here's your money. I never lost it. I may have lost my lunch, but I never lost the money."

"Better you had lost the money and kept your lunch. Sit down."

She gazed at the cheap stools pulled up to the room-divider lunch bar between kitchen and living room. "I guess I can still do stool dances."

"Not with me you can't."

"You don't like me?"

"I do like you, so you can forget that crap."

"What do you want? I don't get it."

"I want you to drink this really foul coffee so I can think I'm doing you some good, then I want you to go to bed—"

"Oho!"

"Oho. Oh no. I want you to go to bed and sleep it off, and we'll talk in the morning."

"Talk?"

"Talk."

She rolled her eyes and sipped the brew, rearing back because its heat seared even her numb lips. "Raf is gonna kill me."

"Not if you never go back."

"But I gotta go back!"

"No one's 'gotta' do anything. Ever. Remember that. Here. Take your cup with you."

He guided her to a bedroom—he wasn't sure if it was hers, but that didn't seem to matter around here from the haphazard arrangement of the place.

When she was settled, sitting on the edge of a lumpy unmade bed with her knees together and the purse at her hip and both hands on the coffee mug like it was a very fragile teacup, Max went back into the living room and threw himself down on the couch, also lumpy and way too short for him.

He hadn't learned a dam thing, except that Raf Nadir was an angry man and he would be formidable if not caught by surprise.

HAIR APPARENT

"YOU DID THE DISHES."

Max looked up from wiping Rorschach patterns of spaghetti sauce from the microwave interior.

She stood in the archway between hall and kitchen, barefoot, wearing worn jeans and a knit top (no bra, and the better for it). He hadn't heard the shower, but she had washed her face (no makeup, and the better for it). She looked like somebody's sister.

"I chipped out some more instant coffee. Want some?"

"Oooh. I guess. If I can find something to go with it. Toast, maybe. Sorry the place is such a mess. With three of us coming and going . . . "

She edged onto one of the stools, content to let him forage.

Which he did. The bread was moldy, but he found a couple of frozen waffles and a crumb-crusted toaster.

"What's your working name?" he asked when he put the plate of waffles and a steaming mug of black coffee in front of her. The milk in the refrigerator was rancid.

She giggled. "I feel like I'm at a lunch counter. I use 'Mandy.' "

Mandy. From the upbeat seventies song by Barry Manilow? Mandy, who gave without taking? Elevator

281

music now, wordlessly familiar, if you were old enough to remember.

"You were right last night, Mandy. You can't go back."

"No." She pushed her hair behind one ear. "I'm a bad girl. Broke the rules and got caught leaving with a customer. They don't want us hooking.

"And you know why? Not on moral grounds. They just don't want you making money for yourself on the side.

"Listen. The girls are a great group. They've been so nice to me. Strippers aren't hookers, honest."

"Usually not, but they're not winners, either."

"Hey, the money is better than hooking."

"Yeah, you can make some money, but pretty soon it's gone on booze, or some biker boyfriend with a habit, and then there's that baby that just happened, or the two kids left over from that marriage right out of high school, and the money goes and there's nothing to show for it but this." He lifted his own coffee mug to toast the jumbled apartment. "And then, if it isn't drugs, it's drink."

She hung her head, hid behind the tangled hair. "I was shy when I started."

"You're still shy. And you're still not a drunk, or you wouldn't get so blown on those watered-down drinks. You could get out."

"And do what? At least at Secrets I'm somebody. I'm a dancer, in the spotlight. We all have our fans. We do!"

"At Secrets, you're somebody else. Some body. Mandy, who six months from now may be . . . Delilah at the place six blocks down the street. You want to wear high heels and look good and meet men? Get a job cruising the casinos with free drinks for players. It

282

doesn't pay like stripping, but you wouldn't have to get bombed to do it. And you wouldn't be under the thumb of some ugly customer like Raf Nadir."

She had picked up one of the warmed waffles, but bit her lip instead. "Why are you interested in him?"

She eyed his chest and Max suddenly remembered what he looked like: gold chain nestling in the requisite macho chest hair, velour top, bad hair.

"I'm not. Someone I know is. You know if he worked Tuesday night?"

"He works every night. He likes what he does."

"What hours?"

"I come in at nine, and he's there. He's there when I leave, usually one or so." She nibbled some waffle, then frowned. "He wasn't there one night, though. Was it Wednesday? Are you an undercover cop or something?"

"No."

"I know! A P.I."

He shrugged. Let her think what she wanted to.

"What'd Raf do?"

"Something bad, maybe. Who'd be able to swear he was gone Wednesday night?"

"Gosh, we all come and go. Larry the manager, I guess."

"What about Nadir? Was he gone that night?"

"No! That I remember. This NCO from Nellis got drunk and started pushing some girls around. Raf was in there like a tiger shark. How come you decked him?"

"I'm stronger than I look."

The phrase hit her in the morning-after mood. "I wish I could say that."

"You can. But it won't be easy, or pay well, or give you the false encouragement of sawbucks in your G-string. You'd have to quit the strip-club circuit and the alcohol, find a straight job, think about going to junior college maybe, find out what you're good at besides taking off your clothes, and develop that."

"I'm not very good at taking off my clothes, not like some of the other girls. Some of them are real pros."

"I know. Dancers. Then why don't they get a job in a casino show? Chorus girls don't wear much more than strippers and they're stars."

"Maybe my friends weren't good enough."

"Good enough dancers, or good enough to themselves? Mandy, I knew a guy who made a living photographing performers, including strippers. He said he never met one who hadn't been abused as a child."

Her eyes panicked and she took a quick swallow of coffee to hide her sudden terror.

"I know one thing. You can't make any of the changes I mentioned—and I think you could do all of them—until you deal with what's really scaring and scarring you."

"I can't afford a shrink!"

"There are counseling programs—"

"They stick their noses into everything. I don't trust them. I don't like talking about me. They always want to know your real name."

"And that's what you're running away from." Max nodded. He knew that game. "Think about it. Where are you going to dance tonight?"

"Oh, there's a club on the other side of town. I know some girls who work there. I can come in as . . . Delilah. That's hokey, you know?"

"I didn't have much time to think up a name. Listen, you really should talk to someone." Max felt a fiendish inspiration coming on. "Why don't you call one of those radio talk-show shrinks? That's as anonymous as you

284

can get."

"Dr. Laura would tear me to shreds."

"There's a local guy on WCOO. Mr. Midnight. That's when he's on."

"Midnight? I heard one of the girls saying something about that. Maybe. If I was near a phone where nobody could hear. Sometime. Oh—wasn't he the guy who . . . that girl in the motel? She was nuts, poor thing. I heard about that."

"See? He kept her from hurting someone else besides herself. That could have been you."

"I'm not nuts."

"No, but a few more years of this life and you will be."

She said nothing, her silence admitting the truth he'd spoken.

"Oh." She dug into the plastered-on jeans, finally tugging something from one front pocket. Max thought that this unconscious act was the most erotic move he'd seen her make yet. She held up the wad of ten dollar bills. "Sixty bucks. And you didn't get a dance, except with a bouncer. Here."

"No. You can keep it, if you don't spend it on booze. Maybe it's a nest egg for something else."

"I don't take money for nothing."

"I don't give money for nothing. I appreciate the information."

"I'm not a snitch either."

"How about it's a birthday present, for Delilah."

"Delilah! Well, I guess I'd give you a better haircut, if I could."

Max laughed. "Then do it."

"Really. Here? Now?"

"Maybe I'm launching a cosmetician."

285

"I do all the girls' hair." Something glimmered in her eyes. Hazel eyes that could focus perfectly well.

"Maybe. I'll have to wash that goop out."

"Just so long as you don't shave me bald."

"You'd really trust me to cut your hair?"

"Sure." Hair, unlike self-esteem, always grew back better than ever. "That's all you want me to do? Cut your hair?"

"Well, you could call Mr. Midnight. Tell him . . . tell him Mr. Magic sent you."

HAIR YESTERDAY, GONE TODAY

Su and Alch stood before Molina's desk, the not-quite-original Odd Couple. Both wore the strangely serene expressions of detectives who have done their duty and come back with something concrete, or at least interesting.

"Tell me about it," Molina said.

"She was everything we thought she would be . . . would have been," Su said. "Modest bungalow—"

"Quiet neighborhood," Alch put in.

"Kept a cat."

"There's something odd about that—"

"Nosy neighbor."

"Love those nosy neighbors."

"This one had a key to the place."

"We had no trouble getting in—"

"And, we may have found the actual murder scene."

"Or abduction scene."

Molina clapped her hands to end the recital. "I love it

when you two are in perfect harmony, but why do I get the feeling that some unanswered questions remain?"

"Because they always do, Lieutenant," Alch admitted happily.

"So what's wrong with this picture?"

"The neighbor lady, for one," Su put in sourly. "Noticed Miss Orth was gone, knew she hadn't mentioned anything about going out of town or looking after her cat or taking in the newspaper, but still didn't do anything about it."

"Not until the cats started acting up," Alch added.

"Miss Orth's cat and what other cat?"

"Well . . . "—Su consulted her notes—"this neighbor, Rosemary Jonas has this cat named Fanny, which was quite a pal of Miss Orth's tiger cat, Wilfred. Fanny began acting funny when Wilfrid wasn't coming out to play with her—"

"When?" Molina wanted to know.

Alch nodded. "The day after Miss Orth's body was found."

"So," Su said, "Miss Jonas just figured Miss Orth had taken off and left the cat at the vet's . . . until these two strange black cats—"

"Wait a minute." Molina planted her hands on the desktop. "Strange in behavior, or strangers to the neighborhood?" She knew her voice had gone taut.

"Both," Su said triumphantly.

Molina glanced at Alch, who shrugged. He no doubt remembered her remarks about the presence of black cats from the death-on-the-Nile scene at the Oasis not long before.

"So what did they do, these two black cats?" Molina asked in resignation.

"Now this is very interesting, Lieutenant. They both

287

went over to Miss Orth's house and kicked up a ruckus."

"How? Did they throw cherry bombs at the front porch? Slide down the chimney disguised as soot?"

"Well, first Fanny howled to go out, so Miss Jonas let her. Then, half an hour later, these two black cats she'd never seen before were yowling and jumping at the window that Fanny liked to sit in to watch for Wilfrid."

"Wouldn't stop," Alch put in.

"So Miss Jonas gets it in her head that the cats are trying to tell her something."

Alch leaped back in. "Every time she comes to the window to give them hell, they quit howling and run over toward Miss Orth's house, then stop halfway there and look back at her house."

Su: "She figures that Fanny has somehow gotten trapped in or near Miss Orth's house. So she gets the key—"

Alch: "And trots over after the cats."

Su: "Once she gets in—"

"And the door was unlocked, so the cats have eeled in with her," Alch says. "You know how cats will wrap themselves around your ankles and slip right into where you don't want them?"

"Yes, I know." Molina sounded even more resigned.

Su shot Alch an aggrieved look: This was her shaggy cat story. "The house smells musty and closed-up. A little ripe, too, like tomatoes left out on a countertop. Anyway, the cats are scampering through the rooms like they own the place, and lead her right into the bedroom."

Here Molina felt her spine stiffening. Scene of the crime coming up, stage-managed by her favorite feline suspects, Louie and Louise. Had to be them. Didn't know how, but it had to be them. Rats!

"That's when Miss Jonas starts to worry, and that's when she spots the dead body."

"Another dead body?"

Su nods, grimly satisfied. "Middle-age male, hazel eyes, average weight, about twelve pounds." After a second's pause, she giggles.

"Alch, get your partner something to sober her up. So the dead body is feline. Fanny?"

"I forgot to mention that Fanny was a"—notes consulted again, and then quoted—" 'such a gorgeous girl, all white with one blue eye and one gold.' "

"Wilfrid," Molina diagnosed. "And getting a trifle rank? Then he'd been dead since the victim was last at the house. Was he . . . a case for the LVMPD, Su?"

"Maybe a victim of death by misadventure. Maybe not. Because Miss Jonas ran home to call animal control to pick up the body. And when the pound people got there the next day—you know pound people—"

"The cat was gone." Alch stole the punch line.

Su sighed mightily and frowned at him.

"Dead cat walking?" Molina wanted to know. "And what became of those two black tattletails?"

Su shut her notebook with a dramatic slap of cardboard on paper. "Vanished, Lieutenant. Like they'd never been there. Like the dead cat. Except that the absent Wilfrid left a distinct odor of Old Mice."

"Your theory?" Molina eyed each detective in turn.

"Either the neighbor lady was a tad hysterical and mistook a rag rug for a dead cat," Alch said.

"Or someone removed the dead cat's body," Su suggested, "maybe to disguise the time of death. Er, Miss Orth's, not the cat's."

"Or the cat wasn't dead and walked out on its own,"

289

Molina added. "Hair and Fibers ought to have a high old time on this one. I hope nobody on that detail is allergic to cats."

"Then you want us to treat the house like a crime scene? Even if the only victim, maybe, was a cat?"

"I want H & F to go over it like it was the last crime scene of Jack the Ripper. And tell them I don't want one hair—and especially one cat hair—overlooked. If we can do DNA on human hair, we can do it on feline hair."

"DNA!" Su was alarmed. "You wouldn't, Lieutenant. We'd be laughingstocks."

"I will if I have to, so I suggest you figure out what went on there, and to what species, from the physical evidence alone. Got it?"

Su nodded and escaped into the hall.

Alch leaned his hands on Molina's desk and spoke confidentially. "What is it with you and cats? First the Oasis; now here."

Molina answered as confidentially, with a grim smile. "You ever think maybe I'm a witch, huh, Alch? I bet I've been called that around here before now. You know, upwardly mobile via broomstick?"

He backed off, and beat a hasty retreat with Su.

Molina took a deep breath. Stupid as it would seem, those cats had been up to something. She had a feeling that if the feeble humans figured out what, they would be a little closer to when and where Monica Orth had been killed. Maybe even why.

Sure, the conviction was nuts, but a cop went on instinct, and these particular cats had given her plenty of reason to have instincts about their often-bizarre behavior.

So Su her.

290

STAKEOUT

NIGHT HAS FALLEN BEFORE I SEE HIDE OR HAIR OF
Midnight Louise again, and I would not have done that,
except that the canine version of a night light, Mr. Nose
E. Byrd, is trotting alongside her.

I have the sensitivity not to ask what trash
compacter they hitched a ride in, and greet them in the
Circle Ritz parking lot after a wearing day of checking
on the whereabouts of Mr. Matt Devine every hour or
so.

"Where have you two been? Reno?"

Nose E.'s tongue is hanging down to his droopy ear-
ends. "Where is the national emergency, dude? This
spitfire has herded me here like a sheep to the
slaughterhouse."

I can see that Nose E.'s coat is sadly bedraggled. His
long, usually silky white locks twist and kink as if he has
been rode hard—through the Caesars Palace fountains,
for instance—and put up wet.

I nod at Louise. She looks like something you try not
to see flattened by the side of the road.

"Do not ask and we will not bore you by telling,"
Midnight Louise snaps.

The normally amiable Nose E. adds his own snap and
growl for emphasis. "Our only choice of transportation
was a bottled-water service van. Not only did we stop
at every other house, but an irresponsible left turn
broke a water container. I nearly drowned."

I tsk-tsk my sympathy, but the fact is that an
overturned teacup would almost be enough to drown
Nose E.

"If I had not nipped him by the scruff of the neck," Miss Louise says, "and clawed my way atop a carton, he would have drowned. Unfortunately, he weighs a lot more sopping wet than he does dry!"

"I fear that my coat is permanently crimped at the nape." Nose E. turns to present his rear. "Is that true, Louie?"

"A trifle . . . bent. Nothing that a good mother's lick would not cure."

"That is the trouble! I do not have a mother any more, and Earl E. is too nearsighted to notice. I do not suppose that you—?"

I jerk my head at Louise. This is woman's work. She scowls, but leans over to lick Nose E.'s neck hairs into a wet, slicked-down condition that should dry straight.

"Here is the deal," I tell the game little professional sniffer. "I know that Mr. Matt Devine has been near the same scent that we all detected at the scene of Wilfrid's death. Mr. Matt Devine obviously does not know he has been rubbing pant legs with a murderer."

"What is wrong with these human noses?" Nose E. bursts out. "Are they blocks of salt? Stone? Granite? I do not get how they can rule the planet with such deficient senses."

"It is deficient *sense* that is their greatest lack," Midnight Louise sniffs, lying down to slick back her toe hairs.

I cannot disagree, but have no time to debate human failings.

"I cannot tell you why humans have such poor excuses for snouts, just as I cannot tell you why dogs have noses a thousand times more sensitive than a human's, and cats have the edge in the brains and personality department. It is a fluke of natural selection, so I have naturally selected you, Nose E., as the key figure in our desperate attempt to right wrongs and save lives human and feline, and maybe canine."

While Miss Louise continues administering her best tongue-lashing, I inquire, "You do sport the usual dog collar under all that hair, right, Nose E.?"

"Arf course," he admits, then growls, "Damn red tape."

"Looks blue to me," I note as I glimpse the phantom collar through a blizzard of white hair. "With the usual rabies tag listing the date of injection?"

Nose E. whimpers in humiliation. "The ace drug-and-bomb-sniffer in the country, and I must be certified sane and disease-free! You would think I had a social disease, just for being a dog."

Well, if the stereotype fits . . . but I say nothing. Sometimes a dog can be useful.

"And do you also wear a bright blue aluminum metal tag on which your name and your, er, affiliate's phone number are emblazoned?"

"I would be picked up and subjected to unmentionable indignities if I did not. Besides, because of my sensitive work clearance, all my papers must be in perfect order."

"Stop badgering the poor little rug-rat sniffer!" Midnight Louise bursts out. "Of course he is collared and labeled. He is a dog. He cannot help it!"

I nod. "He cannot help it. And therefore he will be of inestimable value in this case."

Nose E. starts panting hopefully. "Really?"

"Really." I almost give him a cat smile. Almost. Cat smiles are extremely rare, and best noticed in passing, like mirages. Like the Purr of Power, cat smiles are potent beyond imagining, and I rarely employ them.

Only in matters of life and death.

I nod, one last question to be asked. "And I also suppose that Earl E. is careful enough to have you wear a tag that lists your name, address, and phone number, if it does not reveal your undercover status?"

"Yes, yes, yes!" Nose E. is panting with impatience now and bouncing up and down on the pads of his feet. "Now that I am here, what is my job?"

I glance up at the blank windows of the Circle Ritz. Behind one of them lurks our target.

"The timing is awkward," I say. "Perhaps it would be better to wait until morning."

"Wait until morning!" the pair chorus in pipsqueak indignation.

"After all we went through to get here?" Louise demands all by herself.

"In the meantime," I tell Nose E., "you can put your schnozzola to work and see if you pick up the scent I do, and if it leads where I think it does."

"Hmmf," he yaps, bending head and nose to the ground. After a few circles in the parking lot he snuffles along like a pig after truffles to the small shed at the rear of the lot.

"Sweet smell. Sickly smell," he declares.

"A dead smell?" Miss Louise wonders.

"Tut-tut. Nothing of the kind. It is one of those smells that some humans adore, and that other humans loathe. Odd lot, humans. Dividing smells into likes and dislikes, when they are all of equal use. Of course, their nasal abilities are nil. I do not know why they even bothered to grow noses. They might as well not have them, for all the olfactory skill they exhibit."

"Yes," Louise says. "We know how superior your nose is. If it were any more superior it would be so

294

high in the air you would trip on your ears and never get anywhere at all."

I can see that several hours in each other's company under stress has raveled the relationship.

"Hush," I admonish. "This shed is locked, but it contains a motorcycle. If we could follow its trail into the past, I am sure that we would ultimately find the human who bears the sick-sweet smell."

"I have not heard of any time-traveling motorcycles," Miss Louise notes. "World-class nose or not, we can only go forward in time. Nose E. cannot follow the trail all through Las Vegas."

He is now in the regulation Sherlock-Holmes-human-bloodhound posture, crawling over the ground, nose only centimeters from scraping itself off. "I could follow it for some distance, but once too many scents overlay the trail, I would be as lost as any housecat. Or even a human."

I ignore the jibe at housecats, because neither Miss Midnight Louise or myself is one, not by any attenuation of the imagination.

"We can only hope that Mr. Matt Devine will once again be in contact with the scent-bearer."

"We can only hope?" Miss Midnight Louise's huge golden eyes regard me with astonishment. "If you are right, we are to hope that Mr. Matt puts himself in the vicinity of a murderer."

"It will not be the first time," I answer briskly. "You forget that he has had that dubious honor before, and survived. Now. Nose E., I want you to follow that scent into the Circle Ritz and to whatever door it leads you."

Marching orders do much for the notoriously undisciplined dog. Nose E. puts nose to the ground and makes circular snail tracks right to the round building's side door.

"You know where he is going," Miss Louise points out from her position at my side.

"I want to make sure that the Nose knows where he is going. If we are going to rely upon a dog, I want to ensure that he is in working order.

"Now," I tell Nose E., speaking slowly and clearly. "I will introduce you into Mr. Matt's domain. It is up to you from there on. You must . . . doggedly . . . you do understand the expression 'doggedly'?"

"Oh, yes, Mr. Midnight." Pant, pant, pant.

Well, they can be disgusting, but they mean so well.

"You must doggedly cling to the scent I mentioned— the scent on his pant leg. You must stop for nothing. You must be indomitable."

"Yes!"

"All right, Sergeant Nose E. I will lead you to the arena. Remember! Sniff, cling, and be cute!"

He nods, sending his topknot into a cascade of cute.

Four pounds. I could snack on him. But there is that world-class nose. Touch not the Nose. *Quelle domage!* as the Divine Yvette would say.

"What a sucker," Midnight Louise observes as she watches Nose E. trot up to the Circle Ritz door. "I must say that you have a way with canines, old man."

"Experience," I admit.

Nose E., of course, has no notion of how to open the door. He just sits there as if waiting for Santa Claus, who will not be passing this way again for around eleven months.

"That is the human door," I tell him. "The cat door is thisaway, up the palm tree to the third-floor balcony."

"Palm tree?" he squeaks. "I may have some rudimentary nails, but these claws were not made for climbing. I will have to find another way in."

Louise snorts. "There is no sense in all of us waiting out here until morning. It can get chilly."

"And my undercoat is still damp," Nose E. adds with a ferocious sneeze. "I am not used to alfresco adventures. I am an indoor dog. I could catch pneumonia."

Louise and I exchange glances. The little canine is right. We do not want the best Nose in the business sniffling its last on the stoop of the Circle Ritz.

We realize what we must do, distasteful as it is.

We curl up next to Nose E., one on one side, one on the other.

"Go to sleep," I tell him. "We will get in tomorrow morning when someone comes out and lets us in."

"I am used to sleeping alone in a flannel bed filled with cedar chips."

"You *are* sleeping alone," Miss Louise informs him. "Think of us as guard-cats. We are virtually invisible at night. Besides, I will uncrimp your neck hair again in the morning."

"Oh, thank you, thank you! I cannot bear to have my coat mussed. I will try to sleep, even though I have strange bedfellows."

He is almost instantly wheezing softly through his precious nose.

Louise and I shake our sagacious feline heads. What we do for the greater good!

We put our put-upon heads down upon our paws and drift into instant sleep, an Oreo cookie of fur. Only those who have dozed next to wet dog hair know what a sacrifice we are making.

WORKING IT OUT

MAX FACED THE VARIOUS APPARATUSES IN THE corner of Gandolph's den with the trepidation of a heretic being confronted with the torture instruments of the Inquisition.

There was nothing medieval or even magical about this gear: a gleaming steel jungle-gym arrangement of weights, pulleys, and hand grips. A home workout center.

He could tell by a hitch in his shoulder, a strain in his leg, that the months of inactivity since he had deserted the fanatically fit condition of a practicing magician were beginning to show. No more shrugging off an attacker without feeling it afterward. It was only sensible to prepare for more of same.

Still, this was a momentous occasion: For the first time in his life, merely keeping busy doing what he did wasn't keeping him in shape. Like all sedentary people in their mid-thirties, he would have to work at it.

Max sighed, aimed the remote control at the big-screen TV across the room, and zapped it with enough oomph that he might as well have been shooting at it. Being forced to consider exercise for its own sake made him want to shoot at something. But, no, he would make like a traveling executive in a hotel exercise room and blend the morning news with his morning routine.

Max began fiddling with settings and weights, trying to decide where to begin. He had heard enough about working out with weights that he felt confident enough to avoid the ignominy of a local health club. Besides, he needed to keep out of sight as much as possible. He had found Garry's workout sweats in a closet, and though his late mentor had been a much bulkier man, the gray shorts tied with a cotton string adjusted to any width.

Now. All he had to do was get some sweat on the sweats.

Max sat down on the bench and began with arm presses, three sets of ten, breathing in on the out-stroke, out on the in-stroke.

The president, a perky female newscaster was informing him, had made headway during trade talks with Korea. The perky male newscaster came on soon after to narrate footage of a celebrity golf tournament at Caesars Palace.

You would think these were still the Reagan years.

Max rearranged himself facing away from the TV to do some leg lifts. After the first couple of lifts, he paused to add an extra twenty pounds of weight.

"Another death overnight . . . " the male anchor was droning . . . the dead stripper—"

Max turned so fast to face the TV that he felt the sudden burn of a neck spasm. Wouldn't you know he would get a sports injury watching television—

" . . . has been identified as Cher Smith. She was making her first appearance at Baby Doll's last night when she was killed."

The screen flashed the color photo from Cher's driver's license.

Max stared at the TV long after the cheerful female anchor's impeccably made-up face had replaced the pathetic assembly-line photo of a face he had first seen only thirty-six hours ago. He knew his hand was absently massaging his twisted neck, but he couldn't feel anything, pain or relief, only numbing disbelief.

And then anger.

He got up so fast the suspended weights crashed to

ground zero like a freight train hitting a metal wall.

Even the harsh sound couldn't penetrate his almost self-hypnotic state.

Furious, and thinking furiously, he only knew he needed more information—fast. He had always needed more information, he realized with the sick certainty of hindsight, and Molina, damn her, had not seen fit to give it to him.

She would now. Whether she saw fit or not.

THREE FOR THE RAILROADED

"TEMPLE. I MUST SEE YOU. RIGHT AWAY."

"Max! Well, sure, but—"

"I'm sorry, I can't explain over the phone. It's a matter of life and death. Don't worry," he added bitterly. "It's all over. Both the life and the death. You've got to help me."

"Max, I will. Your place or—?"

"Yours. Getting myself there will distract me. Twenty minutes."

He hung up, and Temple stared at the receiver.

Something terrible had happened.

She glanced at her watch. Getting there might distract Max, but what could she do to make the minutes fly? She went over to the tape machine and rewound it. She'd started recording Matt's show, having missed the really important one, his debut. Nothing like recording the horse's hooves after it had tap-danced out of the barn.

But now was as good a time as any to see—nay,

hear—what Mr. Midnight was all about.

Temple sat cross-legged on the floor by the machine, still in the living room where Matt had played the fateful first tape from Ambrosia only a week ago, and listened.

Listening to talk-radio counseling was like eavesdropping, she decided five minutes into the tape. That illicit act was doubly enthralling for being able to hear Matt's counseling technique. Knowing him, she didn't quite know him as radio shrink, but he sounded good, and his advice seemed sound, and, from the number of female callers he got, Ambrosia had been right that she had needed to provide something for the girls.

No life and death fireworks animated last night's tape. Temple's concentration broke. Life and death. Whose life and death were "all over," and why was Max so upset?

She clenched her hands and sneaked a peak at her watch, which she had resolved to ignore. Ten minutes gone; ten more to endure. Just close her eyes and listen to Matt . . . Max would be here when he said he would. He knew the road time between her place and his the way a good magician knew his illusions down to the split second.

One knock. Imperative. On the dot. Twenty minutes.

Temple unwound herself—ouch; her left leg had gone to sleep—and hobbled to the door.

Max sprang in when she opened it like a jack-in-the-box desperately seeking release.

"I could strangle Molina," he confessed, starting to pace in her hallway and continuing into the living room. "You've got to explain that dame to me. I thought I was playing a genteel game of chess with her, and now she's made me into a murderer."

"Max, for God's sake! Calm down. Sit down." Temple hustled to keep pace with seven-league strides back and forth in the living room.

"What's the matter with you?" He stared at her leg as if it were a prime suspect. "Are you hurt? Is there something you're hiding from me? You weren't attacked too?"

"Only by pins and needles."

"And what have you got on the air?"

"A tape. Of Matt's show."

Max finally stopped still to stare at her, as if *she* were mad.

"Matt Devine."

"I know his last name."

"He's on the radio."

"Well, then turn him off. We need to talk."

Temple hastened to do exactly that. "About Molina?" she asked while on the run . . . or limp, rather.

Max was striding back and forth again, running nervous fingers through his hair. His hair.

"Max, what on earth did you do to your hair?"

He stared at her as if "hair" were a foreign word, then his agitation collapsed into despair. He sank onto the sofa, driving his face into the palms of his hands as if they were very welcome blinders.

Temple sat, gingerly, beside him. "Max." Her voice was barely a whisper. "What's happened?"

"My hair. A tale that hangs on a hair." He turned hollow eyes on Temple. She had never seen him so haunted, not even when he had discussed his Irish past. "I let Molina use me, thinking I was using her, and now somebody's dead."

"Who?"

"Did you hear or see the news this morning?"

"No, but I've got a morning *Review Journal* I haven't looked at yet."

"It may have happened too late to make the newspaper. Probably well after midnight. I'd bet she was waylaid in the parking lot, like the other victims."

"Other? You're not talking about . . . Strawberry Lady and Church Parking Lot Lady?"

Now Max gazed at Temple as if she were mad in her own turn. "You know about those murders?"

She nodded, slowly. "Yes, but how do you?"

"Molina." He might have been saying the word *hemlock,* it came off his lips with such a bitter twist. "She recruited me to do a little discreet snooping. I figured if I did her a favor, I could get some favors from her in the future. She said he was a fringe suspect. Out of L.A. An ex-cop gone bad. I confirmed all that, and then I tracked him here to Las Vegas."

"So that's what you were doing when you were gone and said you couldn't tell me why! Working for Molina?"

Max nodded glumly.

Temple studied his downcast head. His hair wasn't so bad if you were willing to accept Max in that semi-punk look, which she wasn't. But after the bullet had restyled his ponytail, she could see why he'd had it cut.

"Did that Strip shooting have anything to do with this guy you were trailing for Molina?"

"Could have. Could be something else. Anything else. You know my fabled ability to make friends and influence people."

"Max." She curled her hand over his knee, shook it slightly. "Don't be so hard on yourself. Just tell me how you ended up working for Molina, of all people!"

He flashed her a rueful glance, with some of the usual

bite. "I didn't tell you because that was the terms of working for Molina, and . . . I didn't want to admit I'd gone over to the enemy, even just a little. I know how hard-nosed she's been with you, but she's a necessary evil, Temple, and she knows enough about some of the stuff going on in this town to be useful. I thought."

"So, what went wrong?"

"I'm glad you can stick to a rational exposition of the subject. Okay. This guy seems to be everything Molina said: a low-profile trouble-maker, but not a major player. I tracked him to a strip club, where he worked as a bouncer."

She nodded, not wanting to disrupt his story. But she was thinking: *Bouncer? Strip club? Max?*

Max was wringing his hands, wound up with tension, washing his hands like Pontius Pilate.

Oh, God, Temple thought. *This is really serious.*

Suddenly his wringing hands burst apart, like freed birds.

"I found a 'source' at the club. A young stripper. Not even a stripper. Some girl trying to drink enough to pretend to be a stripper.

"She was easy to ask about Nadir. So I did. And, then, I felt sorry for her. They can seem so brassy, but they don't have much self-esteem, strippers."

"I know."

"How do you know?"

"I did PR for a strippers' contest. While you were . . . gone. In some ways they're liberated ladies; in some ways they're perpetual schmucks. Really confusing."

He nodded. "Maybe that's why I got confused. Was I an undercover operative, or a social worker? I decided to get her out of there. Part of it was I wanted to interrogate her privately. Part of it was, she was really drunk, and I thought if she needed to be that drunk to do this, maybe she could do something else."

"So—?"

"I didn't learn that much. But Nadir confronted me when I picked her up. I . . . blew her welcome there. She had to go to a new club. I never did learn anything much from her." Matt stared at the magazines and mail on Temple's coffee table as if they held the Holy Writ of the Synth and needed decoding. "I planted some suggestions for a normal life. I left. She was going to have to work at another club the next night. When she did, she died. It said so on the morning news."

"Oh, Max."

"You're not . . . dubious about my consorting with a stripper?"

"No. I wanted to take a few home myself."

"Temple. You are incredible. I came over here half-ready to explain myself, and you already know."

"So why are you so mad at Molina?"

"Probably because I'm so mad at myself. But she didn't indicate this guy could be a serious candidate for the parking lot murders. She was so laid back: 'Just find out what happened to him in L.A., where he's gone . . . "

"He's gone, all right! Gone all the way to Las Vegas. And now I can't help thinking—him being the control freak that he is, and my snatching away one of his docile charges—he might have tried to get her back the only way he knew how to make sure of her. Dead."

" 'He's gone,' " Temple repeated, as if in a trance. "Not so different from 'she left.' "

"Yeah, she left. She left the club. With me. Now she's dead. She was just a kid, Temple. Just a baby."

"Shhh." Temple was thinking. "The woman who was

found dead in the Blue Dahlia parking lot—did you know that the words 'she left' were found on Molina's car door, beside the body?"

"Yeah, I heard that. But that's such a signature of the abusive male." Max lifted his head, inhaled air as if it were a drug. "Yes! The same pattern. Damn bloody Molina! A third, and probably unnecessary, death."

"Maybe. Maybe not."

"Why do you say that?"

Temple took a deep breath. "I think we should bring Matt in on this discussion. Matt Devine."

"I know the bloody name! I don't know why we should bring him in."

"Because Molina hasn't just been calling you in on the case. She's been using Matt, and me, too."

"Bloody hell!"

Temple nodded. "Maybe we've all been patsies. And maybe Molina is a patsy too. Let me try to call Matt."

"Oh? It's so difficult to reach him, one floor above?"

"Jealousy does not become you. While you've been busy working for Molina, Matt's been busy becoming a media celeb. Oprah wants him."

Max frowned. "*That* Oprah?"

"The very one." Temple had picked up the phone on the coffee table and was dialing. "But maybe he can manage to make a little time for us." She winked.

Max just shook his head. But his eyes had focused beyond his own guilt and grief. Wild Irish Grief. Temple was glad she hadn't been there when his cousin had died . . . and then she was sorry that she hadn't.

Matt was in, reluctant to come down for a consultation with Max without knowing why, but finally game.

"So." Temple hung up the phone. "Tell me about the

hair."

He shrugged. "I had it cut, badly, on purpose, for my role of sleaze-about-town at Secrets." His expression softened. "Then I was talking to Cher, and it seemed she had once cherished ambitions of being a cosmetologist. So I let her clean it up. She really did a good job. You should have seen it before this."

"I'm glad I didn't." Temple carefully touched his hair. "You only tried to help her."

"And may have killed her."

"Maybe not. There's a bigger picture to all of this, Max, and I know, because I've glimpsed it from several angles. Your story just added a new one."

"What bigger angle? These killings are visceral; the work of one madman."

Temple's shrug conceded nothing. "We all have different pieces of the puzzle; yours is just the newest. I discovered who victim number two was."

"Is that the woman you call Parking Lot Lady?"

"Umhmm. Found in a fringe church parking lot. A real Las Vegas type, Spandex leopard-skin leggings and plastic surgery scars." Max made a face. "Don't typecast her, you may have known her once."

"I might know another victim?"

"Her name was Gloria Fuentes." When he continued looking blank, Temple went on. "She used to be Gandolph's assistant, for years, when he was practicing magic."

"No, I didn't know her. But I've seen photographs. She'd be . . . fifty-something by now."

"Only her plastic surgeon knew for sure."

"How did you manage to identify her?"

This time Temple wrung her hands, with hesitation. "Well, you were out of town so much, and I was concerned about those weird messages on your computer, so I went to the UNLV to consult Professor Mangel. He has a history-of-Las-Vegas-magic exhibit over there. In the meantime, Molina had put a sketch of the unidentified victim in the newspaper, which I always read assiduously, and there she was, waiting on the wall for me to identify like a suspect in a vintage lineup."

"But, but if Gandolph's former assistant was a victim—?"

"Then the killings could tie into Gandolph somehow. If only we knew who the first woman killed was. But I did learn something else very interesting from the professor: The same cast of creepy characters from the Halloween séance are all in town right now; there's a psychic conference going on at the Opium Den."

Max's face registered a rainbow of emotions ranging from surprise to suspicion to rejection. Before it had run through the full spectrum of expressions, the doorbell rang through its mellow changes.

For once, Temple wanted to scream at it to shut up after the first note, but she jumped up and raced to the door instead.

"We've had some upsetting news," Temple greeted Matt, by way of warning him. She rolled her eyes toward the living room.

She watched the wariness in his eyes become extreme wariness.

"There's been a third woman killed," Temple explained, not wanting Max to have to go through a personal recital again. "She was found in a strip-joint parking lot, and this time her ID was left on her. Max knows who she was. He ran into her while looking into something. And the second victim? I found out that she used to be Garry Randolph's assistant; you know, the stage magician Gandolph."

"The guy who was killed not long ago?" Matt sat down on the sofa without exchanging any territorial looks with Max; he was too taken aback to worry about it.

Temple nodded. "It looks like two of the three victims have a very remote connection to . . . us." Matt didn't know that Gandolph had been Max's mentor in areas magical, and otherwise. Nor that Max was living in the house that had belonged to Gandolph.

"Then"—Matt was still flabbergasted—"it's even worse. Molina told me she'd figured out the identity of the first woman from the Blue Dahlia . . . and she was a former nun."

"Did you know her?" Max asked.

"I don't think so, but I might have run into her. Molina's checking into her background. She was beginning to think the killer was stalking the ex-religious, but this magician's assistant wasn't in the convent ever, was she?"

"Highly unlikely," Max stated. "But look at the range: an ex-nun to a stripper, and a showgirl in betwcen. 'She left.' A nun had to leave the convent. A former magician's assistant left the profession. The stripper had just left working at one place, for another."

"Was she strangled?" Temple asked.

Max was still trying to piece together a pattern. "Who?"

"The stripper."

"I don't know. The newscast didn't say."

"It's even weirder," Temple added. "The words 'she left' appeared on the body of Gloria Fuentes after the autopsy. It looks like a magic trick."

"Or an afterthought," Matt said quickly. "But who would have known the details of the Blue Dahlia killing but the killer?"

Temple looked from one man to the other. "We need to find out how much the latest slaying imitates, and differs, from the previous two. The best source of that information is Molina. Who wants to ask her?"

"Me." Max spoke grimly. "That woman owes me answers."

"I don't know, Max. She *is* armed and dangerous, after all, and I might be inclined to look toward my own self-defense if ambushed by you in the state you're in now. Besides, I doubt if she'll respond to your kind of pressure. Matt—or even I—might baby it out of her more readily."

Max stood. "This has gone past the point of babying anybody." He glanced from Temple to Matt, and back. "I'll tell her I'm representing a collective." He strode out of the room and a moment later the front door snapped open, then shut. Like this case sure wasn't.

Temple let out a long breath.

"He seems edgy," Matt noted.

"He's more than edgy. He had . . . interviewed the dead stripper just last night."

"Interviewed her? He was planning to hire one? Why?"

"He was making private inquiries for our dear Lieutenant Molina."

"That's ridiculous! She wouldn't trust him to investigate her trash bill."

"Yeah. I couldn't believe she'd do that either. And I wish she hadn't." Temple found her lower lip between her teeth and released it.

"Why?"

"Max feels the stripper's death is his fault."

"Is he right?"

"I hope not," Temple said. She started to sit down in Max's vacated sofa spot, then remembered it was the scene of an indiscretion and managed to sit on the arm instead. "So. What's happening with you, besides fame and fortune?"

He looked as if she'd just threatened to hold the soles of his feet to burning coals.

GONE YESTERDAY, HAIR TODAY

"WE'VE GOT A SCENARIO, LIEUTENANT."

"Then sell it to Hollywood," Molina told Alch. He was on the phone.

"We thought you might want to come out here and look it over for yourself."

"So you've got a weird scenario."

"This *is* Las Vegas, after all."

"I know where I am. I just hope you and Su do. Okay. What's the address again? I'll be there as soon as I can. Do we need to send any cat hair to Quantico?"

"Negative. We've got enough of it here to do the job."

It was nearly five P.M. before Molina could get away from headquarters. She'd questioned the detectives on the previous night's stripper slaying. Was it related to the other parking lot deaths? But the victim's purse and driver's license had been left at the scene, and the strangling looked manual. No knife in the throat.

Women were accosted and killed all the time. This murder didn't seem to be related, thank God. Then the Captain had wanted to know her progress on the previous two deaths. He was not particularly intrigued by the missing cat corpse on Randall street, but she hadn't expected him to be.

She took her own car out to the crime scene. Mariah was at Delores's house (and complaining bitterly about not needing a "sitter" anymore). Maybe they'd go out for pizza tonight. Someplace loud with hijinks, though Mariah would protest that she was "too old" for kid stuff. Well, her mother was too old for kid stuff too, but sometimes there was no way out of it.

Molina was pleased to see the Hair and Fibers van still there. At least *they* were taking this seriously.

She parked by the curb and moved toward the simple one-story house, rented probably. "Modest" hardly described the genteel poverty of life on this block of mostly aging owners, people who had been lucky to have homes of their own after World War II, and who had grown old and out-of-date with the neighborhood.

Rocks on the roof. Molina loved that desert habit, that innocent, pre-ecological use of nature as a shelter against the heat. The lot's soil was sandy and weedy, not the thick mats of green bought at the cost of piped-in water in the trendier suburbs.

That's why she lived in the city. It had character. It showed its wrinkles and was proud of them. Wrinkles were history.

And this house had a history. A recent history, written by the events enacted inside. A cat had died. Maybe. A resident had died, certainly. But where? And why?

Su and Alch greeted her like shining schoolchildren paid a visit by the principal. That was spelled as in your

312

"pal," not "ple."

"You were right, Lieutenant," Su said, beaming. "The cat hairs tell the tale."

"Oh?"

"Look here." Su led her into the bedroom. Alch followed.

Molina had donned a pair of her latex gloves, though she wasn't sure she'd be handling anything. Never hurt.

"The cat was definitely dead," Sue reported happily, indicating the bedside rag rug. "We've found fluid stains on the rug. It's only February, but still warm enough that decay sets in on its inevitable course."

"Could be a title for the screenplay," Alch suggested. *"Inevitable Course."*

Su's glance was scathing. "A very interesting thing, Lieutenant." She was all business: rookie detective graduated from efficiency school. "Several hairs on the rug: yellow, brown, black."

"Obviously from a tiger cat."

"Thank you, Detective Alch," Molina said, "but I'll wait for the obvious to be pointed out to me by Detective Su, who's so good at it." Smile.

They grinned. They had gotten into her improbable "scenario" of tracking the cat hair, and it had produced results. Now they prepared to exhibit those results in all their incongruous glory.

"Also found on the rug were three gray hairs."

"Monica Orth's?"

"We think so. And a number of . . . stray black hairs."

"The murderer's," Molina suggested delicately.

"The cats'," Alch put in, impatient. Men had no finesse when it came to the ridiculous.

"The rug has been moved!" Su was so proud of herself.

313

"Moved. Very good, Su. Where?"

"The trail leads to the side door."

"And?"

"And back again," Alch put in like a prosecuting attorney making the fatal point.

"Back again?" Molina was surprised.

"What if someone . . . some entity," Su corrected, "had dragged the victim—"

"The feline victim," Alch was quick to amend.

Molina nodded, listening.

Su gathered herself for the final revelation. "Had dragged the, er, dead cat, to the door and rolled it out, and then dragged the rug back to the bedside."

"I'd say you had a very inexplicable scenario. Why?"

"So as not to raise suspicions."

"That's good. Always a viable motive. So what happened to the dead cat?"

"We think it was buried," Alch said, with a gulp.

"Buried?"

"On the premises," Su added, squaring her shoulders.

"By the . . . draggers."

"Oh, definitely."

"There was more than one dragger?"

"From the quantity of hairs, yes." Su produced a plastic Baggie in which reposed a few fine curves of black hair, long and short.

"Aren't any of the hairs on the scene, besides the obligatory gray ones, human?" Molina had not meant to sound wistful, and deeply regretted her tone.

Su and Alch exchanged consulting glances. "Yes. We have three. Brown, but not from the feline victim."

Molina nodded. That's what detective lieutenants did a lot of.

"Getting back to the rag-rug trail," Su said. "We have

indications that the feline victim was rolled down the stairs and into the rear yard—"

"Where another variety of hair was detected," Alch put in.

"Another variety of hair." Molina was intrigued. "In color or in . . . species."

"Both," said Sue. "It was white."

Molina could have spit up a hairball. With the precision of the trained investigator.

"These hairs were white—"

"White?"

"Yes, Lieutenant, and they were not feline."

"I don't think I can take much more suspense."

"Nor should you have to," Alch agreed. "The hairs were long, fine, and . . . canine. According to Wertz in H & F."

"Canine. Did anyone witness—?"

"No." Alch huffed out a breath like a winded horse. "Luckily, no. But . . . digging was done."

"Show me."

They took her to the edge of the rear yard, a scraggly affair of ungoverned cactus and islands of ground cover.

"An attempt was made to brush leaves over the gravesite."

She nodded at Alch's observation. "And we will find below—?"

"The late Wilfrid, I am sure of that." Su gathered herself for an official verdict. "I believe that, from this poor animal's death, we will be able to establish the time of the attack upon his mistress, and the time of her death."

Molina nodded, looking at the innocent plot of ground.

"Do you recommend an autopsy?" Alch asked.

She stared at him in disbelief. "What do you think, man? We owe Grizzly Bahr the autopsy of a career."

They grinned.

"And tell him I want a complete report."

"And the black and white hairs, Lieutenant?" Alch inquired humbly.

"You drink, don't you, Detective?"

"Er, once in a while. Off duty."

"Then I think you owe yourself a good stiff black and white this evening. Off duty. And take Su." Molina turned to leave, then paused. "And, please. No catty stories about this investigation behind my back, right?"

"Absolutely, Lieutenant." Su practically put up her hand in the Girl Scout pledge position. "Our lips are seal-pointed."

DEAD RECKONING

IT'S A TERRIBLE THING TO DRIVE A DUMP TRUCK FULL of righteous rage with no place to dump it all day.

Max's suppressed energy level would have fueled a Titan rocket, but there was very little he could do about confronting Molina until he could get her alone.

First he drove by and into the police headquarters parking garage. The challenge shaved off some of his raw edges, and he was pleased to note her repainted Toyota station wagon wedged between a Datsun and a Chevy.

Dreadful car, but nobody would steal it.

His own car for all of a day, a beige Acura, purred as it idled out of the garage. Nothing like mounting a nefarious expedition at the heart of police headquarters for soothing the savage soul.

316

He then drove home, went to the computer, and pulled up her home address from the police personnel files. He'd never be a world-class hacker, but his tutors in the underground had made him just competent enough to be a danger to other people, and himself, for that matter.

He liked picturing the drama of confronting her at the Blue Dahlia again, maybe even showing up for the evening's musicale and sitting there like a hanging judge through the whole act . . . but there was no guarantee she'd be slipping out as Carmen tonight, and she'd have to stop at home first anyway.

So, since he couldn't predict her working hours, staking out the place from four P.M. on should work. The notion of waylaying an officer of the law was satisfying. He wasn't really a renegade, but after all his years of working without a net, he had developed a tinge of contempt for the official detective, bound by rule books and Miranda rights. Breaking and entering for a good cause had always been the best part of his odd avocation.

In fact, he could greet her *inside* the house; that would catch her off guard. No, Temple had been right. Molina was armed and dangerous, and for all his risky history, he had rarely gone armed; better not to aggravate the dragon inside her cave, where he had less room to maneuver.

He called up a street map of Las Vegas to confirm her house location; very near Our Lady of Guadalupe Church.

A NOSE FOR NEWS

"GOODNESS, HOW ABSOLUTELY CUTE!"

I awake, cringing, to these demeaning words.

Daylight has broken to reveal Electra Lark and muumuuu standing in the open doorway, looming over us like a Hawaiian moon that has been into the Easter egg dyes.

"Louie and Louise, together again. And who is your little friend?" she croons.

Louise and I disentangle ourselves as swiftly as dignity will allow and leave Nose E. standing alone, like the cheese of song and fable.

He hops to his feet, shakes his disreputable mop and lets his topknot sag over one eye. How absolutely cute.

"Why, it is a little dog! I thought it was a hamster or something. What are you three doing on my doorstep? Do you want to come in? Why, certainly."

Easy as pie (except for being repeatedly insulted in cooing tones), we are in.

"Imagine you using the *door*, Louie! This is quite the red-letter day. I suppose you and your guests want to visit Temple. Yes, hop in the elevator. I will hit 'two.' You do know enough to get out when the elevator door opens . . . ? Well, thank you very much for the glare, Louie. I was just trying to help."

The doors ease shut on Miss Electra Lark's jolly face.

"We want 'three,' " I point out sourly, "but we can take the stairs the rest of the way."

"You have never been gracious to those who assist you," Miss Louise observes, staring fixedly at the numbers over the door as the lit-up one fades and two

318

begins to glow.

"I prefer the elevators at the Crystal Phoenix. At least the ride lasts fourteen floors."

The doors open and Nose E. is the first to leap over the dark crack plummeting down to the Ritz's hidden basement depths. Louise and I check each other for failing courage. We cats hate to jump elevator gaps, a foolish superstition no doubt, but inbred.

We leap together, to find Nose E. trotting away from the service stairs.

"Wait!" I holler. "We want to go up one more flight."

"Following a trail, following a trail," he carols happily.

So we follow the perky plume of his tail cocked over his back like a horsehair fly-switch.

He disappears down a cul-de-sac near and dear to me.

"That is interesting," Miss Louise observes. "Apparently Mr. Matt visited Miss Temple after he had picked up the murderer's scent. You would have thought she might have noticed something."

"Scents are not her strong point; suspicion is."

Nose E. retraces his steps, nose to carpeting, to veer back down the hall and to the stairs we were supposed to climb in the first place.

The fire door is shut, but Nose E. stops obediently at the barrier. Dogs really are startlingly shy of initiative.

"Back off, I am coming through." With a running leap, I bound into the door, which swings wide.

While Nose E. sits staring at the phenomenon, Miss Midnight Louise encourages him to spring through the temporary opening with one well-aimed swat to the posterior.

A moment later, Nose E. turns with a belated snarl,

319

which dies on his little black lips as he sees the door swoosh shut.

"That could have caught my tail," he whines.

"Not if you move fast enough," I say. "Now, mush upstairs. Follow that trail."

He does, and we do, and shortly after we are standing before the door to Mr. Matt Devine's digs.

After some heavy pawbeats on his door, Mr. Matt Devine opens it to admit Nose E. and me and Miss Louise.

"Hey, Louie. Have you found a friend?"

Stooge is more like it, but I practice my cat smile for the greater good of several species.

"This dog is a purebred."

Yeah? So we cats are not? I am pure black, am I not?

"Hey, little fella! Quit jumping up my leg! Are you wearing Slinkys for shoes, or what? Hey—!"

When Matt Devine bends down, Nose E. is licking his face like it is a stamp. What a pro!

"You must be lost, a purebred like you."

Like cats cannot be lost because we do not have a pedigree? Please!

Mr. Matt Devine sits down on his long red couch (so like a giant, lolling dog-tongue!), on which I recently reclined to great photogenic effect, and plops Nose E. on his knee. These Lilliputian dogs will stick at nothing to curry favor.

"Let us see, little fella. Do you have a tag?"

Does Nose E. have a tag? Does Bastet have whiskers?

I wait impatiently for the obvious to unfold, while Midnight Louise slinks into place beside me.

" 'Nose E.' Odd," Mr. Matt says. "Someone ought to have come up with a more appropriate name for you than that."

Yeah, and Mr. Matt Devine is such a great expert at naming things?

He laughs as Nose E. slides down his leg to worry tooth, nail, and nose at his pant leg. "Come on. No wiggling. Got to read this thing—ah, a phone number." Muttering the numbers over to himself while trying to keep Nose E. corralled, Mr. Matt also tries to punch the telephone buttons one-handed.

I watch in stupefaction. Who says humans are manually dexterous? But finally my hero has the phone receiver pinched between his cheek and numbing shoulder, has Nose E. penned in his lap, and is waiting for an answer.

I am waiting anxiously myself. I do not know what hours Earl E. keeps or where he hangs his hat when he is not selling wax-museum platters.

"Hello," Mr. Matt says suddenly. I notice that since he has become a radio idol his voice seems to be deeper and more deliberate. Pretty soon he will be sounding like a Crawford Buchanan clone. You do remember Crawford Buchanan? The sleazy reporter for the slimy *Las Vegas Snoop* who always has it in for my Miss Temple.

"I have a"—he pauses to rear back for a good look at Nose E., to make sure he has the species right; cannot blame him—"a small dog here. Called 'Nose E.' Oh, you do. Yes, well, he showed up on my doorstep just now and he is sniffing and chewing the devil out of my pant leg. Uh, no, I am not 'smoking dope.' "

A long silence.

"I can understand the dog is valuable to you; it looks like some kind of . . . purebred. Well, I work nights, so I do not know how I can get him to you so fast. Um, is this address near downtown? Uh-huh."

Human conversations! So unoriginal. So stop-and-start. So hard to interpret from one side of the fence only!

"Actually, he was with a couple of cats that *are* known to me. One's from this neighborhood and one is from the Crystal Phoenix up the Strip. Does not usually like cats? They seem to get along fine." Another silence. "I would rather not give you my phone number just now. Ah, I work a high-profile job and I like to keep it as private as possible. An entertainer? I guess you could say so. Oh. The saxophone. Cool instrument. Well, Nose E. seems fine, other than digesting my clothing. Let me call a couple people I know and I will see if someone can get him back to you tonight. I know you must miss the little guy; he is quite . . . active. Yes, I know he is very valuable; I will take care of him, and call you back in a half hour or so."

He hangs up and addresses me for some reason. Perhaps it is my wise, nonjudgmental expression. "Whew. That guy was a little too anxious for my name and address. Should not be so suspicious but . . . a dog. Sort of. Hey, cut that out! I know—"

Mr. Matt looks both happy and inspired as he picks up the receiver again. In a moment he is smiling, though not for us. "Temple! You are in, thank God.

"I have acquired a dog. Or it has acquired me, rather. Little white thing. Looks like a long-haired rat, maybe three or four pounds. Maltese? If you say so. Anyway, Louie and Louise escorted it to my place. It looked a little lost and it is eating my khakis. I called the number listed on the ID tag and the guy there, I do not know. He sounded kind of . . . fishy. Do you think you could—? Great!"

322

Mr. Matt dumps Nose E. into my and Louise's custody and runs around the place stacking newspapers and moving coffee mugs into the kitchen. Like Martha Stewart was coming up for a white-glove inspection or something. I am just glad I am not in the apartment below watching my Miss Temple scurry around.

About five minutes later, a discreet knock at Mr. Matt's door has all our ears pricked. She is so thoughtful. No doorbell gongs to disturb Nose E.'s tiny ears. Mr. Matt opens the door cautiously so Nose E. does not run out, but Nose E. is too busy having conniptions over the scent on his trousers to run anywhere but at the nostrils.

"Matt! Is this the dog? Or a renegade cotton ball?" Miss Temple storms in, a pair of dangly earrings swinging at her neck and her high heels clicking, and is on her knees to Nose E. as soon as you could say "pushover."

"What a darling dog. Definitely a Maltese. Well, it certainly likes you."

"Not me. My wearing apparel. How do you suppose it got here, and in such good company?"

It is only then that Miss Temple deigns to notice Midnight Louise and myself. "Louie and Louise . . . Louise is a long way from home. Maybe the dog lost its owner at the Crystal Phoenix, and Louie somehow picked the both of them up and led them here."

"No." Mr. Matt has sat down on the sofa again, happy that Temple's petting has kept Nose E. at bay for a while. "The dog's owner lives, or works, near downtown. I have the address and phone number, but the guy was weird when I called. Asked if I was smoking dope at the moment, like I might be crazy or something."

Miss Temple sits back on her heels, the better to fawn over Nose E. One would think sitting back on high heels would be like cozying up to a beaver-tail cactus, but I have never tried such a feat, either sitting back on high heels or cozying up to a cactus.

"And then," Mr. Matt adds, "he wanted my address and phone number in the worst way. Kept saying the dog was invaluable."

Miss Temple frowns, already showing the suspicion she is justly famed for. "Might be some kind of 'lost-dog' scam. You go to the address like a good citizen to collect your reward for returning the dog, and they jump you and take all your money, *and* the dog."

"Very creative," Mr. Matt says approvingly, smiling at her like she has just delivered the answer to the year-2000 computer glitch.

Meanwhile, Nose E. is trying to lunge from Miss Temple's custodial grip and shouting the obvious to all who would listen. "The sick-sweet smell. It is all over him. I cannot be sure, but there is even a trace in his hair. Let me at 'im; let me at 'im."

"Nose E.," Miss Temple notes, disinterring the tag from the animal's plentiful hair. "You would expect anyone who names a little fluff-budget like this 'Nose E.' to be weird."

"Yeah. So I put him off about giving my name and phone number and called you right away. What is going on here?"

"The dog might be legitimately lost," Miss Temple says sensibly, "and Louie took him back here to hit up the local patsies. It worked before," she adds significantly, with a long look at yours truly.

At last I am getting some credit for masterminding

this operation, even if she only sees the surface of my grand plan.

I must admit that it has a ways to go. Somehow, we must lead these incredibly dull-wilted humans to the conclusion that what Nose E. finds so attractive about Mr. Matt's pants is the trace of a killer and that Mr. Matt must lead us to everywhere he has been of late, so Nose E. can finish his sniffing duties before poor Earl E. thinks he has been kidnapped.

While we are all contemplating worst-case scenarios, one that nobody has yet thought of makes itself painfully clear.

The faint shriek of police sirens—nowadays a scale of loud and soft yodeling that would chill the blood in a crocodile—comes hurtling toward us like a meteorite.

Apparently Earl E. is no dummy, and he has concluded that Nose E. is in the hands of a dangerous drug lord or a mad bomber. That little hairball is about to get the Circle Ritz surrounded.

OUR FLAG IS STILL THERE . . .

TEMPLE HAD NEVER BEEN SO HUMILIATED IN HER LIFE.

First the entire population of the Circle Ritz had been rousted and forced outside, until it was all too clear where a certain white Maltese dog resided for the time being.

Even the police had retreated at this revelation.

Then bullhorns had blared forth for everybody left in the apartment to come out, their hands empty.

That meant leaving the cats and Nose E. behind.

She and Matt faced the audience of ousted residents, including an Electra Lark whose face had gone as white as her pixie hairdo. While uniformed officers corralled them near a squad car, bomb squad experts in what looked like beekeepers' outfits rushed past to storm the empty building.

Temple and Matt were not searched, but they were asked pressing questions about Nose E. and how he had come "into their possession."

Why was Matt unwilling to give his address and phone number to the dog's rightful owner?

"The dog's rightful owner had sounded a little odd on the phone. Asked if I was smoking dope."

And were you?

Matt shook his head. "Never in my life."

"He used to be a Catholic priest," Temple explained in rapid-fire PR-person-ese. "Until very recently."

Then had *she* been smoking dope?

"No! Why would this weird guy who owned Nose E.

even suspect such a thing? He sure couldn't tell it over the phone."

"Nose E. is not just any dog," the young policeman said solemnly.

They waited.

"He is a drug-and-bomb-sniffing ace. If he wandered off, he was probably on the trail of either illegal drugs or incendiary devices."

"He was on the trail with my cat, who is still up there," Temple said. "Cats do use catnip. Perhaps Nose E. has been suckered by a perfectly legal odor."

This caused the first frowns to develop on the mustached officers' young and tender faces. The frowns deepened when the guys in the jumpsuits, gloves and face-masks came down to pronounce the building all clear, except for two black cats and a white dog in 3B.

Officer A was uneasy. "I don't know what to do," he admitted.

Temple decided that strong, even odious, measures were called for. "Get in touch with Lieutenant Molina in Crimes Against Persons."

"These are two cats and a dog, ma'am."

Temple *hated* it when men, especially young men in their twenties, called her "ma'am." She was only thirty-and-a-half herself. She drew herself up to full, three-inch-heel-implemented height.

"I am *thinking* of crimes against persons, particularly against police persons, that haven't happened yet. Like wrongful detention lawsuits."

What a difference twenty minutes makes.

The unmarked car drove up; Molina got out and walked past the assembled, currently evicted residents, past the beekeepers' apprentices, past the boys in the uniform, past Temple and Matt. She spit one word in her wake: "Follow."

Obviously, she had been briefed.

Temple scampered after her, Matt coming along more deliberately.

The building was eerily quiet. Not even an aging faucet squeaked somewhere while someone ran water for the dinner vegetables.

They saw or heard no trace of Molina ahead of them as they "followed," not even the flicker of the third-floor elevator light.

"Why did you have them call Molina?" Matt asked as they rode up in the empty elevator.

"Because I think this is relevant to her cases."

"To Strawberry Lady and Church Parking Lot Lady?"

"And maybe Stripper Lady."

"So it's a trio?"

Temple nodded grimly. "Three women strangled to death within a week of each other. The stripper hadn't been stripped of her ID, but the other two sure seem like mirror slayings."

"But . . . the cats, the dog. Surely, no one would take anything they did seriously."

By then they were outside his open door.

Inside, they could see Molina squatting in front of Nose E. She wore latex gloves and was pulling a short muzzle hair from the dog's perky little face.

He whimpered and jumped back.

Molina deposited a few hairs in a plastic Baggie, straightened, stuffed it into her pocket, and turned. "Good. Round up the cats. I need samples from them too."

"Couldn't this be considered invasive?" Temple asked. "Don't you need permission to take hairs for DNA testing?"

"DNA I don't need. Just the species will do fine."

"You don't have to pluck the cat hairs. Just pet a cat, your hand will come up with several loose specimens."

"You contemplating a police brutality suit?"

"Among other things," Temple said.

While the women were word-sparring, Matt had done sensible things like shutting the door and picking up Louise.

He offered the pretty, semi-long-haired cat to Molina. "I think a couple loose ones are already hovering." Like bombs bursting in air?

Her pale-gloved fingers pincered onto a couple of likely specimens. With perfect gravity, she put them into their own plastic Baggie, labeled it, then glanced at Midnight Louie, who was under the sofa. "His Majesty next."

His Majesty was not so sure of that.

He had chosen well. The sofa was just wide enough that no human arm could quite reach in far enough to capture a furry body. Oh, a fingertip could flirt with search and seizure. A hand might brush a soft swath of fur. But curl around and extract a feline extremity? Never!

Temple felt like Nose E. (who had again attached himself to Matt and his pant leg) as she crawled from sofa front to back to side. Each time Louie impeccably adjusted his position so that he was utterly out of reach.

"Louie! This is the end! No more Free-To-Be-Feline for you if you don't come out this instant!" she bellowed.

Underneath the couch, Louie seemed to smile like the all-but-disappeared Cheshire Cat.

Ooooh!

"I'll trick him out," Temple swore, rising to study the

329

landscape of Matt's apartment like a sneak thief. "I need a tassel, a cord, a tape measure, a ribbon, a . . . " She leaped upon Nose E. and undid his collar.

Moments later, she was shivering the short length along the sofa edge.

Louie wouldn't budge.

"Smarty pants! You're in trouble," Temple threatened, quite emptily.

"That does it." Molina spoke in the voice of authority. "Devine." She nodded at Matt, who came to stand at the sofa's opposite end. They lifted, Molina swung the bulk sideways, and Temple dove onto the stranded cat.

Matt had to help her upright, since holding twenty pounds of cat didn't leave a hand free to lever herself up.

Temple shut her eyes. "Please be quick."

A moment later Molina announced, "Bagged."

Temple opened her eyes to see a third plastic bag vanishing into Molina's bottomless jacket pocket, along with the latex gloves.

Matt waited patiently by his post at one sofa end, Nose E. happily gnawing his pant leg, for Molina to pick up her end and swing the sofa back into place.

All three humans collapsed on it, having at length defeated the three nonhumans.

"Do you mind explaining the hair scavenger hunt?" Temple asked.

"I do mind," Molina admitted, "but I see no help for it. I've had my best investigative team on the Blue Dahlia strangulation case, and there is no question that the victim's house contained long, white hairs, and black hairs, both long and short. I would like to think that she was done in by a salt-and-pepper-haired killer, but the inescapable conclusion, given eyewitness testimony in the neighborhood, is that two black cats were in the house, certainly after the time of death. Miss Orth's cat had also died, or more likely was killed. The evidence indicates that someone dragged the cat corpse out of the house and buried it in the yard. Marks in the disturbed soil and sand show the tracks of four nails, either a human with his or her thumbs folded under into an exceedingly awkward position, or of quadrupeds definitely larger than a squirrel but smaller than a coyote. Unfortunately, whatever body was there has been removed. Maybe by coyotes.

"I have been forced, much against my better judgement, based on all the evidence, to conclude that these black cats, specifically, were in the death scene area, and that later they were possibly joined by an animal of white coat. And that a human, whose hair was also white or gray, was recently in the vicinity.

"Therefore—" Molina pushed her hands into her jacket pockets, gazed at the magical undulating Circle Ritz arched ceiling. "I am forced to examine the animal behavior here tonight in the light of evidence. Apparently the white dog was Nose E., who is known to me both in his capacity as professional snitch and record-store dog, and apparently his activities on the death scene have spurred his recent fetish for Matt Devine's pant leg. So. I have to ask you, sir; where has your pant leg been in the past few days?"

Temple sat upright, alert as an attorney working on a contingency fee. "Lieutenant, you have gone too far. A man is not responsible for where his pant leg has gone."

"When and where did I last wear these pants?" Matt looked bemused. "I don't have that many pairs." He glanced down at the damp bottom of one leg, still clutched in Nose E.'s face. "And will have fewer soon. I don't pay any attention to what I wear when or where! I've only been here, or at ConTact briefly. Or at the radio station."

"The radio station." Molina digested that. "You come into contact with any people with white hair there?"

"Uh, no. Most of the people at a radio station are pretty hip and therefore pretty young. Unless they bleach their hair." He glanced at Temple, the germ of an idea leaping between them like Ebola.

"Nance!" Temple said. "She was right here. And those were the pants you wore for the photo shoot, weren't they?"

"Yeah. I guess. I hadn't worn them since, come to think of it."

"Nance?" Molina inquired.

"The photographer," Matt explained. "I don't know if it was natural or not, but her hair was snow-white."

"In one of those buzz-cuts," Temple put in. "Kind of like that Aussie actor who used to sell batteries a few years ago. Jacko, or Jocko."

Molina's expression grew analytical. "Then this 'Nance' must have been a bit—"

"Butch to the bone," Temple said promptly, precluding any hemming and hawing on Matt's part. "Even had a really pumped tattoo on her left bicep. I mean, this was one barbed-wire babe. She also seemed like a hell of a photographer."

"How old, would you say?"

"Hard to tell with that hacked-off Harlowe hair . . . pretty old. Even forties, maybe."

"Even forties. Hmm." Molina was looking intrigued. "I hadn't considered a female perp, but gay relationships can get as abusive as straight ones." She was beginning to buy into the theory. "In fact, gay

332

sexual violence can be particularly vicious. The knotted ligature could be some fetish object. 'She left.' It fits."

Matt was frowning. "Yeah, but . . . the victim you described, an ex-nun librarian in her fifties. I don't see—"

"It fits," Molina interrupted. "You and I both know that there were a lot of unadmitted gays among the clergy."

"Not a lot . . . "

"Didn't you say forty percent, once?" Temple reminded him.

"Forty percent of new recruits to the priesthood, they think, but there wasn't anything like that number in the old days. Then, years ago, most people never guessed they might be gay, much less dreamed of leading the lifestyle. You don't know the environment: a vocation was a blessing and an honor, and the celibate life was held up as a higher form of behavior."

"Besides," Molina added, "getting married and having fourteen kids didn't look like a picnic to everyone. Girls with intellectual ambitions had no choice but to look to the convent. Those days are dead. And good riddance."

"I still can't see this woman even hanging out with someone as up-front as Nance," Matt said. "And just because Nance's looks seem to announce her sexual preference, that doesn't make her abusive, or a murderer. You're stereotyping, both of you. People with in-your-face façades are often the most insecure of all about themselves."

"Thank you, Mr. Midnight," Molina said caustically. "When I want a profiler, I'll call Quantico. How can we get in touch with this Nance?"

"Ambrosia would know. That's my broadcast partner.

Her off air name is Leticia Brown. You can reach her at WCOO."

"Oh, we will." Molina stood, gazing down on the three animals with fond wonder. "Amateurs," she muttered.

Whether she was referring to the four-footed or the two-footed of that dreaded species was up to the hearers to decide.

"You going to take Nose E. back to Earl E.?" she asked Matt.

"Sure. I mean, he must be worried that the little fella has been in the hands of international terrorists or something."

"Good. I don't want to get dog hairs in my car. Might mess up the evidence. Thanks." She glanced at Temple, but didn't say anything, and then . . . she left.

"How weird!" Temple declared when she and Matt were finally alone, except for the three animals, who regarded them with the rapt attention of those requiring feeding shortly.

"Which part of weird are you talking about?"

"Hey, I had to be honest! You're kind of upset about that Nance angle, aren't you?"

"I hate to see the dead libeled, and the living too. We don't know that Nance is gay, and we certainly don't know that she's dangerous. Besides, none of these victims was sexually assaulted. Or Molina isn't saying so, and I don't see her holding that back with us. We know too much about the fringes of this case."

"Strippers can be lesbians too, like hookers. You know, women who've been abused by men often go the other way in their personal lives."

"I've heard that too. All this makes committing to a life of religious celibacy sound like a real sensible course, doesn't it?"

"For the first time I understand it," Temple admitted. "Maybe you had the right idea in the first place." She grinned.

"Maybe I had the right idea at the time, but now—" He shook his head.

"I hope I'm not totally disillusioning you."

"You are, but it needed to be done. In fact, I'm meeting with an ex-priests' group that has an openly gay member. It's been like the military decided up to now: don't ask; don't tell, but—Omigod!"

"What?"

"I just realized. You want white hairs, come to my ex-priests' group."

"I don't think I'd be welcome." Temple glanced at the furred triumvirate on the floor. "But maybe this Earl E. would let you take Nose E. if we both asked him very, very nicely. And explained what we had in mind."

"It would be a scummy thing to do."

"It's what Nose E. does all the time: go undercover for the greater good."

"I'm surprised you didn't hold Max up as an example of same."

She wagged her head from side to side. "I didn't think you'd appreciate the reminder."

"I don't."

"But . . . Nose E. Who can resist that furry little two-faced face?"

"Louie won't like being aced out by a dog."

"I kinda think Louie has resigned himself to it. Who do you think sprung Nose E. from downtown?"

"Lou E.?"

"Man, you are getting into the undercover lingo. Now all you have to do is get into the spirit."

MAD MAX

MOLINA PULLED INTO HER DRIVEWAY AT SIX-THIRTY, animal hairs turned over to Hair and Fibers, and visions of a long-delayed chorus line of pepperoni slices dancing in her head. The only fibers she wanted to see tonight were long strings of hot, melted cheese between her plate and her palate.

She was famished.

She was bemused.

She was appalled the case had come down to plucking hairs off household pets at the Circle Ritz. But she was proud of Alch and Su for pursuing the unlikely scenario, and hopeful of finally making headway on the Blue Dahlia and church parking lot slayings.

Cats, God bless 'em. She had two of her own, after all.

She got out of the car, depressed the lock, and slammed the door shut. No need to pull into the garage. She'd freshen up, collect Mariah at Delores's house across the street, and they would go eat pizza, diets be damned! Daughter could play video games and Mother could have a big, frothy mug of beer . . .

She moved, lost in thought, toward the front walkway she seldom used.

As she passed the corner of the garage, a figure materialized in the dusk.

"You!"

Max Kinsella nodded slowly.

"What are you doing here?" After surprise, came anger. "You are out of line! Not on my premises. Not ever."

"I agree. Not on my watch. Not ever."

"Watch? What are you talking about?"

"Cher."

"Cher? Her ex-husband, 'he dead.' Cher? What? Are you crazy?"

"A little."

The steady, absolute sanity of his tone worried her. The absolutely sane were the craziest of all.

"Look. I don't know what you think you're doing, but you are not to come here. Get it?"

"Too late," he pointed out, quite logically, still with that eerie over-controlled tone that she mistrusted with every instinct in her suspicious history.

"What's your problem?"

"You."

"Besides the obvious. I've never hidden the fact that I'd love to nail you."

He nodded. "You have this time."

"Enlighten me."

"That man you had me looking into."

"So."

"You didn't tell me he was a murderer."

"I didn't *know* he was a murderer." Molina's throat squeezed shut with sudden dread. "Is he?"

"First, *who* is he?"

"I gave you the name and the facts. You ought to remember."

"Oh, I remember just perfectly swell. What I need to know is who he *really* is. To you. To whatever case you think you're working on."

" 'Think' I'm working on?" She tried to brush by, but he stepped in front of her. She pulled back, unhappy about retreating, but not ready to try anything else. Talk was always good while you were thinking of something else.

337

He seemed to think so too. "I don't know whether you're so stupid you don't know what you're doing— what you've done—or you're so dangerous you sent me out there to get that girl killed."

"What girl?"

"Cher Smith."

"The stripper. So what?"

"So everything! I pointed him right at her, thanks to my investigative work for you. She wouldn't be dead if you hadn't used me as your Judas goat."

"Wait a minute. Are you saying this—the stripper killing—had something to do with Nadir?"

"Are you saying you didn't suspect in advance that he might be involved in the earlier killings?"

"Look. I've had a long day—"

"So have I. And I had a long night before that."

"I just asked you to check out this guy. He was a very remote suspect."

"Now that's where we differ. I don't think he was that remote a suspect. I think he was a too-close-for-comfort suspect. I've had a little talk with your other 'helpers.' "

She remained silent; no one knew better when to ignore leading questions, or statements, than a cop.

"You've really been relying on the Circle Ritz gang on these cases. That's not according to your past M.O. There's some reason you're desperate enough to rely on amateurs."

"Look. I'm sorry she's dead, but I don't see any way this can tie into the two earlier murders."

"Except through you."

"Me? What about the second woman? The magician's assistant? Ring a bell, mighty Mystifying Max? She used to work for a magician around town years ago. Gandolph the Great. Ever hear of him?"

He was silent for a long moment. Then he pulled her into the dark of the entry courtyard with him. She could feel his fevered breath on her cheek.

"I don't care about your deaths one and two. I don't care that you think Cher wasn't the third. I only care that she wouldn't have died if I hadn't come hunting your prey. This Nadir guy. You've been notably off-the-record on these murders, Lieutenant. You've asked me to bird-dog for you, you've invited Matt Devine and even Temple into your inner sanctum of evidence. Why? Why were you so suspicious of this guy? Why were you driven to use me, when you knew what a two-edged sword I could be? I don't like having dead girls on my conscience."

"And why do you?" She pulled away, though it took all her strength. "How did it come to dead stripers?"

"He's a bouncer at a strip joint."

"At Baby Doll's?"

"No, at the place Cher worked two nights ago. The place I got her out of."

"How, 'got her out of?' "

"I went there to get information on Nadir. She was working the club, an obvious rookie, drunk as a duck on champagne. She knew a little about his whereabouts on the nights of the parking lot killings, so I suggested she sneak out and I'd meet her. He caught us. Cher said that she'd find work at another club, that it'd be all right. But she died the next night leaving that club. Guess who probably did it?"

"I don't know who murdered her, but you've just given me plenty of reason to look into your story, because you're probably the last man she had anything to do with the day before her death."

She cut him off before he could finish drawing breath

339

to speak again. "But what I find most unbelievable in all this is your stupidity. I'd expect it of a new uniform. They're always going soft on some pathetic hooker or stripper, and trying to get her off the streets. I thought you were a bit beyond that. That is such a rank, amateur thing to do—

"Don't talk to me like I'm one of your rookie detectives. You have no idea what I do, or did, or who I trashed or saved. I'm saying you sent me in there blind, without enough information, and I want the right stuff now."

"I see."

"No, you don't see." He came closer, grabbed her arm, hard. "I got her to leave because it suited my purpose . . . your purpose. But it made this guy of yours mad; he acted like he owned that club, and everybody in it. He didn't like eating gravel and watching her leave with me. He wasn't the type to let it be. You didn't tell me he was capable of murder. You said he was just a pathetic tough, not a killer."

"I didn't think he was!" She wrenched her arm free. The skin burned even through her gabardine sleeve.

When Max Kinsella got hold of a thing, he didn't let go easily. But his words still dug in when his fingers no longer did. She couldn't fault his fury. In his position, she'd feel it too. Was Nadir a killer? Had she had any suspicion that he was when she had asked Kinsella to find out about him?

"I basically expected you to clear him," she said, rubbing her arm. "That's all. I needed to know he wasn't responsible. And you still can't prove that he was."

"I'm the one who saw him in that parking lot. He had me from behind, an elbow across the throat. A

340

stranglehold. He could have killed me if I hadn't been ready for him. He could have killed Cher in a heartbeat."

"She doesn't show the pattern! Her killing is unconnected. It's gotta be."

"Because that's the evidence and your professional opinion? Or is that what you need to believe to clear your conscience?"

"Evidence." She bit out the word. "So far," she added reluctantly.

But her hedging seemed to shear off some of his edge. Even stone-strong evidence could develop splits and chips.

Kinsella leaned against the stucco garage wall, mollified enough to ease off a little. "All right. I agree that the ID left on her implies another type of killer. But Nadir might just be that other type. You wouldn't have had me look into him if it weren't a possibility. What I want to know, need to know, deserve to know, is why you suspected this guy from L.A. in the first place."

She thought. She thought for a long time, maybe a minute-something, and he waited like a cigar-store Indian: wooden, relentless, wearing the weight of the wrong she'd done him like a cloak.

And she had used him precisely because she wouldn't have to explain her motivation, as she would to one of her detectives. Now, here she was, having to explain in spades, and hating every second of it. This was her own worst scenario in living color. The only person it was worse for was Cher Smith, and she was dead.

She spoke at last, trying to keep her voice flat and expressionless.

"It's simple. Read my lips. 'She left.' On my car door; beside the first body. You noticed that something had happened to my car. Murderous graffiti. The only clear-cut case of the words 'she left' being left at the scene of the crime was at the Blue Dahlia. The body, which evidence now indicates was killed elsewhere and brought to that setting, was placed near my car. I had to assume a possibility that the placement was personal. If the dead woman had 'left,' had I also 'left?' Yes, I had. The man I asked you to investigate was the man I left, years ago, in L.A. That's who he is. Rafi Nadir."

His silence lasted longer than hers had. One upmanship must be his middle name, except that she now knew all of them: Aloysius Xavier and who-knows-what else.

"You and Nadir?"

"A long time ago in a place far away, he used to be a good street cop, back when he was younger and felt less challenged. He started to change, and I left."

"I'm sorry. I just don't buy it. You and Nadir?"

She shrugged. "I evolved, he devolved. What more can I say? People do change."

"Still. Why not burn him? What can he do to you now except embarrass you?"

"Embarrass? You think this is because I don't want to admit I ever associated with such a loser? Hah! I'd testify to shacking up with Jack the Ripper rather than go slip-sliding around trying to use a quasi-unreliable amateur like you! Except for the fact that this lowlife is the father of my daughter!"

"Your daughter?" he stepped back, finally giving her the space she needed. "You have a daughter?"

"Don't sound so shocked. Even the Virgin Mary had a child."

"Your daughter. I never figured that. How old is she?"

"No. My daughter is off limits. To him, and to you. And I'll thank you not to ever show up on my daughter's doorstep again." Shock gave her the upper hand, and she used it, backing him into the house's entry area until the security lights blared on.

He lifted a forearm to his eyes. It was like having a suspect under the hot lights of *The Front Page* era, and she pressed her advantage, quite literally pushing him to the wall.

"Yeah, I know you can find out what you want to find out, but you're not to show up on my daughter's doorstep ever again. I can handle you wherever or whenever you choose to materialize, but she's not fair game to you, and if you ever try to use any information about my kid, you try to blackmail me, or whatever, and you are . . . well, I'll let you imagine what you'd be. Roadkill would not be a bad guess."

Kinsella hardly heard her threats. She could watch his mental wheels turning, doing a 180-degree shift on one plane while they kept on whirling in another.

Finally, he reconfigured his suppositions. "Nadir. He never knew he had a daughter."

She was silent.

"He didn't know you were in Las Vegas, with her."

Still as the grave.

"Not until now. Maybe."

She had nothing to say.

"You *were* between Everest and Gibraltar, weren't you?" He pushed off her garage wall, backing her up, facing her. "Okay." His tone was brisk, businesslike. "I want, need, deserve to know what's happening in the Smith investigation. I'll pursue it in my own fashion, which is to say, I hope you get something on Nadir, because if you don't, and you can't do anything about

343

him, I can and I will."

"Don't bother. If he's involved, my history is public property."

"You could lose your job."

"Sometimes it's hell."

"So's mine," he said lightly. "I won't tell, unless you won't tell, and I think you need to."

"Don't hold your breath. If he does know anything, he'll come after my daughter next, and I'll do whatever is necessary then."

"No, I wouldn't want to be walking in your shoes. But then, neither would Temple." He passed her, gingerly, on the way to the driveway.

"Miss Nose E. of the Mojave Desert."

"She tries to help. Just like me."

Molina nodded wearily. Sometimes you needed a little help from your worst enemies.

"Say, Kinsella!" she called after the shadow he was becoming.

The shadow paused.

"What the hell happened to your hair?"

He was silent for a long moment.

"I had a brush with the devil and a haircut from an angel. Care to give me a polygraph on that?"

"No, I'll take your word."

"I think that's a first, Lieutenant. Better watch yourself."

She stood there for a long while, listening for a vehicle to leave that never did. He had parked out of sight and out of sound, of course. He wasn't an amateur; she had just accused him of behaving like one, because she was coming darn near herself.

If Raf Nadir had killed Cher Smith, then he had devolved into the worst kind of over-controlling misogynist, and it didn't matter if he'd had nothing at all to do with the Blue Dahlia and church parking lot slayings.

He was as dangerous as death anyway.

NOSING INTO CRIME

WELL, I AM NOT ABOUT TO DESERT NOSE E. JUST WHEN he gets to star in the solution of the crime.

So when Mr. Matt Devine picks up the little whimperer and prepares to go out, I goad Louise to join me in standing by the door, where we caterwaul like the Second Coming is imminent and Mr. Matt needs to open the door to the Heavenly Host.

"What is with you cats?" he demands, cradling Nose E. against his chest.

Perhaps we do not like to see dogs getting all the free rides.

"This is serious," he adds.

We both produce long, lugubrious faces, as if to demonstrate our essential sobriety.

"Oh, all right. If you are so attached to the little dog—"

Yeah, we are attached, by gum. By a claw!

First we are loaded into Miss Electra's pink Probe.

It seems that Mr. Matt has arranged for formal transportation now that he is toting a lap dog around. What a disgusting breed! I refer to lap dogs, rather than Mr. Matt's species, but perhaps they are interchangeable.

We make a pit stop at the Reprise record store, where Mr. Matt endeavors to introduce himself, restore Nose E. to his proper owner, and in the same breath beseech Nose E.'s services on his next stop.

Earl E., an elderly, stooped individual with laser-sharp eyes and the instincts of a Doberman when it comes to dogs, cats, and homo sapiens, eyes Mr. Matt up and

346

down.

Nose E. wags his bedraggled tail to show that he is game.

Louise and I, we narrow our emerald and amber beads to mere slits, and will Mr. Earl E. Byrd to do our will.

He shrugs. "I have never seen such a committee before. But I want Nose E. home before midnight. He needs a bath and a pedicure after his adventure."

"Fine," says Mr. Matt, much relieved. "Nose E. is the only one who can dismiss a suspicion that I hope is not genuine."

"Nose E. knows his business, and does it," Earl E. says. "I try not to interfere."

With that we are gone in the borrowed car, heading out of Las Vegas into the Great Black Nowhere of Night.

I love traveling through the empty desert like this! Although I enjoy the bright lights and many amenities of the Strip, there is something to be said for venturing into the Great Unknown. Even Louise, city-bred brat that she is, arches her neck and sniffs the desert air. Nose E. pants out the half-open window, his ridiculously long ears blowing back in the wind.

"I-am-getting-there, I-am-getting-there," he is singing in Dog. They always were an operatic breed—all that baying at the moon, as if the moon would care.

"There" is more civilization: crowded home sites and corner churches.

Our corner church looks like a 7-Eleven with altitude to match its attitude.

Mr. Matt pulls into the parking lot, shuts off the car, and sighs.

I wish he would speak Cat, or even Dog. But he says

nothing, merely picks up Nose E. and leaves the car, barely leaving us cats room to exit with dignity.

I can see that he is pondering issues of great moment.

Inside is a naked room: bare tile, bare walls, blinds. Nothing soft for the savaged soul.

I smell that noxious brew, coffee. I smell that other noxious brew, guilt. Nose E. is not the only evil-sniffer among us.

"What is with the menagerie?" a man asks, laughing.

"Pet-sitting," Mr. Matt answers. "I guess we formerly employed have to do what we have to do."

The gathered men nod. They are all displaced persons, I gather, all formerly of Mr. Matt's stripe.

I gather that not all the likely suspects have arrived, so I shepherd Miss Midnight Louise to an inconspicuous spot just outside the circle of empty chairs.

"I do not wish a seat on the sidelines. I wish to be in for the kill."

"Face it. Our job here is as mere witnesses. It is up to Nose E. to finger the perp."

"Do you think he will find the scent we have traced from Wilfrid's house?"

"Only if the person who carried it there, at the scene of the crime, is here. Nose E. cannot conjure the criminal; he can only sniff one out."

Midnight Louise sniffs in disgust. "Then we are just window-dressing. I call that small reward for wearing our footpads to nubs all over Las Vegas. And then the dog gets all the credit."

"Sometimes it is enough just to see justice done."

"Not for me. We female felines have hung back and let someone else hog the glory for far too long."

"Am I hogging glory? I ask you, am I? Face it. We do

348

not have the sniffers for this particular job."

"I detected the scent that Nose E. follows."

"But could you swear to the source?"

"Maybe."

While we have been having a quiet exchange of hisses under the chair legs, Mr. Matt and his performing wonder dog have been gathering the usual coos and chin-chucks. The only thing worse than a cute little dog for hogging the attention is a human baby.

"What is his name?" one guy asks.

I can see Mr. Matt hesitate. He does not like to lie, but saying Nose E.'s name is like giving away his game. "Ah, Chauncey," he comes up with.

I wince. A wimpy name for a wimpy dog. Nose E. takes it like a canine, without a whimper. They are so disgustingly eager to please; you could name them "Doormat" and they would come running. When will dogs realize that they will not get respect until they demand it? Obviously, this species takes way too much abuse; they could use a bodyguard. In fact, maybe I sniff a new business venture in this somewhere: Midnight Louie's Canine Advocacy Service: Our Claws at Your Command. Our Claws in Your Cause. Our Claws . . .

Oops. Another guy has entered the room.

I can see why Mr. Matt's suspicions have moved in this direction. I note a lot of snowy thatches on the heads present that still have hair. The poor sinned-against human male! How demeaning. To lose one's hair right at the apex of your physical profile. I mean, who would mind a few patches off, say, where nobody can see, like one's inner thighs? But right on top of Old Smoky? Cruel, the ways of human aging. That alone would be enough to turn a male rogue, one would think. Luckily, my breed just goes gray around the muzzle and ears. Very distinguished.

I, of course, have yet to spot the first white hair—unless it has been left upon me by some feline of the female persuasion—so I can afford to sympathize. It is no fur off my chin! Perhaps that is why men with shrinking scalps cultivate chin and cheek hairs. What melted like the snows of yesteryear up top can still flourish on the lower slopes.

Oh, well. It is their problem, thank Bast. Not mine.

While I am ruminating on these Serious Male issues, Miss Midnight Louise is pacing back and forth behind me like a penned panther.

"This is ridiculous. Get to it! I am waiting for Nose E. to sink a fang into the villainous creature who is willing to kill two species."

"Then you are waiting for naught, Girl. Nose E. does not do anything obvious that would give the game away. His signals are subtle, sort of like those in baseball."

"Baseball!"

Apparently I have touched another nerve, but then, that is what I am best at in relating to Midnight Louise.

She hisses quietly. "I do not understand this fetish for worshiping a sport in which human males spend so much time *thinking* about moving a ball around."

"Uh, it has a certain gender symbolism, if you will."

"I will not! It is stupid. And so is this exercise in waiting for Nose E. to do something."

At this moment, the door opens, and another dude ankles in.

As I had tried to tell Miss Louise about Nose E. (whom I have seen in action ere this), his job demands the subtle cue, not the noisy, media-friendly takedown one sees so often on *Cops*. Bad boys, what you gonna do when they come for you? Especially if they are nose-hounds.

He begins struggling in Mr. Matt's arms. Mr. Matt obediently sets him on the floor on his four fluffy little pins. Nose E. trots around the circle of gathered men. The chairs are full now.

Nose E. sniffs and accepts pats. He is rather like a royal personage off to press the flesh, or off to have *his* flesh and fur pressed, rather.

At one man's feet he sniffs for a long moment. Then he sits, cocks his head, and raises his right front foot.

In Nose E.'s world, this is the equivalent of the Judas kiss, or maybe I mean sniff-off.

I stare at Mr. Matt, whose face has gone still and cautious and very, very sad.

EVIDENCE OF THINGS NOT SEEN

MOLINA LOOKED AT MATT AND TEMPLE, SITTING SIDE by side on her office chairs.

"I know *what* Nose E. is," she said. "I don't know what the hell Nose E. thought he was scenting. Unfortunately, we detectives don't sniff our way to glory. So a drug-and-bomb-sniffing pooch pointed a paw. This case has nothing to do with drugs and bombs.

"What did the dog smell? I don't know. You don't know. You want to take this to court, with a Maltese as the main witness? I don't think so."

"There's a reason," Temple insisted. "Those animals were on that trail for a reason."

"What? They want to nail a killer? They're animals. They can be trained, but they can't reason."

"Oh, I don't know. I've seen Louie's wheels turning."

"I've seen windmills turning. I don't ask them to testify in court."

"Look," said Matt, "why not investigate this man? His background, his possible motive? Isn't that what you do all the time?"

"Yessss," Molina hissed in frustration, "but there is usually a little thing called evidence, physical or behavioral evidence, that gives the police some reason to investigate."

"What about animal instincts?" Temple asked. "That's behavioral."

Molina's eyes narrowed to laser-blue slits. "So is piddling on the rug. We don't build cases on it."

352

"What about human instincts?" Matt asked. "I know one of the men from my ex-priests' group called the radio station, talked to me on the air."

"Did you recognize a voice?"

Matt grimaced. "We all develop that institutional pulpit voice. I recognized the syndrome, yeah, but not a specific voice. Not well enough to point a finger."

"Well, then. You do not have a dog's keen hearing. And you"—here she glared at Temple—"do not have a dog's keen sense of smell, Strawberry Lady or no Strawberry Lady. We have three murders here: three women dead who came from wildly different spheres of life and experience, in one case, of age as well. Each was strangled. Each somehow . . . was punished for leaving. Something. This is beyond doggie sniffing."

"Would you take my request seriously if I told you I think I know the murder weapon?" Matt said, like a man who had committed to a great risk.

"You do?"

"At least in the first murder. Your murder, Lieutenant."

"It is not *my* murder, any more than it is your murder. But what weapon are you thinking of?"

"It may sound farfetched, but, if my idea has a possibility of being right, will you look into the dog's . . . suspect?"

"You give me a feasible murder weapon in the first case, and I'll investigate Lassie." She glanced from one to the other, expecting nothing.

Matt took a deep breath. "A rosary."

"A rosary? Much too small. The average rosary is— what? Fifteen inches around. You couldn't even slip it over someone's head."

"Large beads on a chain. Nodules. Regular."

Molina rubbed the back of her neck with an impatient hand. "Yes, the general pattern, but—" She grew suddenly quiet.

Temple edged forward on her chair seat. What? she wondered. She didn't know a rosary from a string of pearls, but she knew a sudden insight when she saw one a-borning.

"Matt?" She glanced at him.

He was even more intent on Molina than she was. Temple understood that he was playing her, as Max would play an audience—that Matt knew the answers and was making Molina face them despite herself.

When had he become so certain? When had Molina become vulnerable enough to be wrong? To need help to see the obvious?

"The Catholic rosary," Matt said softly to Temple. "Ten spaced beads, a central single bead between two larger spaces, then ten more beads, for a total of five, 'decades.' Not barbed wire, but not unlike it, in a way."

"But the size—" Molina broke in.

Matt's eyes remained on Molina's face. "The size is too small, unless—"

Molina waved away his unvoiced explanation. "Unless you're talking about the oversize rosaries some orders of nuns wore with their habits. They were strung on an extremely sturdy cord. So, is a nun the suspect?"

"Anyone with access to such . . . artifacts would be."

"Look, I concede that you know your religious artifacts, but who would keep such an antiquity today? Nuns haven't worn those old habits for more than thirty years."

"Are thirty-year-old guns incapable of being fired?"

"Who would hang onto such things?"

"Who indeed? Maybe you should look into certain

354

people's backgrounds, Lieutenant, and you might start where the dog suggested."

"Idiots!" She stood. "You are both idiots. And I am an idiot for even considering this wild goose chase. I'll look into it, all right? I'll put valuable person-power on this crazy theory of yours. But then how do the other killings fit in?"

Temple stood too, although she was not nearly as impressive as the almost six-foot-tall lieutenant. "Maybe they don't. Maybe assuming they do fit is trying to link the unlinkable."

"That's . . . unthinkable."

Matt stood. "Murder always is. Let us know if we can be of help."

"Of more help," Temple amended.

Molina snorted in disgust and did not look up from her desk when they left.

She sounded like Nose E. on a roll.

BEAD COUNTING

"DID THEY REALLY MAKE ROSARIES THAT BIG?" Temple wanted to know as she trailed Matt out of police headquarters, holding her arms as if embracing an invisible barrel.

"Well, almost. For nuns. Hung from their belts."

"Wow."

"Wow. It was another time and another place."

"Rosary belts. Sounds kind of kicky. Fashion, maybe. Crosses were big a couple seasons back."

Matt stopped. "An oversize rosary could be a pretty fiendish weapon. I hope Molina takes me seriously enough to reexamine the ligature marks on that first victim's neck."

"You think Nose E. is on to something."

"I don't know about Nose E. It's a cute dog. Maybe it smelled . . . menthol or eucalyptus leaves or tanna leaves to raise the mummy of King Tut. I don't know. But I have a bad feeling, ever since I heard the Blue Dahlia victim was an ex-nun, a nice, harmless ex-nun. It struck me that whoever killed her throttled the vocation, not the person."

"But she wasn't a nun anymore."

"Exactly. And she sure isn't an ex-nun now."

Temple sat down on the low concrete rim edging the weirdly decorated wall towering in front of police headquarters. "Matt, what if I'm right and the murders are philosophically but not physically connected? Like Leopard Lady. She left, all right, left the vocation of being a magician's assistant. And we've seen signs that it's not safe to leave magic."

"We? You and Max, you mean?"

Temple's nod only increased Matt's obvious unease.

"It was bad enough to learn after your recent kidnapping that Max has a counter-terrorist history he can't walk out on. Now you tell me that leaving his front profession could be as dangerous. He's really not safe to know."

"He never was. Hey, don't look at me like that. If what you're saying is true, it's not terribly safe to leave Mother Church, either."

Matt sat beside her, rubbing his neck as unconsciously as Molina had done earlier. "True. Fanatics are fanatics, whether they espouse a religious or a political cause, or even . . . hocus pocus."

Temple remembered him pointing out that the magical term originated in the Catholic mass, and

356

smiled. "Maybe all those things are connected. Call it mystical entertainment. Okay. Let's assume the murders aren't connected. Where does that leave us?"

"With one fingered, or pawed, possibility. With a couple of mystery deaths."

"Aren't all deaths a mystery?"

"Now you're sounding theological. Pretty serious stuff for a Unitarian."

Temple nodded glumly. "I hope Molina takes you seriously, because I sure do."

"I wish you took me seriously on matters other than murder."

"Hey, you wanta go somewhere with me?" Temple asked as they approached her car at the curb across the street.

Matt paused for a moment not so much to consider the invitation, as to relish it. "Yeah."

"As part of the case, I mean."

"Molina wouldn't like you calling it that."

"You mean it's her 'case' and our 'conundrum?' " Temple pushed up her jacket sleeves as if mentally preparing to duke the difference out. "I want you to meet some people. Look them over."

"People?"

"Well . . . assorted psychics."

"That's a change of scenery from what I've been used to lately."

"The Halloween séance gang just happens to be in town for a conference. I'd like to renew auld acquaintance and ask them some questions. And I'd like your opinion of them. And, I'd look more . . . innocuous if I showed up with an escort."

She had managed to select the car key from the jillion-thousand keys on her ring (Temple had never met a key she didn't like the shape of) and unlocked her door, but Matt opened it and held it until she was seated.

He shut it and came around the back to the passenger's side, while she started the car and wondered why he made her so nervous lately. He certainly acted calmer himself, sort of dreamy calm around her. Maybe his newfound fame and fortune, relatively speaking, was good for him.

She smiled, nervously, as he got in the passenger side. "You haven't said whether you'll come or not."

"Of course I will." His smile was slow and sweet. "I'm always interested in what you're up to."

That blanket approval, of course, made her undercut her own impulses for the next four blocks.

"Well, I don't know what I hope to accomplish. I'm not going to find, you know, a suspect. It's just that it's awfully coincidental that they're all in town just when Gandolph's old assistant is killed. Well, she wasn't that old, although she was well over forty. Former assistant, is what I mean."

"I know what you mean. You want someone else to look over the suspect pool."

"Right. I . . . we never did buy that one of these sleight-of-psyche artists didn't cause Gandolph's death. And now, with his former assistant killed—"

Matt nodded affably.

"You don't have to agree with everything I say!"

"What's bothering you?"

"Ah . . . I guess I should tell you that we—Max and I—have discovered that there's this secret society among magicians. It makes sure their secrets stay secrets, the inside info on all the illusions. Gandolph wasn't just unmasking phony psychics. He was planning a book on the subject. Max decided to finish it."

358

"Write a book? Kinsella?"

"*Wrote* a book. Yes, he did. Don't sound so dubious. It's not bad."

"But, Temple, psychics aren't magicians. What would this group have to do with this sinister society of sleight-of-hand artists? Whew. Try to say that fast three times."

"Try it after you add the name of the society. The Synth."

"Sinth? As if you want to say 'since' and you lisp?"

"It's spelled with a *y*."

"Kind of like that designer drug, Hyasynth?"

"Exactly. Maybe the Synth was behind that smuggling operation. Well, they do exist. I've seen documents from them."

"What kind of documents?"

"Threatening letters. On parchment in Old English script. Like—"

"Like props in a high school Shakespeare play?"

"Maybe, but I've also seen threatening computer messages from them."

"Where? At home?"

"No, at—On Gandolph's old computer. Max showed one to me."

"This 'Synth' sounds like all shadow and no substance."

"It could be just that. Or not."

"What's really bothering you, Temple? You're talking a mile a minute. I don't think a couple pretentious messages from this Synth could do that."

"Well, there's another reason I'd kinda like you along on this outing."

"You don't have to tell me why."

"It's just that I'm not really, really keen on visiting

the Opium Den again."

She could tell he was searching her expression with a sudden concern she'd rather not look straight in the face. It reminded her of that awful night out on the highway, and what had gone before.

"I'm not crazy about it either," Matt said, "your visiting the Opium Den again. Even though she's gone. Shangri-La is a fraud and thief for sure, and maybe even worse."

"Matt!" Temple hit the brakes, realized that her rear view mirror showed a van close on her tail light, accelerated rapidly enough to jolt them both, and finally pulled over at the first empty stretch of curb she spotted.

"Matt? Do you know what you just said?"

"I said that Shangri-La is a bad lady, but nothing to be afraid of anymore." His face tautened, as if he had just remembered a secret he wished he had never known. "She left."

" 'She left!' Yes! The message on Molina's car."

Matt's face remained empty of every emotion but concern and confusion. "But . . . the ex-nun had nothing to do with Shangri-La, or magic."

"But the Leopard Lady did! Gloria Fuentes. Gandolph's former right-hand woman. And the 'she left' showed up on her body in the morgue. Okay, at the medical examiner's. But I still like 'morgue' better. It has class, 'morgue.' "

"I don't see what you're so excited about."

"Well, you might think the second strangling was an imitative killing. Copycat, they call it. But maybe the *message* was the copycat part, not the killing. Somebody knew, or learned of, the message on Molina's car, and duplicated it, after the fact."

"Why? Just to bug Molina?"

360

"Maybe. Wouldn't you like to bug Molina now and then?"

"Not really. She's done a decent job—"

"Oh, come on. She rides right over whoever she pleases to get what she wants."

"It's her job."

"Is persecuting Max her job too?"

"Maybe. He's been involved in some dicey things. If you'd just look at him with a little distance—"

"Oh, like from he's on Alcatraz and I'm in Las Vegas, is that enough distance for you?"

"Not. Quite."

"What would be? Aldebaran in the Hyades?"

"Huh? Temple, you're getting overexcited."

"Of course I am. It's what I do best." She leaned back in the seat, let her hands fall from the steering wheel. "Molina and Max aside, the fact is that those words appearing on the Leopard Lady's corpse are pure . . . theater."

"Magic."

"Magic, if you will. So, say the murders aren't connected."

"I don't think they are, because what I think happened to the woman Molina found . . . well, I know who did it, Temple. Nose E. thought so too, for whatever reason. Some smell. But we're just humans. We can't convict a man on something only a dog can smell."

"We can on DNA." She checked her rear view mirror again. "Look. Help me check out these ESP types at the Opium Den, and I'll go back to church with you and we'll try to smoke out your murderer on the homeboy front."

"You think we can?"

361

"I think you can, if you just set your mind on it."

"Temple."

"Yes?"

"Let's go. Wherever. But . . . I'm sorry you lost your ring."

"My ring—? Oh."

He was silent for an International Coffee moment.

"Well," she said, sighing, "I am too. It went so well with your pendant."

When he looked up, amazed and hopeful and appalled, she was absorbed in putting the car into gear and pulling away from the curb.

The sudden acceleration knocked him back in the seat.

THE USUAL UNUSUAL SUSPECTS

IN DAYLIGHT HOURS, THE OPIUM DEN'S BRASH NEON marquee was a gray-white expanse as dull as dead skin cells.

The tawdry sex-and-skin-parlors on either side seemed painted on canvas by a circus circular designer.

Matt inhaled deeply. Revisiting a place where Temple had recently been so endangered, and he had been so helpless, was like walking into an elaborately unreal dreamscape. In fact, Matt felt he was entering a cartoon-factory set, with nothing behind the exaggerated façades but empty cels.

Yet the interior surprised him.

The Opium Den's gaudy lobby bristled with booths and Celtic lettering. Incense spiced the air. Bells, drums, and Moog synthesizers swelled the sound system.

Temple stood beside him, surprised too, and subdued.

She hadn't expected the scene of her most recent trauma to have been transformed into a New Age Renaissance Fair.

"Okay?" he asked.

"Okay. Hey. I kinda dig this. Maybe we can play we're tourists."

"Aren't we?"

"Gauche, but true. Now, where are our most-likely-to-murder candidates?"

"I doubt they're advertising." Matt gazed in some wonder over the scene. "This is an alternate spirituality universe," he decided. "A little Asian, a lot flaky, and kinda charming, in a naïve way."

"Yes. But it has a dark underside. Never forget that."

He laughed. "Doesn't everything?"

"I guess so. So! Vere are my prey?" Temple curved her lacquered nails into exaggerated claws.

"You tell me."

So they wove through the booths and tents, pausing at appropriate stops.

"Ossss-carr Granttt," she hissed, pulling Matt to a sudden stop. Matt eyed the well-coifed, dark-haired man she indicated. He reminded Matt of a well-fed cobra who hosted a televangelist hour on the side. And maybe did faux-diamond infomercials on the other side.

"Looks like Crawford Buchanan after a personality-suction."

Temple giggled. "He is too, too serious, but let's ask him some leading questions."

They sidled over.

"Are you *Dead Zones* watchers?" the man asked them first, before he had even fully turned to acknowledge the presence he—eerily—sensed.

"Only in Las Vegas," Temple said.

"Temple Barr! The stage manager of our last, least-conclusive séance!"

Close up, Grant looked more than ever the young-George-Hamilton clone: razor-cut, tanned, brunette as a plump hotel-breakfast prune.

Matt felt his hackles rising, although he shouldn't have worried. Temple had a built-in sleaze detector. Still, worrying about what he shouldn't worry about was one of the best features of his current state.

"This is my friend Matt," she said, omitting his last name so no belabored greeting rituals would be necessary.

Matt didn't mind; Oscar Grant struck him as someone who was always playing a role.

"What brings you to our gathering?"

"I was going to ask you what brings you back to Las Vegas?"

"Oh, my show does quite a few episodes here. Know any good psychic phenomena I should look into?"

"Well, there's always the Crystal Phoenix Ghost Suite."

"The hotel has a ghost?"

Temple nodded. "The manager swears to have seen it. Jersey Joe Jackson, a shady character around Las Vegas before it was more than four motels and a casino, lived in the seventh-floor suite of the Joshua Tree before it was remodeled into the Crystal Phoenix. Now, the hotel is adding an underground theme park and ride based on Jersey Joe's reputation for hiding treasure underground all over Vegas."

"Terrific! Kind of a dematerializing Yosemite Sam character. I could get a seven-minute segment out of that."

Temple whipped out her business card. "It so happens I'm handling publicity for the Phoenix on the project."

"Really?" Grant's ooze quotient went up several points. "It would be great to work with someone who's sensitive to psychic issues for a change."

"Speaking of psychics, I understand some of the Halloween séance gang are here."

"All of them. Somewhere." Grant's languid, beringed hand waved to the surrounding booths.

"Thanks." Temple started to leave, then, Columbo-like, turned back to Grant. "By the way, have you ever heard of something called the 'Synth?' "

Matt was impressed by Grant's self-control, but the pupils flared suddenly in his dark eyes, as if they were registering an adrenaline rush.

"Sinth when?" he joked. "Or, I should say, synth what?"

"It's supposed to have something to do with magic."

"Oh, magic. That's merely the fringe of my interest area. Some booths here have magical paraphernalia and books, but this show is geared mostly to genuine phenomena."

Temple thanked him and moved on.

"The only genuine phenomenon here is him," Matt remarked. "Phenomenally fake."

"Then let me find someone I don't think is a fake." She wove ahead of him through the crowd, peering into booths.

"Aha!" Temple stopped so suddenly that Matt walked right into her, not an unpleasant experience. "Uh, sorry I didn't use my brake lights, but look: Birds of a feather flock together."

Matt studied the trio of figures Temple's red-headed

nod indicated. One was behind a booth table; the other two had paused in front to talk.

If these were birds, the two in front were common sandpipers, strangely muted middle-aged women. The one behind the counter was a snowy egret: an Elvira, Mistress of the Dark clone, but all in white, from flowing long hair to flowing robes.

"The two genuine ones are in the aisle," Temple briefed him under her breath. "D'Arlene Hendrix has a pretty good record at finding dead bodies and will often help grieving families out at her own expense. Agatha Welk looks like she walked out of a 1930s Charlie Chan movie, but she read my tea leaves and made some eerily accurate calls."

"And the bird of paradise behind the counter?"

"I thought even you couldn't resist that presentation. Slick, huh? She has a black bird's name, but dresses to the contrary, always in white. Mynah Sigmund. She has a husband, William-something, around somewhere."

"He sounds less essential than her nail file," Matt said, eying the mother-of-pearl lacquered fingernails that telegraphed her frequent hand gestures.

"I don't see him anywhere." Temple went on her tiptoes to crane her neck around. "Let's ask the ladies."

Mynah Sigmund, despite dominating the conversation, fixated her eyes on Matt when they were still thirty feet away, and addressed him when they came within ten feet.

"Here comes someone who could no doubt enlighten us." The whites of her eyes gleamed as luminous as her fingernails. "D'Arlene was discussing whether self-delusion projects its own positive energy, a kind of Egyptian ka, or shadow-soul."

Matt absorbed this borderline gobbledegook, trying

366

not to show confusion. It was Temple who had met these people, not he.

Mynah's smile was sleek and self-satisfied. "You should know," she prodded him. "Mr. Midnight."

Now that took him aback. "Are you talking about that sad incident?"

"Exactly. D'Arlene says the spirits of murder victims call to her, project some last fragment of their living selves. Who did you talk out of infanticide? The deranged girl, or some surviving fragment of her sane self? You let her rename herself, so in a sense you were dealing with a split personality, or even a split soul."

"You . . . must have heard the actual broadcast."

"Absolutely," Mynah said. "I always listen to Ambrosia. I find her very . . . New Age."

The other women were not looking blank, as they should have at what would have been a cryptic conversation to most people.

D'Arlene, to whom Mynah had nodded earlier, was gazing harder at Matt than he was comfortable with. "You two are intimately connected with a death," she announced. "More than one. The answer is no."

Agatha, a seventyish woman with a plain, oversensitive face, was looking both fascinated and frightened.

"No?" Temple finally got over her own shock to speak up again. "No to what?"

"Whatever question plagues you surrounding the deaths that you are concerned with." D'Arlene shook her graying Brillo-pad-permed head. She was an unassuming woman dressed in a hand-painted jogging suit, with glasses on a pearl chain.

"Does the word 'Synth' mean anything to any of you?" Temple asked.

Agatha and D'Arlene shook their heads. Mynah, unlike the bird whose name she bore, wasn't talking.

"Has this been a productive outing?" Matt asked when they stood outside again.

"Productive in the sense that Professor Mangel predicted no one would say anything about the Synth. I guess we're supposed to believe in something all the more because everyone denies knowing about it. Not too logical. What did you think of the psychic femmes?"

"Weird. You say you think D'Arlene's abilities to find dead bodies may be genuine?"

Temple nodded. "Some psychics have helped some police forces in some cases, and she's one with a track record."

"She probably deduced the question about the bodies from your past encounters of the murderous kind. As for what her out-of-the-blue 'no' means, it's like all prophecies: too vague to believe, or to disprove. I sure would like to know how the Mynah-bird knew I was Mr. Midnight, though. That was rather . . . nonplusing."

"And Agatha Welk was so strangely silent, just staring at us like we shouldn't have been there, especially after I mentioned the Synth."

"So you didn't learn anything."

"Not a thing."

"But I did get an idea. If I'm supposed to be this super-counselor, Mr. Midnight, why don't I take over the regular ex-priests' meeting and pry a confession out of Nose E.'s suspect?"

"Because it's impossible to do?"

"I can call the leader, and get him to go along with the idea, I'm sure. So the taking-over isn't hard. It's the prying-out. I suppose I should record it, but it wouldn't be legal. What do you think?"

"I have a baby tape-recorder I use sometimes; cigarette-pack-size. But anything you got on a concealed tape recorder would be illegal. I think. I'll, uh, ask Max."

"Yeah. I bet he's one wired guy." Matt grinned. "I'll ask Molina."

"Can I come?"

"You don't look like an ex-priest."

Temple made a face. "I could pretend to be a reporter, wanting to do a story."

"Great cover. The suspect would be sure to blurt out incriminating evidence in front of a reporter."

"Oh."

"No. It's got to be just us guys. I can use the dynamics of the group to put pressure on him."

"You can?"

"I hope so. At least I know something none of them does, and that gives me an edge."

"Which is?"

"That one of them had to be at the dead woman's house, and left a distinguishing scent."

"Pretty thin evidence, Devine."

He smiled. "I'm an expert at extracting confessions, remember? And every suspect in that room should at least have a conscience to examine."

"Killers are conscienceless, aren't they?"

Matt shook his head. "Not in this case."

"Wow. Another costly little gadget I can't live without."

Matt was in Temple's apartment, examining her tiny tape-recorder that took mere thumbnails to move its Nose E.-size buttons. The casing was blush-colored metallic, rather like a cosmetic case, but the tiny cassette inside turned like it meant business.

They had practiced recording with Temple moving around the room to determine mike setting and range.

In the course of her rambling, she had dislodged Midnight Louie from his usual sprawling zone on the upholstered loveseat. When he moved to a nice sunny spot in front of the French doors, Temple's high heels had shortly after relocated to this vicinity as well.

He rose to rearrange himself on the faux goatskin rug, and shortly thereafter found himself in the path of yet another of her testing positions.

He finally lumbered off to the kitchen and jumped up on a counter.

"Poor Louie," Temple said when she noticed his defection. "Why do cats always arrange themselves just where you are going to want to be?"

"Because they know all the comfy spots." Matt, fascinated, was still playing with the Lilliputian controls. "This is incredible. It picks up from quite a distance, even through my jacket pocket."

"Molina, or even Max, could probably get you something really professional."

"I don't need a body wire. These are fellow ex-priests. They trust me. Or they do now."

AND LOUISE, SHE HAS SECRETS TO CONCEAL...

MIDNIGHT LOUISE IS ONE OF THE MOST DISGRUNTLED operatives I have ever worked with.

Of course, I have never worked with many operatives, for the simple reason that I work best alone. But sometimes even a lone wolf needs a female of the species. Among wolf-dogs, such are called bitches. Draw your own conclusions.

I find Miss Louise back under the usual oleander bush, in the unusual-for-her Mandarin Position of Patience Eternal: lying down with her forelimbs tucked before her. An ant is wending its way up the left side of her nose.

"You would think I was guarding Buckingham Palace," she hisses, looking somewhat cross-eyed at the ant. "Come on, you six-legged tourist! Just try to make me smile."

"Cats do not smile," I reply.

"Particularly when they pull nanny duty," she sniffs.

"Is the, uh, little nipper doing well?"

"As well as can be expected. Why?"

"I may need a witness."

"Do not we all!"

"No. Off the premises."

"I do not know if your witness can travel."

"How can you find out?"

"Move the poor bugger, and if it lives . . ."

"I could use a more optimistic projection than that."

"Then rent a movie! Preferably not *Titanic*."

"You are certainly tart today."

"I have been squatting here on and off for days, when not called away for your dog-herding detail, engaged in the feeding and care of an invalid, on no more say-so than you can come up with. The ground is hard, the food is literally lousy, and the ambiance would give an insomniac narcolepsy. What do you expect?"

"How about you move your assets—and your, uh, charge—to this address?"

Miss Midnight Louise eyes the coordinates I scratch into the dusty ground before her. "That is one long hitchhike, Daddio."

"I think you can do it."

"With dead weight?"

"With whatever."

"Humph. And what is the payoff?"

"The payoff is a confession of murder."

"Murder is a contradiction in terms among our species."

"We are lucky. Humans are a lot less lucky."

"I know. They are not feline."

I nod. There is no arguing with a dame, especially when she is sitting on your best witness.

FOOTWORK

SHE FELT LIKE A SCHOOLTEACHER WHO HAD JUST found a shiny red apple on the middle of her desk.

There were Su and Alch in their places with bright, shining faces: standing before her desk, with an in-depth report on the man the little dog from Reprise Record Shop had cocked a clever head at.

"Any idea what tipped the dog off?"

Alch and Su exchanged a disappointed glance. They wanted to start their recital with triumph, not dog tricks.

"Never mind. It wouldn't hold up in court anyway. So. What's his story?"

"Incredibly apt," Su said.

"She means he's tied into this killing like twine around a stack of newspapers," Alch translated.

"They don't use twine to bundle newspapers anymore." Su radiated the disdain of the under-thirty for the over-fifty. "It's plastic."

"Well, they did when I was a paperboy."

"Either way," Molina intervened, "neither substance was the murder weapon. The lab has confirmed that it could be a string of pearl-onion-size wooden beads."

Alch nodded. "The religious angle. We got a lot of tie-ins, whatever the substance. First, Reno."

"They both lived in Reno until recently."

"They both had used a dating service. Get this: Blue Heaven."

Molina leaned forward. "Weird name. What was its clientele?"

"Middle-aged people with Christian backgrounds," Alch said promptly.

373

"Christian? That encompasses every denomination, but usually fundamentalists claim the term. You're sure it wasn't Catholic backgrounds?"

Su shook her head. "No. Christian. But Catholics were included, obviously."

"Okay. Enough suspense. Any evidence that they did date?"

"Plenty." Alch was happy. "Not only do the Blue Heaven records indicate the usual meeting in the neutral public place, but shortly after that both quit the service."

"Naturally," Su added, "the service checked up with both of them, because there's nothing a dating service likes better than a satisfied customer, unless it's two."

"And—?" Molina prompted. A provable relationship between the two would be, well, heaven-sent.

"Everything okay," Alch said, flipping through his notebook. "Except . . . the former neighbors of Monica Orth said about a month after that, she became very withdrawn and agitated, and a month after that, she was out of her apartment and down here in Las Vegas with a new job and a new place."

Molina sat back. "So she left."

Alch and Su nodded.

"Not only the church, but Reno, and the relationship, whatever it was, with this guy."

"You could say she got outa town fast, Lieutenant."

Molina nodded and sighed at the same time. "Woman on the run. But not far enough. Anything else interesting?"

Su's blackberry eyes sparkled like a brandy spritzer. "A couple even more interesting things. About him."

Molina leaned forward over her desk.

Alch and Su leaned over her desk.

If the figurative apple Molina visualized atop her

desk were actually there, and were a microphone, it would have picked some A-plus tidbits from these prize pupils.

WHEELS

I MUST ADMIT THAT I DID NOT THINK MUCH OF MISS Midnight Louise's master plan.

But I did not have much time to argue, it being plain that Mr. Matt Devine was going ahead with a master plan of his own, with no regard for my carefully laid devices. The fact that he was totally ignorant of them is no excuse. People are all too often oblivious to the machinations of the superior species. In most cases, that is to our advantage.

Anyway, this hair-brain shirt-tail relation of mine has come up with a risky, arduous, and pretty impossible scheme.

Naturally, I am all for it (mainly because the snip thinks that I cannot do it "at my age and weight").

So here is what we have been through.

First, she and our surprise package have to get to the Circle Ritz. Let me tell you, I take plenty of heat hearing about how hard that was. I have to admit the package looks pretty warped around the edges.

Next, we have to break into the locked shed in which is stored that awesome Hesketh Vampire motorcycle. (I call it Hesky for short. Rhymes with Pesky.) This collector's edition chromium critter is previously owned by Max Kinsella himself. (I cannot guarantee that in that instance it was "gently used.") Since then it has been in the custody of Miss Electra Lark, the Speed Queen landlady of the Circle Ritz. Out of the goodness of her heart (of which there is much of both: goodness and heart), she has of late lent it to Mr. Matt Devine, who came into this world (Las Vegas, that is) without wheels, a grievous lack in this flat-out, salt-flat part of the country.

So, anyway, Mademoiselle Louise and I dull our nails on the weaker members of the shed's boards until we are inside the shadowed interior. I have left a lot of shiv casings behind, but far be it from me to cavil when it might be interpreted as whining by Miss Midnight Louise!

Then we have to breech the accessory storage bags that sit to either side of Hesky's saddle. At least they are the black-leather variety, rather than those meat-locker-style metal jobbies that could smother a hitchhiker of the furred kind.

For that is our mission: undercover hitchhikers on the road to Truth or Consequences.

I would hate to arrive asphyxiated, as I stress repeatedly to Miss Midnight Louise.

"Save your breath, Pops," she replies, not encouragingly. "You will need it."

"Where is the safety belt in this arrangement?" I ask when we have loaded our cargo, such as it is, and leaped into our saddlebags.

"Loop your tail around a strap and hold on: It is going to be a bumpy ride."

I recognize the Bette Davis line (that dame had lion-eyes), as well as the reference to early air travel. Since the Hesketh Vampire is a motor vehicle, I sincerely hope that we remain firmly on the ground.

All I can trust to is the solid driving skills of Mr. Matt Devine.

Who will be highly distracted tonight, on an undercover mission of his own.

Why could he not pilot a bicycle? It worked for E.T.

That is my last rational thought before I hear the

shed padlock unlocked and the footsteps of Mr. Matt Devine approaching.

After that all is a turmoil of speed bumps, speed, noise, speed bumps, and confusion.

We arrive in one piece, which is pretty good, as there are three of us.

The next problem is breaking into the joint, and when to make our entrance.

DECEPTION, LIES, AND AUDIOTAPE

MATT PARKED AND LOCKED THE VAMPIRE, STEPPING away from the motorcycle and feeling the road vibration still thrumming through his frame.

That was a given effect of riding canned heat. That was the buzz motorcycle riders loved.

He could take or leave that disorienting aftershock, but something else far less physical, and therefore far more upsetting, shook his soul tonight.

He stood for a moment in the empty lot, studying the church's sharp prow of glass gleaming in the fading light. Distant gulls seemed to squeal over Lake Mead. The sun set behind the western mountains. It always disappeared before its own last rays, most evenings leaving behind it a flat, cold light that only a landscape painter could love.

How could you stand in the light and feel such a chill? Only if the thought of what you were about to try put your soul on ice.

He remembered the hectic, surreal twelve minutes he had spent on the phone with "Daisy." *Daisy, Daisy, give me your answer do. I'm half crazy, all on account of you.*

The Gay Nineties love-ditty rang in his mind with unromantic Grim Nineties irony. He had gotten what he needed out of a frantic, addled girl about to commit delusional murder.

Could he get what he wanted to out of a clever, twisted killer who had committed delusional murder and wanted to survive it?

Just how good *was* Mr. Midnight at his new job?

Time to find out.

The sun's last, icy light glared off the gilded glass, cut through the stained-glass cross like an arctic laser.

This time Matt regarded the bare, plain room with a different eye.

The lack of upholstery and curtains would bounce sound, add an automatic echo to every word said.

Best he sit tonight somewhere other than the usual spot. That would disrupt the circle; all people in groups commandeered a small, rote territory—the place first sat-in—and returned mindlessly there like lemmings heading for a favorite cliff into the sea.

Matt's moving would upset that natural order. Would upset the neat expectations of his target. Would be an advantage.

He claimed a seat one down from Nick, the group's unofficial center, and pictured how the others might adjust, especially Norbert, whose seat he had usurped. Norbert already felt an outcast.

Good. With Norbert unsettled at the outset, the tenor of the whole evening would be off-balance. Confession was only good for the off-balance soul that had to be honest despite itself.

Matt also knew the role he had to play. He had to seem the victim, not the perpetrator of tonight's revisionist arrangement.

He *had* the problem; he was not the problem.

When Nick came in, alone, Matt leaped up from his claim-jumped chair. "I'm glad you're early. I thought we could talk—"

But Jerry came in before Matt could establish

anything more than his presence in someone else's seat, and a certain agitation.

"Sorry." Jerry stopped dead, his genial smile fading. "Am I interrupting something personal?"

"No," Matt said, too quickly. "Nothing personal. I'm just a little . . . upset."

"Well, that's what we're here for." Jerry smiled uncertainly, and joined Nick at the coffee urn. St. Caffeine Minor, cousin to St. Nicotine the Greater. "Want some, Matt?"

"Huh? Uh, yeah. Coffee. Be great."

Jerry exchanged a glance with Nick that Matt hadn't been meant to see. Then he poured two Styrofoam cups full of India-ink black liquid.

"Creamer?"

"Huh?"

By now Paul and Norbert had come in together, having linked up in the parking lot. They stopped inside the door, sensing the disorder inside.

"Creamer," Jerry repeated.

"Uh, yeah." Matt didn't have to play at being distracted. He was. "Thanks."

The two newcomers' eyebrows lifted at coffee being delivered to Matt.

They served themselves. Serving another suggested crisis.

They collected their own coffee cups and took their places one chair to the left without comment, respecting the unknown that had elbowed them out of their traditional territories. Something was up.

Damien came in last, pulling off his lined raincoat and light wool gloves. "Getting cold out there. I don't know how Matt can take that motorcycle."

He glanced at the last empty chair to the left of Nick,

the deserted coffee table, Matt in the wrong place, and frowned.

"Come on in." Jerry half rose from his chair (which used to be Damien's chair). "Put your things down; I'll get you a cup of coffee. Plain, right?"

Damien nodded, picking up that the status quo had shifted for a reason. He tossed his outerwear on a folding chair near the door and joined the circle.

In a minute, Jerry brought him the coffee.

They were about to begin.

"A prayer," Nick announced, low-key as ever.

Alcoholics Anonymous had made the Serenity Prayer famous in a paraphrased version as the cornerstone of its twelve-step program. American Protestant theologian Reinhold Neibuhr had created this most popular of generic prayers in 1934, but this Catholic group said it every session. "Oh, God, give us the serenity to accept what cannot be changed, the courage to change what should be changed, and the wisdom to know the difference."

Matt bowed his head, feeling a traitor. He suddenly saw what undercover work was really about: deception, lies, and audiotape.

Nick wasn't one to dance around a problem. "What's the matter, Matt?"

Cue: answer.

"Nothing major, I guess." He let the words drag out of him, the tone belying the meaning. He glanced at his audience. Confusion and concern in every face. Except Norbert's.

Matt allowed a pale smile to escape before he sipped his coffee. "You know that radio rescue I was in on? Yeah, who could miss it, with the newspaper and everything? I just didn't expect the fallout."

"Fallout?" Jerry prompted.

"Fallout. The calls questioning my motives, saying I was excusing the girl. I was just trying to save her!"

"Amen," said Nick. Count on Nick to be super-supportive.

"I guess it was just such a shocking situation," Matt went on. "You don't realize it at the time, while you're in it. You're just trying to think how you can save the situation. Do the right thing. I mean, who would imagine that a girl would call a radio counseling line while about to deliver a baby? I mean, she sounded so young and innocent—"

"They all do," Nick put in, about to say something more.

"It's not your fault," Damien said.

"No, of course not," Jerry added. "You did the right thing. It doesn't matter what other people think."

"I guess," Matt said, "that they think I was excusing what she was thinking she had to do, instead of getting her to do the right thing. Anyway, it's enough to make me sick of even trying. I'm giving up this radio gig. It's too . . . morally ambiguous. It's just not clear what the right thing to do is anymore."

"Nonsense!" Nick sounded angry. "You're being way too hard on yourself. *She's* the one in the morally ambiguous position, not you."

"But isn't that blaming the victim?"

"There's way too much wiggling out of responsibility by calling it 'blaming the victim,' " Damien said. "That's the trouble these days. The center cannot hold. No one can hold to the center. We're all a bunch of wishy-washy wanna-be do-gooders. We've given up on the eternal verities."

"What about eternal realities?" Matt wanted to know.

He took a deep breath. "I was just trying to be unjudgmental—"

"That's just the trouble!"

Matt glanced up. Damien was furious with him.

"You . . . wimp! You can't take people at their least. You must demand their best. What is wrong with the world? She was an unwed mother! She was ready to destroy her child rather than admit her guilt."

"That's not as bad as being ready to destroy another adult human being rather than admit one's sense of guilt."

"You. You . . . child. You don't know what it used to be like when right was right and wrong was wrong. Everything's middle now. Wiggly, weaseling-out middle ground. No fasting for Lent, no mortal sin, no Penance in no Confession. Not even Extreme Unction. 'Sacrament of Reconciliation?' What kind of wimpy theology is *that*?"

Before Matt could answer, an eerie wailing drifted in from the hall.

"What is *that*?" Jerry asked.

Paul just got up and went to check it out.

"Maybe lost souls in limbo," Norbert added with a nervous laugh, "in need of some old-time religious intolerance."

The last thing Matt needed now was comic relief.

WITNESS FOR THE PROSECUTION

BUSTING OUT OF MOTORCYCLE STIR IS NOT EASY.

Miss Midnight Louise and I tumble to the asphalt finally, serving as a landing zone for our "third wheel."

"I do not know, Pop," Miss Louise says. "This one is pretty dazed. We might have been better off with one of the Beanie Babies. You know, we could have made like puppet-masters and talked for it."

"Just being here will make the difference. Come on. You hoist up one side, and I will hoist up the other. Now we have to break into the building, great!"

"A glass door," she notes as we arrive. "Terrific. Do you know how much these things weigh?"

"At least they weigh less than I, according to certain sources," I say pointedly. "Opening it ought to be a cinch for a buff babe like you."

Miss Louise snorts in a most unladylike way. "Then I am for your usual modus operandi when you wish to get into someplace."

"What is that?"

"In this case, a ghostly wail ought to do it, especially in triplicate."

"I am too pooped to wail."

A razor-sharp claw reminds me of the power of the feline voice.

So we set up an ungodly caterwauling.

In time, of course, the door opens. It always does.

The doorman, a tall, portly guy with a surprised expression, stands aside as we stride in three abreast:

385

the good, the bad, and the ugly.

Miss Midnight Louise and I swagger forward (all right; we are still a bit wobbly on our pins thanks to that motorcycle ride, so it is more like a stagger). Between us is our secret weapon: Wilfrid Orth, recovered from his coma, and fresh from several days' private nursing duty at the vigilant paws of Miss Midnight Louise.

His tiger coat looks more like a tortie's; not a stripe is straight. And he tilts a bit to the left like a bum pinball machine. But he walks inexorably into the open space made by the circled chairs and the seated men in them.

Miss Louise and I hang back. This is Wilf's big moment.

He looks around at the first human faces he has seen since being given a would-be fatal blow by one of them.

He is not a four-pound pooch. He cannot be trained to lift a leg and finger a perp on command. He does not have a perky little topknot and long fluffy ears. And at the moment, he is a mess.

But he is still a cat, and he possesses the Infallible Feline Instinct for the human in the room least likely to welcome his presence. He reacts with the swift skill of a seasoned predator.

He takes a couple of running steps and launches himself at the lap of a white-haired man dead ahead.

It is not his fault that his target, at first frozen immobile like he has seen a ghost, stands up and backs away screaming as Wilfrid's ragged form comes bounding at him.

The chair tips over, but Wilfrid is already airborne.

It is not his fault that the object of his attentions has moved and removed the lap that was his original target. Wilfrid lands at chest-level, and, having nothing to catch onto, hangs eight (as the surfers describe their toe-clinging technique) onto the guilty man's shirt.

There is quite a ripping and tearing sound as Wilfrid slides slowly to the ground.

The man is screaming and babbling as the other men rush to attend—or is it detain?—him.

Mr. Matt Devine, being a sensible person of our acquaintance, ignores the human hullabaloo and rushes to us as we rush to attend Wilfrid. He has obviously lost a lot of nail sheaths.

"Louie? Louise?" He seems otherwise speechless, and we certainly cannot comment, other than with a serious expression.

Luckily, the cavalry comes in at this point: Lieutenant C. R. Molina and a Mutt and Jeff pair of detectives. Mr. and Miss Detective go to the aid and custody of the killer.

Lieutenant Molina, being a seasoned veteran, comes to where the action is.

"Did you get enough on tape?" he asks her.

"Plenty, especially at the surprise climax. Did you hear what he was screaming? 'You're dead.' Proves he was on the crime scene."

"I do not see why. And how did these cats get here?"

"Hitched a ride in your saddlebags. We saw them disembark from outside."

"And just let them come in and disrupt things? Why?"

She points at poor Wilfrid, who is sitting ignored and dejected at the center of the empty circle. "That is the missing and presumed dead cat of Monica Orth. Apparently the killer swatted him during the attack and left him for dead. A neighbor lady found the cat and called animal control, but by the time the van came out the next day, the corpse was gone. We found signs of digging in the back yard, and presumed, ah, someone had buried the cat. But when we excavated, there was nothing beneath the disturbed ground but insects."

"So . . ." Mr. Matt looks a bit drained as well. "The cat came here and freaked out—"

"Lieutenant?" A personage as petite as my Miss Temple is standing behind the group, looking like a schoolgirl who just got all As on her report card. "The suspect not only has an awesome set of fresh cat-scratches on his torso, he has scabs and inflammation from a set of *old* cat scratches."

"Awesome," the lieutenant agrees. "Alch can take him in. Call a squad and have these animals taken to the Circle Ritz apartment, care of either resident Temple Barr, or landlady Electra Lark."

The young woman frowns. "The uniforms will not like it."

"Tell them they are conducting a material witness." She glances at Wilfrid, who is licking traces of blood from his wispy foot hairs. "A very material witness."

"It is all right," Mr. Matt puts in. "I will get there on my motorcycle first and can take delivery."

"No, you will not." Lieutenant Molina's voice means business. "I have a date with my daughter in"—she checks one of the ugliest wristwatches I have ever seen, it does not sparkle or have loose little rhinestones or do any tricks whatsoever but tell time—"twenty minutes and I am not breaking it. You can come along."

She has turned to supervise the detectives and uniformed officers who are taking their man away.

Before Mr. Matt can object to her plan, he is

surrounded by the other men, who are clamoring to know what happened. Mr. Matt mentions the operative word: murder.

"Not Damien," they say. "Not one of us."

That is what they always say, and I do not have much chance to hear more, as Wilfrid, Louise, and I are scooped up and held fast against chests clad in beige shirts and lots of metal and leather accouterments of a sinister sort, not to mention buzzing, shoulder walkie-talkies.

We know enough to be utterly docile in custody; besides, Louise and I are anxious to return to the Circle Ritz. Wilfrid, he could not care less where he goes; he has seen his duty and done it royally.

So the cops, who are fretting aloud about not having facilities for our transportation in the squad car, are pleasantly surprised to find that we sit like three little statues in a row in the back seat for the entire ride, and make not a peep the entire way to the Ritz.

"Beats hauling dogs every time," one comments when we arrive.

Higher praise I have never heard.

Our triumphal return to the Circle Ritz finds Miss Temple Barr and Miss Electra Lark in residence, although a bit surprised at our uniformed honor guard.

"Gee, I do not know why," one officer answers when questioned about the details of our arrival. "The lieutenant says deliver these cats here, we deliver these cats here. She does say one is a material witness."

Naturally this causes great cooing between the ladies. There is nothing like a little notoriety for stirring up the ladies.

Anyway, I am received back into Miss Temple's arms,

389

and an officer is drafted to convey Miss Midnight Louise upstairs in our quarters. Apparently I will have to share the place for the moment. An imperfect end to a perfect master plan.

Miss Electra Lark takes one look at the bedraggled Wilfrid and sweeps him into the muumuu-bower of hydrangeas decking her person.

"You poor abused thing!" she cries. "I will take you right upstairs where it is soothing and dark and quiet."

And filled with Karma, I think to myself. Me, I would not want to mess with Karma in a weakened state, but perhaps Miss Electra believes that some psychic surgery is just what Wilfrid's much abused brain needs.

Me, I have had such an exhausting evening, especially in the knapsack affixed to Hesky, that I am even ready to nibble some Free To Be Feline before I lay me down to sleep in my own home, sweet home.

I'LL BE SEEING YOU

"I'VE NEVER BEEN ORDERED TO EAT PIZZA BEFORE," Matt commented loudly. "It's a novel experience."

"Sorry," Molina shouted back across the table. "I didn't have time for amenities. And I thought you'd want to discuss the case."

"Here?"

It wasn't quite Chuck E. Cheese's, but it was a flattering imitation: upbeat music, video arcade adding percussion to the noise, crowded tables, kids screaming, adults consequently screaming at each other, either in frustration, or just trying to talk, like Molina and himself.

"Where's Mariah?" he shouted.

"Games." She gestured to an area of the restaurant that resembled a mini-casino for kids.

Matt picked up his mug of red beer and moved to the empty chair at right angles to Molina. "How does you and me sitting here and Mariah off feeding quarters to video games add up to an outing 'together?' "

Molina grinned and swigged beer from her massive glass mug. "It's the thought that counts. Nowadays, this counts for 'quality time.' Besides, we're celebrating, aren't we?"

Matt leaned his head down; it was easier to hear closer to table-level. Or maybe the beer mugs acted as sound enhancers. "What's to celebrate?"

"The Blue Dahlia killing is solved."

He nodded. Of the three deaths, that was the one that had hit her closest to home. He could see what she had to celebrate. "I'm not in the mood to celebrate. Guess that's where your job and mine differ."

"You were right about the murder weapon. The order Monica Orth had belonged to wore the large, waistband rosary with the habit that was de rigueur when she professed her vows. She probably kept it as a memento and her killer probably took it. We'll find it, if he wasn't smart enough to destroy it thoroughly."

"Why would he kill, though?"

"Now I'm guessing. I think he was attempting to reach out for a first romantic relationship. He connected with Monica through the Christian dating service, looking for a woman whose ethics were as stringent as his. Wouldn't you know he'd click with an ex-nun. She probably didn't tell him until the relationship had gotten physical, or the physical had at least been attempted. Maybe she had to explain herself. But when he found out he'd defiled, or been defiled by—with his mind-set it's hard to tell which—an ex-nun, he freaked, driving her away. But he couldn't leave it alone, of course. He had to punish her to punish himself for being human."

"And why the Blue Dahlia lot?"

"Probably considered it the opposite of Blue Heaven, a nightclub version of Blue Hell. He left her body there both to confuse us as to the time and place of the actual death, and as a statement of what he thought about ex-nuns, and maybe all women, who attempt to be sexual beings."

"Poor woman! The first time in her life she tries to make a connection, and she draws a psychopath."

"Extremely neurotic, certainly, but not psychopathic. I doubt he'd killed before, and I doubt he'd do it again. I told you it's dangerous out there in dating game." Her eyes narrowed. "Make one 'connection' to the wrong person, and it can haunt you for the rest of your life."

"However long that will be." He was thinking of a true psychopath, Kitty O'Connor, and her scattershot sense of vengeance.

"Don't be so glum. Hey! We got our man, and you did a good job of leading him on."

"Yeah, but . . . an ex-priest. It's scary to know one of your peers is so warped."

"Like the news headlines the past few years haven't gotten you used to the idea?"

Matt shrugged. He'd never get used to the idea of clergy of any kind abusing their position.

"Cheer up," Molina ordered, articulating as crisply as Bette Davis in a forties movie to make herself heard over the friendly din. "Damien was never a priest."

"Huh? What? Did I hear you right?"

She nodded exaggeratedly. "That's what Su and Alch discovered. He'd been rejected by a seminary years ago. On grounds that he considered himself holier than any 'thou' in the church. Over-scrupulous to the point of obsession. The seminaries did use *some* discrimination. So he became a priest groupie." When Matt stared blankly at her, she added, "You know, like the doctor groupie guys who masquerade as the real thing? Only this guy was a fake priest. Your self-help group didn't exactly ask for ID, did it?"

"No. But . . . who'd want to pretend to be a failed priest?"

"It was the closest he could come to the real thing. You accepted him, didn't you, despite his over-strict ways?"

"We accepted everyone; that was the idea. So that's why he was so fanatical; he was holier than the church."

"Right."

Matt frowned, hesitating. "What were the animals

393

after?"

"Who knows? That Midnight Louie is a rambling wreck; always has had the run of the town. Maybe he had hung out with Monica Orth's cat."

"But—"

"I do have a theory."

This Matt had to hear. He waited.

Molina looked over his head, chewing. After a long while she said, "Catnip."

"Catnip?"

"It's the crack cocaine of cats. They go nuts over it. Must have been some especially potent variety in the Orth house that got on Damien. They became obsessed with following it."

"And Nose E.?"

"He must have picked it up from the cats after they'h been in the Orth house. That's his job, you know. Drug-sniffing. Dog like that will follow a trail to the ends of the Mojave Desert."

Molina still hadn't looked him in the eye.

"Catnip. So animal obsession brought Damien down."

"So to speak. Speaking of obsession, what're you going to do about Temple Barr's ring?"

"What would I do about it? You've got it."

"For one thing, you could tell her we got it, and where it was found."

"Why? You're not going to give it back."

"True. And I'd rather you didn't tell her, if that very fine-line conscience of yours permits it."

"It would only exasperate her, and I don't see why you care what I tell her."

"Because the ring is evidence, and that second strangulation murder isn't solved yet. Father Damien had nothing to do with it.

"You mean . . . Kinsella?"

Molina shrugged. "Maybe him, maybe someone he knows, or who knows him. Anything goes. One thing's sure; we're not going to crack that one soon."

Matt nodded to save the trouble of talking. It didn't stop him from thinking. He didn't like that ring of Temple's turning up on a murder scene that was going to take some time to solve. It implied that somebody was willing to use her in a larger, longer-range context. Had the ring been left there as a message to Max? If so, not telling him could be disastrous. He wasn't sure who he would or wouldn't tell.

"Cheers!" Molina lifted the massive mug, toasting, "Your new career."

Matt lifted his stein, let the thick glass lips butt with a dull clink. It sounded as hollow as his recent "victories" felt.

A mobile storm landed at their table. Mariah, flushed with Dr Pepper and game arcade triumphs.

"I made three-point-two million, a record. For me, anyway. What are you two doing, whispering?"

"Whispering?" Molina laughed. "We're *whispering* OUT LOUD so we can hear ourselves talk. We were planning to eat all your pizza if you didn't come back in time."

Just then a rangy waitress hip-slung her way through the crowd to lower two trays loaded with deep-dish crusts crowned by everything the Heart Association would most recommend not eating.

"Not so fast!" Molina urged. "You'll burn the roof of your mouth."

Mariah rolled her eyes, but pulled back to nibble just a bit of the crust, rather than sink her upper palate into the steaming landscape of melted mozzarella mountains, an oil-bearing pepperoni landslide, and lots of little hamburger hills.

She had grown taller since Matt had seen her last fall. The long braid down her back was gone, truncated to a glossy short cut. She looked less like a tomboy, and more like a girl.

"Mom, can I get my ears pierced, please!" She glanced at Matt, subtly enlisting a witness for what was probably an ongoing argument.

When Molina hesitated in answering, mainly because she was trying to cut through one of the mammoth pizza squares, Mariah rushed on. "Please, Mom, please! All the girls in school, and half the guys, have pierced ears, and lots of other stuff. You don't want me to look like a dork my whole school life?"

"Sounds like a good plan," Molina muttered to her pizza.

"What, Mom? Did you say yes? You said yes!"

"No!" Molina returned to full bellow. "I said, I'll think about it."

"You think about it forever!"

"I'll let you know this weekend."

"You're always working on the weekends lately."

"Well, the first weekend I'm not working, we'll go to the mall. Look into it."

"Reeelly?" Mariah was so excited she stuffed a chunk of pizza into her mouth, then began pulling it out as the heat got to her.

"*If* you slow down and eat your pizza like someone who isn't going to need a burn ward."

"Okay." Mariah jumped up. "I'll . . . go play some more and let it cool. Gimme some quarters."

"You got all my quarters."

"Oh." Melting brown eyes glanced ever so quickly at Matt.

"I might have some quarters," he confessed, digging in his pockets until Mariah had a fistful.

"Thanks!" She bobbed her way through the scurrying waiters, and disappeared.

Molina eyed him askance. "This is tough love?"

"Peace at any price."

Matt drank some beer, ate some pizza, and listened to the happy havoc all around.

Carmen Molina knew as well as he did that peace didn't come at any price.

Temple sat home alone by the telephone.

Actually, the telephones in her place reposed on the kitchen wall, in the bedroom, and in the office, and she was curled up on the living room loveseat with her male of the moment, Midnight Louie.

He lay like one dead to the world, legs stretched out, eyes closed and refusing to open even when she tickled his tummy.

Why he and his cohorts, including the odd-looking tiger cat, had been dropped off, she had no idea. But Matt's big-time expedition into undercover work must have been successful. He was probably downtown right now, making a statement and being debriefed and undergoing the usual grilling by Molina and her minions. Poor guy. She hoped he got back early enough to call her and tell her what had happened. Because she would call him by—eleven o'clock—if he didn't call her first.

She frowned and tried to read the small print in the big book, same paragraph, one more time. She had picked up some turn-of-the-century tomes on the history of magic at the psychic fair, and were they heavy going, in more ways than one. Not only had she nearly dislocated her arms and tote bag bringing them home today, but they were putting her to sleep just when she should have been on pins and needles about what was happening at the ex-priests' meeting.

She had tried calling Max, for distraction purposes, but he was out, or on the Internet, or just not answering.

Temple sighed. She was sure that the Synth, if it had really existed, would have left a paper trail somewhere. Everything did. If the Leopard Lady murder was separate from the Blue Dahlia murder, and it looked like it was, then the Synth could have been involved. Maybe it had been a warning to Max about releasing Gandolph's book. Knowledge was power. She yawned. So she couldn't be undercover with Matt tonight, and she couldn't be under the covers with Max tonight. She would just open the covers and find the trail and solve the whole thing by herself.

Beside her, Louie stirred, lifted his head and regarded her balefully.

"Well, not totally by myself," she told him. "You're one guy I can always count on."

Max was back.

At Secrets.

The name of the place was scrawled on the bare, boxy wall outside in the hot-pink script of pink neon, commercial graffiti in coy curlicues.

The hot-pink curlicues of the strippers inside seemed tame by comparison with the outdoor fireworks.

He had been forced to take naked disguise to the tenth power. The haircut was invisible under a sweaty biker bandana. His height was flattened by the bulk of a leather jacket tattooed in steel studs. His left nostril bore a glue-on stud too. He slouched like an inchworm, and still he couldn't be sure that Nadir wouldn't spot him.

Here, where nothing but literal sleaze was an adequate disguise, it was hard to portray the Compleat Sleaze without terminally alienating yourself.

Still. Nothing put off the greedy optimism of the tireless stripper.

They came gyrating past, G-strings pulsating like neon. He spent dollar bills like a nickel-slot high-baller. And got not a flicker of humanity back.

"You got a girl here, Mandy?" he asked one frost-haired bundle of edgy muscle, implant, and collagen lips prominent enough to make Donald Duck envious.

"Mandy? 'Fraid not." She hip-swung away.

Max feared she meant that ' 'fraid not' literally. A dead stripper was someone—something—no live stripper wanted to think or talk about.

He hadn't seen Raf Nadir, or the bartender who'd waited on him the other night.

Tonight he stuck to beer. Five-dollar beer as weak as rainwater. Suited his mood. From now on he'd stalk Nadir like a second skin. Find out where he'd been when, and where he was going to be. Even if Nadir wasn't guilty of the first two murders, he was a prime suspect for the third.

Molina didn't dare get too close for fear of giving herself away, but Max had no problems in that area. He was in it to the bitter end.

CASE CLOSED

THE NEXT MORNING BEFORE ANYBODY IS UP, I SNEAK out my usual point of egress and hightail it to the scene of the crime. I must transfer to various transportation modes several times, but finally the neighboring bungalows are in sight, and I hasten my weary steps when I view a blur of white behind a certain window.

Miss Fanny Furbelow welcomes my appearance by sashaying back and forth against the glass, whipping her white plumy fantail from side to side in a most graceful and inciting manner. What a shame that I will have to report that Wilfrid's death was just a hoax.

I mean, it is such a shame that I had to mislead her as to the state of his health.

But I had to hide the only witness to the killing next door, even to digging a false grave in the yard. (Luckily, Wilfrid had dispatched a rat in the house shortly before his mistress was killed, which added an aura of animal death to the premises. And the late rat admirably "filled in" for Wilfrid on the grave site.) Besides, I was not sure Wilfrid would recover from the murderer's wallop, despite Miss Midnight Louise bathing his brow and dragging a McDonald's carton-bottom of water from the hose tap to keep him sprinkled, not to mention the unmentionables she dug up to keep him fed.

Miss Fanny is out of the window and through the front door faster than you can say "Sally Rand." Her white coat sparkles in the sunshine as she sidles down the steps like the showgirl she was.

"Oh, Louie, I am so lonesome."

"Well, you will be lonesome no more."

She stops on a dime and pirouettes saucily to face me. "Oh?"

Hmm. The widow appears nearly ready to ditch the weeds and go for the deeds.

"You have something to tell me, Louie?"

But a private eye is a private eye, and he has to adhere to code, just like an electrician. I sit down, and don my most serious expression.

"Are you ill, Louie?"

"No. But you will be unless you too sit down and take this like a, er, lady."

So I tell her of the deception I had engineered at her expense.

Her gold and blue eyes flash with anger and the tip of her fan flutters furiously, but she says nothing.

I describe Wilfrid's excellent home nursing care and his slow but steady recovery. I throw pride to the four winds and reveal how we used Nose E. to trail the distinctive odor of the killer and how I concluded what that devilishly elusive stuff that gave him away, at least to a connoisseur's nose, was: vanilla-pudding-scented pipe tobacco. I finish up with Wilfrid's triumphal attack on the man who killed his mistress and who tried to kill him. When I am done, I sit back and wait for the usual hysterics.

There are none.

"It was cruel of you, Louie, to leave me in the dark. I understand that you feared I would give away Wilfrid's true condition, but you forget that I was a performer in my youth. I could have been trusted." Her tones are distant and severe.

I feel my ears lowering, more in sorrow than in anger.

"But," she goes on, "you did as you thought best, and you have indeed rescued my darling Wilfrid. How soon do you think the police will let him go?"

"They may want to run his blood type; I saw the detective take some scrapings from his nails last night. Your mistress may have to identify him as the neighbor's cat. I do not believe you will be bothered to testify. The usual red tape."

She shakes her head and straightens her ruff. "So Wilfrid is a hero."

"Er, I suppose you could say that."

"He not only came to his mistress's defense, marking her attacker, but he returned from the dead to stalk, confront, and again claw the killer. What a magnificent fellow! And to think I thought he was only a domestic. He must have been working undercover the entire time."

"I think it is more a matter of being in the wrong place at the right time."

"Nonsense! Wilfrid obviously is far more than you or I ever dreamed he was. You must finish your assignment by seeing that the authorities return him here, and I will work upon my companion to bring him into our establishment."

"I cannot speak for the authorities. I do not think my Miss Temple would let them put Wilfrid into some shelter."

" 'Think!' Then there is a possibility they would separate us by such heinous means! You must go immediately and see to it. Your task is not done until my hero is home with me!"

"But, gee, lady, you have not even paid me for the work I have done so far—"

"Paid you! What kind of ignoble opportunist are you?

402

Have you so little interest in the law of the land that you would let a genuine American hero languish in a homeless shelter? Go on! Find out what is to become of him immediately. Tell him Fanny will be waiting for him."

I back away down the walk.

There is no reasoning with a dame bent on deluding herself. It looks like I am to be Wilfrid's keeper until I can dump him off at home for good and all. And the way she is carrying on, my role in the recent events have been reduced to a walk on, or a prop boy.

I was hoping for a tender, *Casablanca*-style parting scene before I produced the little wimp again, but no go.

So much for the movies. All deception, lies, and videotape.

MIDNIGHT LOUIE FRETS
ABOUT THE FUTURE

It is certainly not flattering, no matter how well intended.

Here I sit, the star of my own mystery series, my name on everybody's lips and e-mail and snail-mail list, and what do they want?

What do they want?

Do they want to know what mean streets I will be impressing with my stealthy footsteps in my next adventure?

No.

Do they worry about the sinister forces gathering on all fronts? The magical Synth, the international terrorists, the lethal Siamese conspiracy?

No.

Do they worry if my midlife energies will be drained by the onslaught of my darling daughter (maybe), Midnight Louise, who seems bound and determined to elbow in on my detecting business?

No.

Do they worry if my human acquaintances will come out of the next episode with their respective epidermi intact?

No.

No, the inquiring public wants to know what only your hairdresser should know, and a private dick should be hired to find out, and then well paid to keep quiet about.

Who is sleeping in whose bed.

This is not Goldilocks, folks. This is not even Puss in Boots. *This Is My Life!*

Can you imagine? There is even lascivious speculation about whether / will end up with the silver sweetheart, the Divine Yvette, or the Sublime Solange, her golden soul sister.

Granted, my amatory exploits would make a good book. Perhaps I will write it one day: Midnight Louie tells all, names names. There may be some household names in the roster, like you remember that sleek little black number on the "Gary Seven" episode of classic *Star Trek?* Well, so do I. Not that I am claiming anything a gentleman should not, but you are free to draw your own conclusions. Those who are good with numbers will realize that there is a considerable age difference. Not that this ever stopped a determined dude. If one will examine the careers of such silver-screen mainstays as Paul Newman, Clint Eastwood, and Warren Beatty, one will see that as the dudes go silver, the dames go jail-bait.

So who ends up with whom is still very much in the air. No doubt there are dames as yet unmet who would be perfect partners for a suave dude such as I. On the other hand, I would not mind tangling with that witch-goddess Hyacinth again, or winning that spokescat position and reuniting with Solange and Yvette, the stunning Ashleigh sisters. I am open to all possibilities. It is just that the humans should get their acts together and settle down to a nice predicable domestic life, one that will not distract from my doings both predatory and amatory.

Of course, that is asking a lot of mere humans.

So, all I can say is, do not despair. I will work things out to my best advantage in the end, and everyone else will be all the better for it.

Very best fishes,

Midnight Louie, Esq.

P.S. You can visit Midnight Louie on the Internet at:
http://www.catwriter.com/cdouglas
To subscribe to *Midnight Louie's Scratching Post-Intelligencer*
newsletter or for information on Louie's T-shirt,
write: PO Box 331555, Fort Worth, TX 76163.

CAROLE NELSON DOUGLAS RUMINATES ON DOING TIME

FOR ONCE I THINK THAT LOUIE HAS A LEGITIMATE complaint.

His feline hijinks have been upstaged by the human gavotte. That is what happens when one species outnumbers another, even in novels. Natural selection.

The observant reader (and aren't we all?) will have noticed that after Louie's debut in *Catnap* and *Pussyfoot*, the series developed a title pattern with *Cat on a Blue Monday*. Cat, and a color, and also an internal alphabet, beginning with B as in *Blue Monday*, continuing with C as in *Crimson Haze* etcetera.

Louie, being a sensitive soul (and also being a midlife male) is worrying about longevity these days, but I want to reassure him that his adventures in this incarnation will last for a total of twenty-seven books (one longer than Sue Grafton's alphabet series, because Louie's third novel started with "B"). Louie likes that bit of feline one-upmanship, but since Sue Grafton likes cats, she shouldn't mind too much.

The passage of time in a mystery series is a subject worthy of study, or at least of a few scholarly monographs.

Some series characters abide in an Eternal Now. No names, places, or brand names date the setting. Think Erle Stanley Gardner, whose Perry Mason dwells in a generic landscape (except for things never expected to change, like men wearing fedoras).

407

Now that mystery series are able to indulge more fully in the pleasures of character development and setting as well as puzzle and plot, time has bent, warped, become a thing of mystery and magic.

Sue Grafton has pointed out that Kinsey Milhone began in 1982 and, because of the time between books, remains anchored in the eighties even as the author and the rest of us approach the millennium. Grafton is now writing recent-historical novels.

The opposite is true in the Midnight Louie landscape. Because of the Las Vegas background, something every tourist can check for veracity every day of every month of the year, time has gone schizoid. While the first Midnight Louie novel came out in 1992, and while the ten so far document the cataclysmic and constant changes on the Las Vegas map, the time elapsed for the characters is only nine months.

Think of it as an early film: the main characters are shown conversing in the foreground roadster, while behind them the background of passing scenery reels by at a cosmic speed.

When a hardcover Midnight Louie book comes out saying New York-New York Hotel and Casino is opening, that is exactly what is happening in the real-time world on the book's first appearance. This is the only way to handle an endlessly evolving setting like Las Vegas: make the physical setting as contemporary as possible; let the characters develop at their own, slower pace.

Time for a pregnant pause: Although ten Midnight Louie books have passed through our hands and before our eyes since 1992, the actual time passage in the books is only nine months. I didn't plan this; like Topsy, it "just growed."

Yet, while writing these books, I've become aware that our culture is becoming Omni-Era-tic. The television shows and film reruns I grew up seeing as a child are still running on cable and overseas, enticing today's and yesterday's children. They are being remade into major film releases for a new generation, a next and future generation of rerun-watchers. *Star Trek. Zorro.*

We are all fluid and coming to share a culture devoid of timelines. So any status quo in any of the Midnight Louie books is bound to change. Except for Louie, of course.

As he knows (and we always suspected), cats are too good just the way they are to change, very much at least. No matter how much time elapses.

Remember. It isn't over until the fat cat sings. Stay tuned.

Dear Reader:

I hope you enjoyed reading this Large Print book. If you are interested in reading other Beeler Large Print titles, ask your librarian or write to me at:

Thomas T. Beeler, *Publisher*
Post Office Box 659
Hampton Falls, New Hampshire 03844

You can also call me at 1-800-818-7574 and I will send you my latest catalogue.

Audrey Lesko and I choose the titles I publish in Large Print. Our aim is to provide good books by outstanding authors—books we both enjoyed reading and liked well enough to want to share. We warmly welcome any suggestions for new titles and authors.

Sincerely,